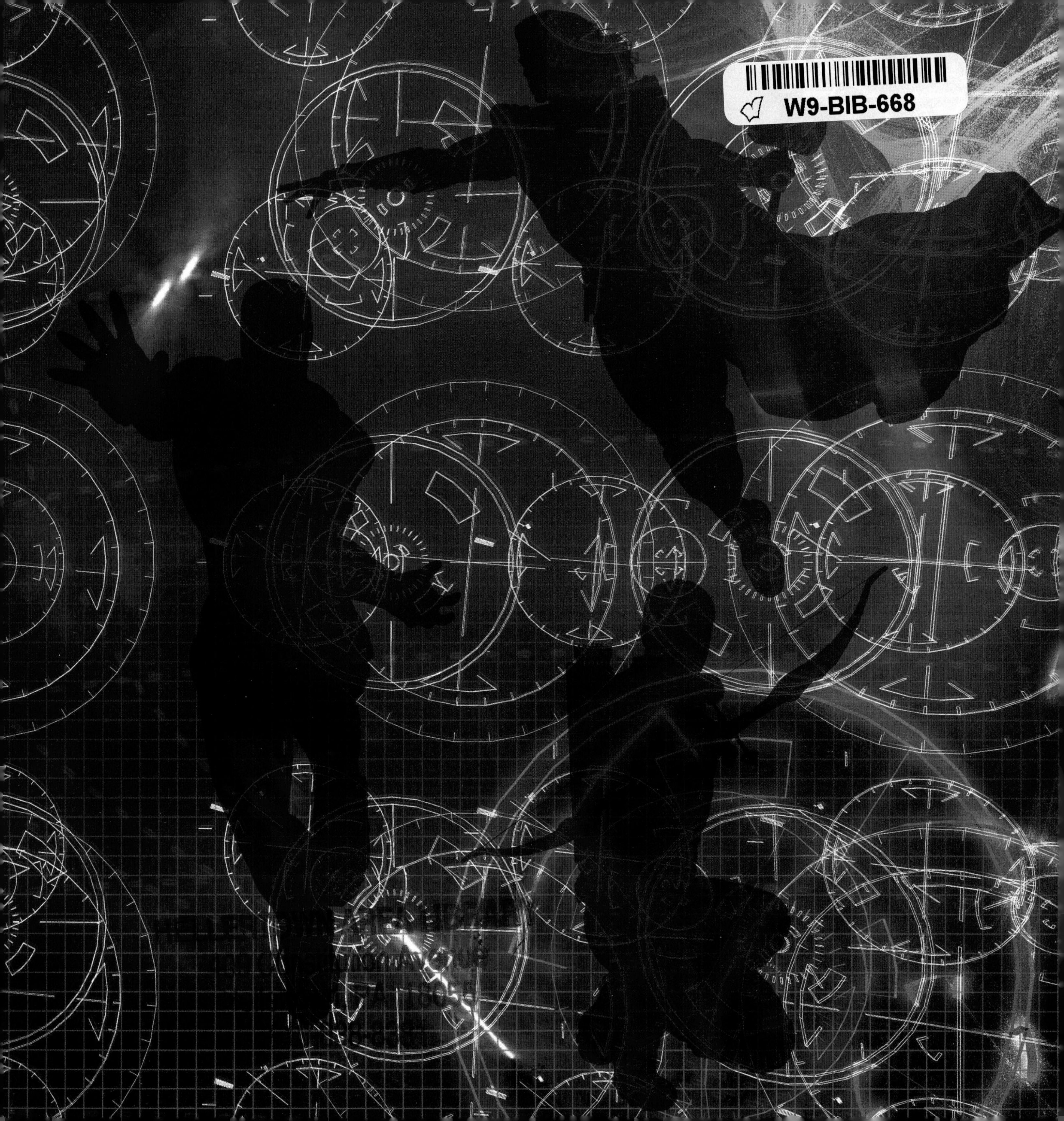

MARVEL

THE AVENGERS

STORYBOOK
COLLECTION

Little, Brown and Company

Hachette Book Group
1290 Avenue of the Americas, New York, NY 10104
Visit us at lb-kids.com

Little, Brown and Company is a division of Hachette Book Group, Inc.
The Little, Brown name and logo are trademarks of Hachette Book Group, Inc.

The publisher is not responsible for websites (or their content) that are not owned by the publisher.

First Edition: March 2015

The Avengers: Battle Against Loki originally published in 2012 by Marvel Press, an imprint of Disney Book Group
The Avengers: The S.H.I.E.L.D. Files originally published in 2012 by Marvel Press, an imprint of Disney Book Group
The Avengers: Return of First Avenger originally published in 2012 by Marvel Press, an imprint of Disney Book Group
Iron Man 2: Iron Man Fights Back originally published in 2010 by Little, Brown and Company
Iron Man 2: Iron Man vs. Whiplash originally published in 2010 by Little, Brown and Company
Thor: The Dark World: Warriors of the Realms originally published in 2013 by Marvel Press,

MARVEL

THE AVENGERS

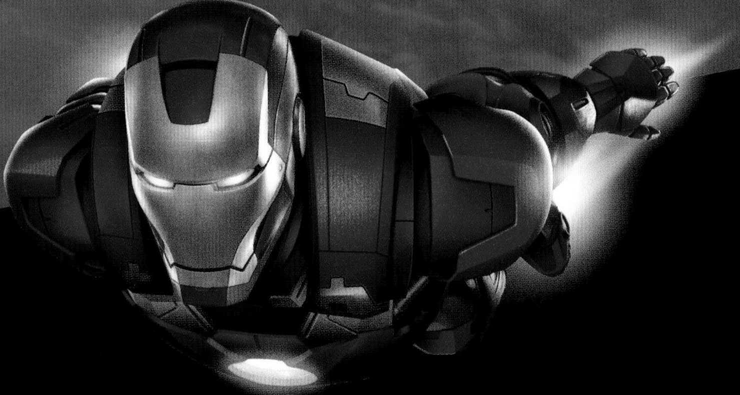

STORYBOOK COLLECTION

LB

LITTLE, BROWN AND COMPANY
New York Boston

MARVEL
THE AVENGERS

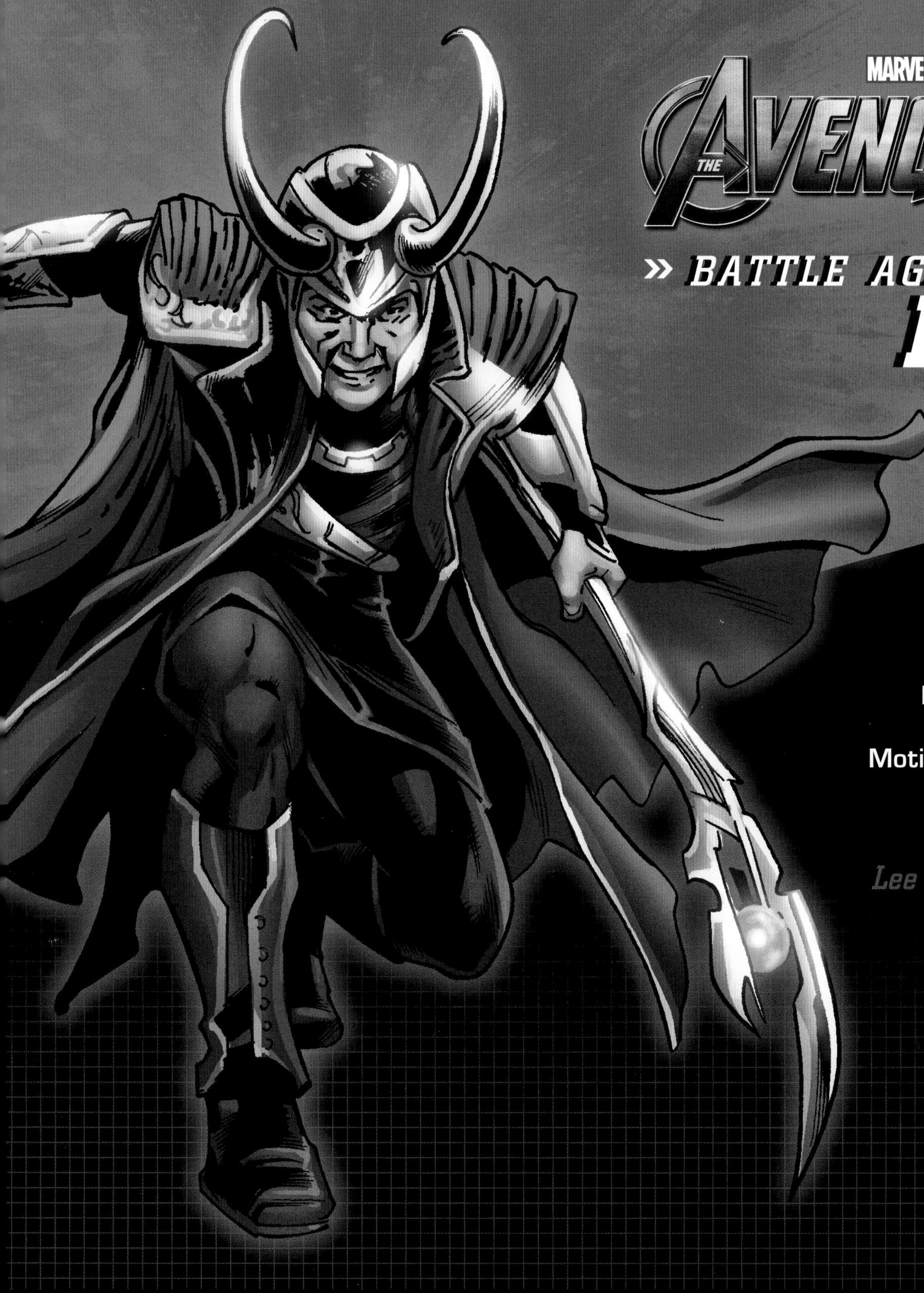

MARVEL

THE AVENGERS

» BATTLE AGAINST LOKI

Written by
Tomas Palacios

Based on Marvel's
The Avengers
Motion Picture Written by
Joss Whedon

Illustrated by
Lee Garbett, *John Lucas*,
and
Lee Duhig

Based on
Marvel Comics'
The Avengers

All Loki ever wanted was to become king of Asgard. And since he could not rule over his Realm, he would gladly take Earth instead.

And with the power he now possessed, taking it was just what he would do!

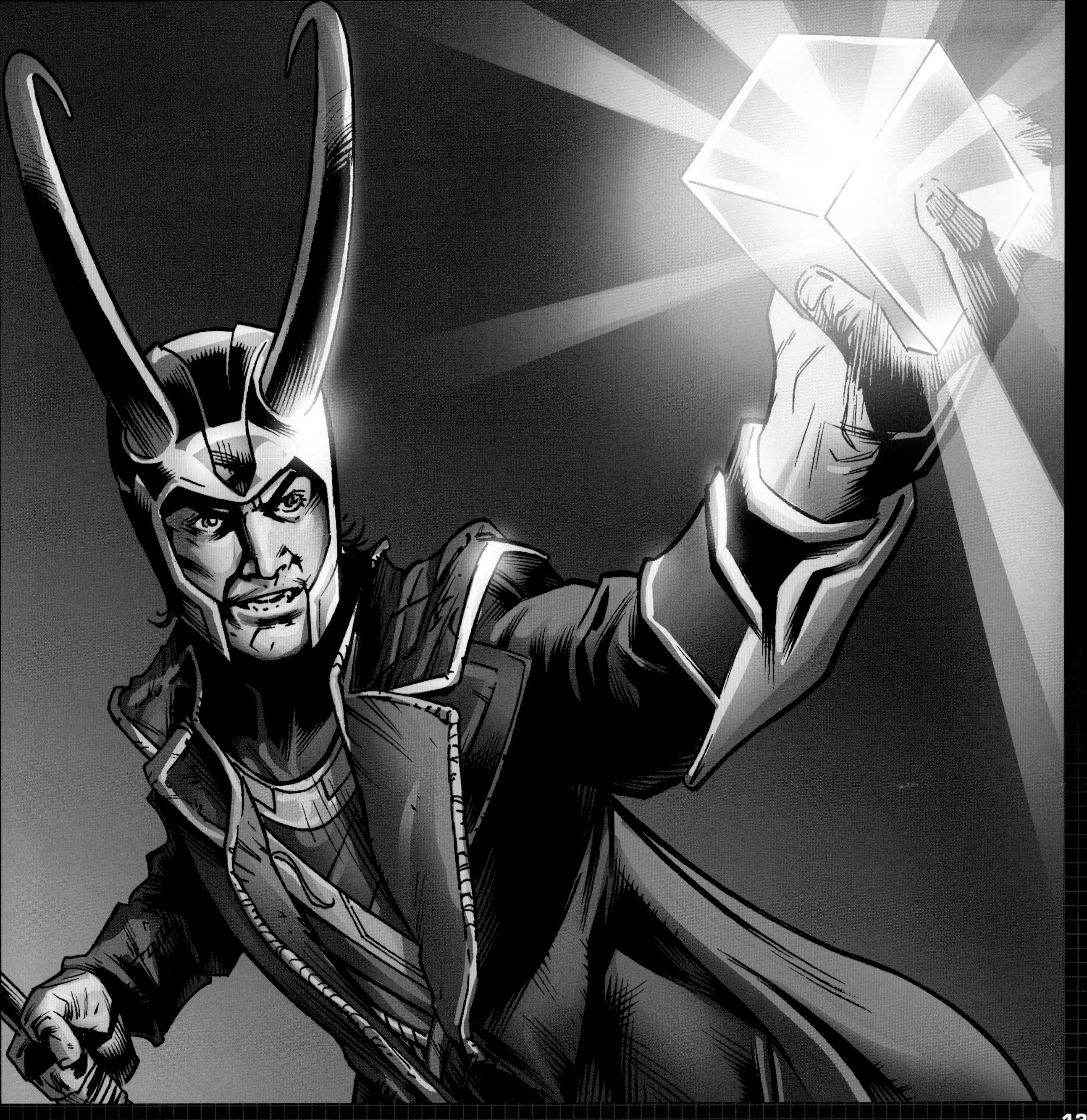

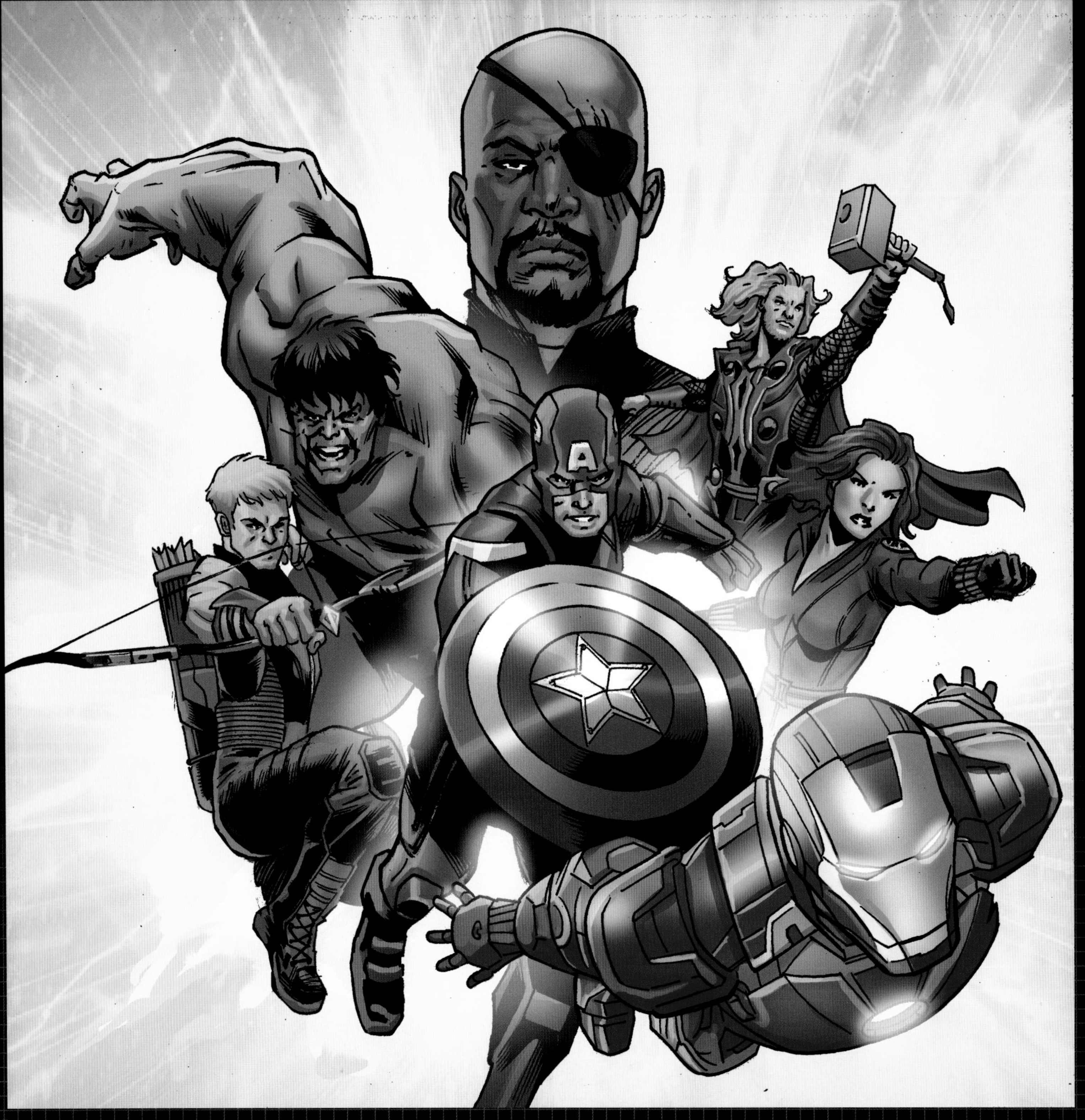

But Nick Fury, director of S.H.I.E.L.D., had other plans for Loki. Fury had been secretly assembling a team of Super Heroes.

There was the invincible Iron Man, the Super-Soldier known as Captain America, S.H.I.E.L.D. agent Hawkeye, superspy Black Widow, and scientist Dr. Bruce Banner, also known as the Hulk! Lastly, there was Loki's own brother, Thor.

By themselves, they were good at what they did. **But together, they were Earth's Mightiest Heroes!**

And on this day, it would be their first battle as a team. But it wasn't going to be an easy one. Loki possessed an object called the Tesseract. It was an ancient artifact that could be used as a terrible weapon.

The Tesseract gave off gamma radiation, which S.H.I.E.L.D. was able to track thanks to **Bruce Banner.** And no one knew more about gamma radiation than he did.

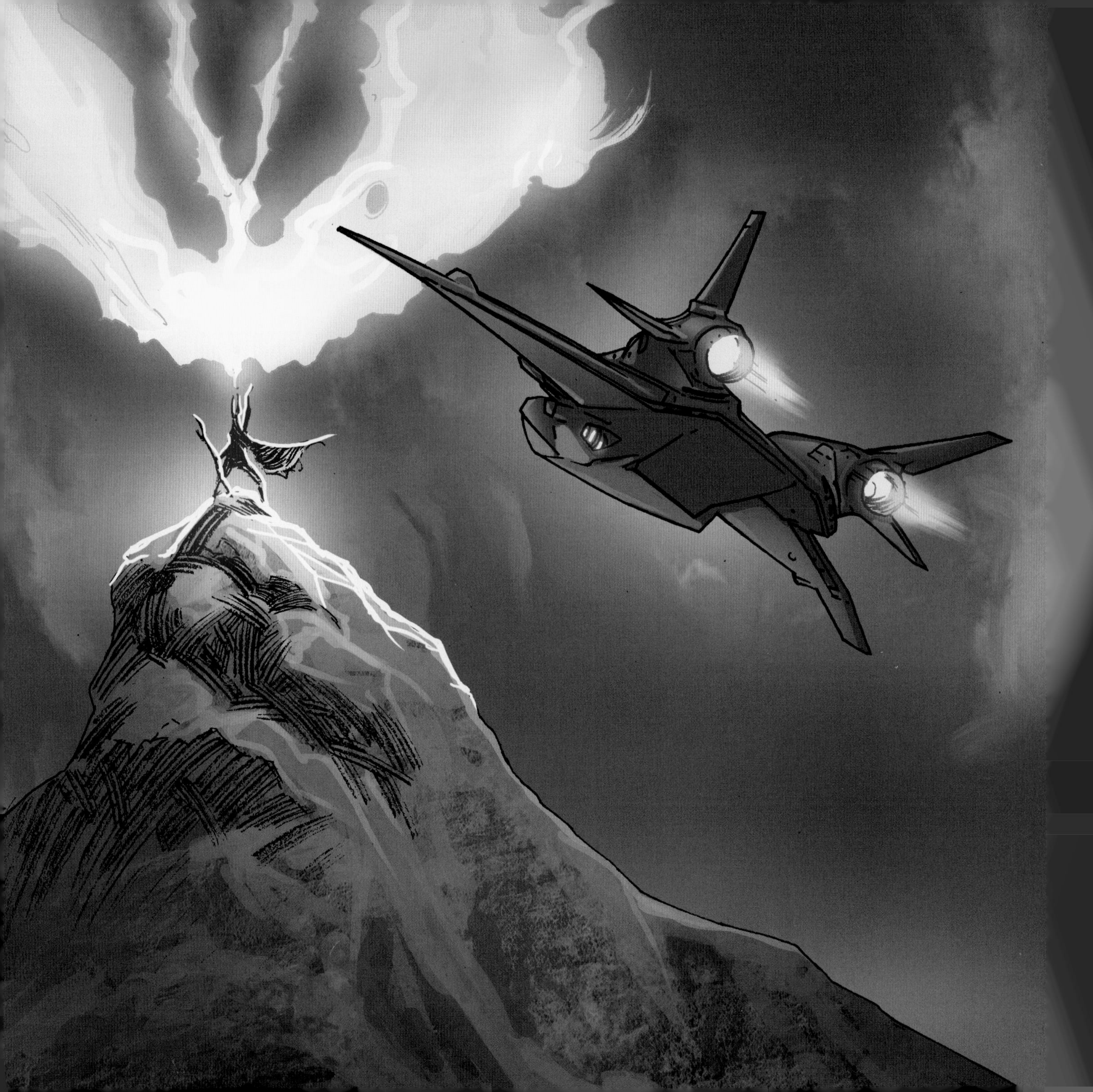

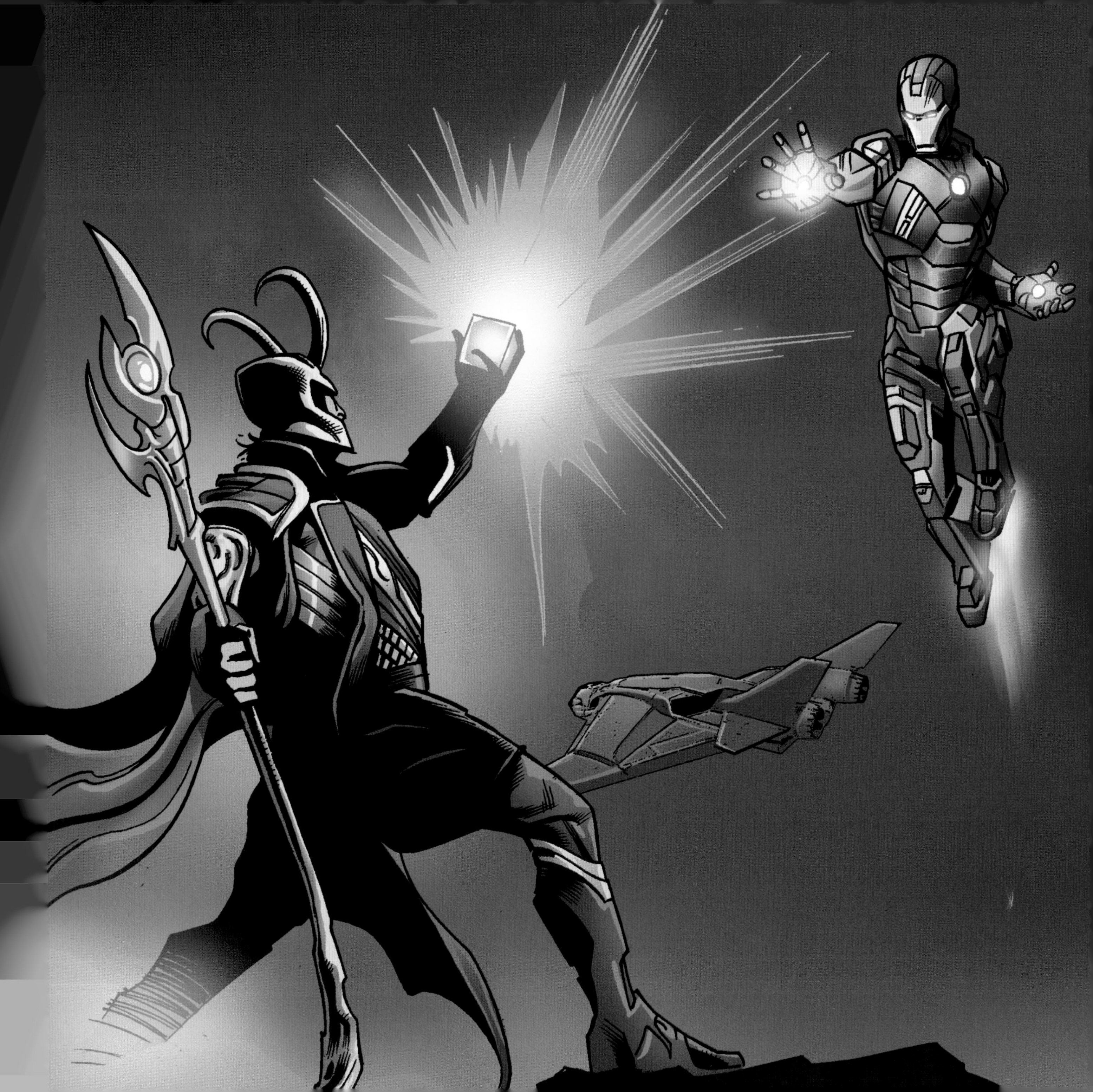

First up was the invincible Iron Man! He rocketed out of the Quinjet toward Loki, ready for battle. Iron Man used his repulsor beams and fired them at the Trickster! **One shot. Two shots. Three shots**! But Loki avoided each one with ease.

Suddenly, Loki fired an energy blast from the Tesseract. But Iron Man was fast! His armored suit warned him, and **he dodged the blast!**

Loki was down, but he wasn't defeated.

So Black Widow jumped into action! Black Widow was a master spy and she knew how to fight!

The S.H.I.E.L.D. agent used her martial-arts skills to clash with the villain. She kicked and punched and punched and kicked. Loki was quick and blocked them all.

Then he fired a blast from his scepter directly at the hero! Black Widow leaped out of the way just in time!

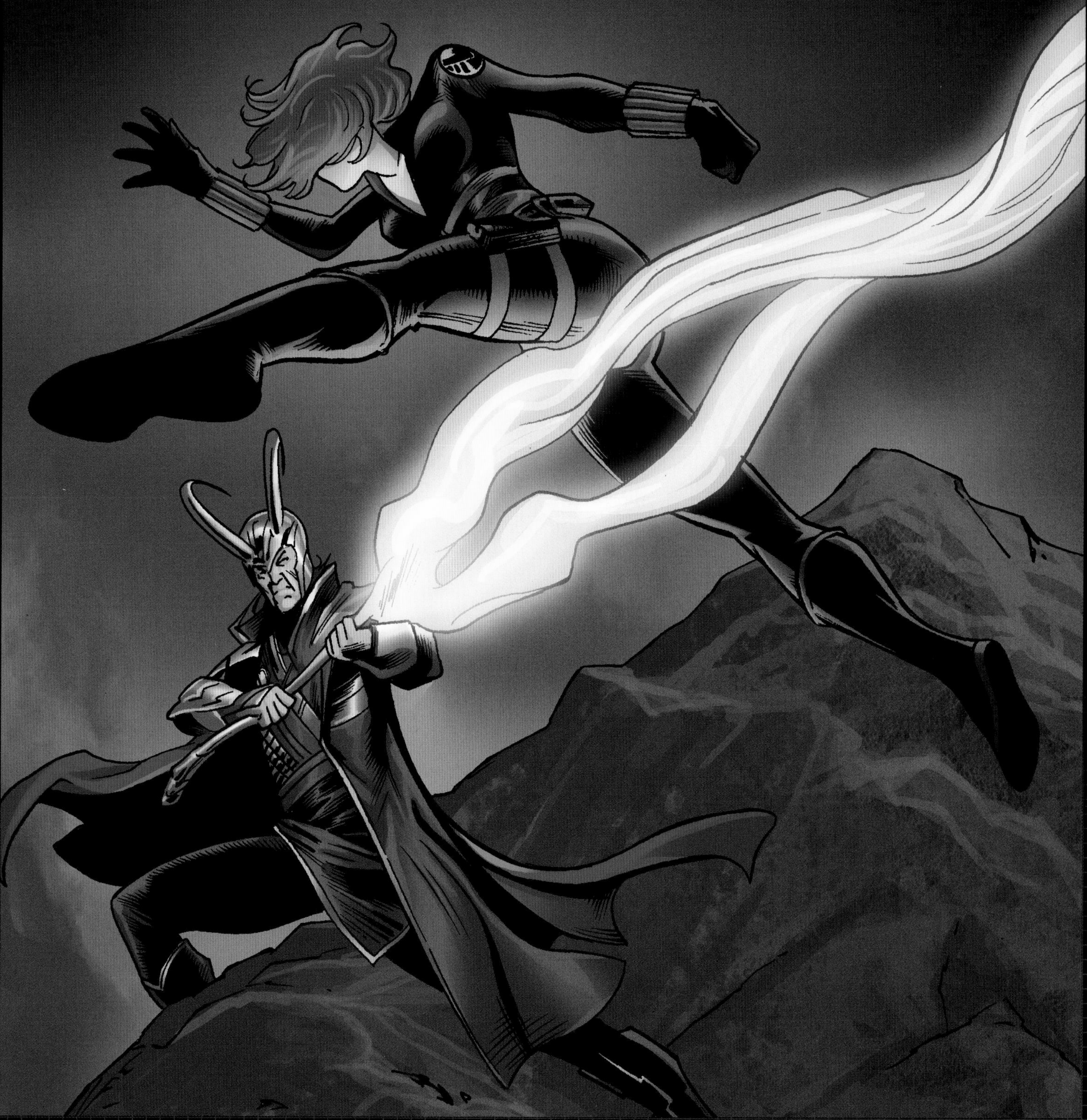

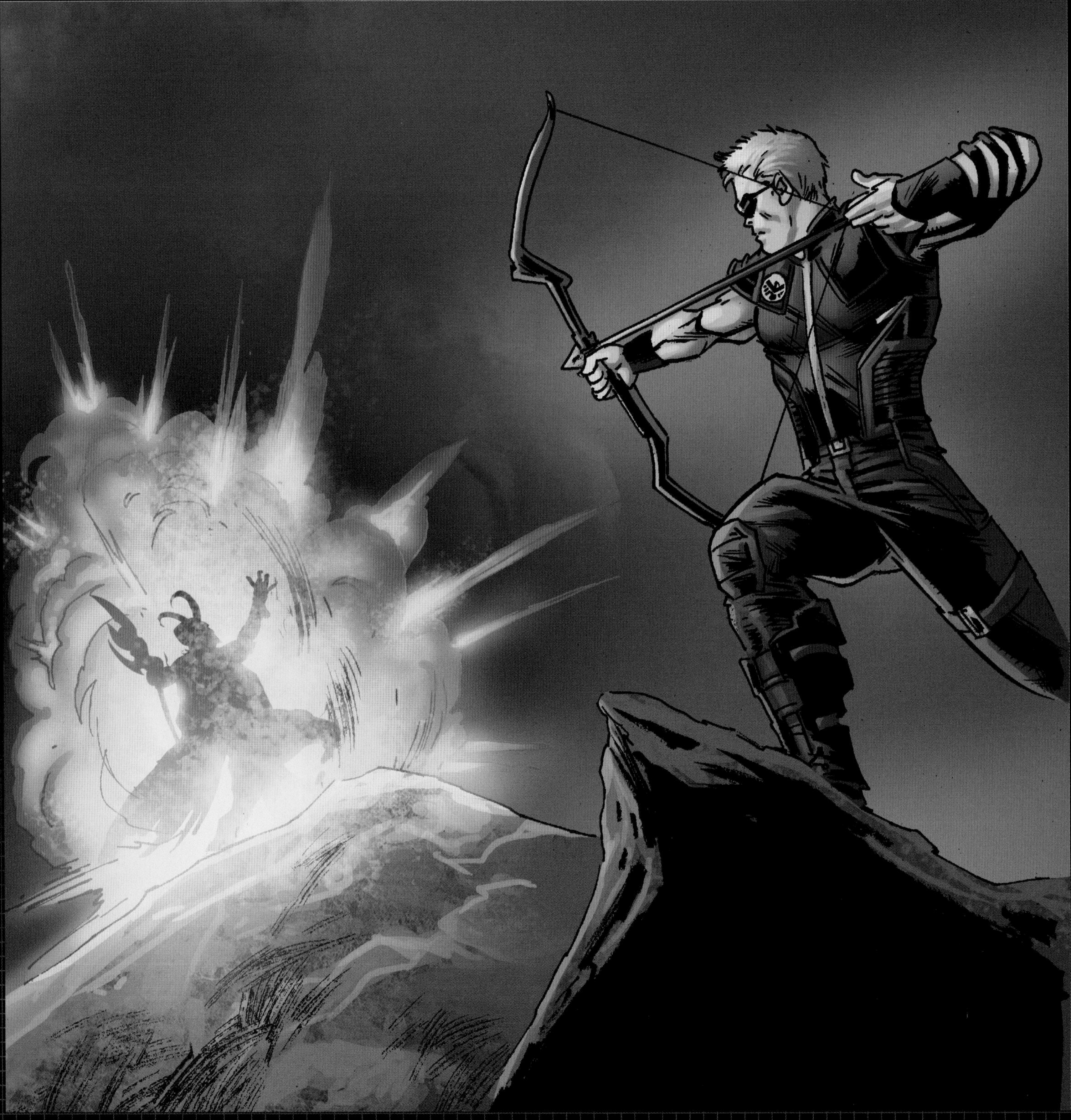

It was now time for Hawkeye to show his fellow Super Heroes what he could do. Hawkeye quickly fired several arrows at Loki. Loki dodged them, and they struck the rocks behind the villain. But they weren't ordinary arrows. **The arrows suddenly exploded,** throwing the villain to the ground. When he stood back up, he saw Hawkeye already firing more arrows in his direction!

Loki created the illusion that there were dozens of him to try to confuse the Super Heroes. But the next person he was about to face wasn't just a Super Hero. He was a Super-Soldier! **He was Captain America!**

Cap grabbed his red, white, and blue shield and flung it toward the illusions, collapsing each into a cloud of smoke. Just one Loki was left. The real Loki!

Cap threw his shield at the Trickster. **CLANK!** Loki was knocked to the ground once again!

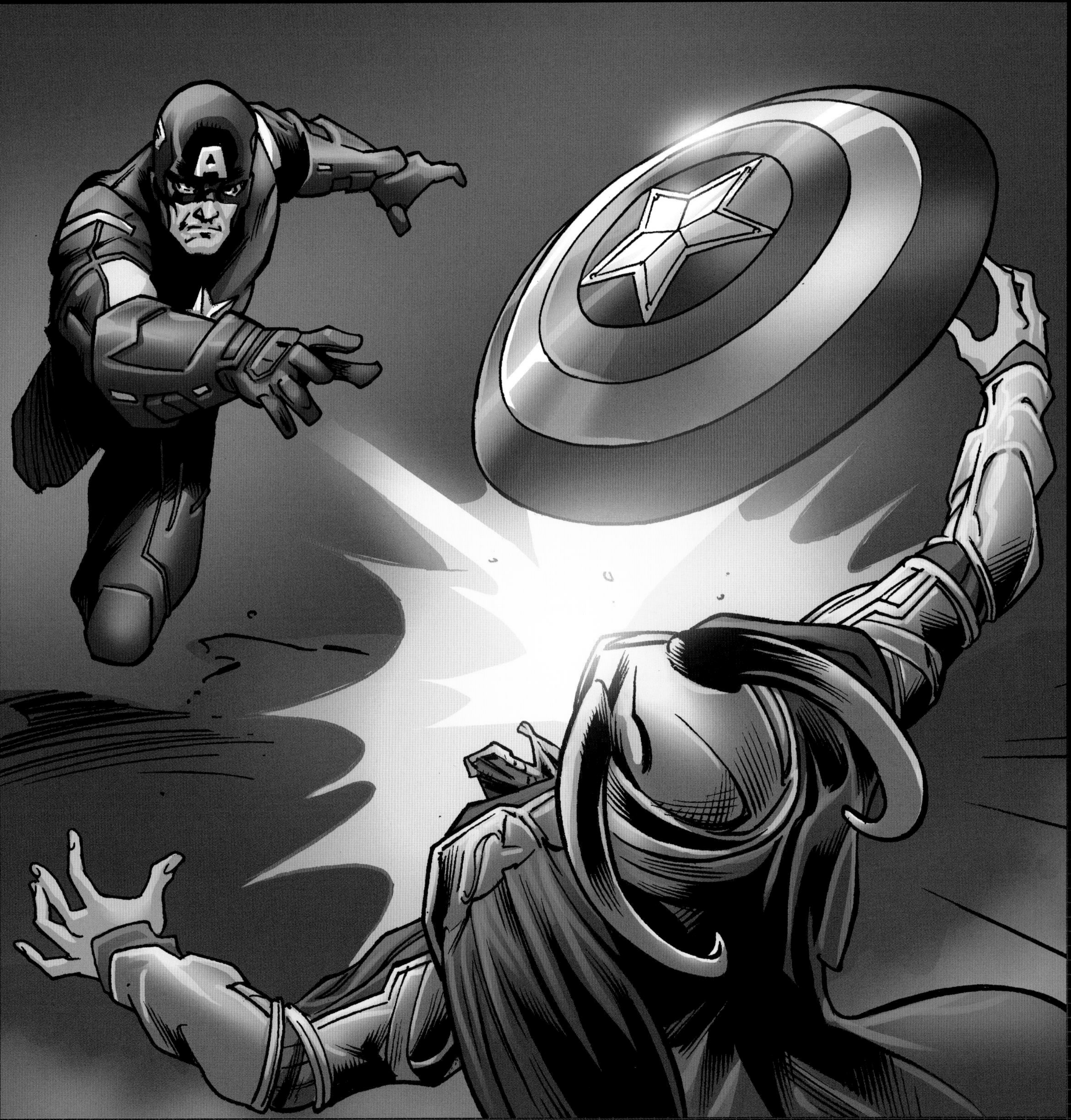

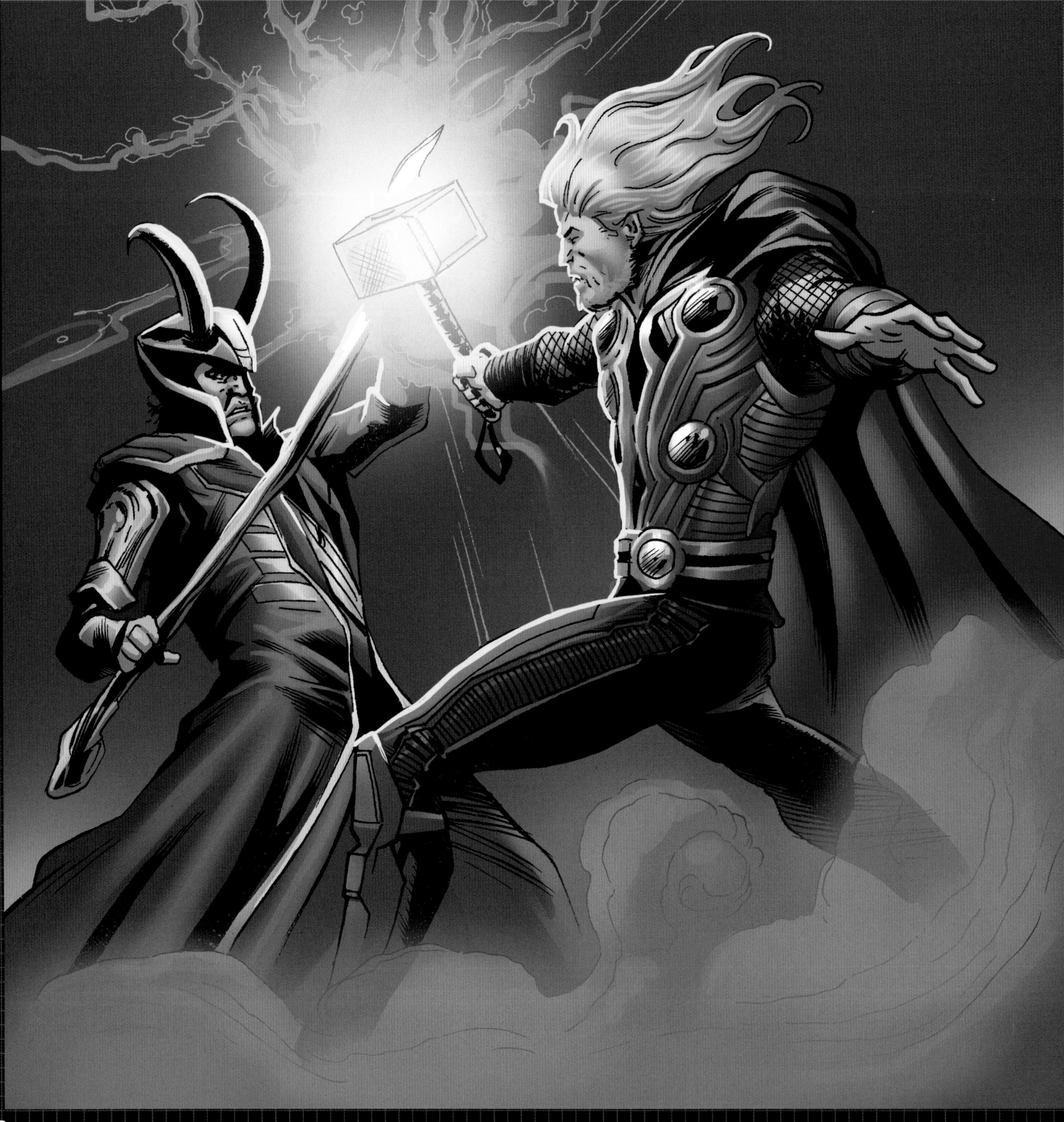

Loki had fought every Super Hero.
But there was still one more he had to face—
his own brother, the mighty Thor! Loki wanted
to beat his brother once and for all.

It seemed as if this would be their final
showdown! Thor hurled his mighty hammer at
Loki, smashing his brother into the mountain.

Angry that he had fallen to Thor once again,
Loki stood and rushed at his brother. Loki's
scepter and Thor's hammer clashed! Lightning
shot down from the sky, striking the villain!

Finally, Loki was defeated! All was quiet. The heroes gathered around the fallen villain.

Alone, they knew they were not enough to defeat the powerful Loki. But as a team, they had beaten the Super Villain and taken back the Tesseract. **The world was safe once again.**

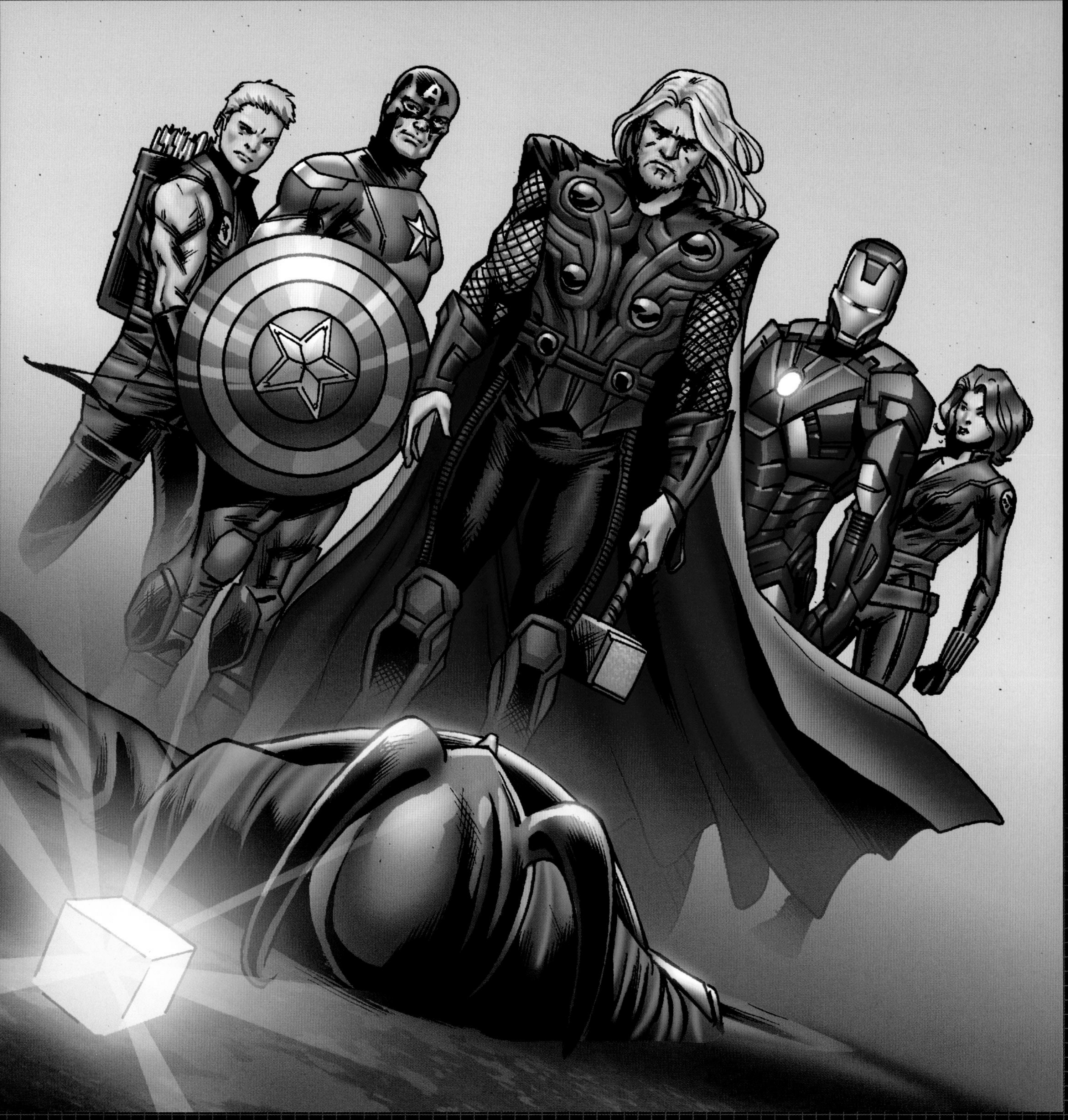

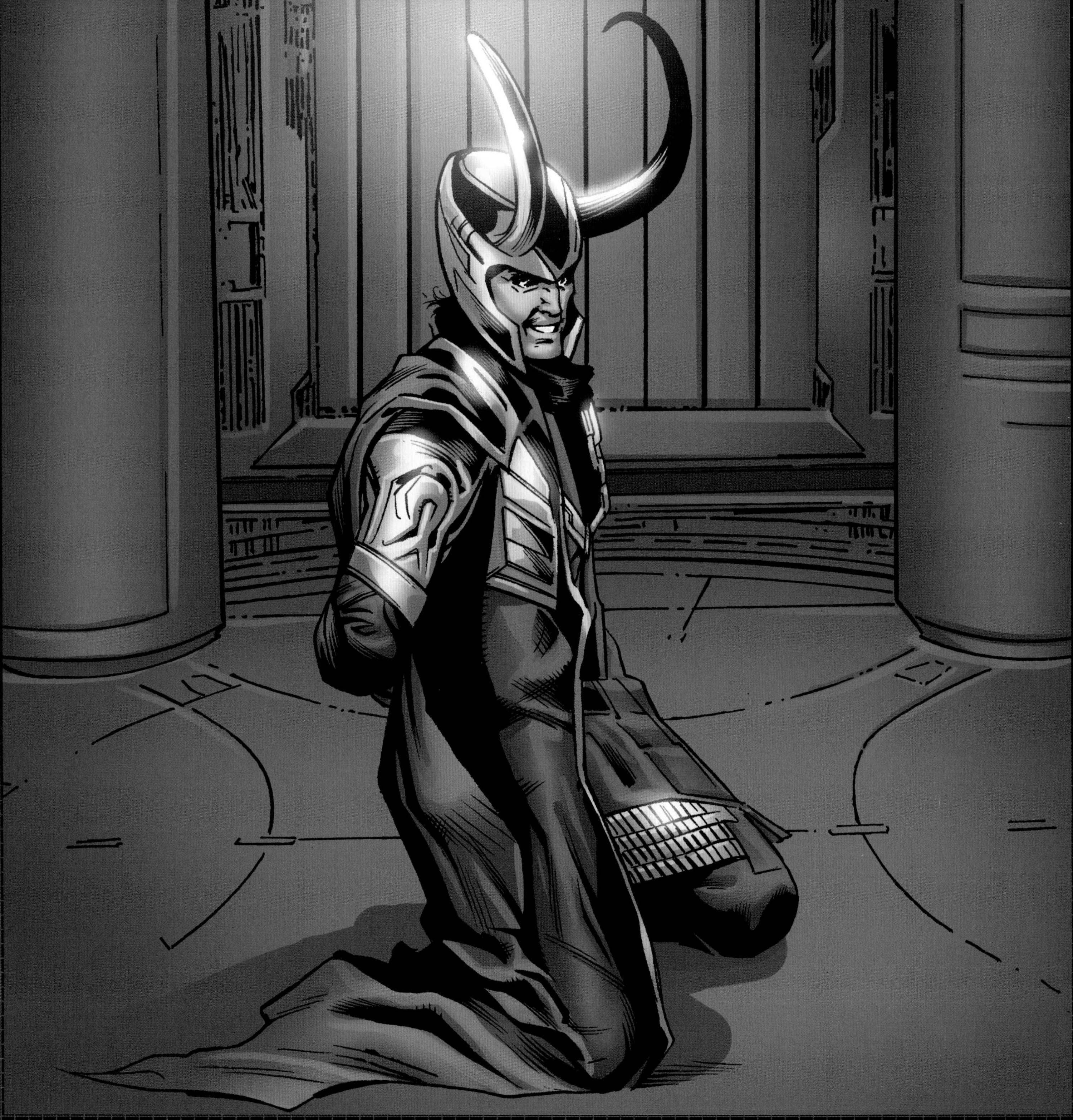

Back on the Quinjet, Nick Fury applauded the heroes for capturing Loki. He knew this team would work, and they had proven that to him today.

But Fury knew that more threats were looming around every corner.

That was why Fury needed one more Super Hero to complete the team . . . a Super Hero who was **big** . . . and **incredible** . . . and Fury had the perfect candidate in mind. . . .

The incredible Hulk! The other heroes looked on in amazement as Bruce Banner changed into the green Goliath. He was huge! He was even bigger than Thor! With this last Super Hero in place, Nick Fury had **assembled the ultimate team.**

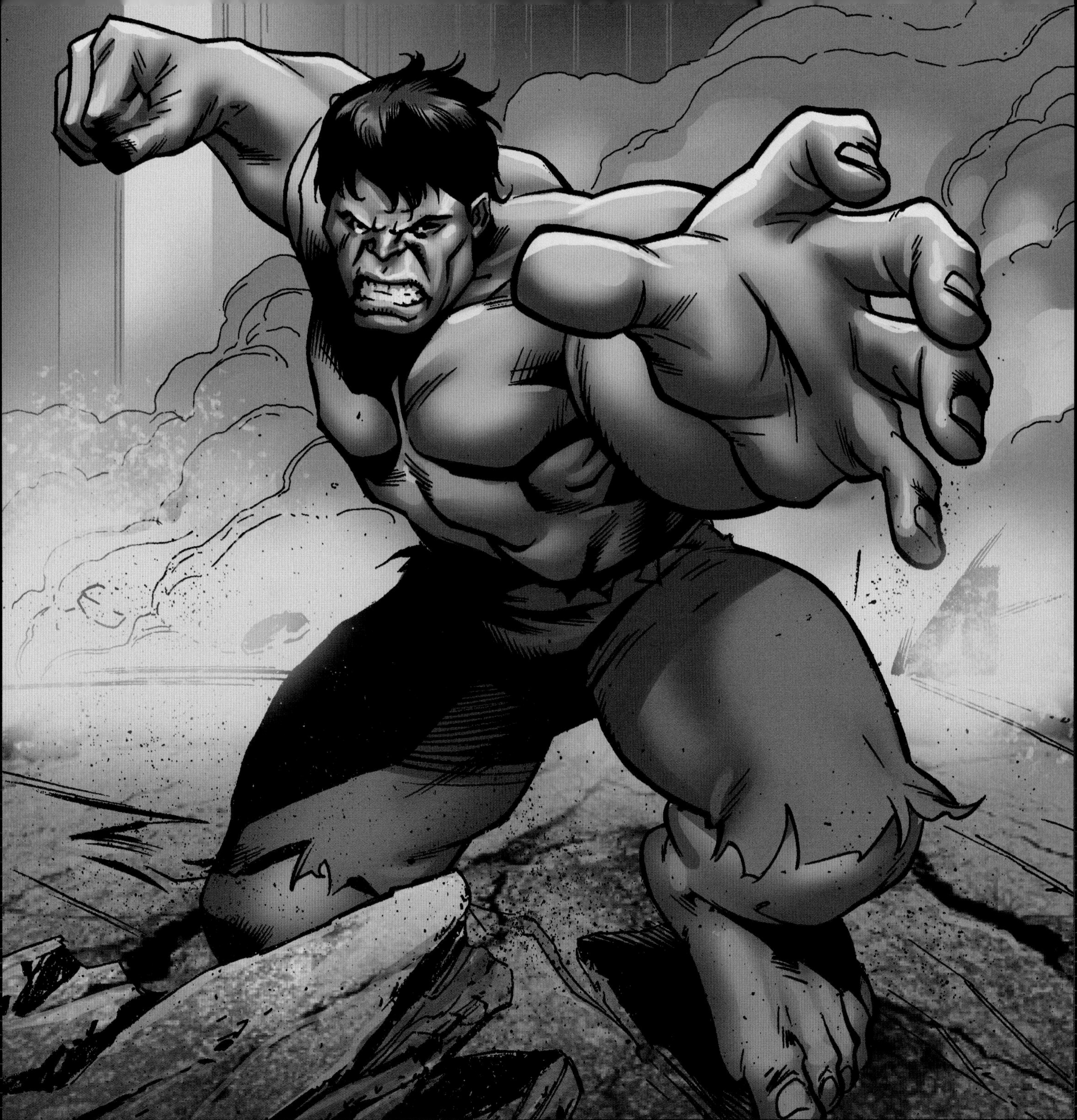

From that day forth, these Super Heroes would assemble and be known throughout the world as

the Avengers!

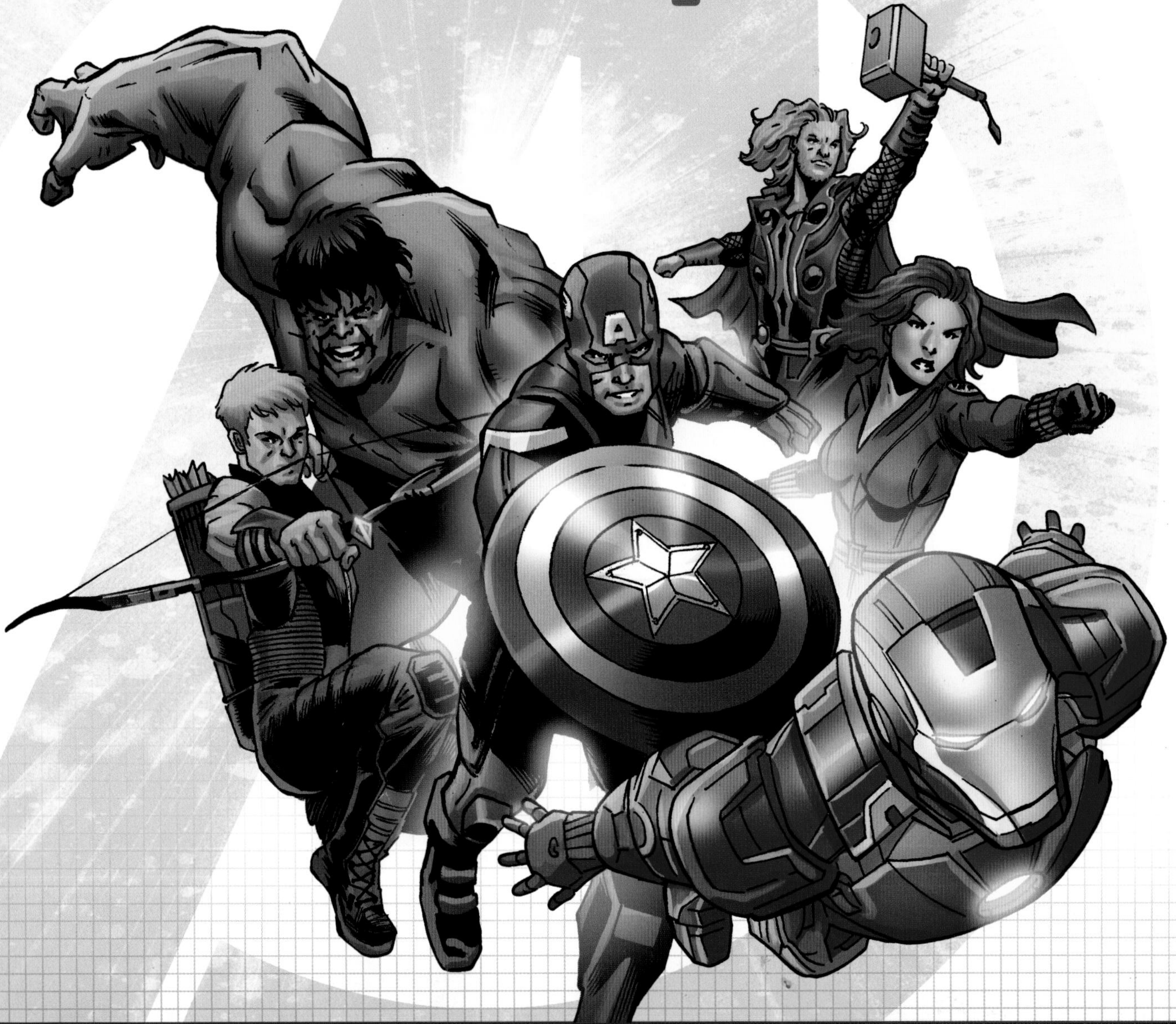

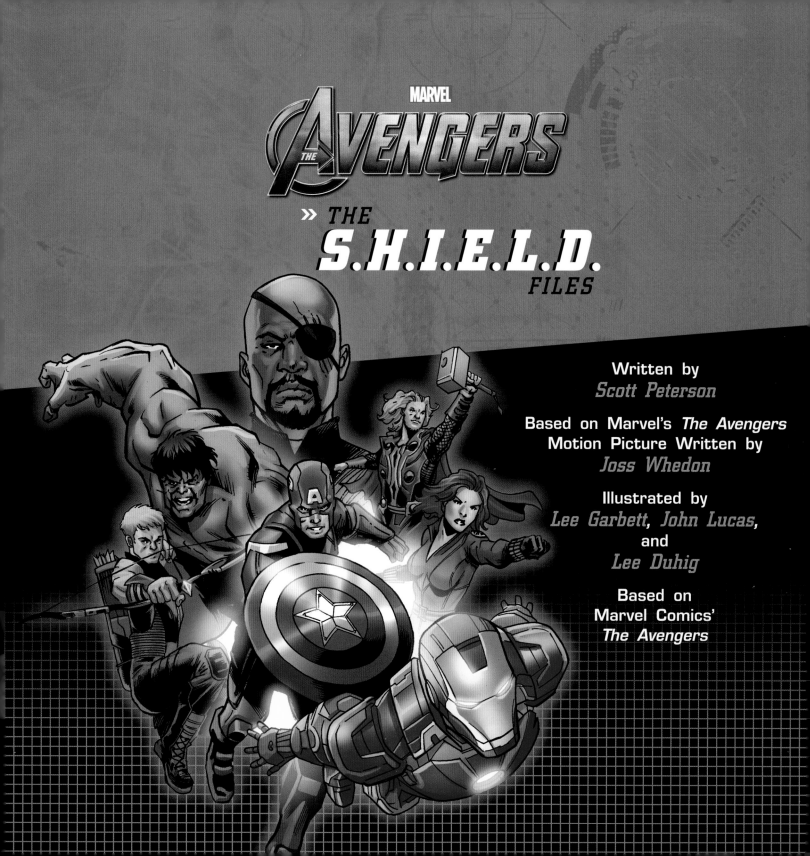

MARVEL

THE AVENGERS

» THE
S.H.I.E.L.D.
FILES

Written by
Scott Peterson

Based on Marvel's *The Avengers*
Motion Picture Written by
Joss Whedon

Illustrated by
Lee Garbett, John Lucas,
and
Lee Duhig

Based on
Marvel Comics'
The Avengers

The things you're about to read are real.

You won't believe it, but it's true.

I'm going to tell you the story of **the Avengers....**

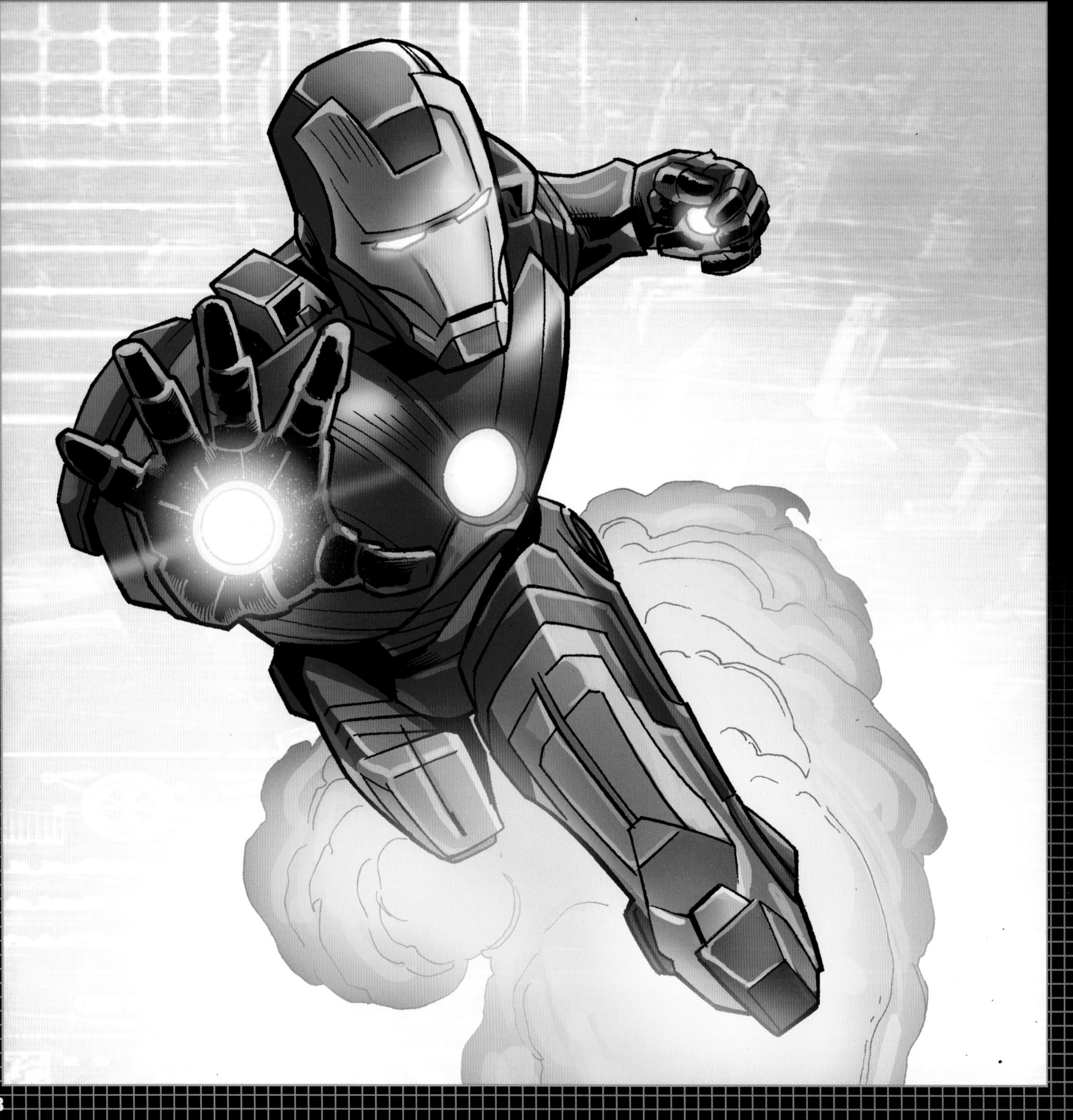

The invincible Iron Man. A red-and-gold knight in a shining suit of armor.

Tony Stark is the man beneath the iron. He's one of the richest people in the world. Owner of Stark Industries. Inventor of half of the coolest things the world has ever known. Most of all: the creator of the Iron Man suit.

Bullets bounce off it. It can fire repulsor blasts that would knock down a small building.

Oh, and it can fly.

Things weren't always perfect for Tony. While driving through enemy territory, his truck was blown up and a piece of metal hit Tony's heart.

He was captured, and while a prisoner **he built the first Iron Man armor.** His chest plate acted like a new heart, keeping him alive. And the armor made him strong enough to escape and beat the bad guys.

Back home, Tony decided to fight for those who couldn't fight for themselves. He also fought against super-powered villains bent on total destruction. With a heart of iron and armor to match, Tony Stark was the perfect fit for S.H.I.E.L.D.'s new team.

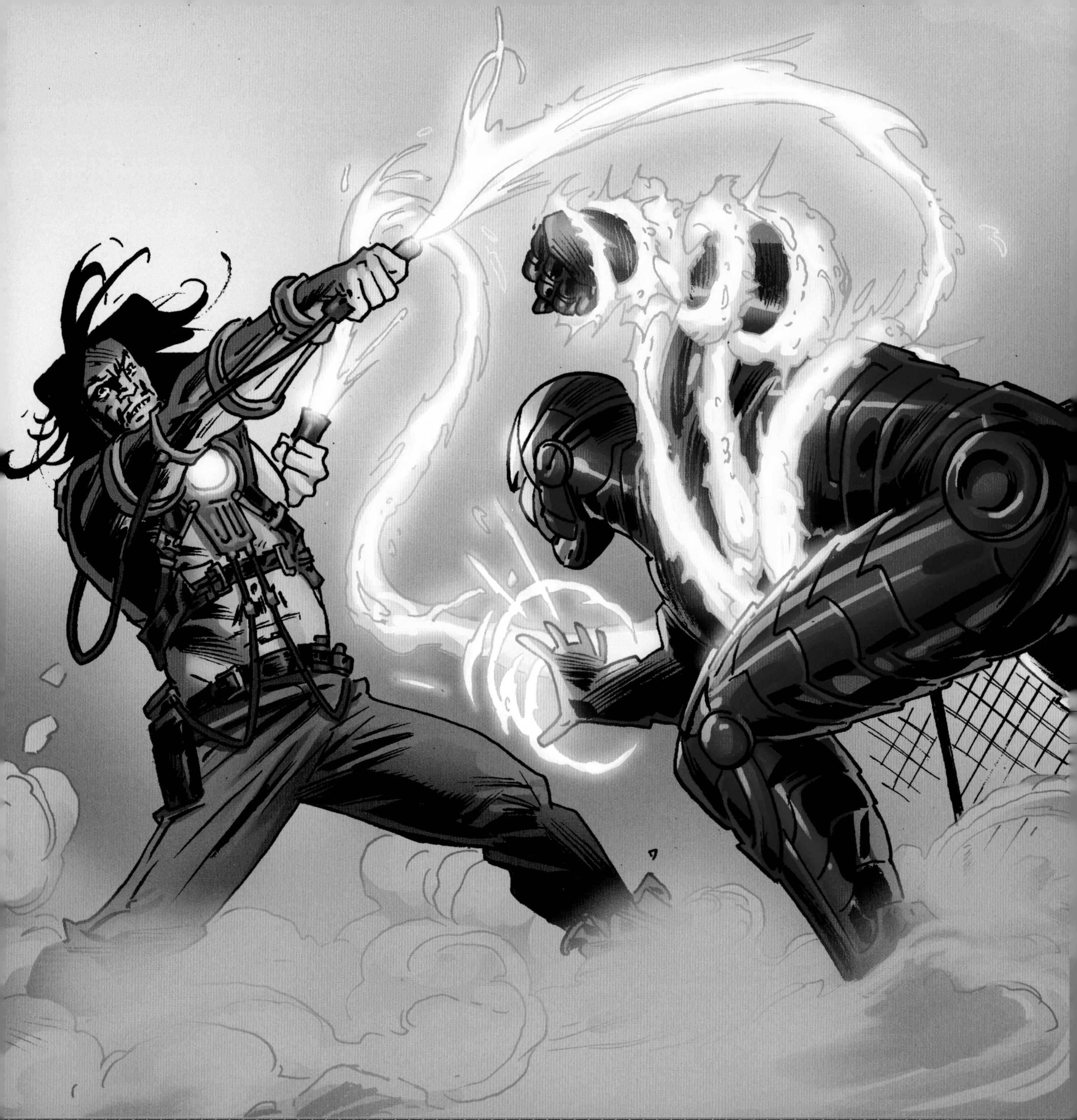

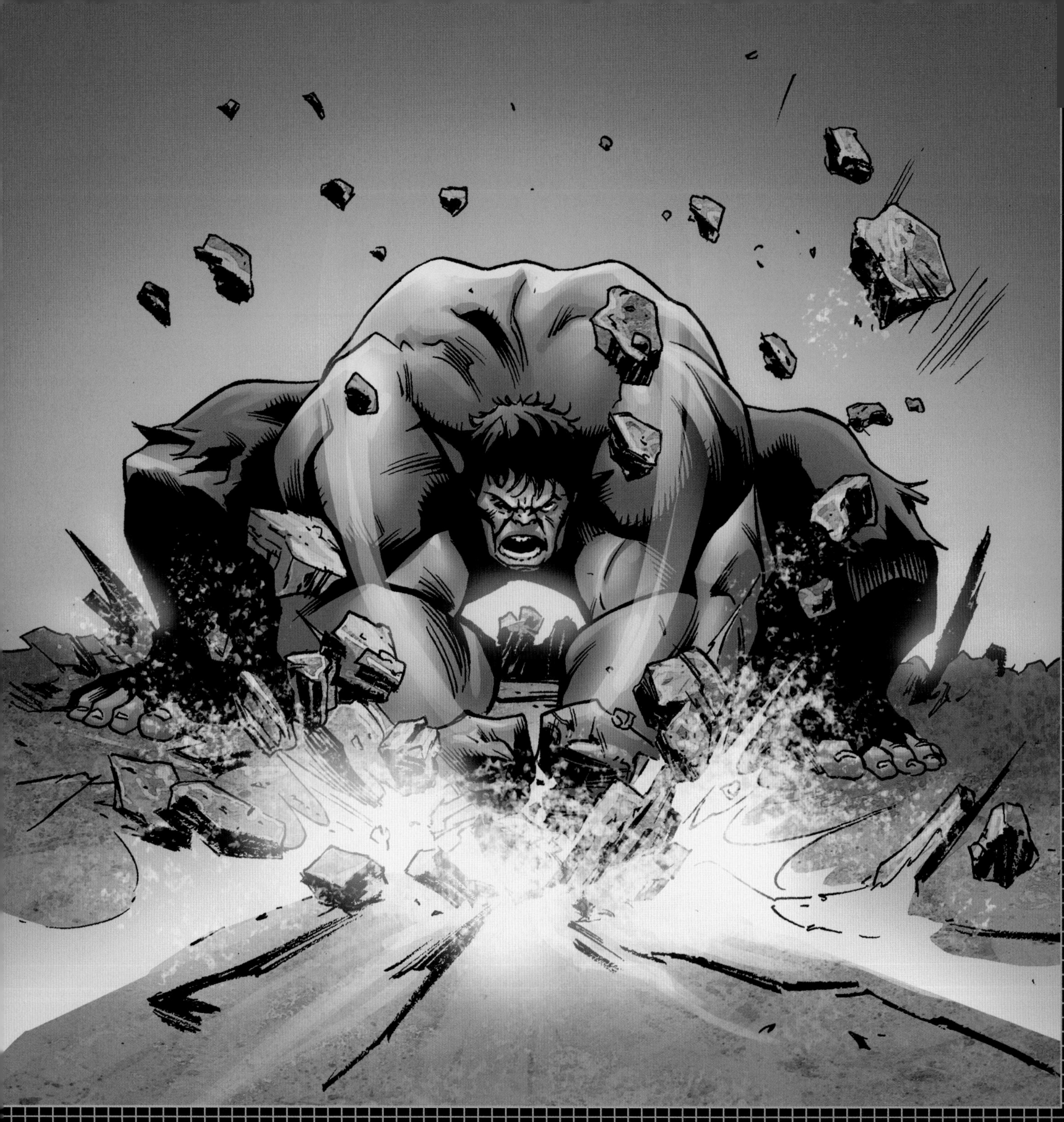

Next up is the creature known as the incredible Hulk. Eight and a half feet tall and a thousand pounds of attitude.

And he's green.

He can punch through a brick wall. He can rip a tree out of the ground. He can throw a truck like it's a baseball, and he can stomp a tank in half. Plus, he can jump more than a mile.

He doesn't say much, but he yells a lot. It's hard to believe the **Hulk is actually Bruce Banner, a brilliant scientist.**

When General Ross, the father of
Bruce's girlfriend, said they wanted to
cure something called gamma radiation
poisoning, Bruce said they could
experiment on him.

But General Ross was really trying to
create another Super-Soldier like Captain
America. It didn't work. Instead of getting
Cap's powers, Bruce turned into the Hulk.

**Now, whenever he gets mad, Bruce
changes into the incredible Hulk.**

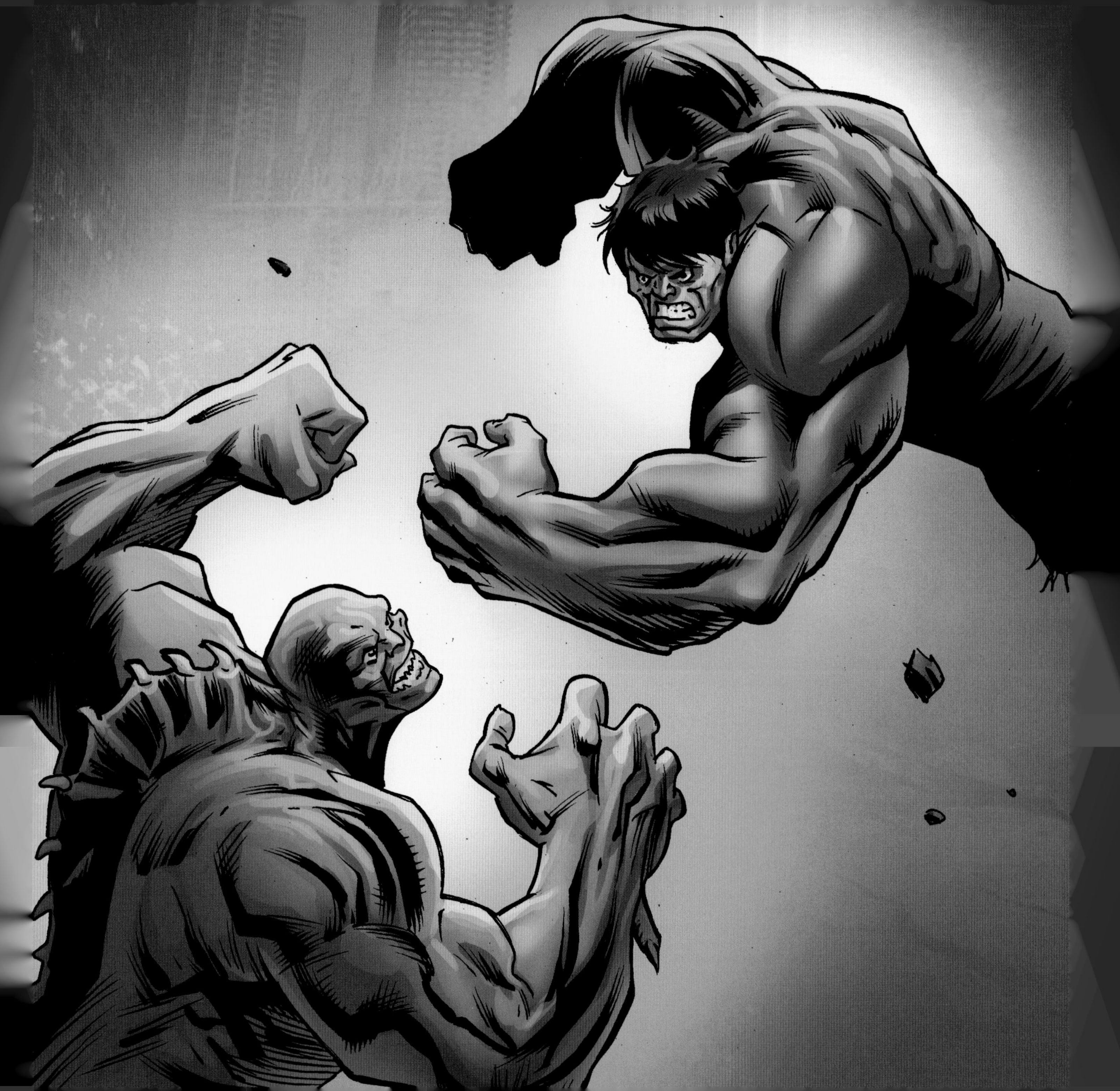

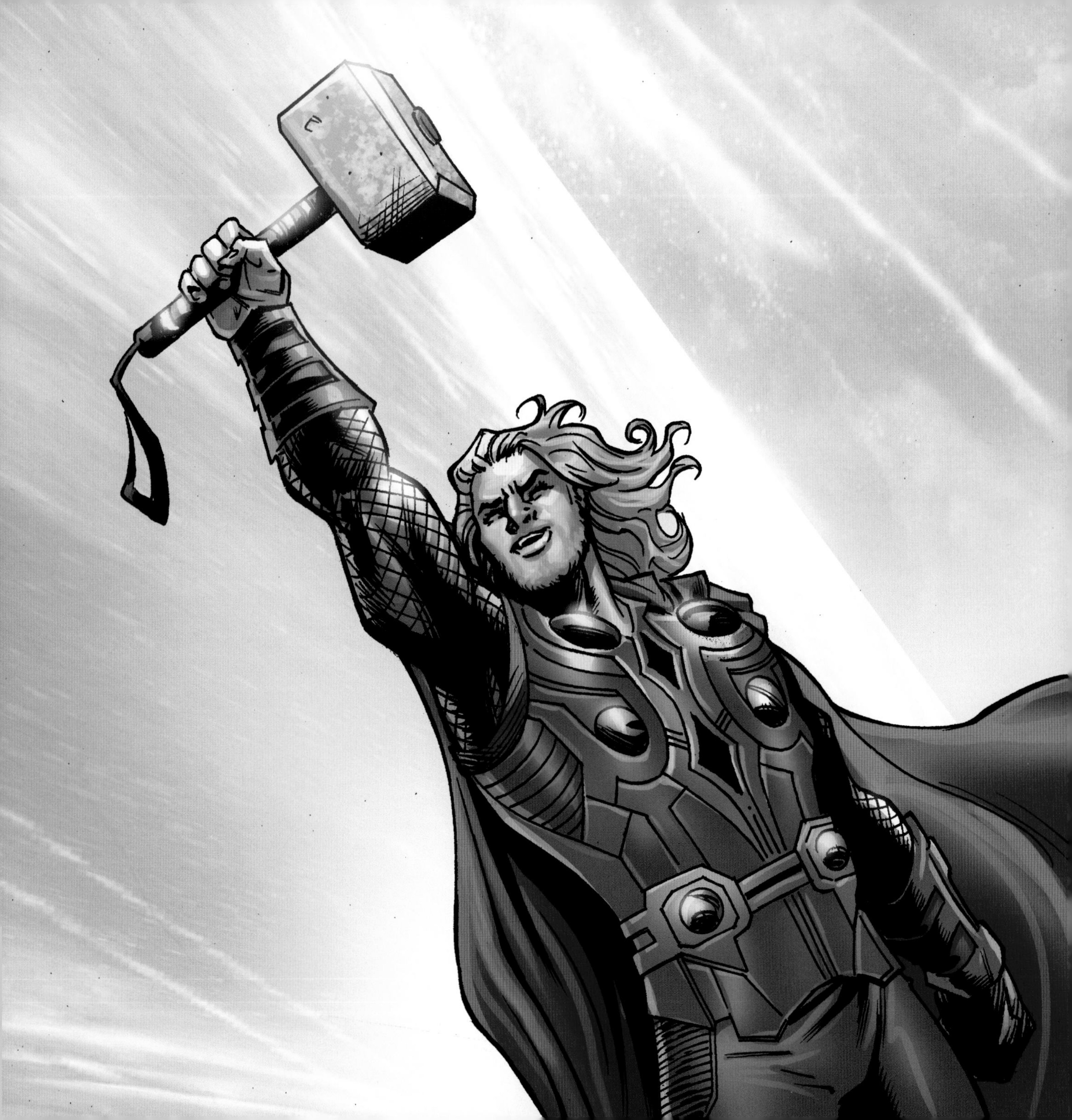

Then there's Thor. Like the Hulk, he is impossibly strong—if there's a limit to his strength, we haven't found it yet.

He carries something he calls Mjolnir—a magical hammer. This hammer cannot be broken—but it seems it can break anything, except for Captain America's shield. No one else can even lift Mjolnir, but if Thor twirls it really fast and then throws it while holding on to its strap, he can fly.

You could say he's...mighty.

Thor doesn't wear a special suit, and he wasn't given some Super-Soldier Serum.

Thor is from Asgard, a place of Norse myth that happens to be real.

And while that sounds silly, it's what Thor believes. Also, S.H.I.E.L.D. hasn't found any proof yet that it's not true. So as long as he's one of the good guys, I don't really care where he came from.

His evil brother, **Loki**, on the other hand, is a master of magic and very dangerous—he's number one on our Most Wanted list.

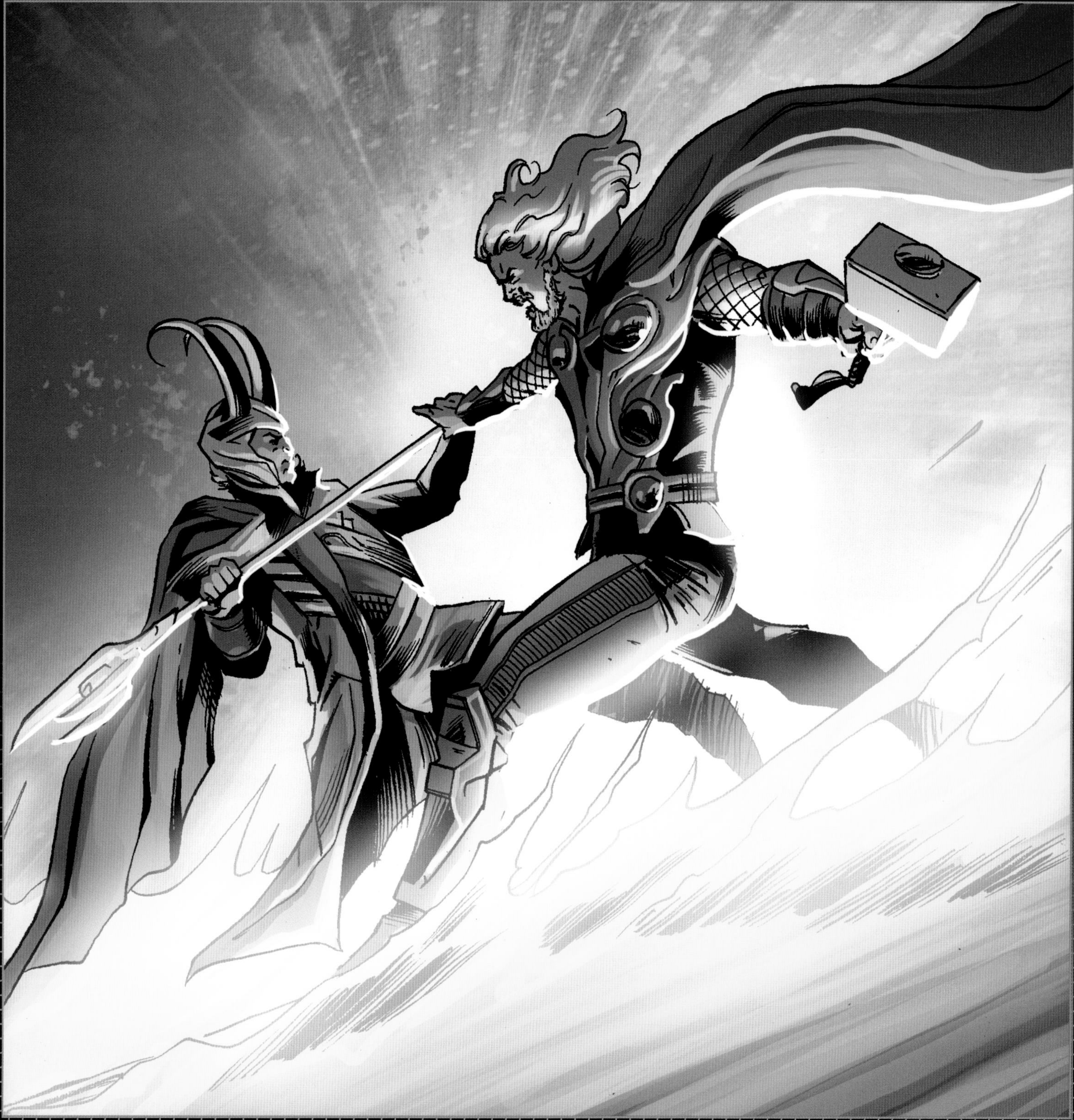

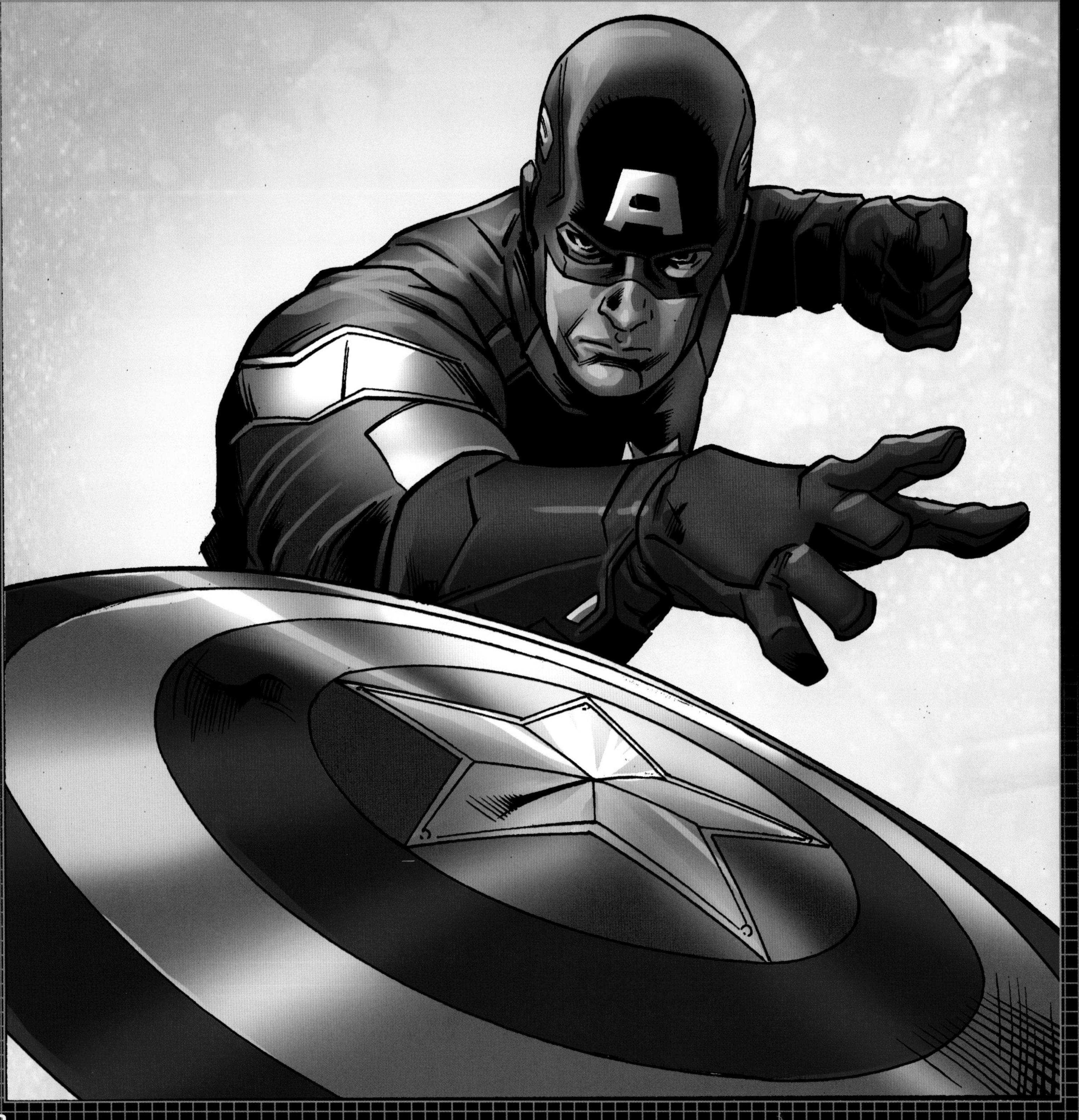

And then there's Captain America.
The ultimate Super-Soldier.

The fastest people can run a mile in three and a half minutes—Captain America can do it in just one. The strongest people can lift a thousand pounds—Captain America can lift twice that. He can't be poisoned or gassed and he almost never gets tired.

And he carries a shield made of vibranium, which cannot be broken.

Yet Captain America was once the smallest, slowest, weakest kid in school.

Young Steve Rogers was smart and nice and tried hard—harder than anyone else. But he was always sickly.

More than anything, Steve wanted to be a soldier. After being rejected again and again, a scientist asked if he would be part of a secret experiment called **Project: Rebirth.** That experiment turned him into the Super-Soldier he is today.

And now Steve Rogers is Captain America, the First Avenger. Cap fights a never-ending battle against evil, which includes the sinister Hydra organization and its leader, the Red Skull!

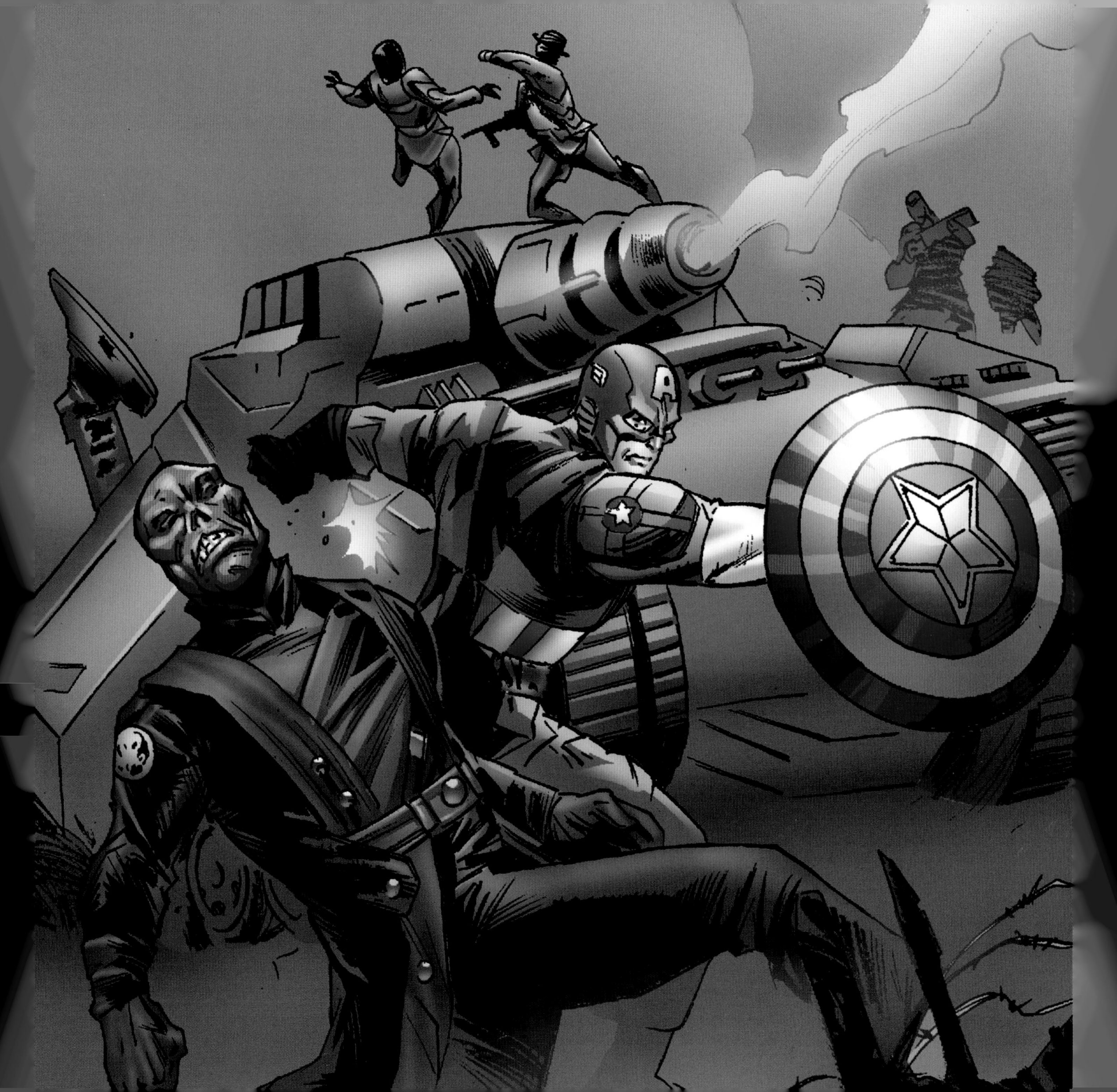

Natasha Romanoff. Tony Stark knew her as Natalie Rushman when she worked for him. But, actually, she was working for me. **I call her Black Widow.**

She's an expert in every form of fighting and an expert with every kind of weapon. She speaks a dozen languages. She's even a world-class dancer.

The thing Black Widow may be best at? Keeping everyone guessing—even me. No one can ever tell what she's going to do next . . . but whatever it is, she'll succeed.

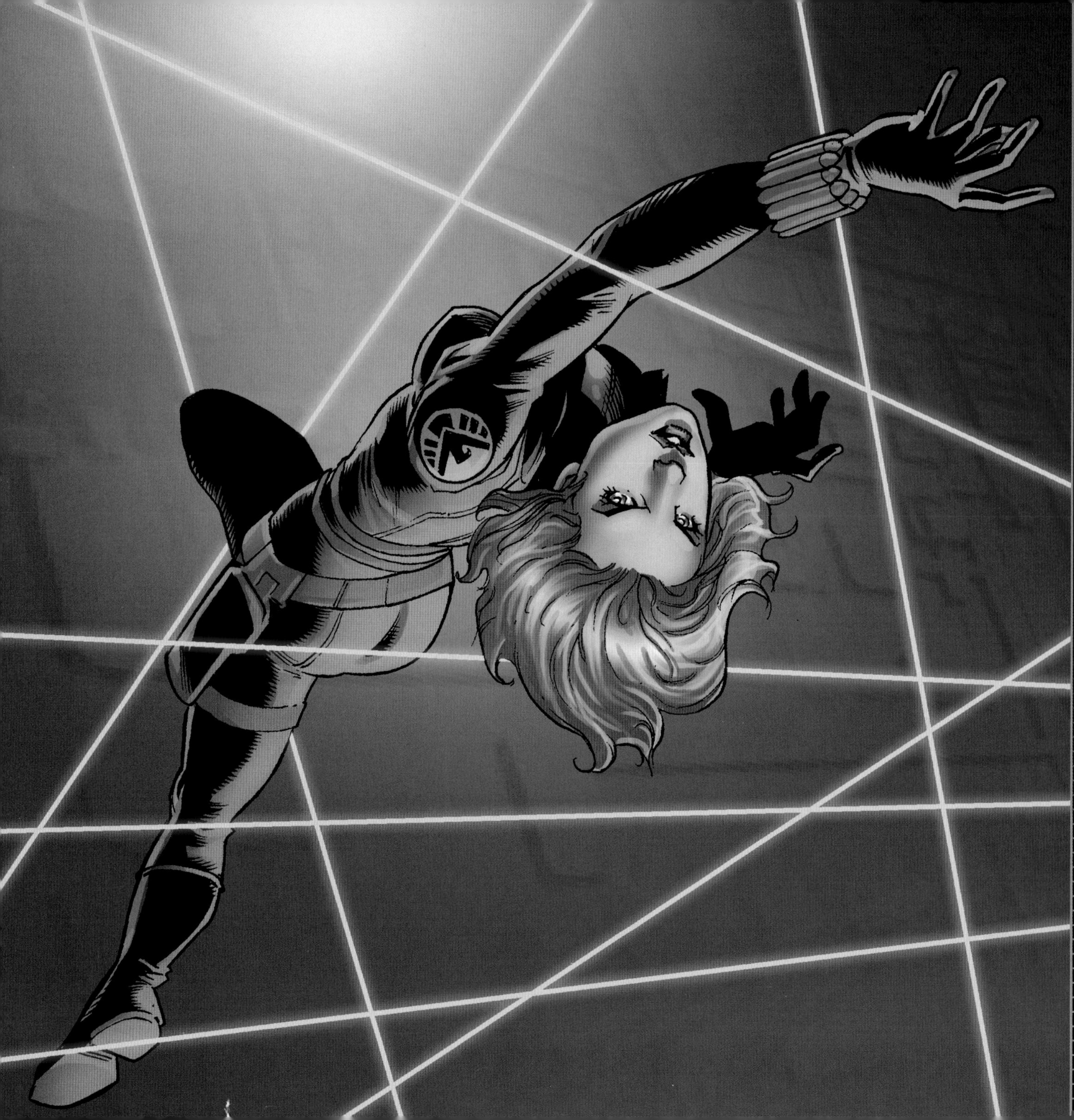

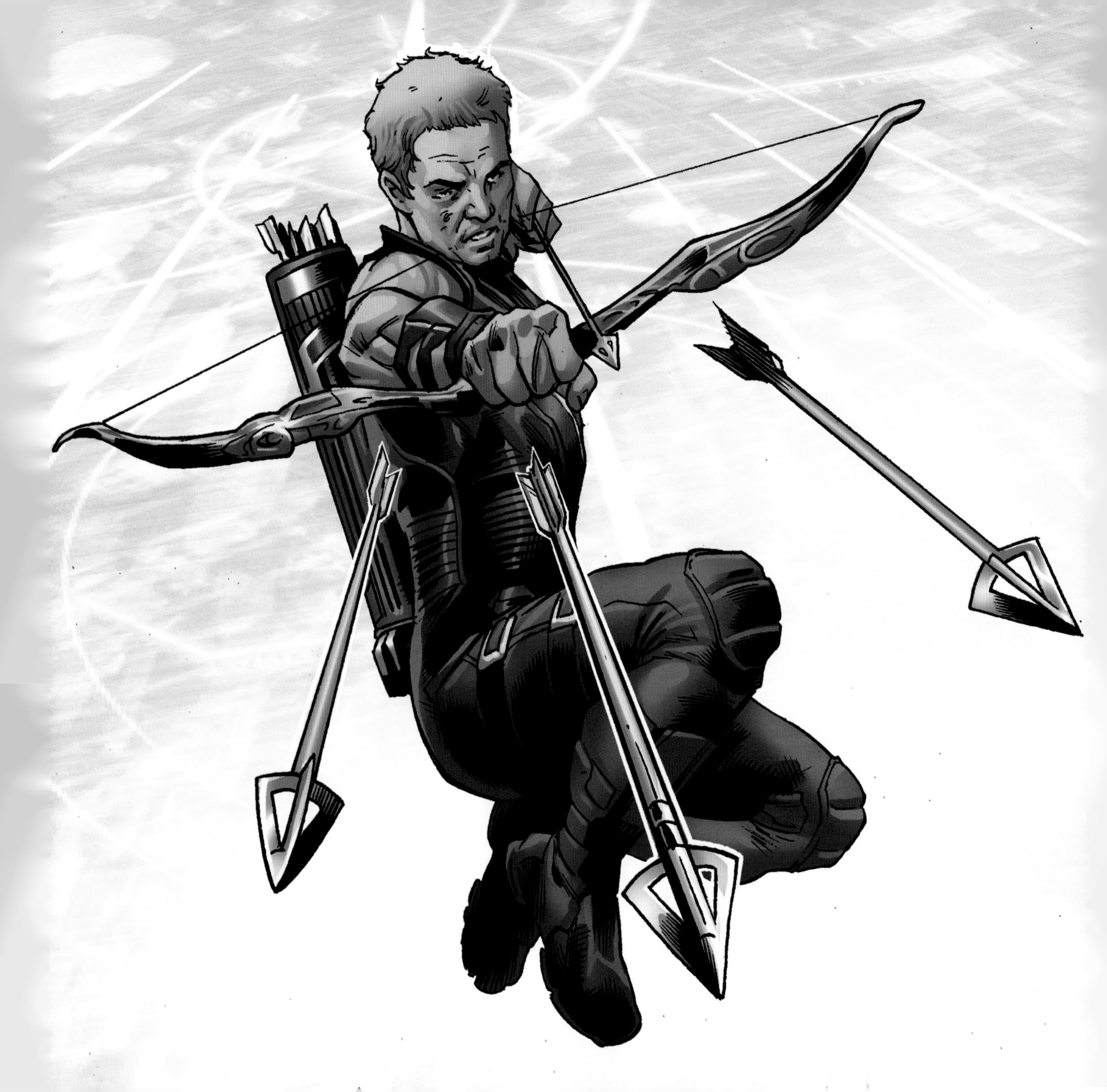

And that brings us to Clint Barton—Hawkeye.

Whenever I can't afford to miss, I call in Hawkeye. He is an expert marksman—especially when it comes to archery.

I've seen him do stuff with a bow and arrow that just doesn't seem possible. I mean, Thor was amazed by some of the things Hawkeye could do—and it's not easy to impress a Norse god.

And then there's me. I'm the guy who knows what's going on. The guy who makes things happen.

I run the Strategic Homeland Intervention, Enforcement, and Logistics Division. We just call it S.H.I.E.L.D.

The few people who know me call me **Nick Fury.**

But I think of myself as the man who assembled **the Avengers.**

MARVEL
AVENGERS

» RETURN OF THE
FIRST AVENGER

Written by
Michael Siglain

Based on Marvel's *The Avengers*
Motion Picture Written by
Joss Whedon

Illustrated by
Lee Garbett, John Lucas,
and
Lee Duhig

Based on
Marvel Comics' *The Avengers*

This is the story of the return of the First Avenger.

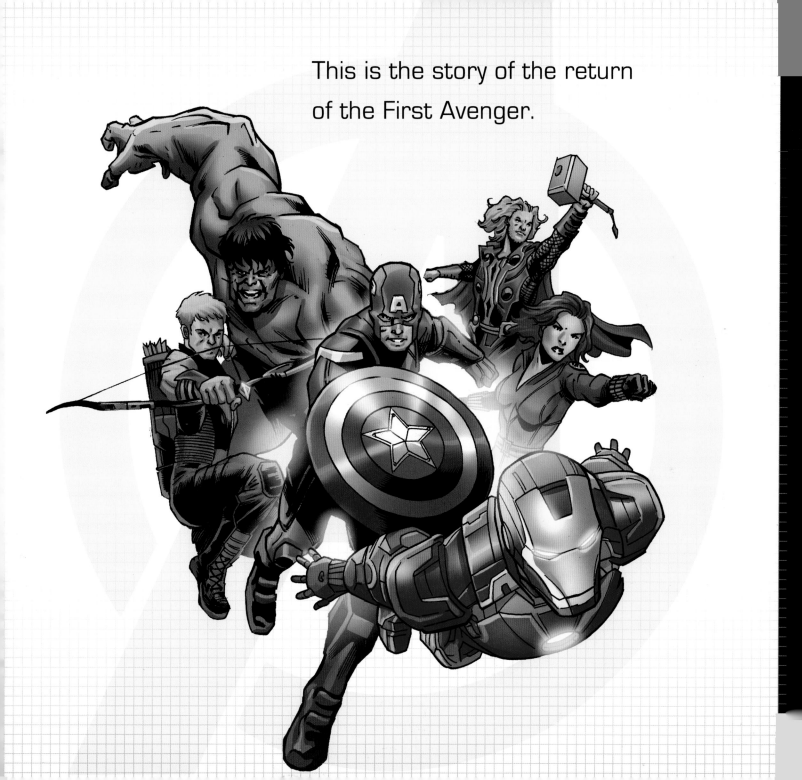

Steve Rogers wasn't always
a Super Hero.
And he wasn't always
known as Captain America.

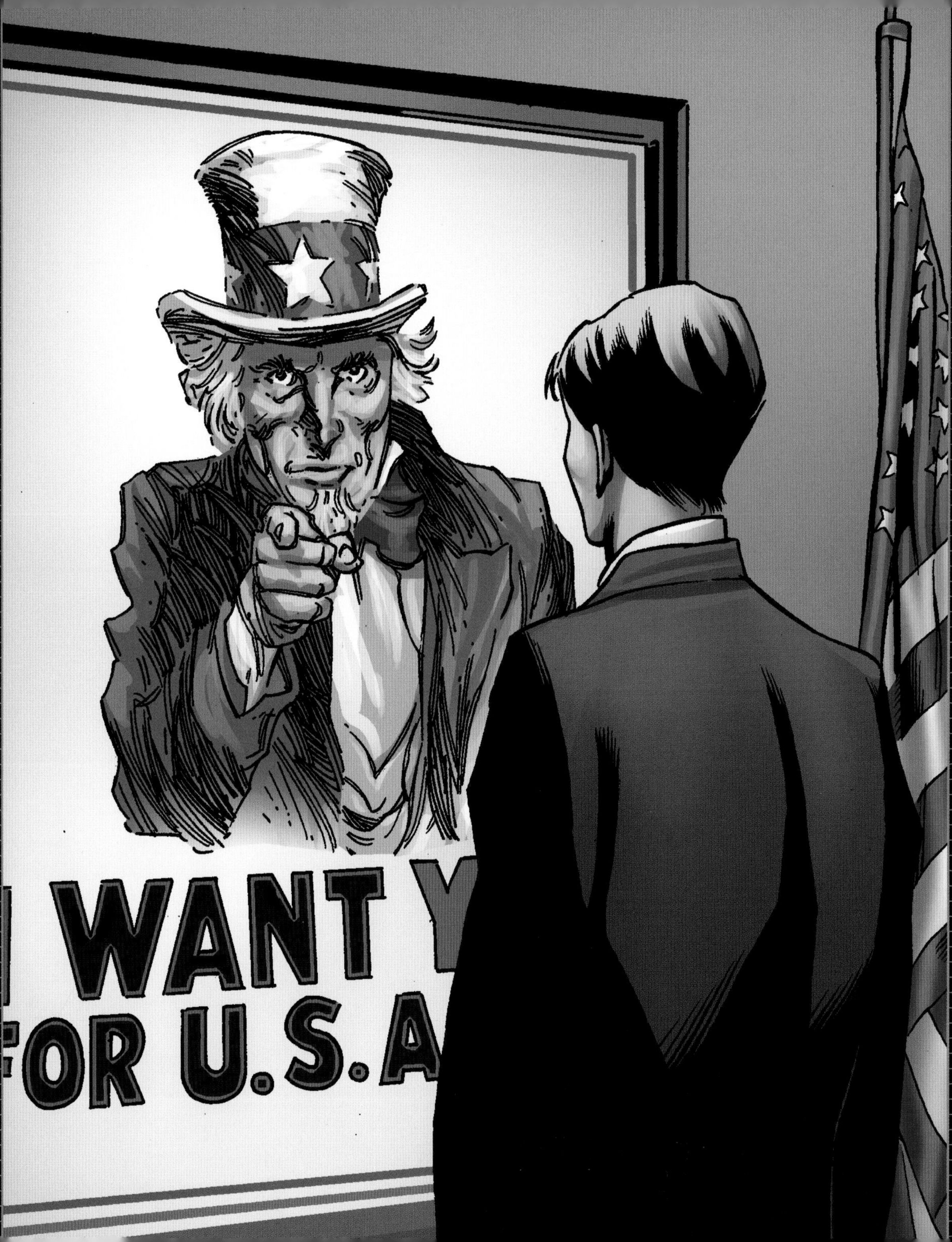
I WANT
FOR U.S.A

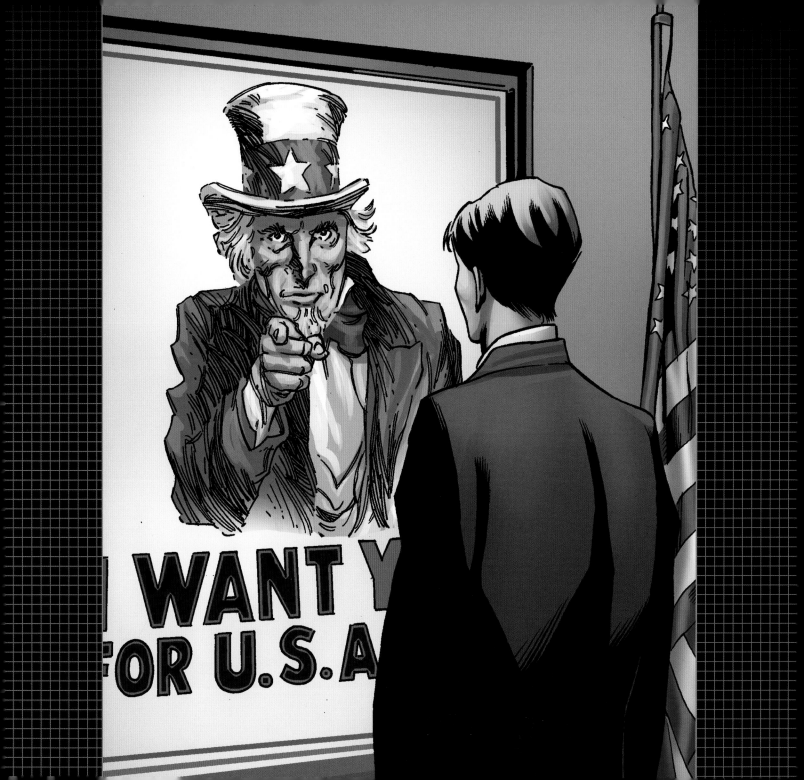

Steve took part in a very
special army experiment
called Project: Rebirth.
It turned Steve from sick
and thin to big and strong.

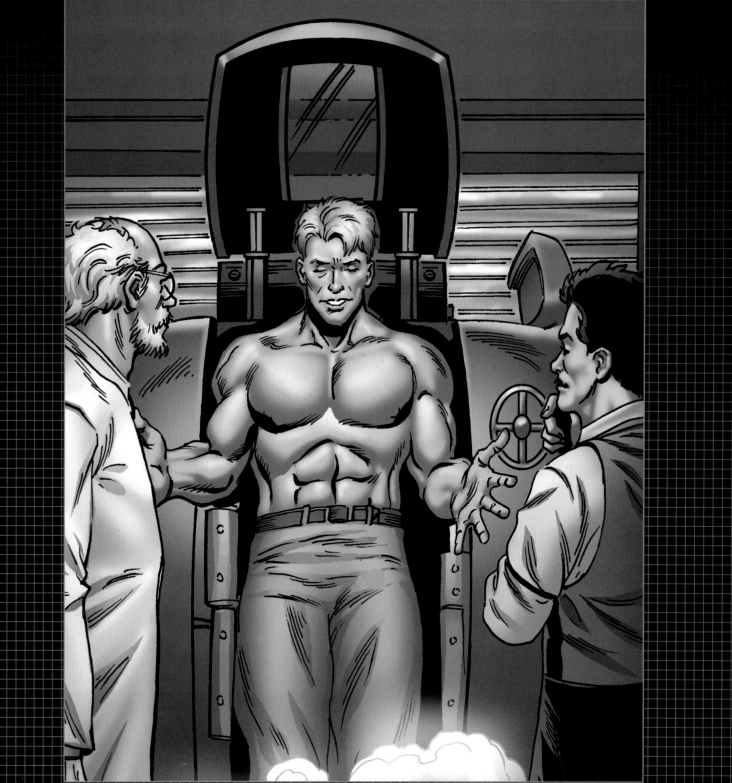

Steve Rogers became America's first Super-Soldier.

He was now known as Captain America, the First Avenger!

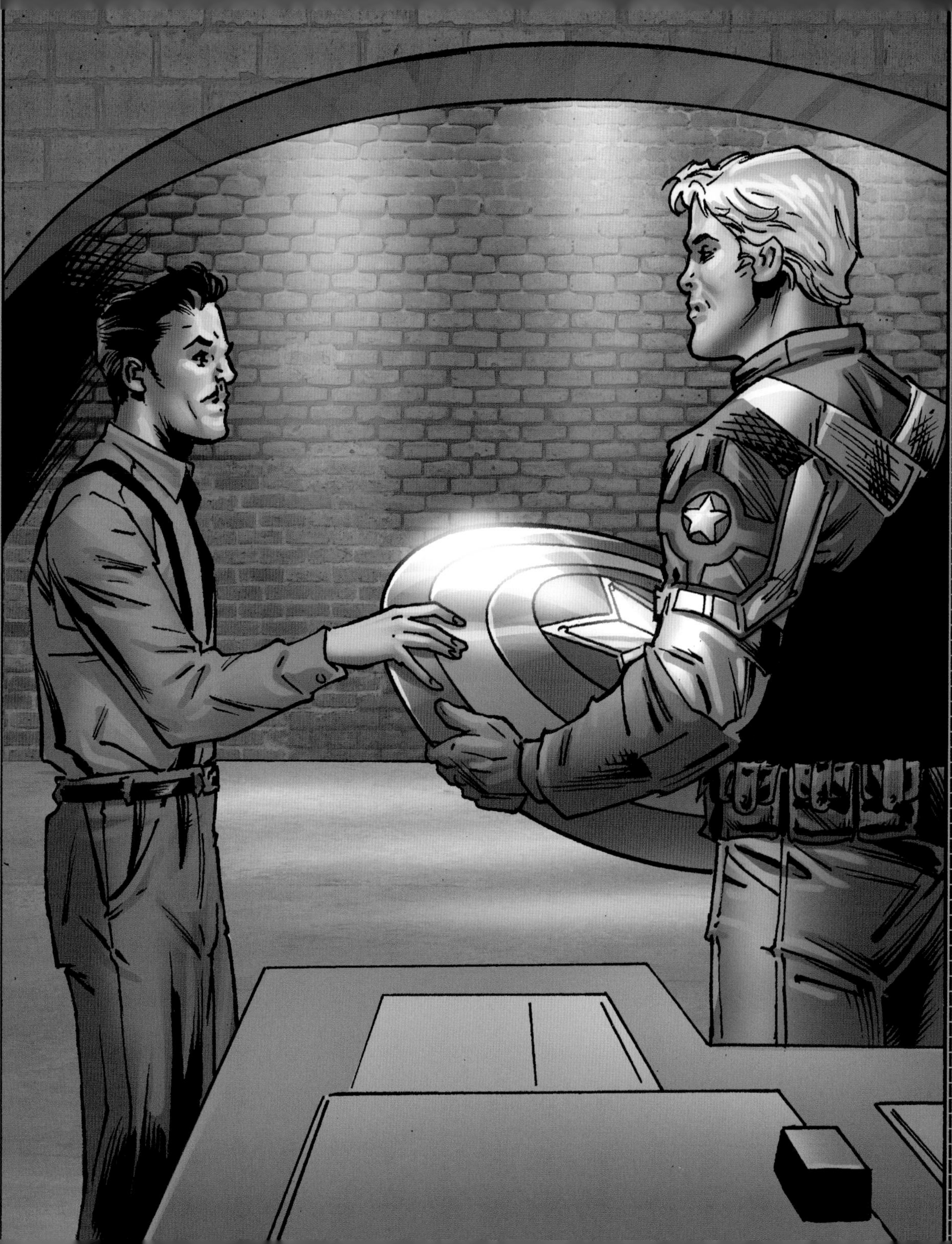

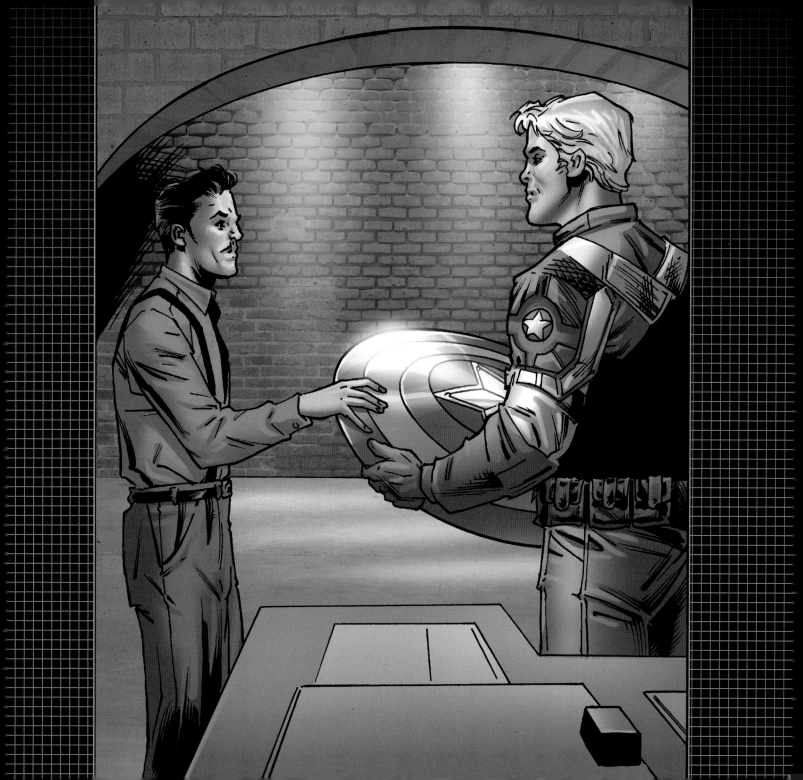

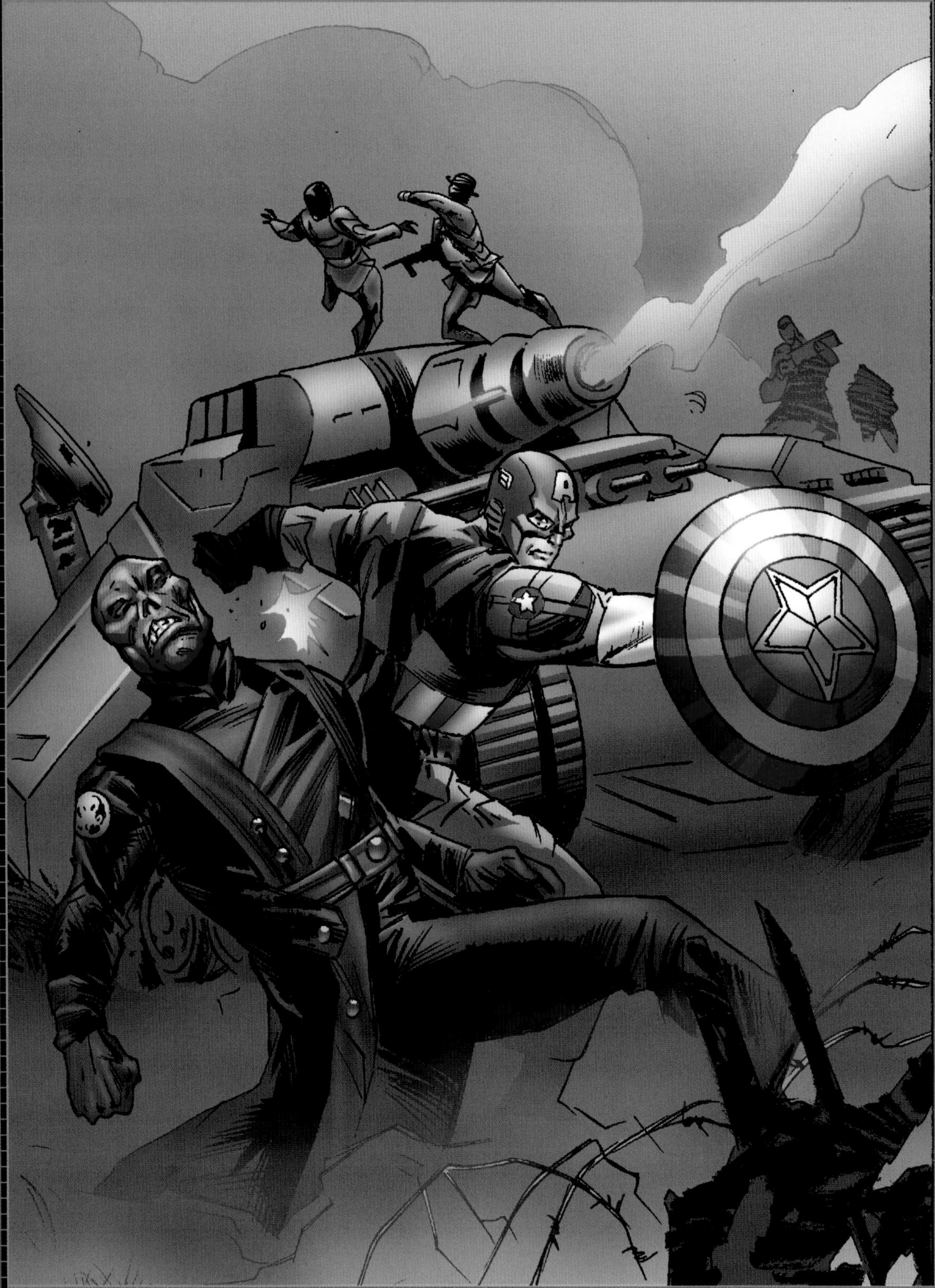

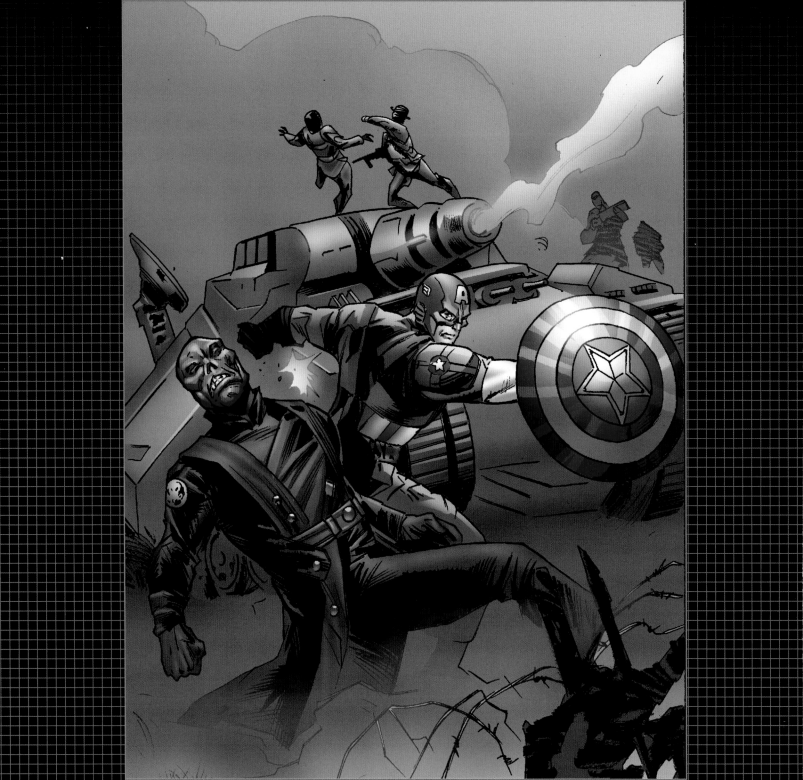

Captain America fought
for justice with the Howling
Commandos against the
evil Red Skull and his
Hydra army!

During World War II, Captain
America was lost in the
Arctic while saving the world.
  He stopped a plane full of
bombs.

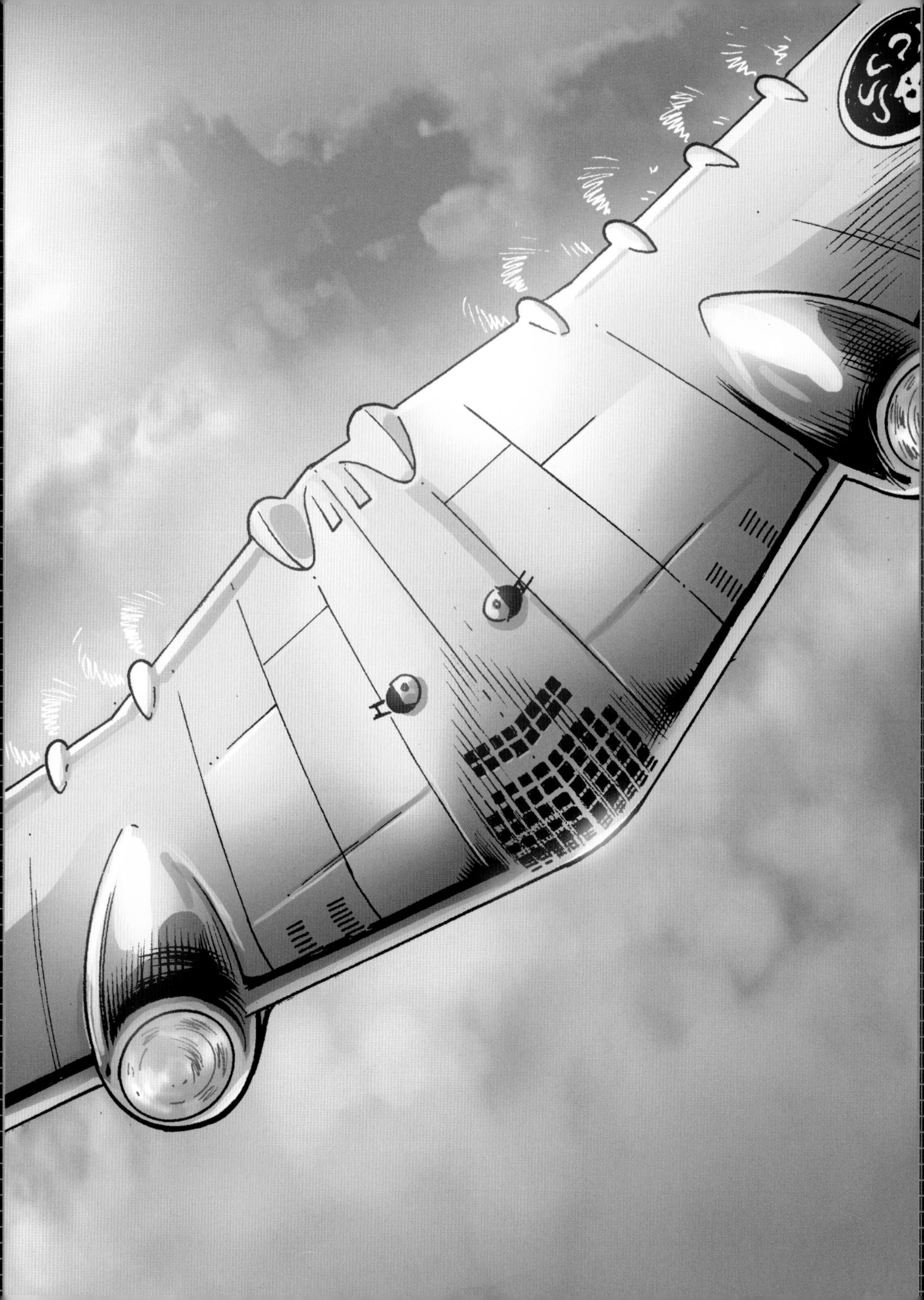

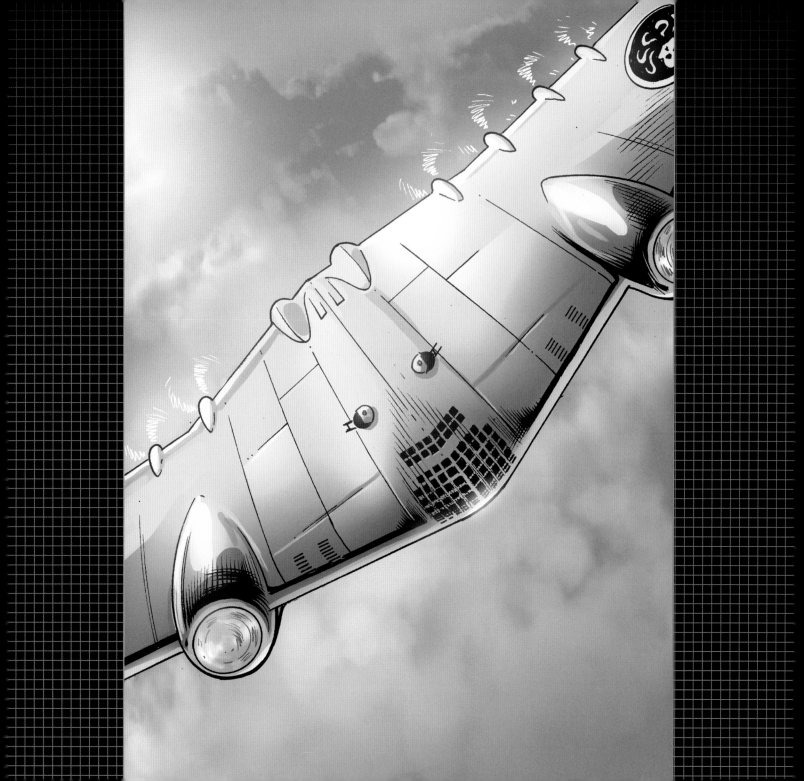

Captain America and the plane he was flying sank under the cold ice. Captain America was trapped inside the plane and frozen in the Arctic for many, many years.

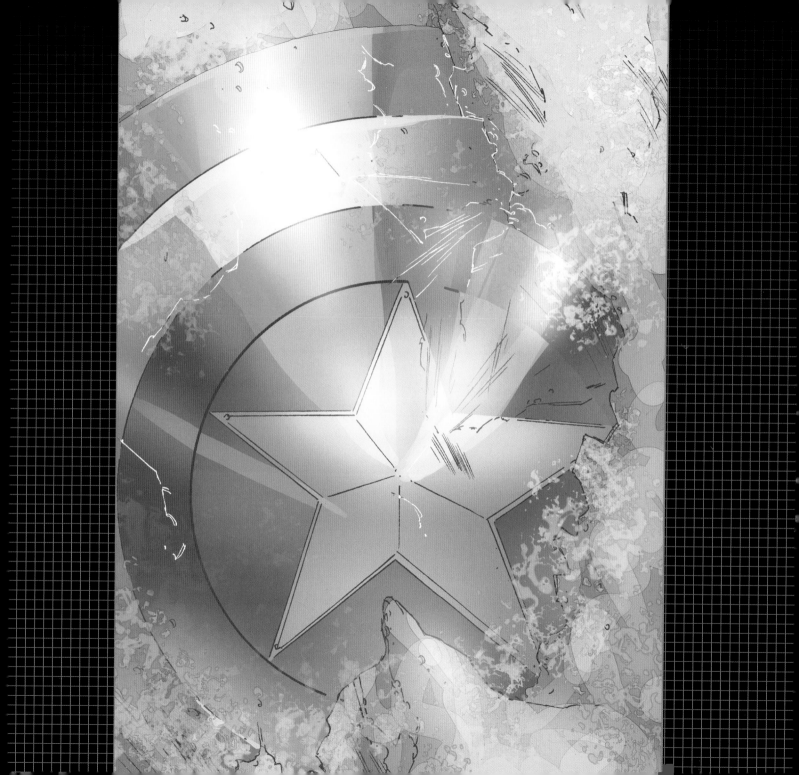

Decades passed, until finally Nick Fury's S.H.I.E.L.D. team found Cap and the plane.

S.H.I.E.L.D.'s plan was to bring Captain America back to life!

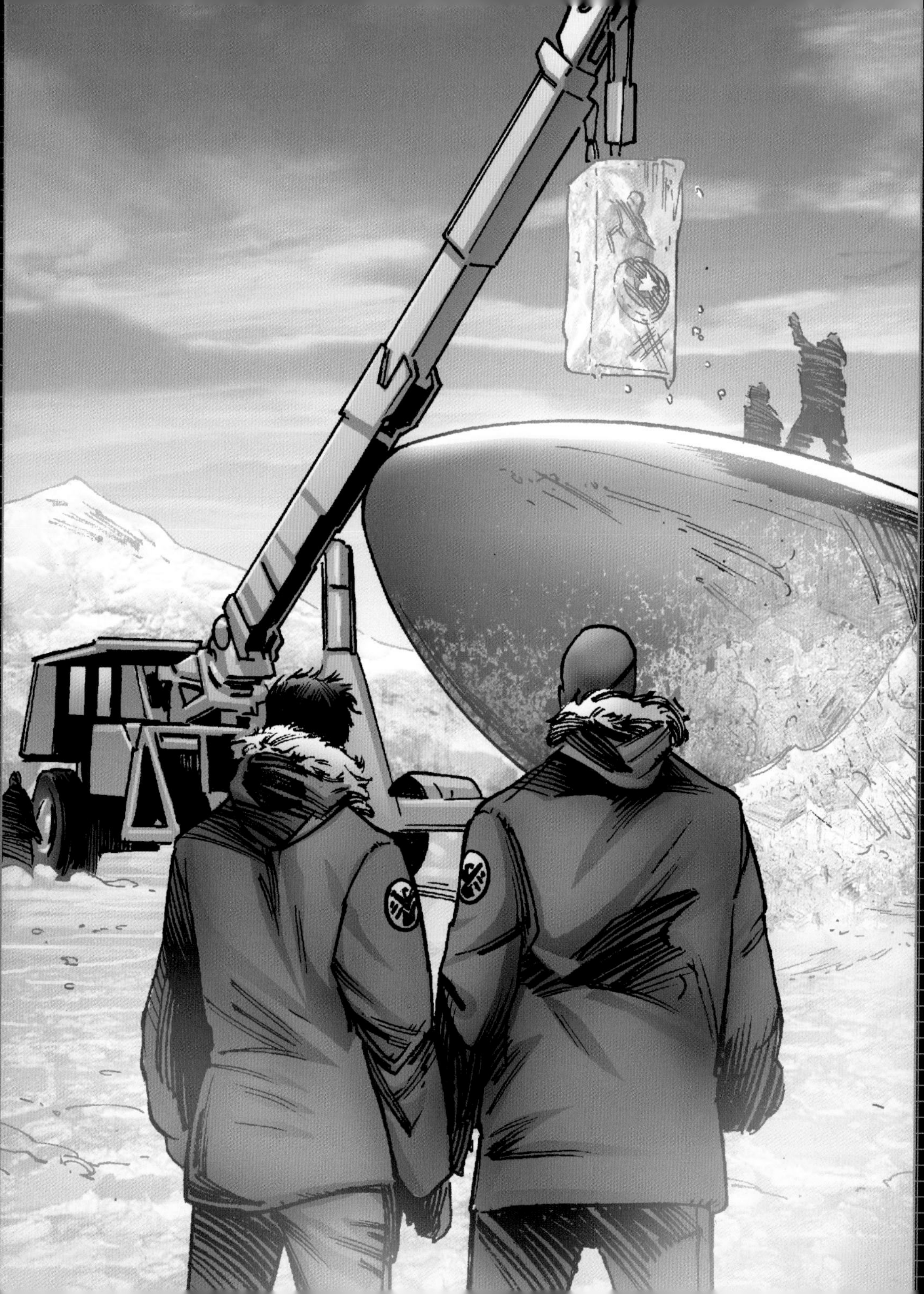

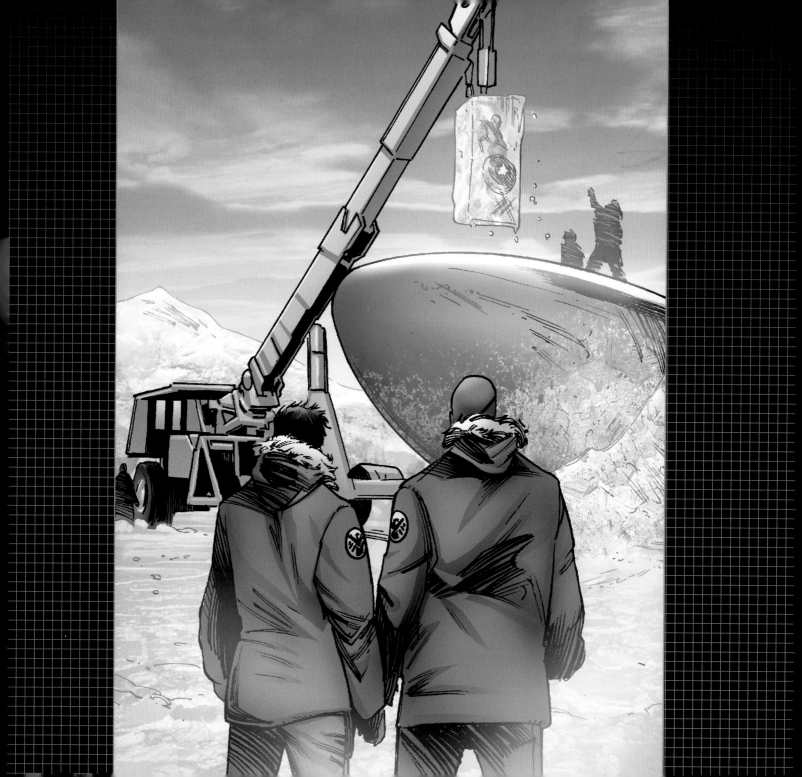

Steve Rogers awoke almost seventy years later.

He was very confused.

Steve didn't know where he was, but he knew he had to escape!

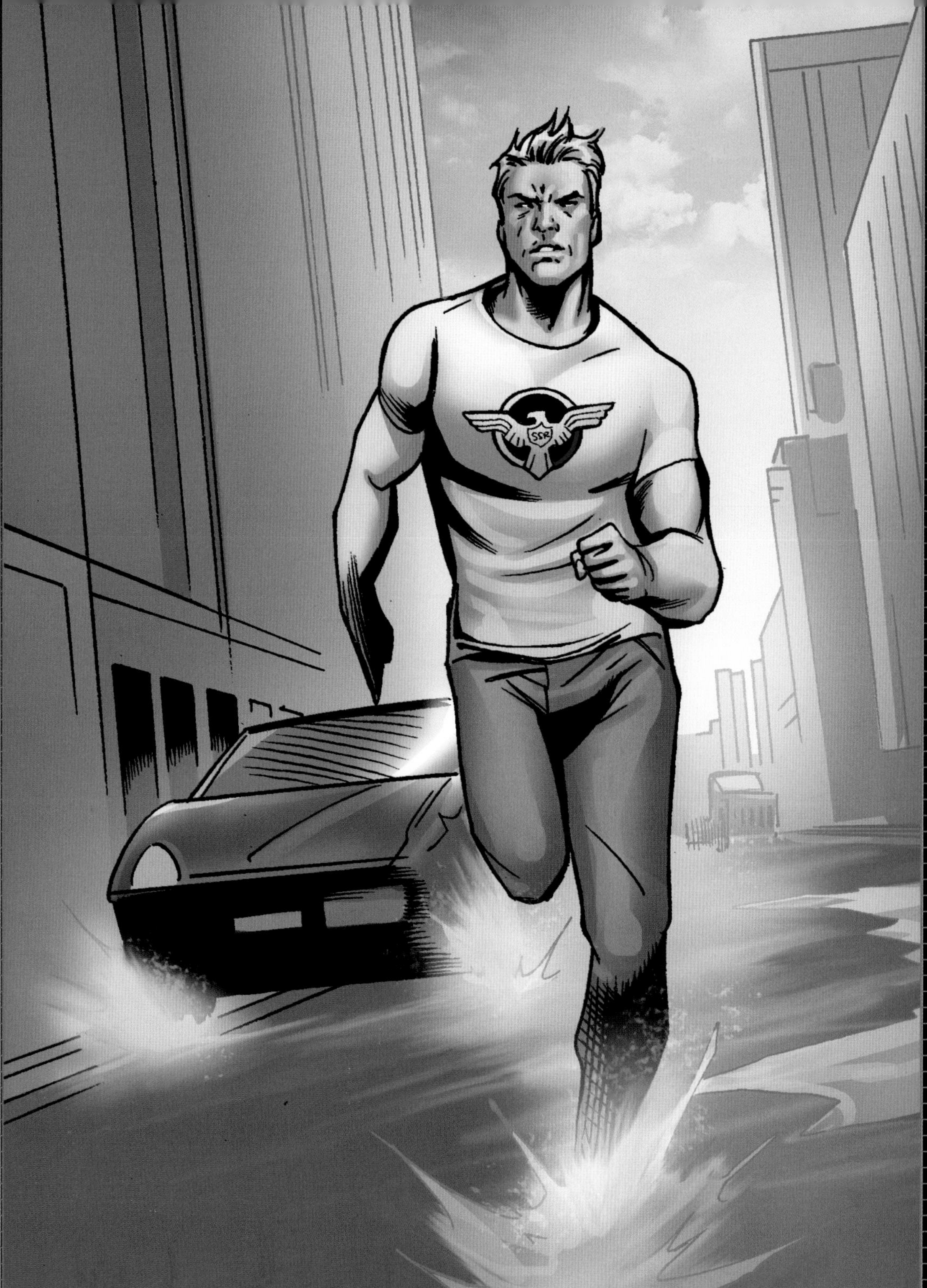

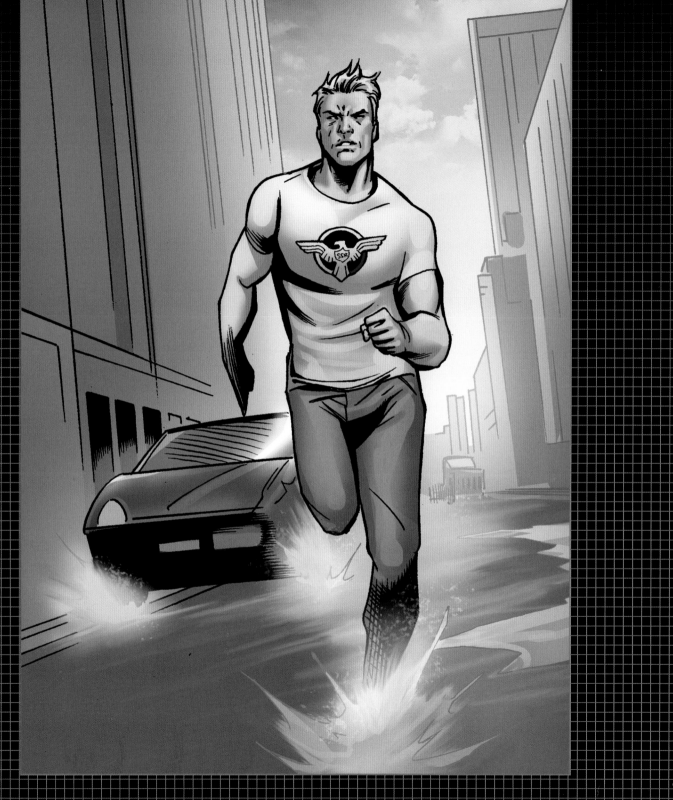

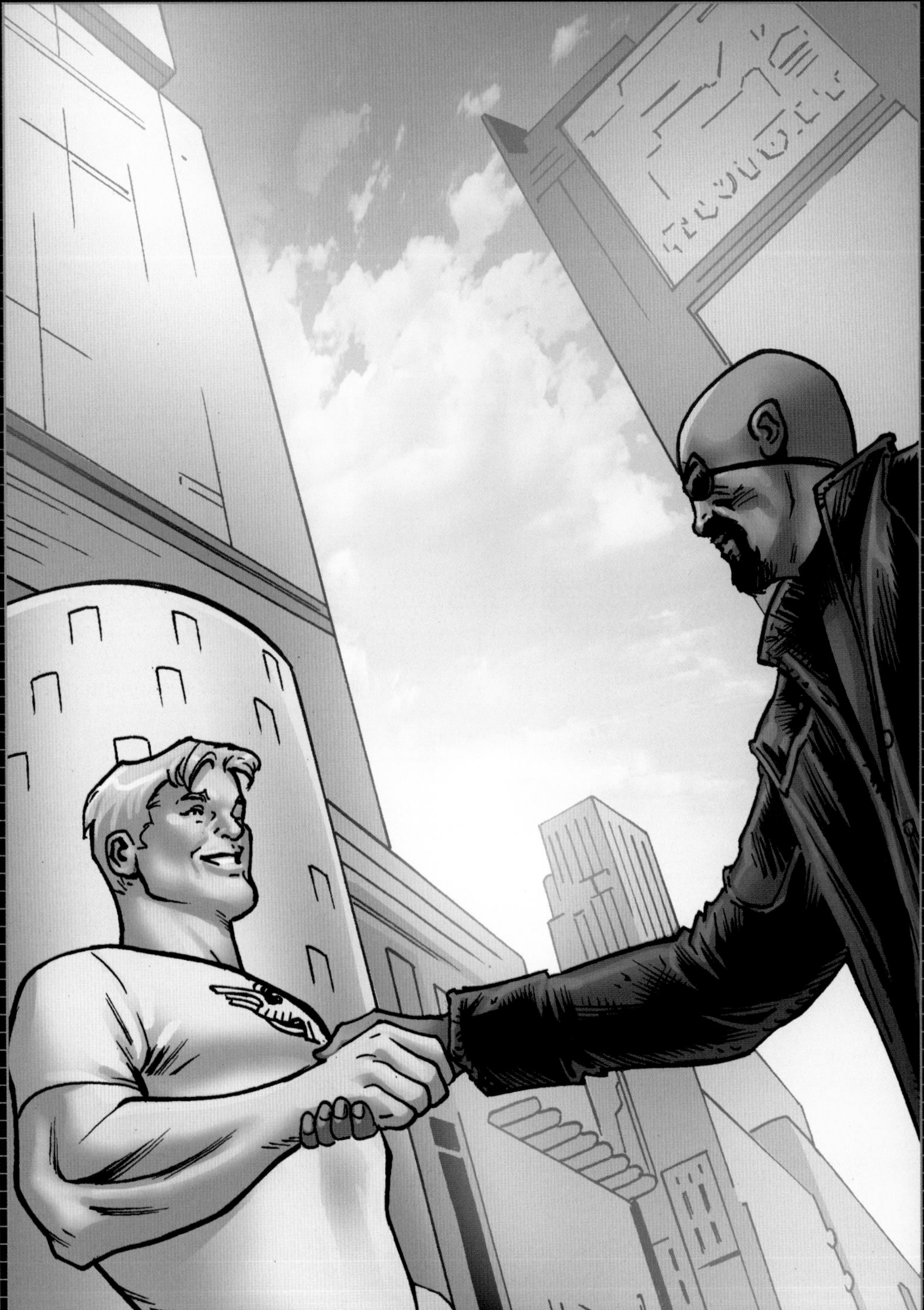

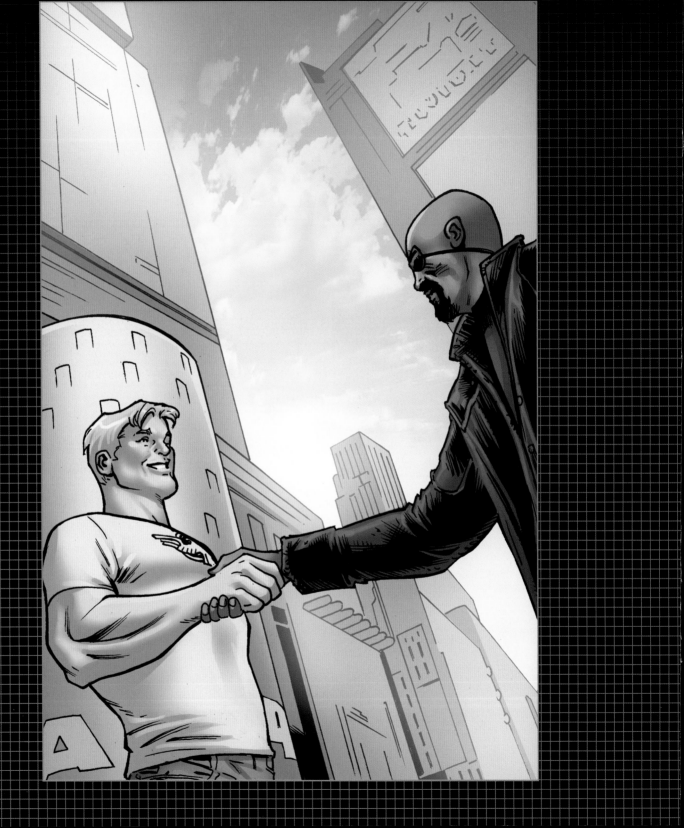

Steve ran into the middle of
Times Square in New York City.
   There, he met Nick Fury, the
director of S.H.I.E.L.D.
   Fury explained what had
happened to Steve and that he
was there to help.

Steve spent a lot of time watching news footage to learn what had happened while he was frozen.

It seemed to him that the world still needed a Super-Soldier.

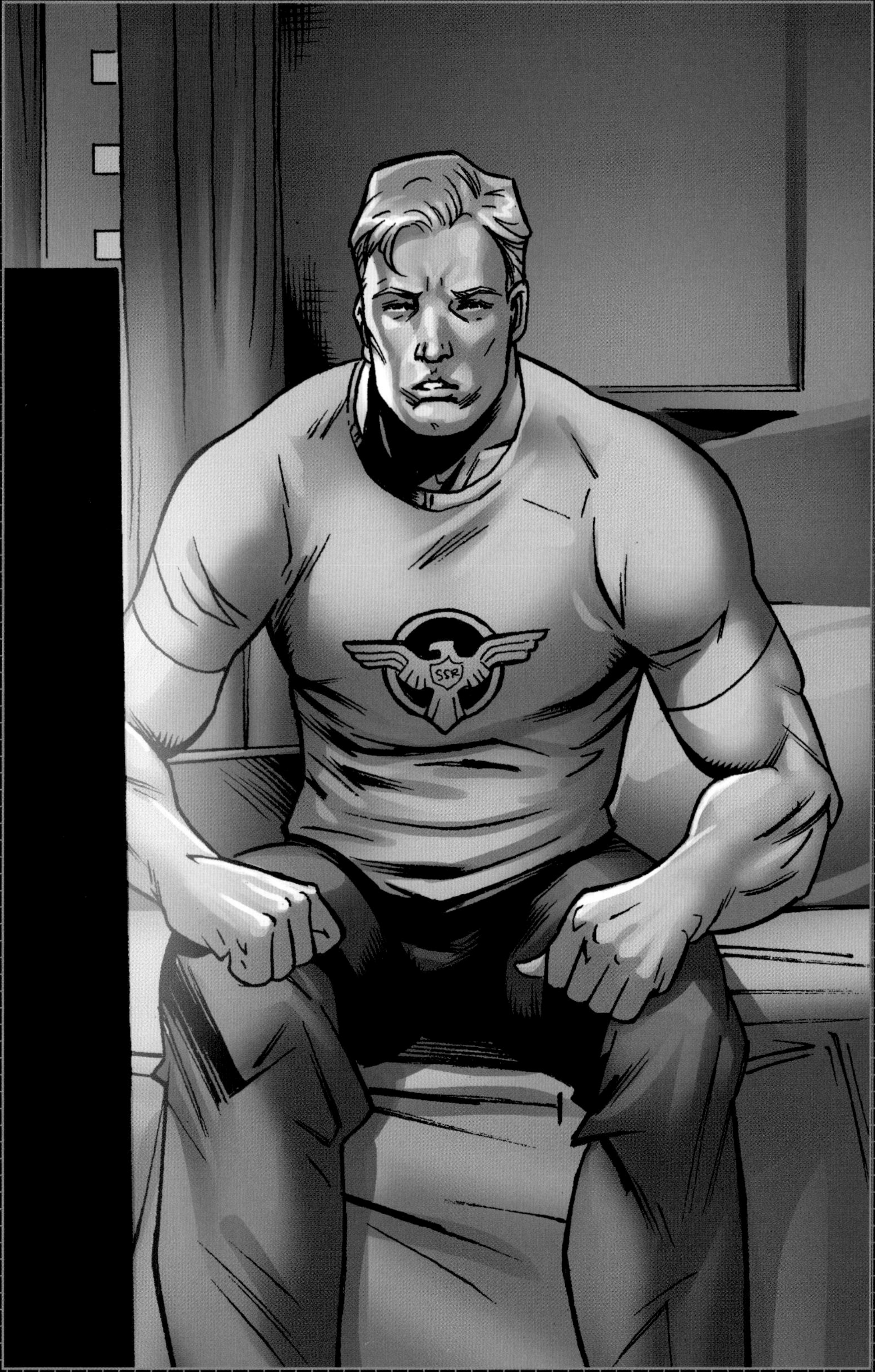
SSR

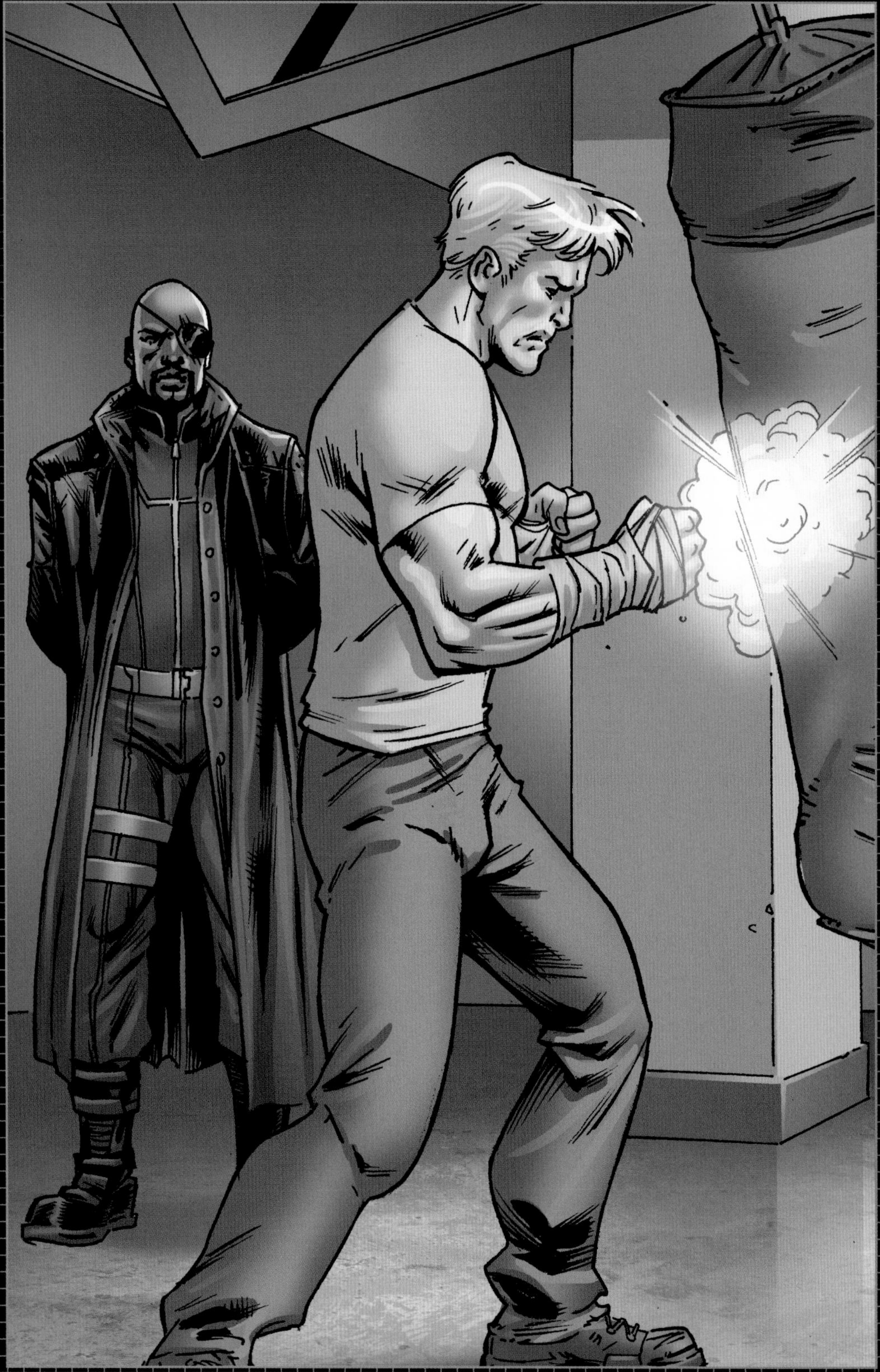

Steve exercised to keep his mind and body strong.

And when Nick Fury asked Steve to join a very special team of Super Heroes, Steve said yes. The First Avenger had returned!

Nick Fury introduced Steve to his new teammates. He met Tony Stark, who is Iron Man; Clint Barton, who is Hawkeye; Natasha Romanoff, who is Black Widow; the mighty Thor; and scientist Dr. Bruce Banner.

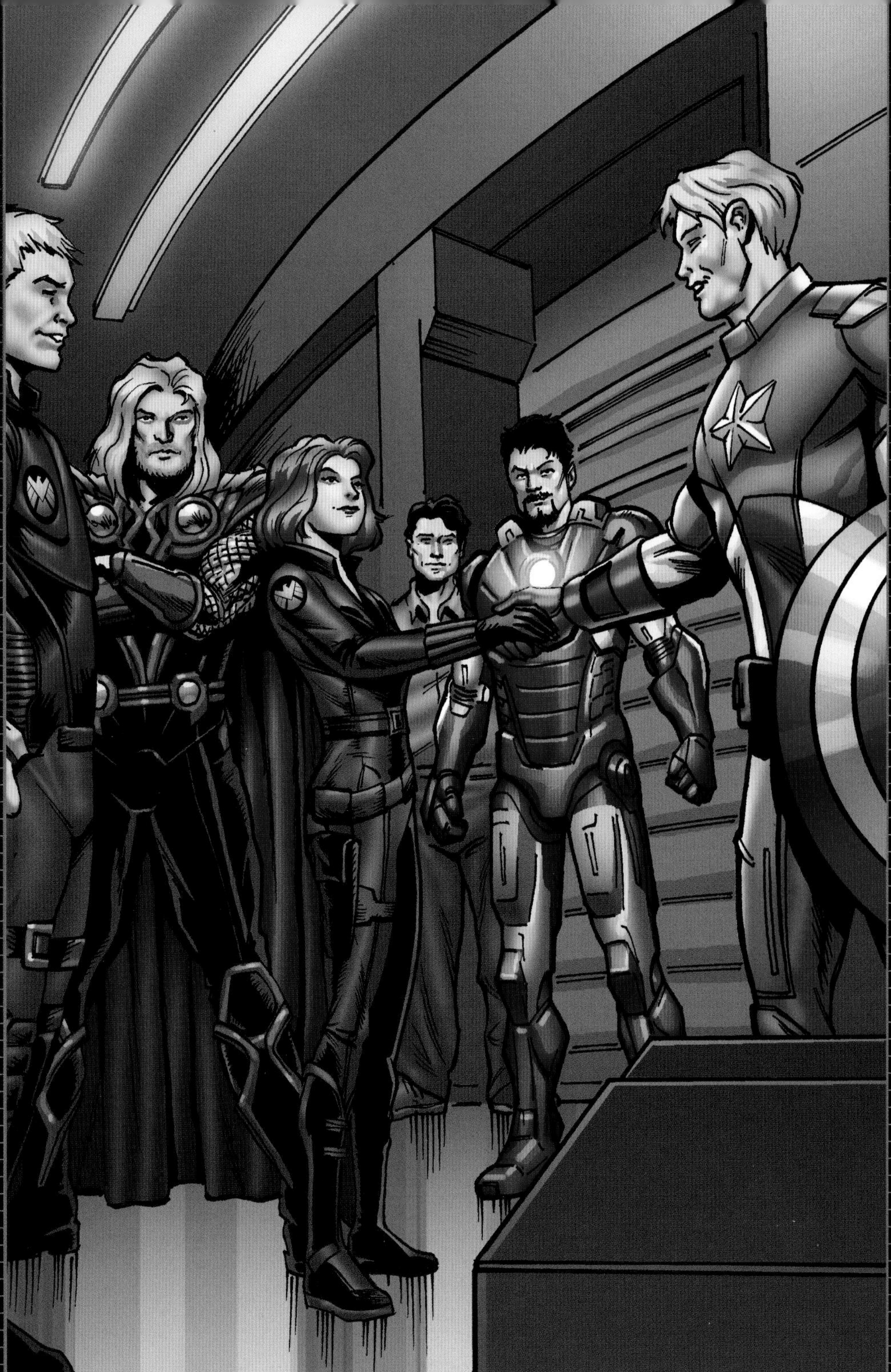

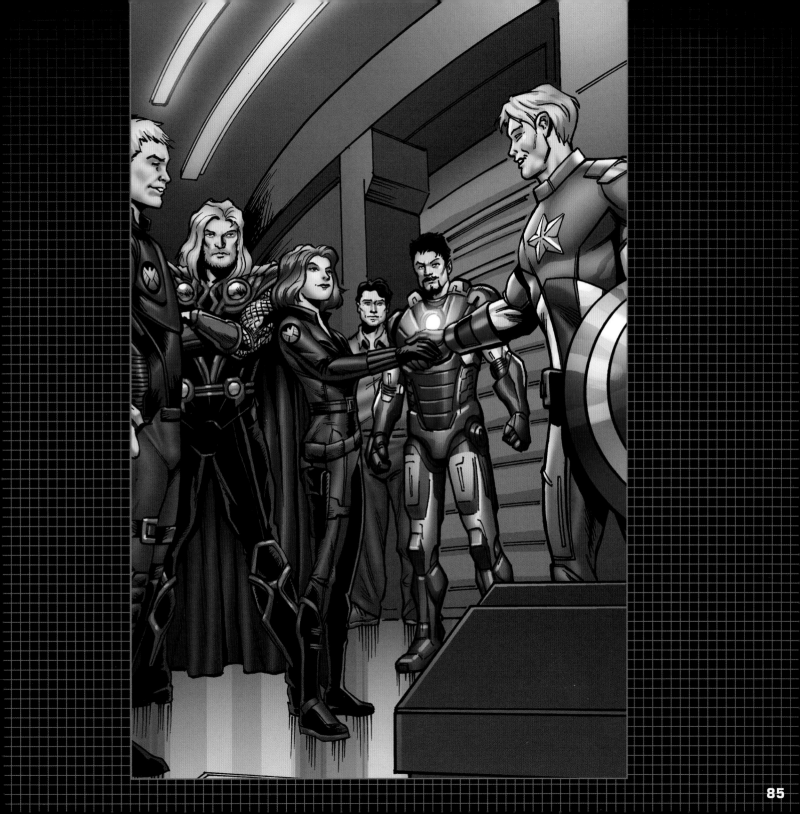

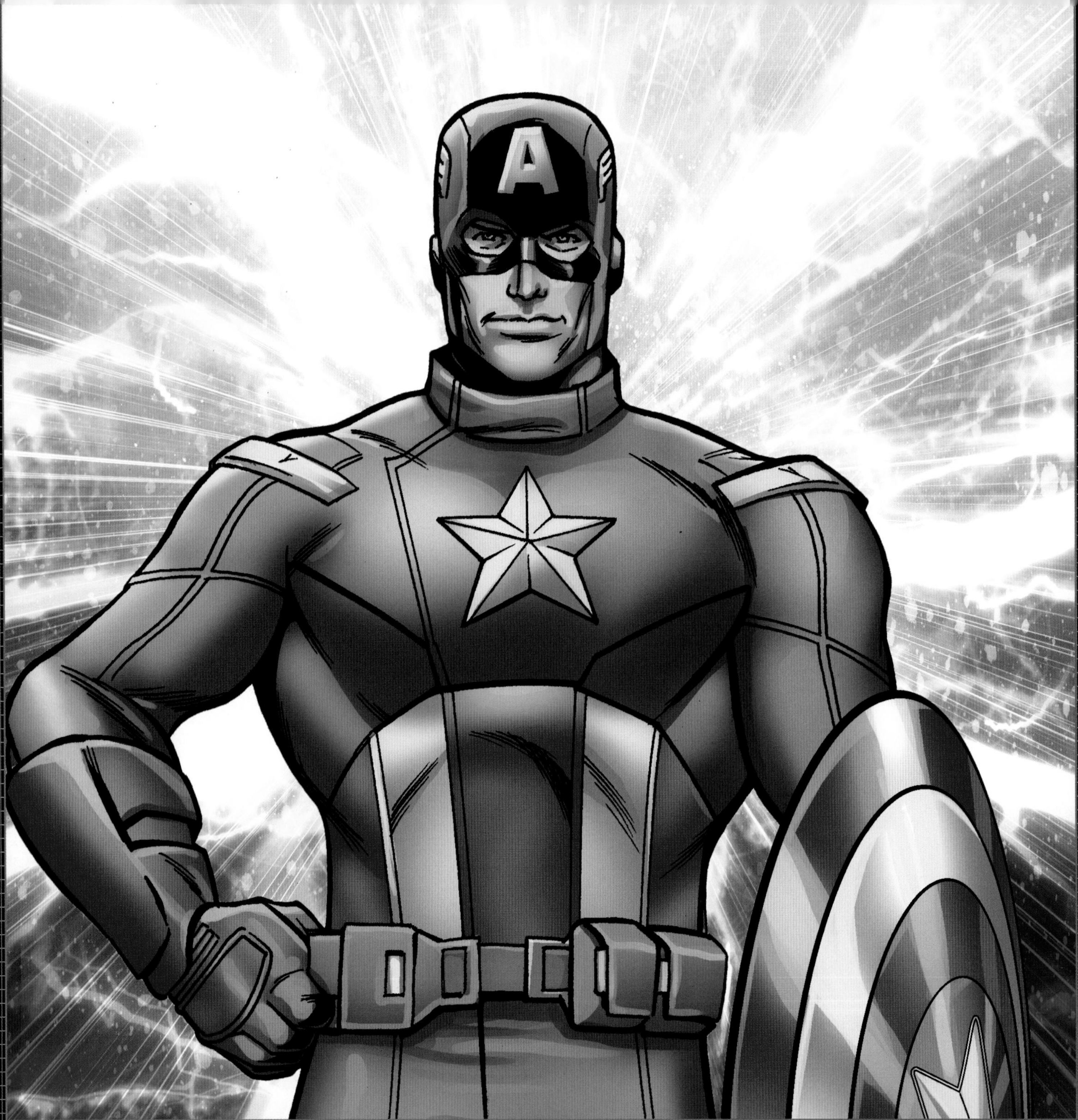

But Steve couldn't go into
battle without a new uniform.
He was given a new suit,
and soon Captain America
was ready for action!

It wasn't long before a
Super Villain threatened the
safety of the world.

Captain America and his
teammates fought against
Loki, Thor's evil brother
from Asgard.

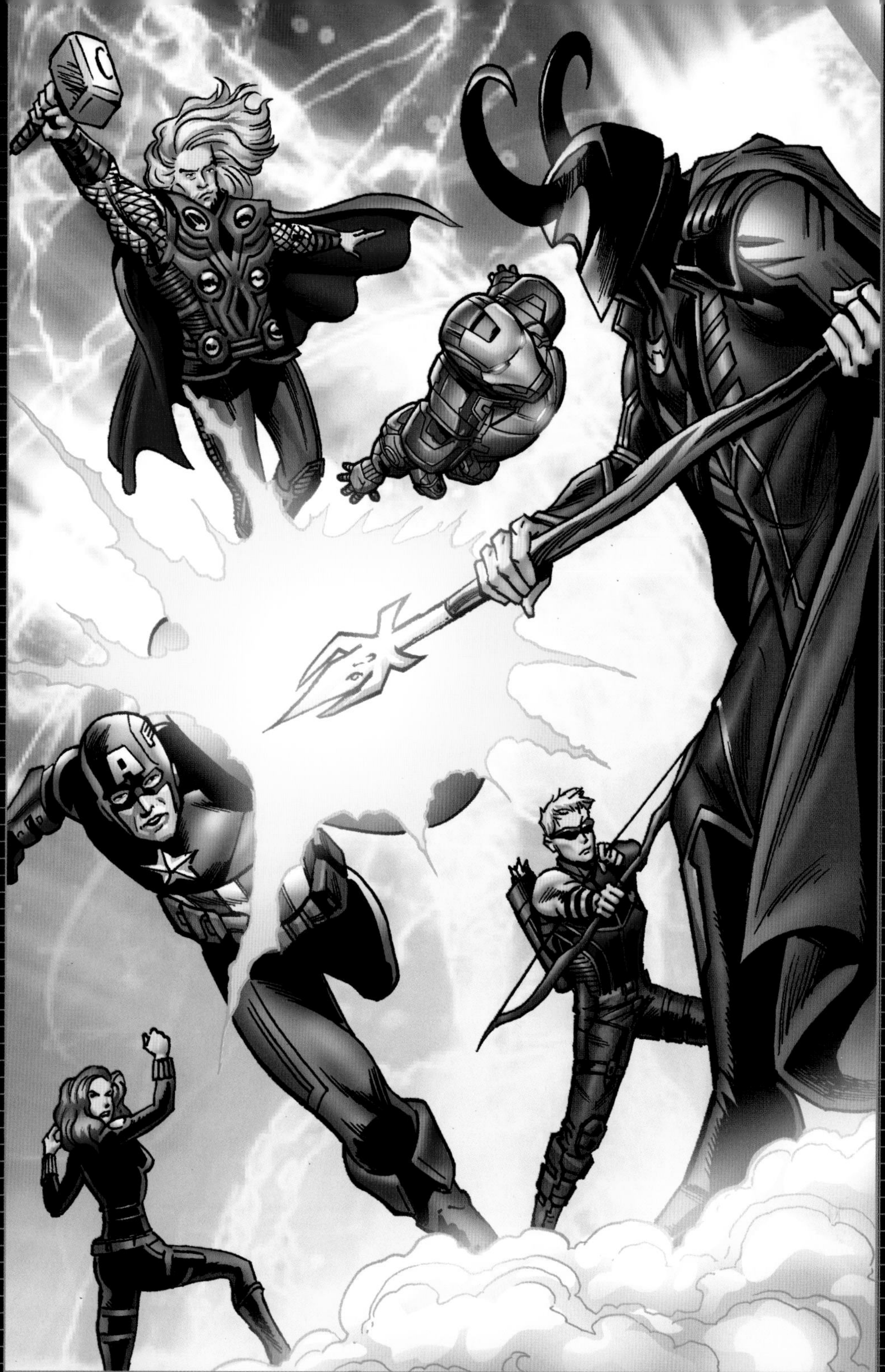

After Bruce Banner changed into the incredible Hulk, the heroes were finally assembled.

Steve Rogers was happy to be fighting for freedom and justice as a member of the Avengers!

IRON MAN 2

IRON MAN FIGHTS BACK

Adapted by **JODI HUELIN**

Based on the screenplay by **JUSTIN THEROUX**

Pictures by **MARCELO MATERE**

A Stark Industries C-17 plane flies swiftly around the world, ferrying a Super Hero to his work. Iron Man zooms out of the plane and through the sky, putting out California wildfires.

Next, he zooms across the ocean, foiling pirates. Finally, he zigzags through the air to destroy missiles. It's all in a day's work for Iron Man!

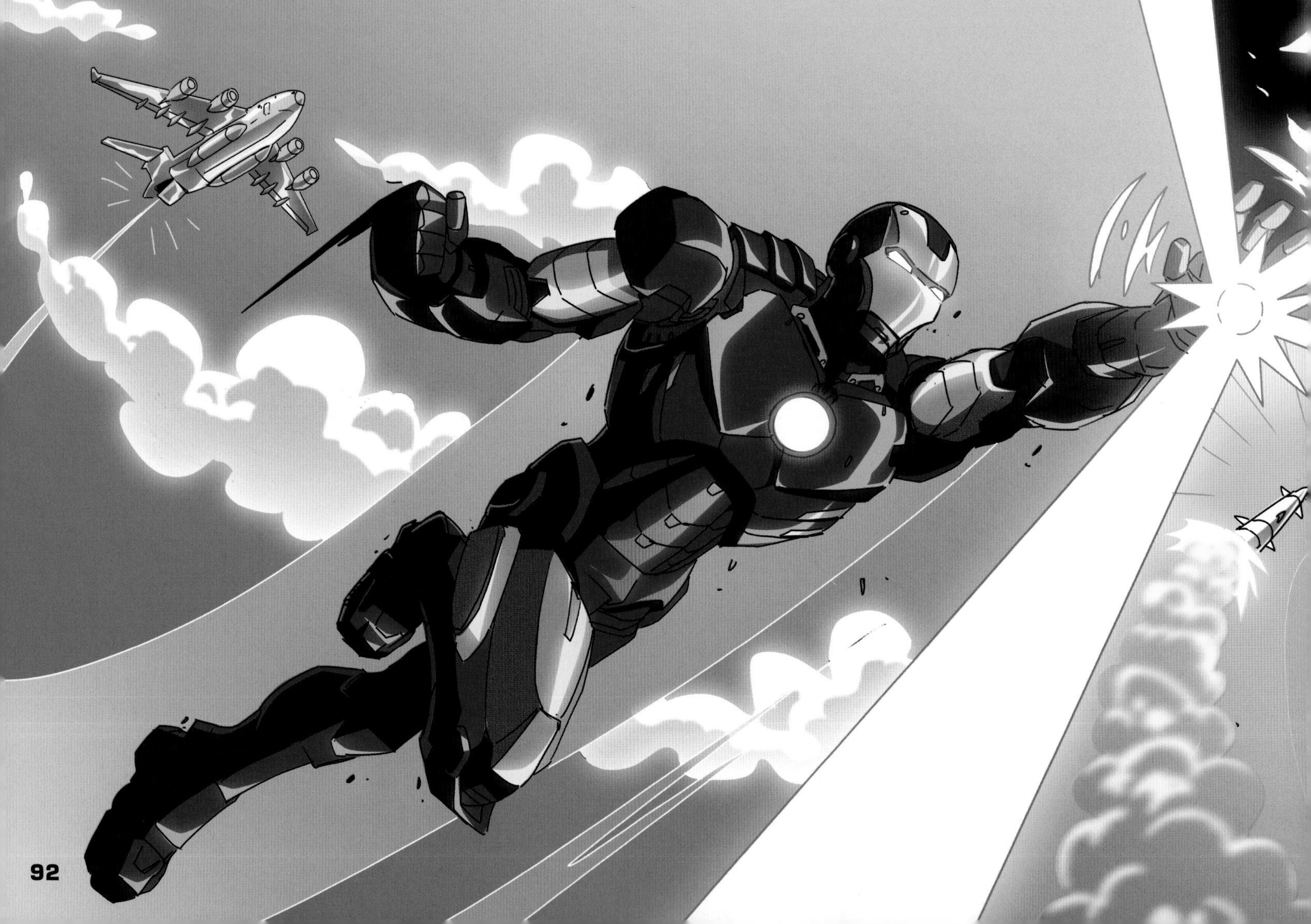

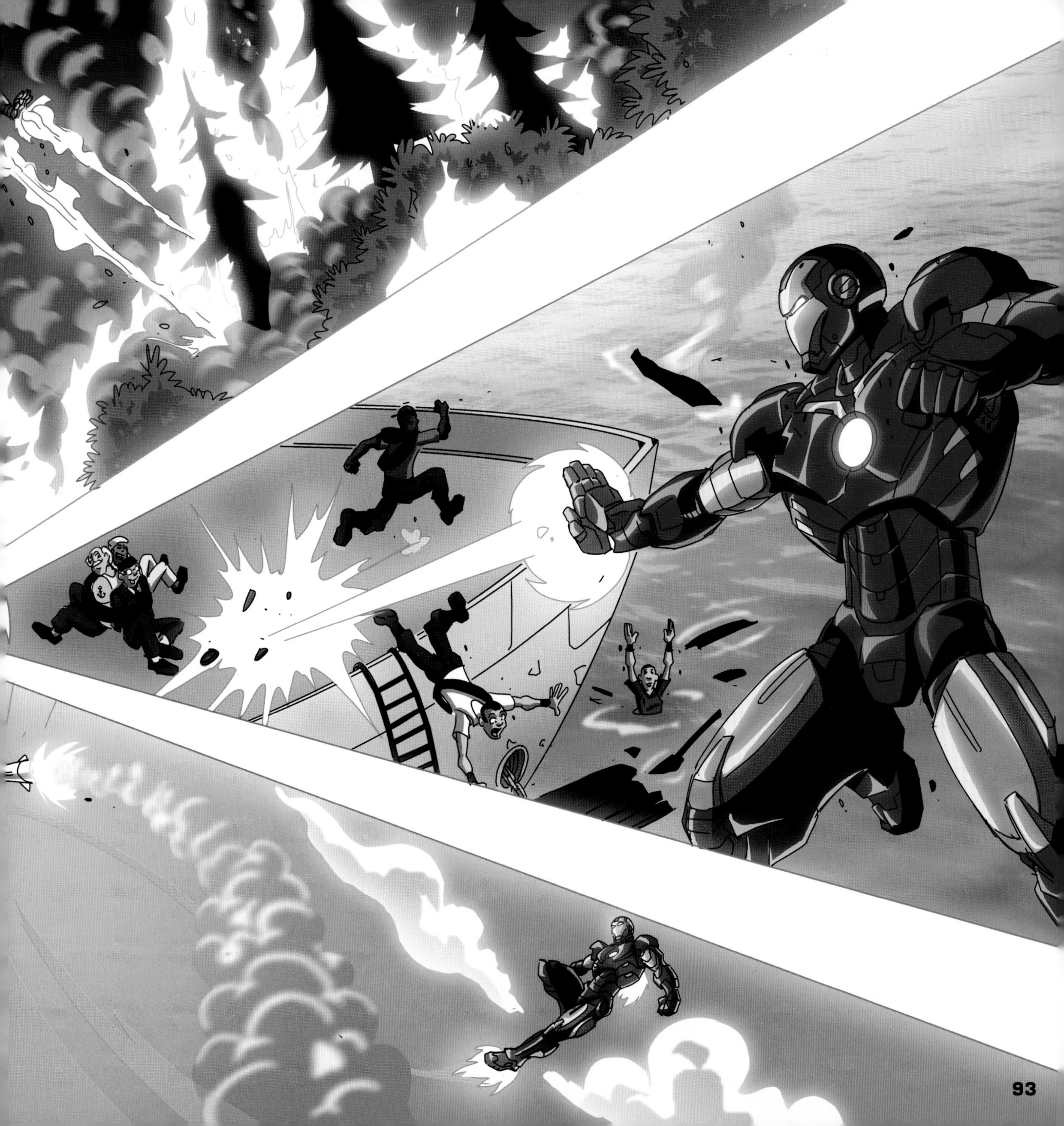

For his final act of the day, Iron Man descends onto a stage in front of a huge crowd. He removes his suit, piece by piece, until he stands before the people in a fancy tuxedo.

The man behind the Iron Man suit is Tony Stark, the CEO of Stark Industries. He welcomes the crowd to the Stark Expo.

"Every ten years, Stark Industries hosts this Expo, where scientists, world leaders, and corporate CEOs come together to pursue better living, robust health, and world peace!" Tony tells the audience.

The Expo grounds are vast, with different buildings, electric trams, and a reflecting pool.

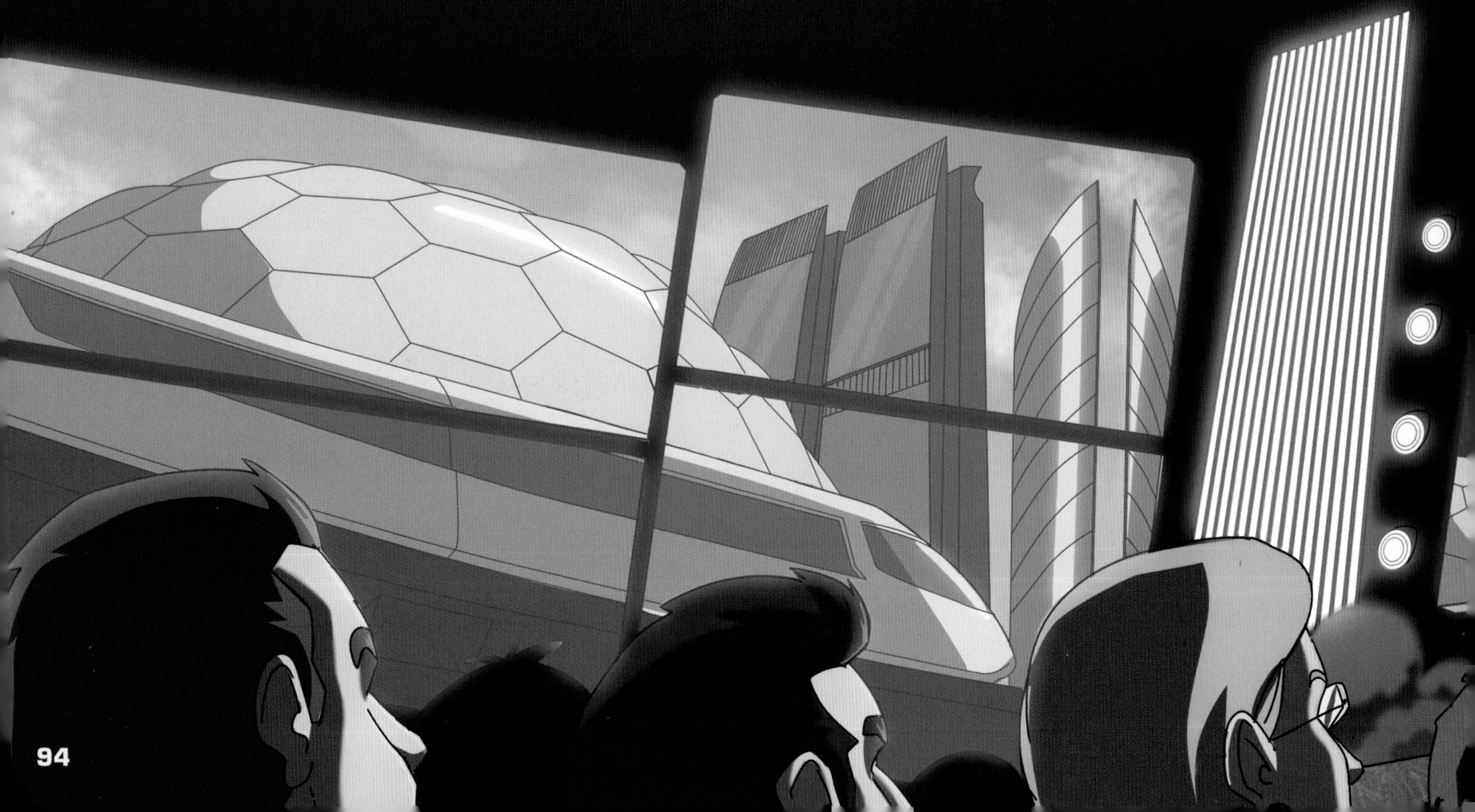

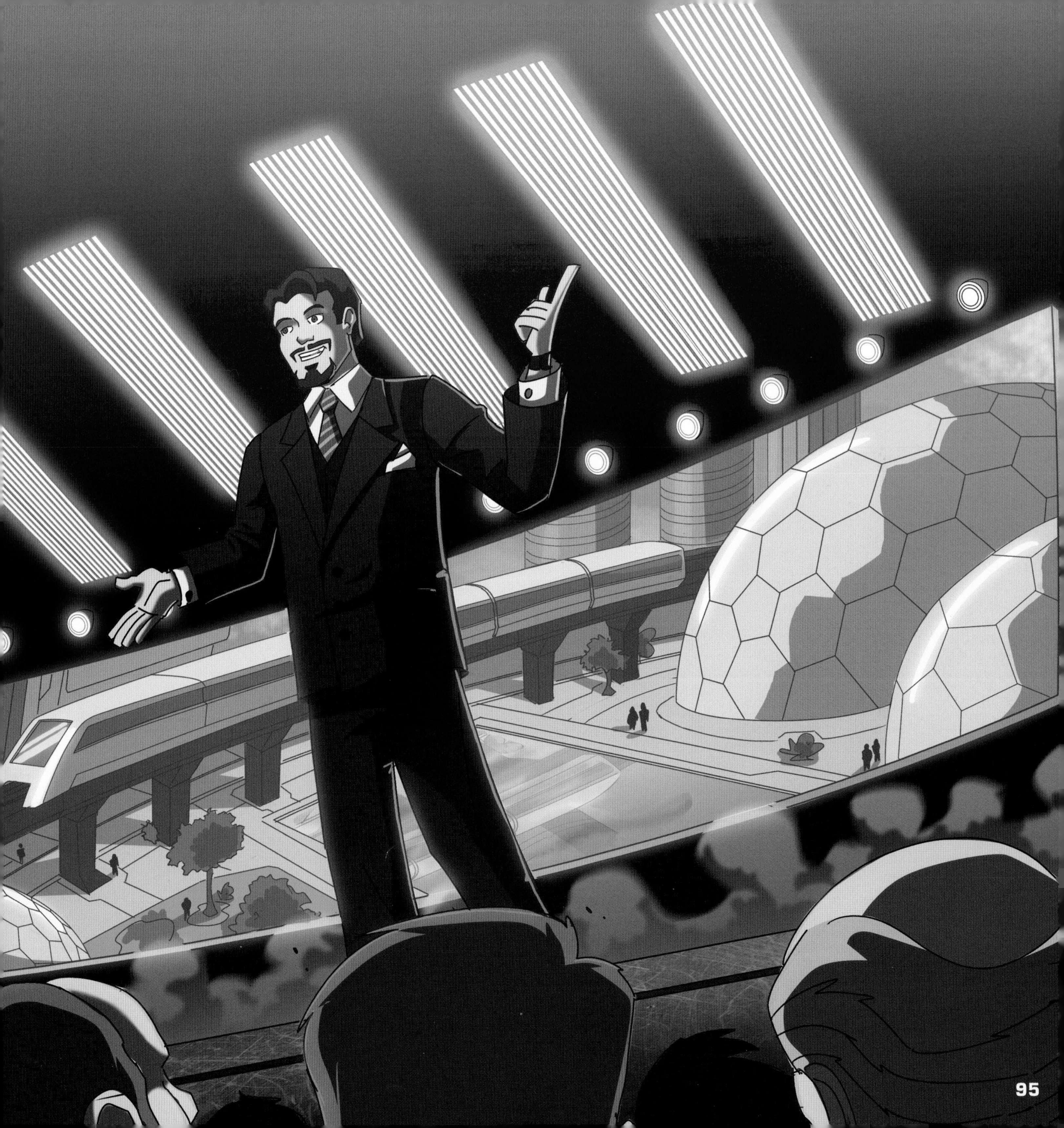

Lots of different devices are presented at the Expo, but the one invention everyone wants to have is the Iron Man suit. Rivals all over the world have been trying to re-create the Stark technology. A big company called Hammer Industries, run by Justin Hammer, has been working on a prototype.

"I hope to have something to show you soon," Justin Hammer tells Tony at the Expo opening.

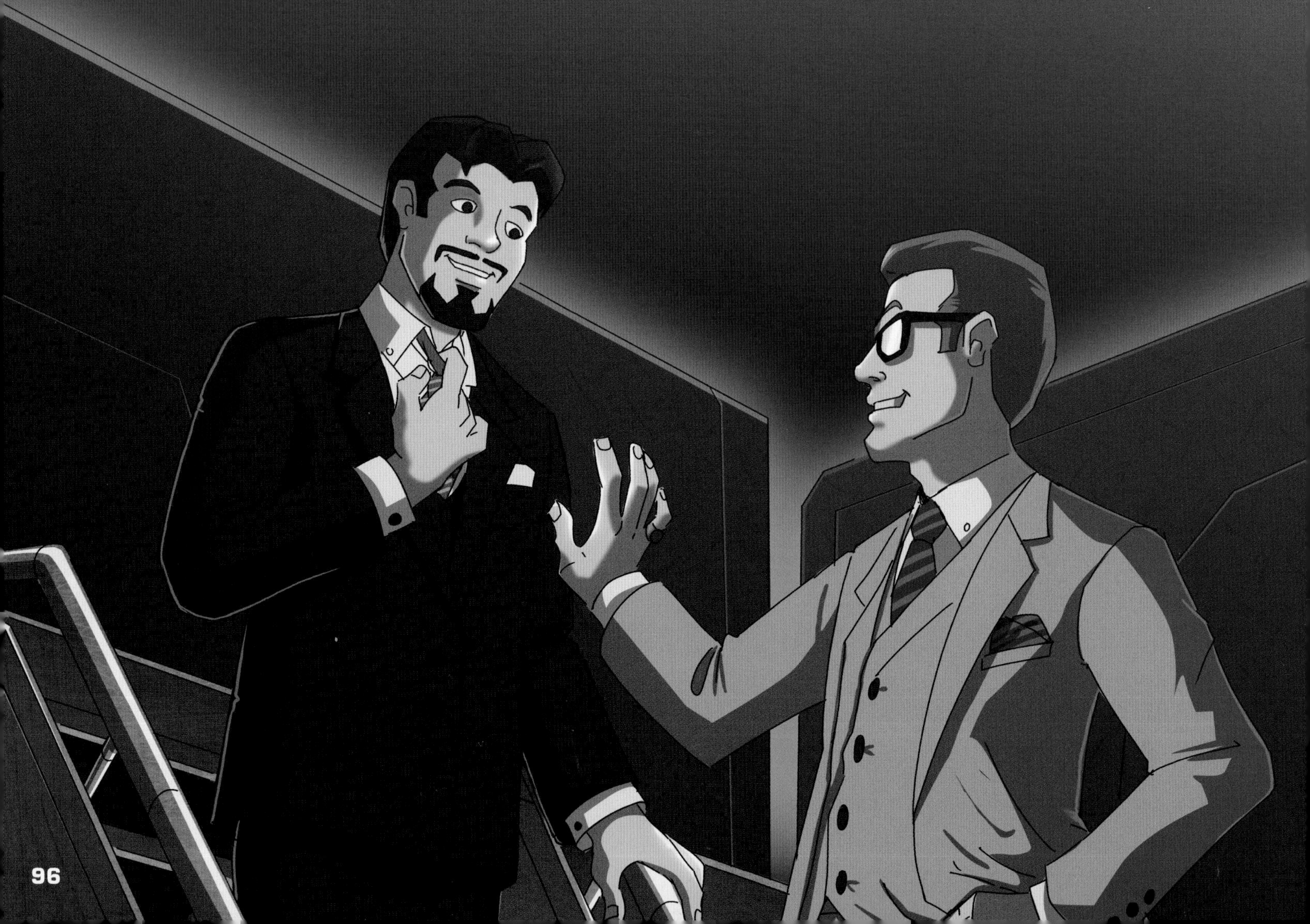

Hammer has a secret warehouse, where dozens of armored suits are being built. He plans to turn them into fighters.

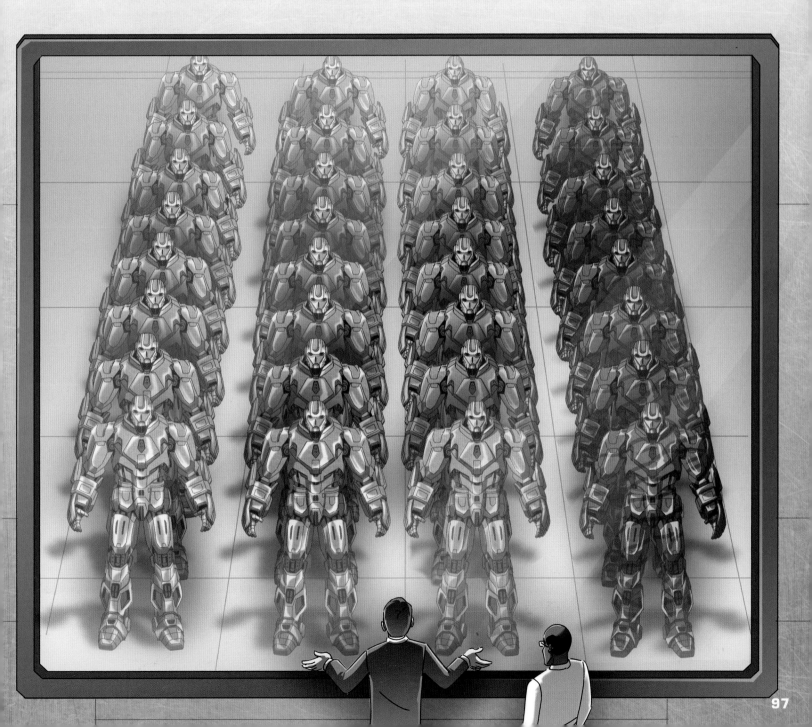

Tired from a long day, Tony goes home. But rest will have to wait: his best friend, Jim "Rhodey" Rhodes, is waiting for him.

Hammer isn't alone in wanting an armored suit. The United States government wants one, too. As a lieutenant colonel, Rhodey works for the Air Force. He asks Tony to hand over the Iron Man suit.

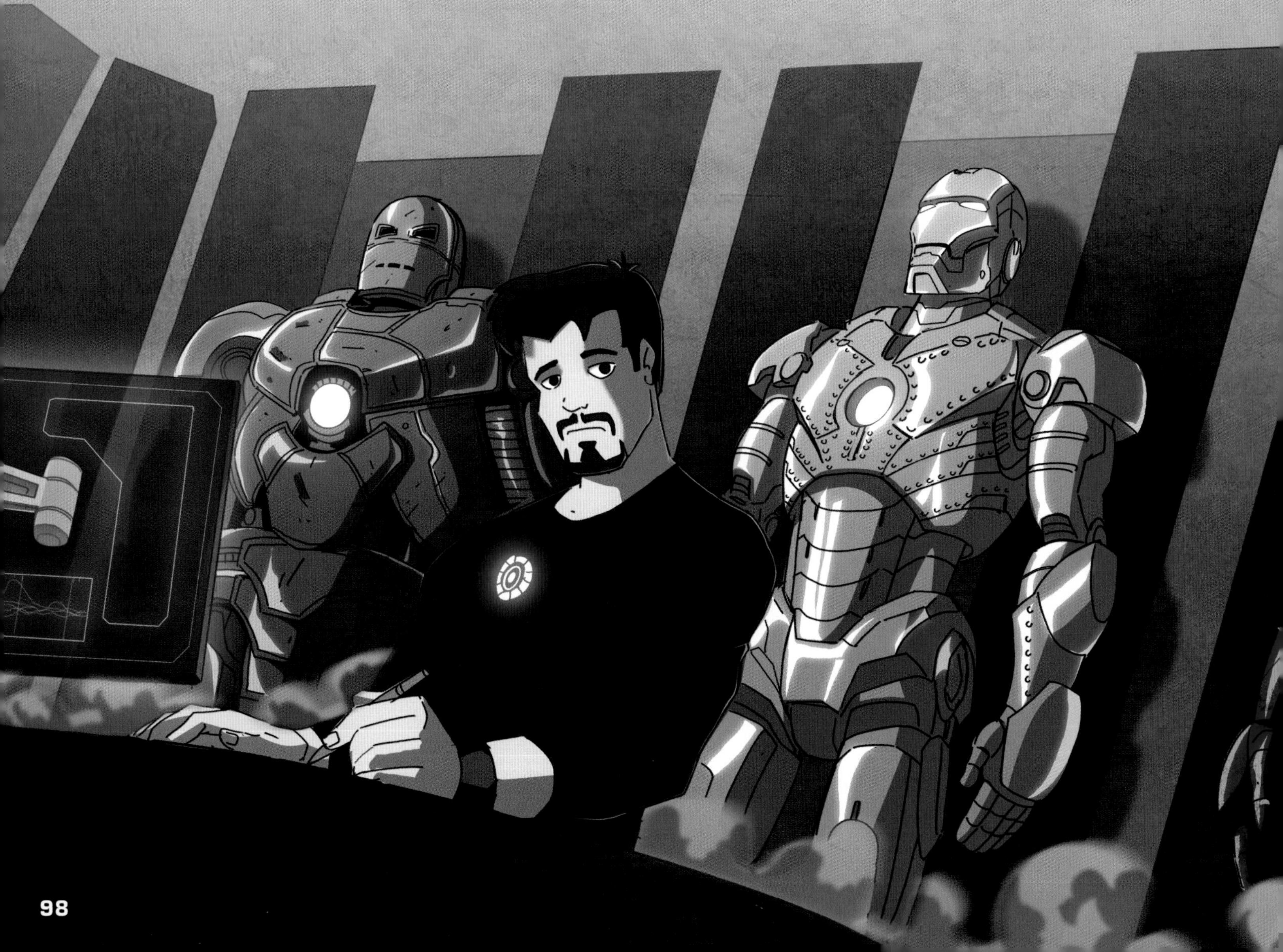

"It will help the country fight enemies!" Rhodey says.
But Tony doesn't trust anyone else with his technology.
"I am Iron Man — the suit and I are one. To turn over
the Iron Man suit would be to turn over myself," Tony says.

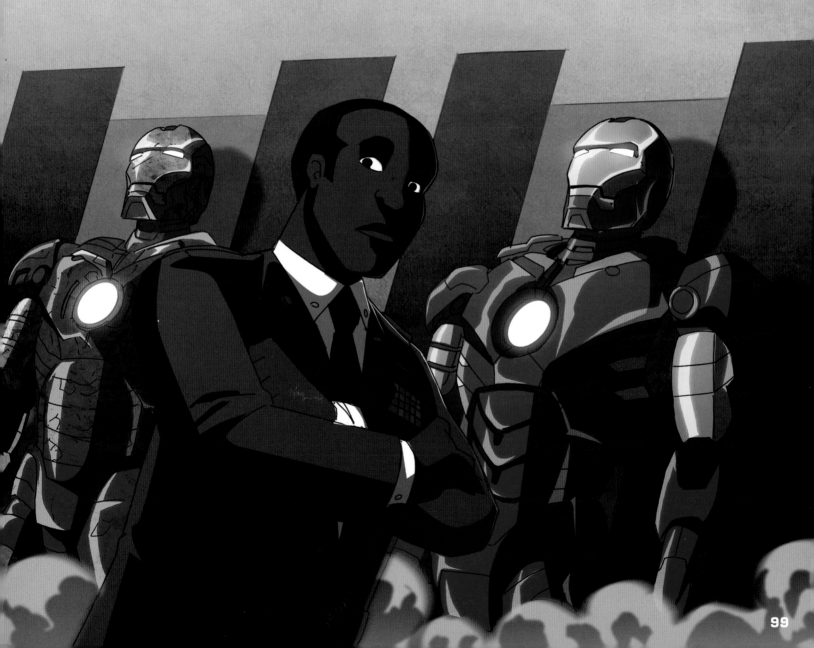

"You need to work with the Air Force, Tony," argues Rhodey. "We need the suit to help us defend the country."

"It's not a weapon," yells Tony. "I'm not giving it to anybody."

"You're making a mistake," Rhodey says. He wishes his friend trusted him with the suit.

Tony just glares. "I'm not talking to you anymore."

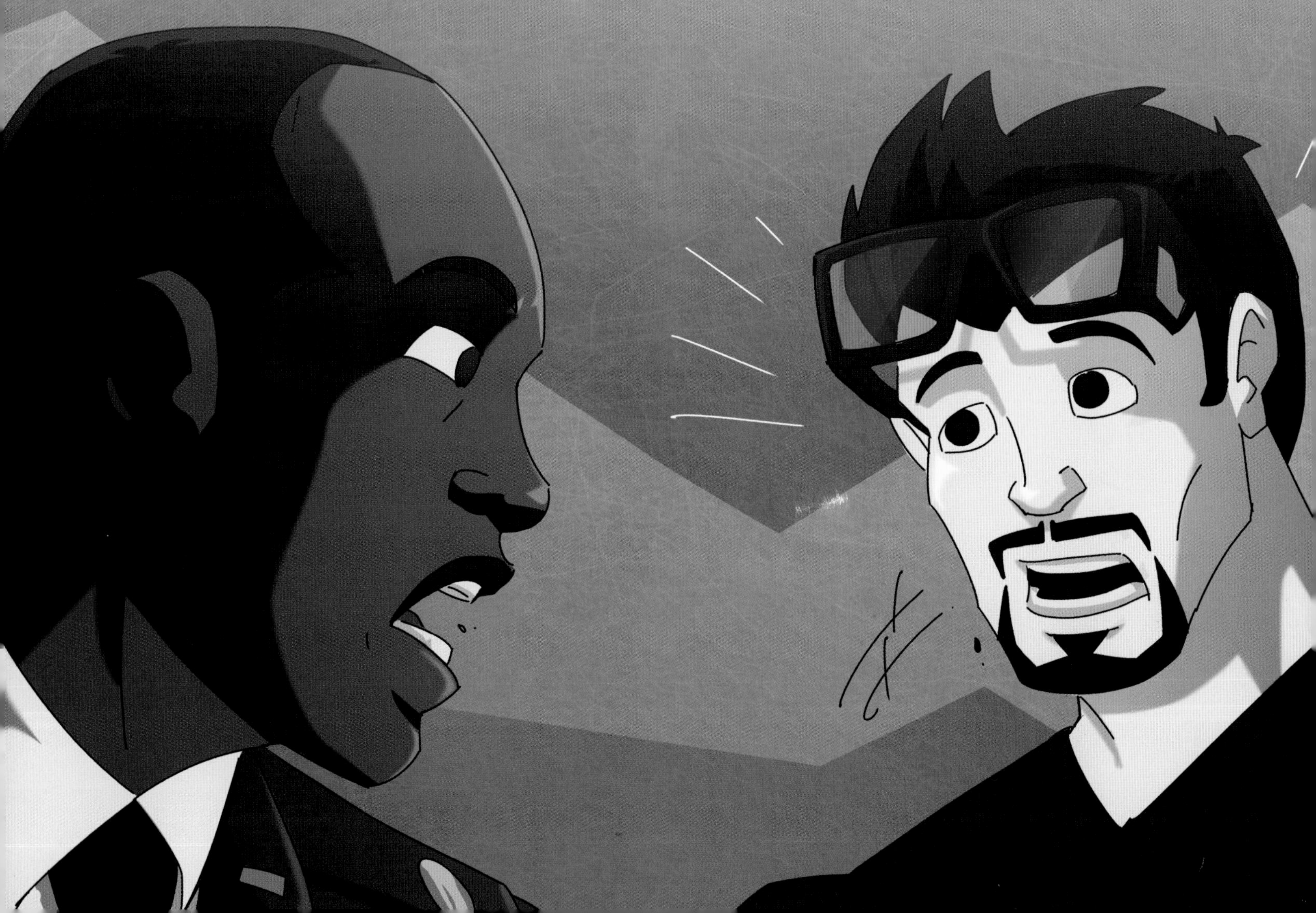

A few days later, Tony throws a party at his house. While Tony entertains his guests, Rhodey sneaks down to the lab. He takes an older version of the Iron Man suit, one that Tony doesn't use. Rhodey knows that his friend will be angry, but he thinks the Air Force needs the technology to keep people safe.

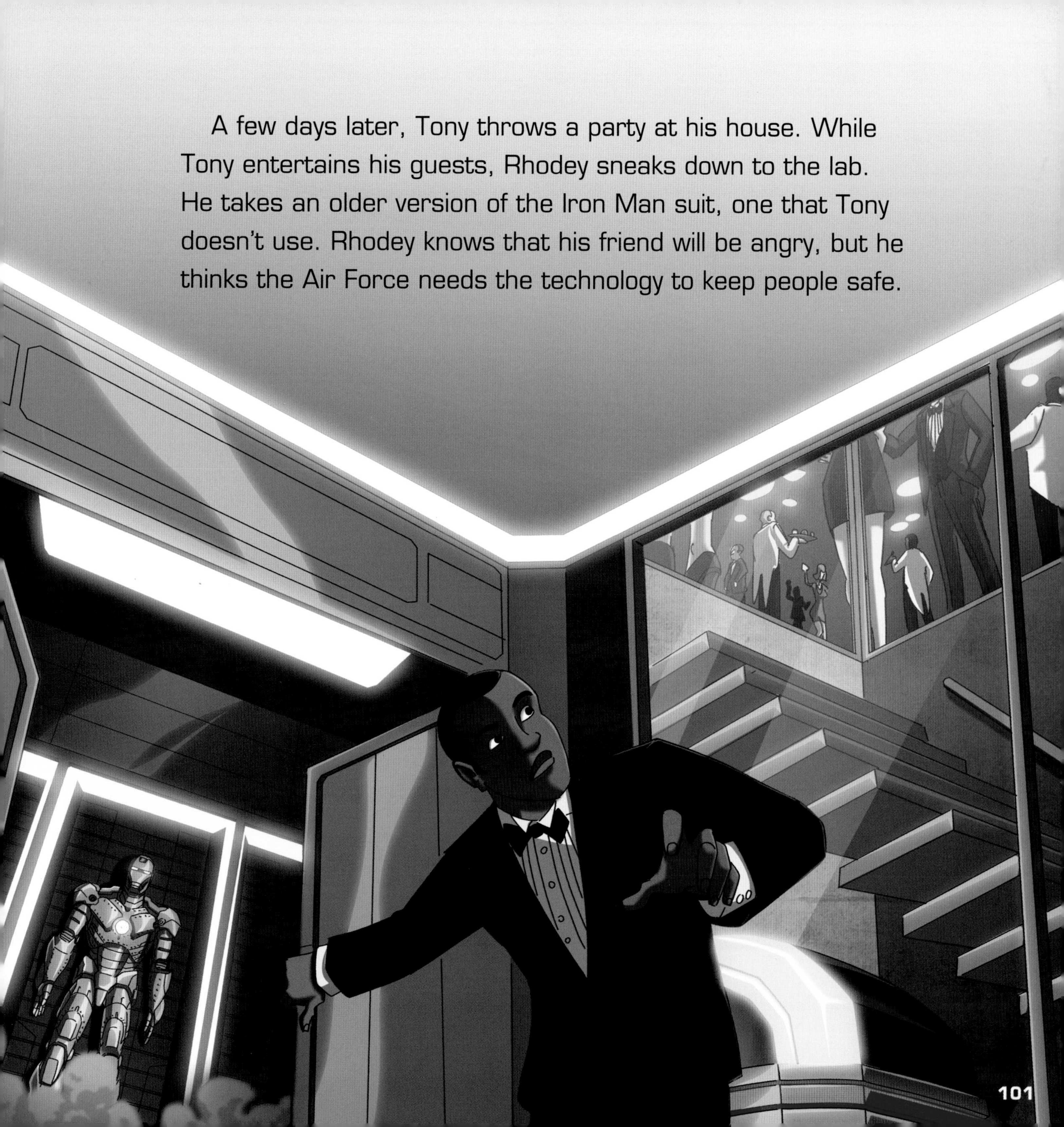

Rhodey puts on the suit and flies off to a United States Air Force base, where he enlists the help of the Air Force's smartest and best scientists. They work in secret, day and night, updating the suit with military weapons.

When they are done, Rhodey shows it to his boss.

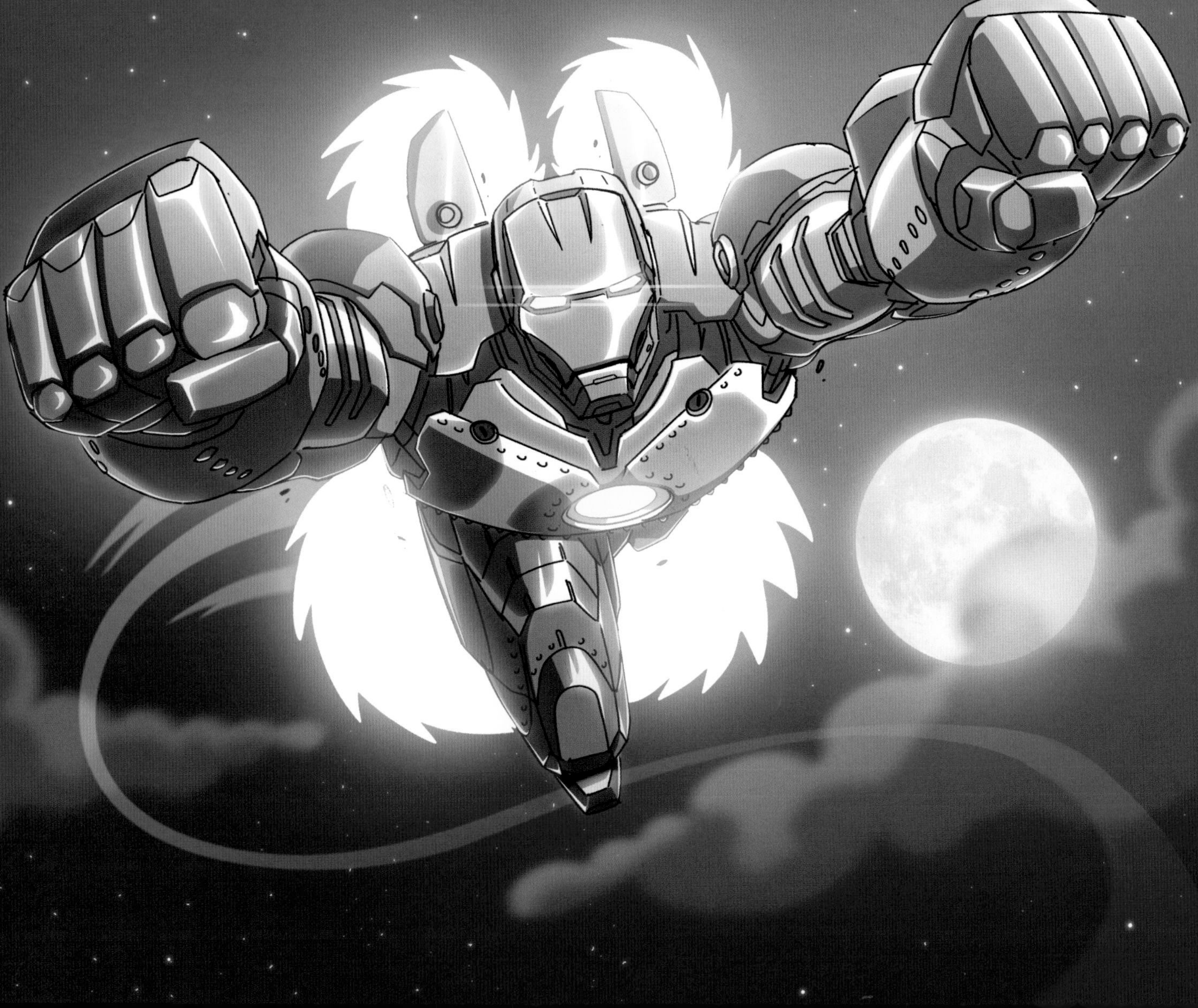

"Meet the War Machine!" Rhodey announces to a general. The general is thrilled. He tells Rhodey that War Machine will be presented at the Stark Expo — along with Justin Hammer's new robots!

"General, I feel strongly that we use the suit only when absolutely necessary," Rhodey says firmly.

"It's an order," the general states. "You've made your country proud."

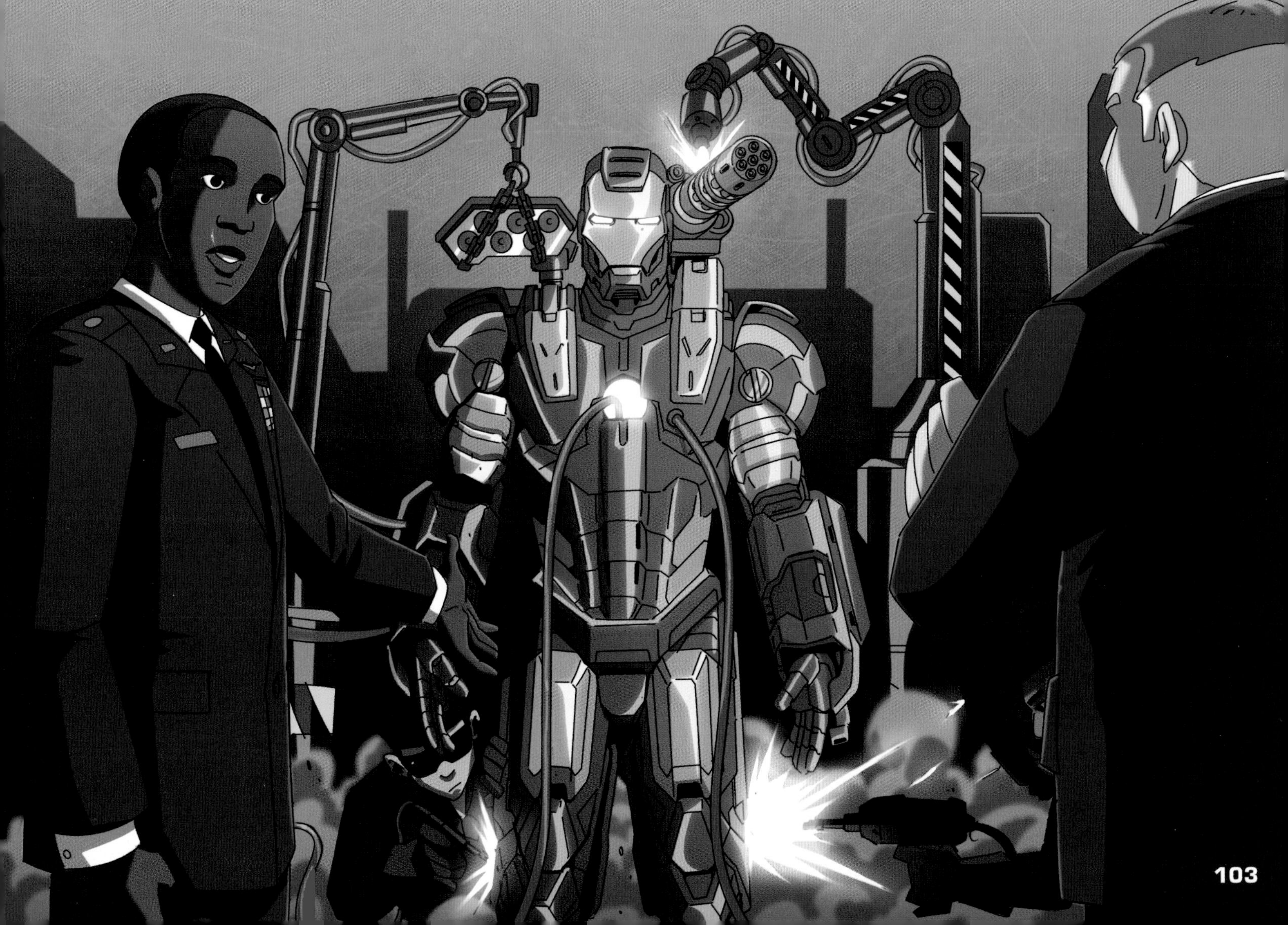

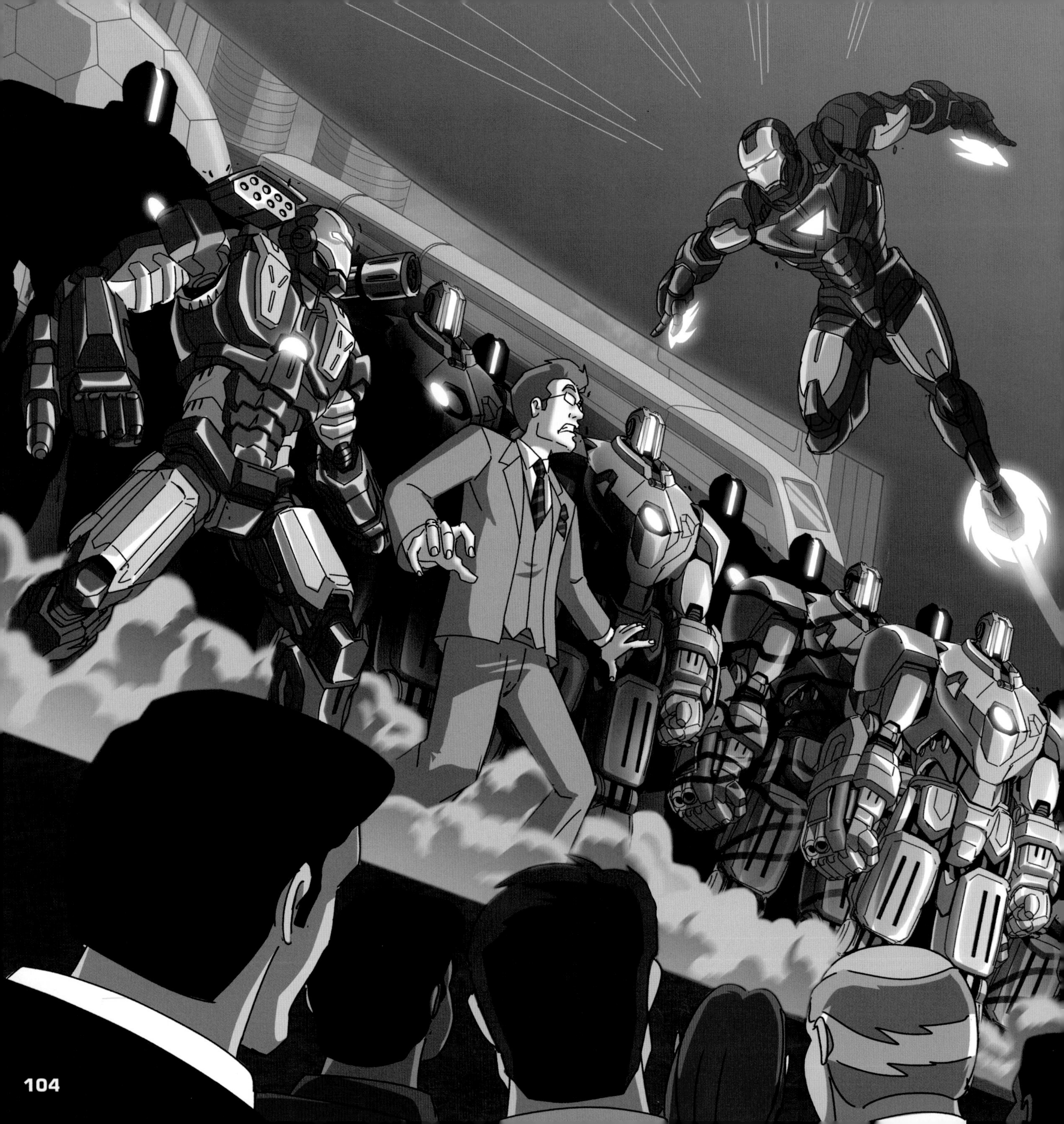

At the Stark Expo, the audience eagerly awaits something grand. Justin Hammer stands on the stage, surrounded by his hulking robots.

A hush falls over the crowd for Hammer's introduction. "Today, I give the world . . . Lieutenant Colonel James T. Rhodes and War Machine!" he shouts into the microphone.

With his repulsor lights flaring, Rhodey descends onto the stage wearing the armored suit. The crowd claps for him.

Then Iron Man suddenly arrives as well!

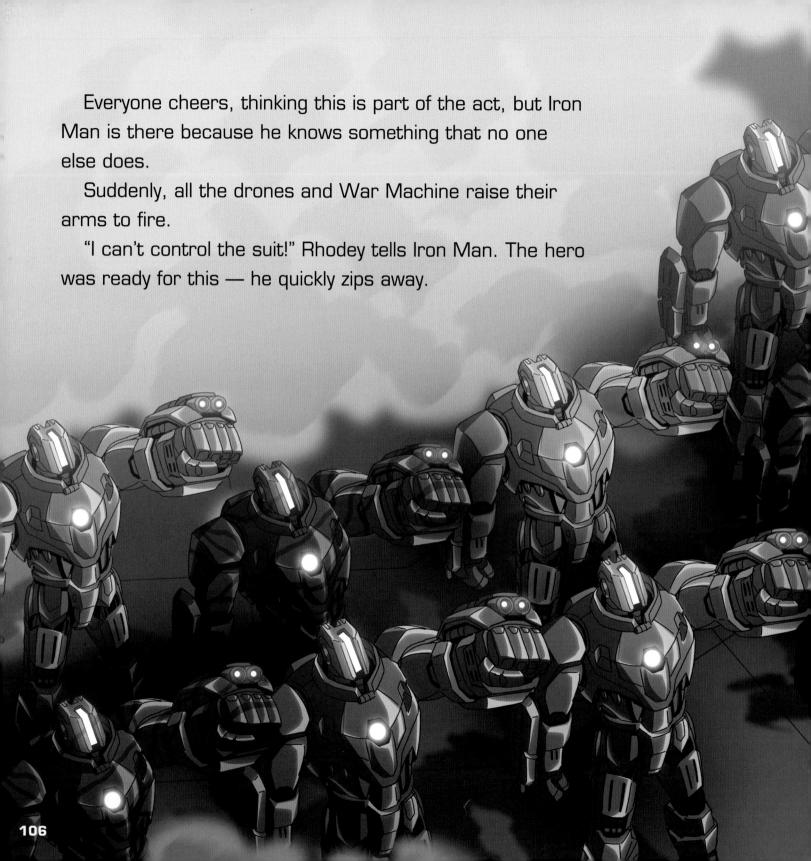

Everyone cheers, thinking this is part of the act, but Iron Man is there because he knows something that no one else does.

Suddenly, all the drones and War Machine raise their arms to fire.

"I can't control the suit!" Rhodey tells Iron Man. The hero was ready for this — he quickly zips away.

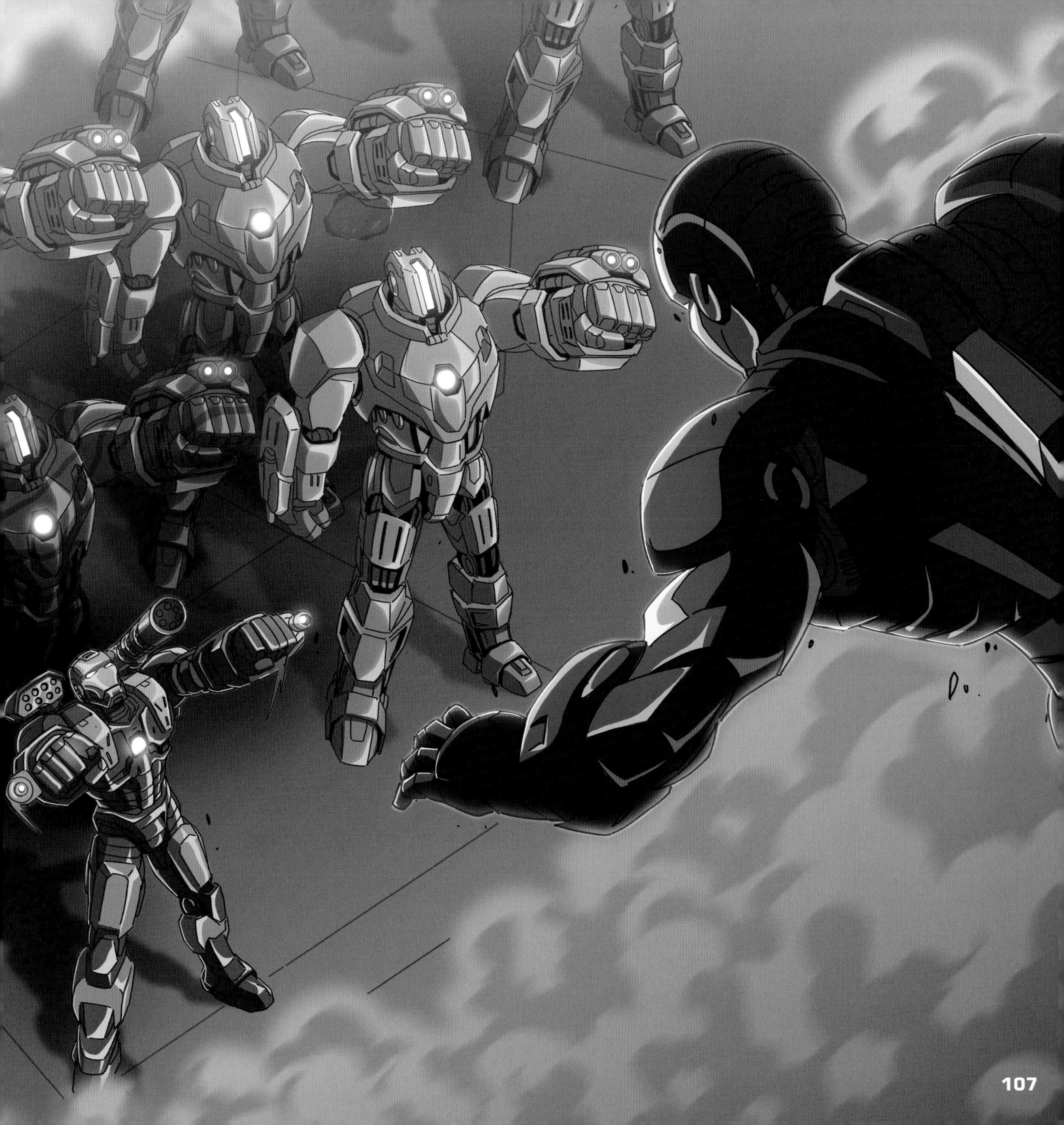

Iron Man flies around the Stark Expo with War Machine hot on his trail and firing blasts. The suit is acting on its own with Rhodey trapped inside! The two smash through a huge glass dome and then crash into the reflecting pool.

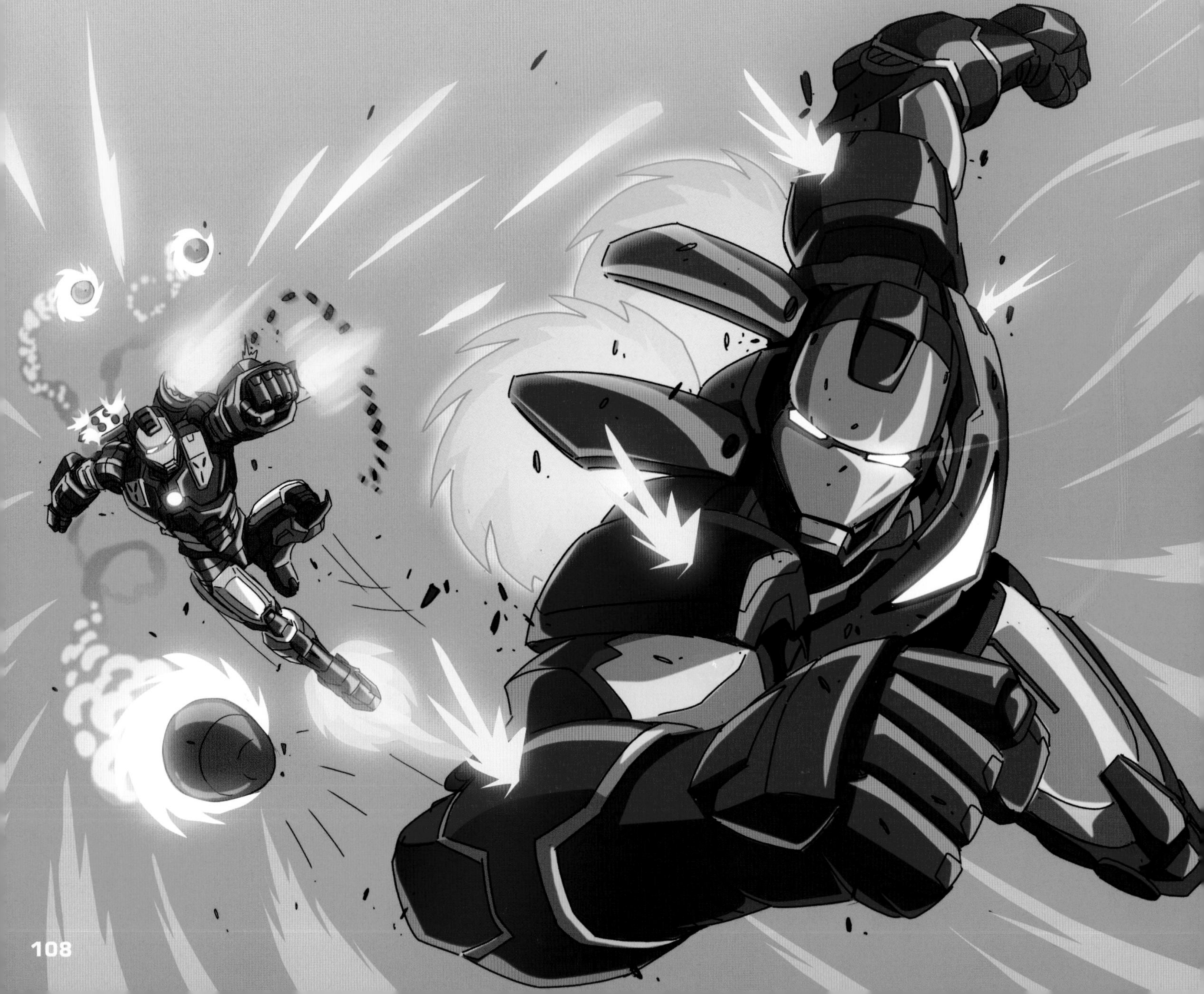

Iron Man jumps on War Machine's back and yanks out the power cable. Then he helps Rhodey reboot the suit. War Machine is under Rhodey's control once again!

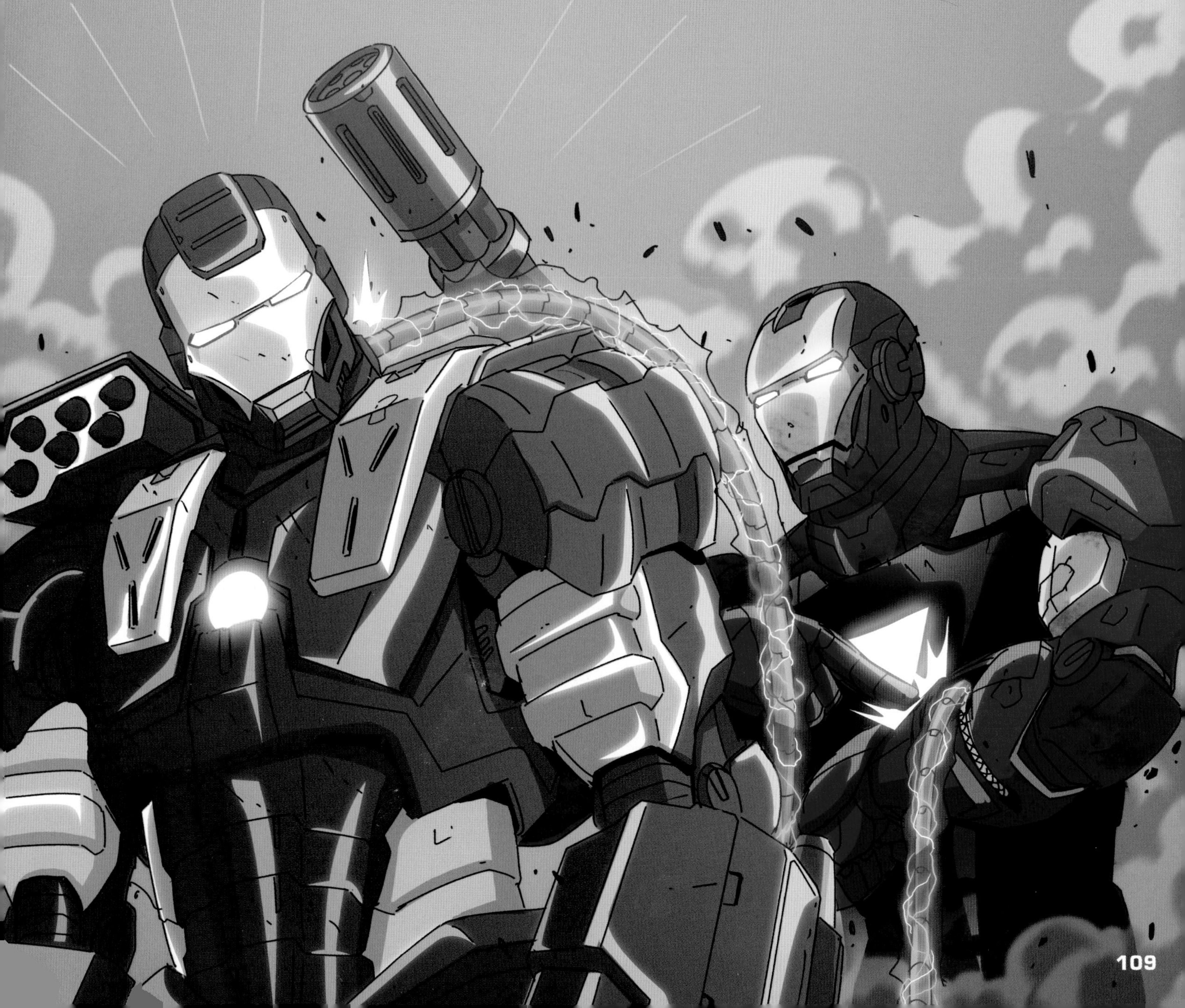

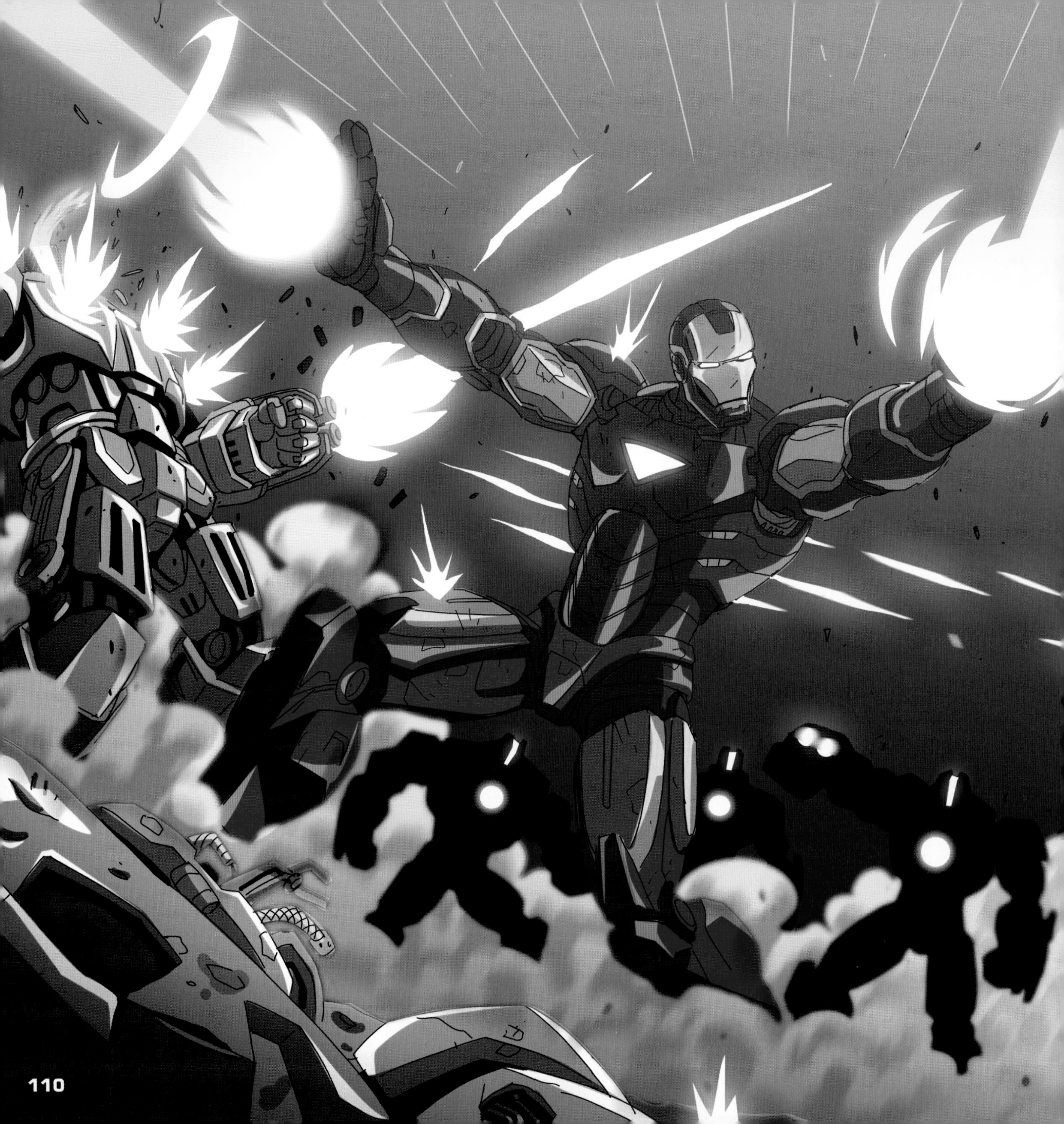

"I am so sorry," Rhodey tells Tony. Rhodey didn't mean for any of this to happen. Tony forgives his friend. He knows that Rhodey didn't realize what Hammer was up to.

The old friends don't have long to celebrate — the Hammer robots arrive and completely surround them. Tony looks at Rhodey, who nods. They know what to do.

The robots begin firing as Iron Man and War Machine stand back-to-back. With both suits firing, they take out each robot, one by one.

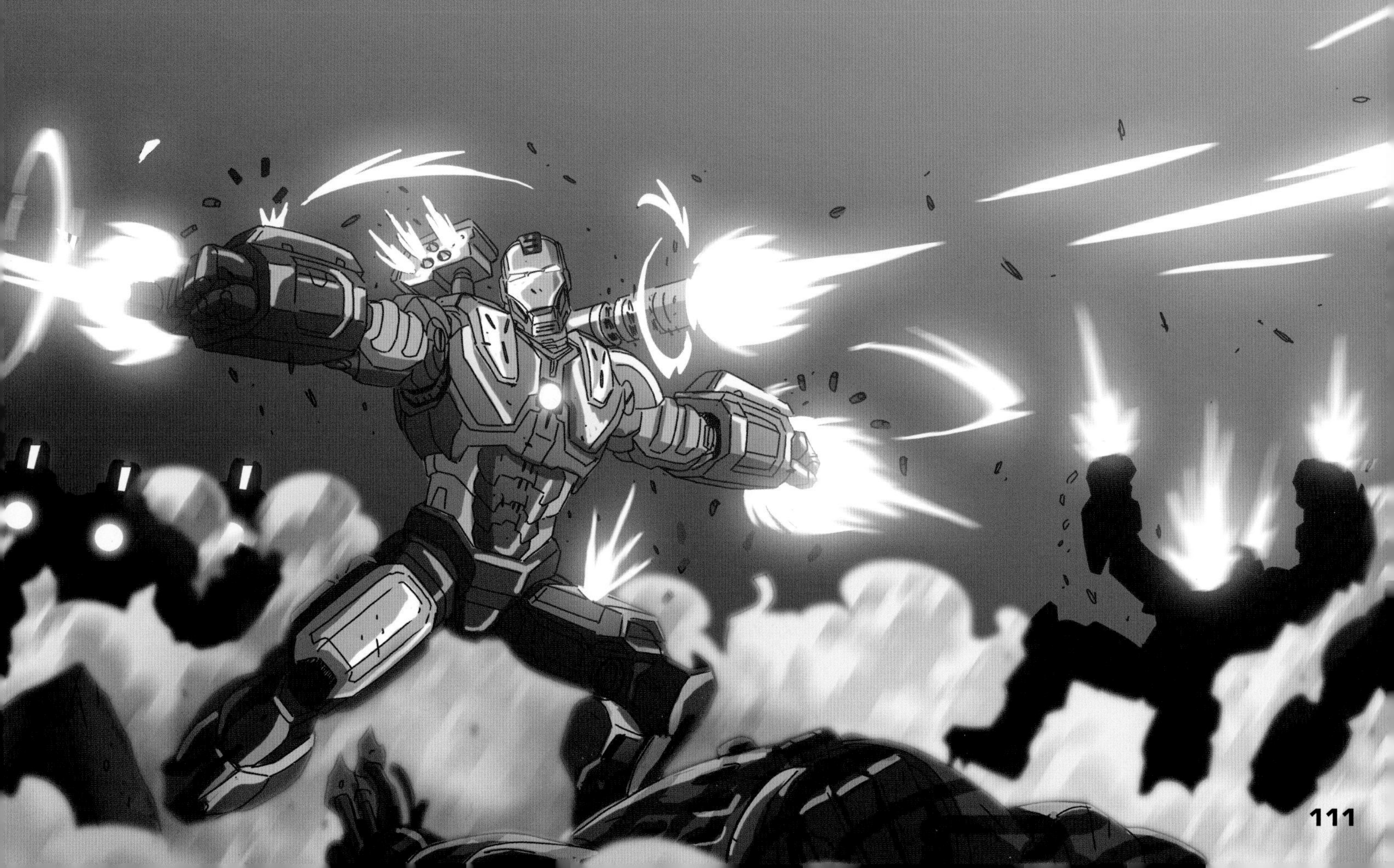

The last robot falls at their feet. Everyone is safe! Iron Man and War Machine live to fight another day — together.

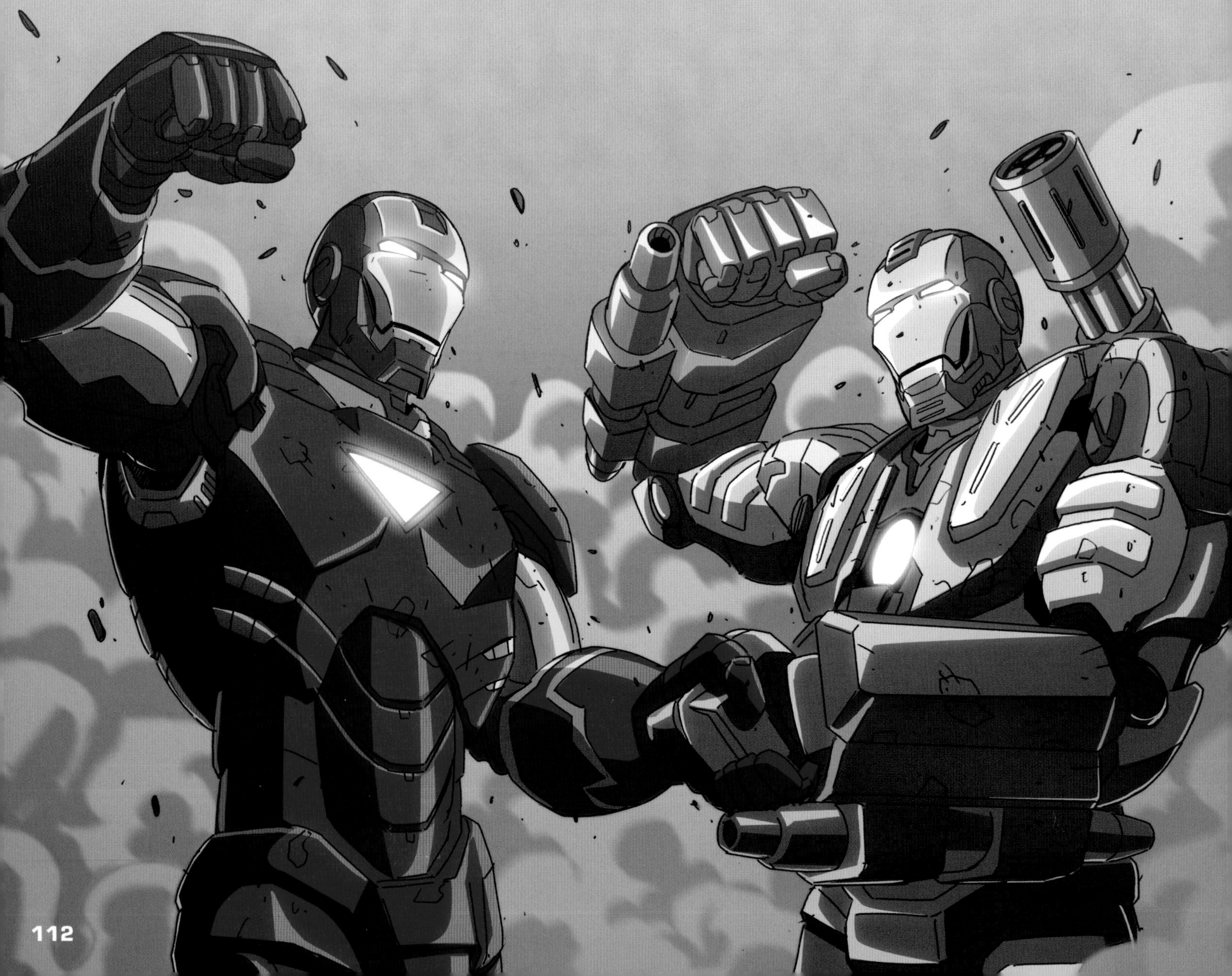

IRON MAN 2

IRON MAN VS. WHIPLASH

Adapted by **JODI HUELIN**

Based on the screenplay by **JUSTIN THEROUX**

Pictures by **SCOTT HEPBURN**

Coloring by **ESPEN GRUNDETJERN**

Ivan Vanko lives in Russia. The famous billionaire inventor Tony Stark doesn't know Ivan yet. But he will . . . and soon.

Tony Stark invented an amazing suit of armor. When he wears it, he goes by the name Iron Man and helps people who are in trouble.

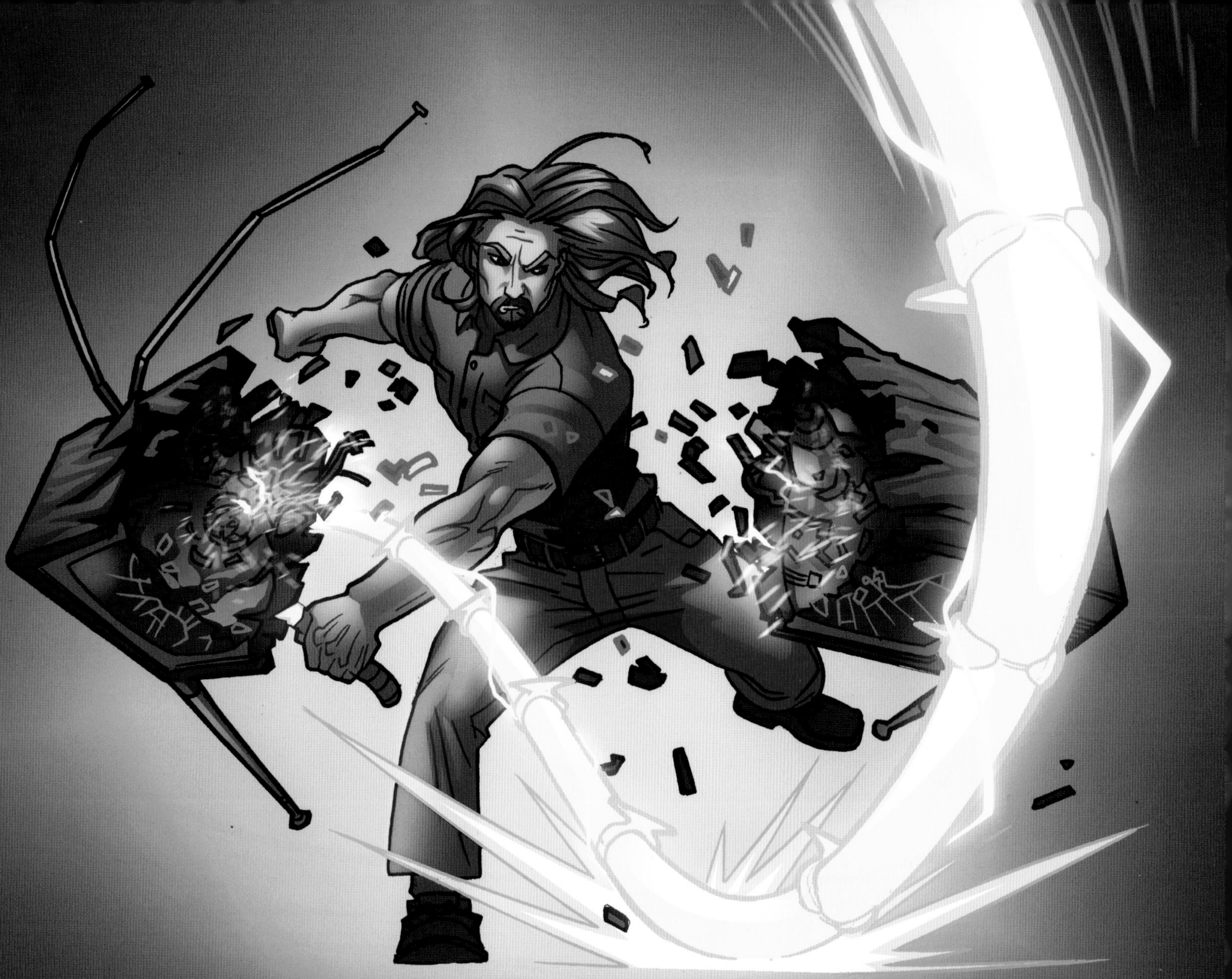

Ivan is also an inventor, and he's working on a device that will stop Iron Man in his tracks. Ivan winds thin copper wire around long cords with jagged teeth on them.

"I'm coming for you, Tony," Ivan says out loud. *SNAP!* Ivan uses the cords like whips to slash his television in half!

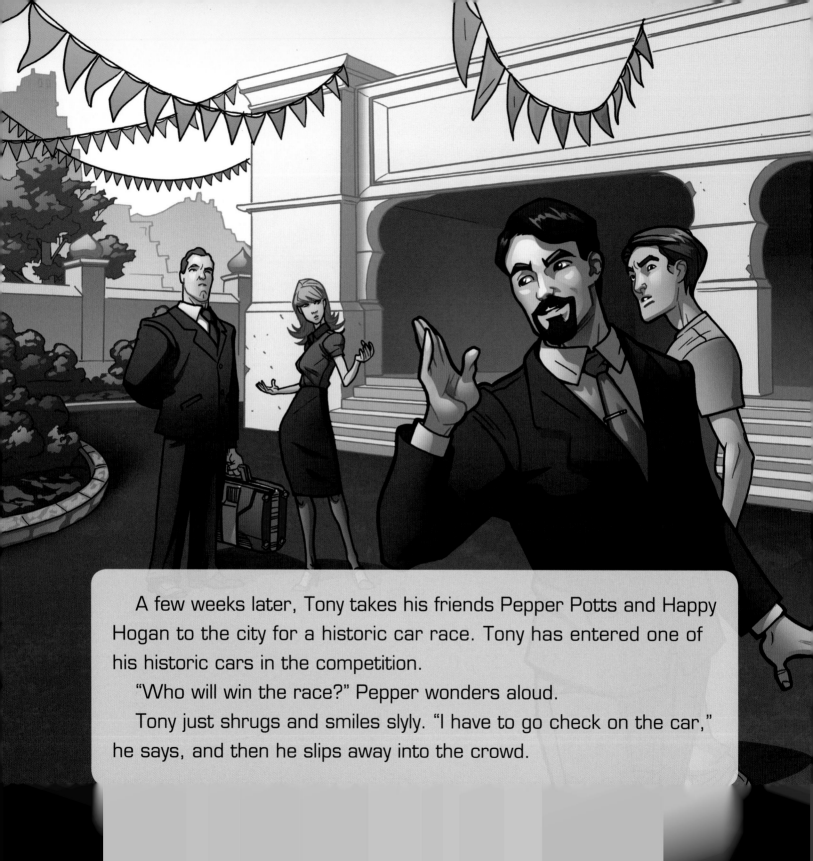

A few weeks later, Tony takes his friends Pepper Potts and Happy Hogan to the city for a historic car race. Tony has entered one of his historic cars in the competition.

"Who will win the race?" Pepper wonders aloud.

Tony just shrugs and smiles slyly. "I have to go check on the car," he says, and then he slips away into the crowd.

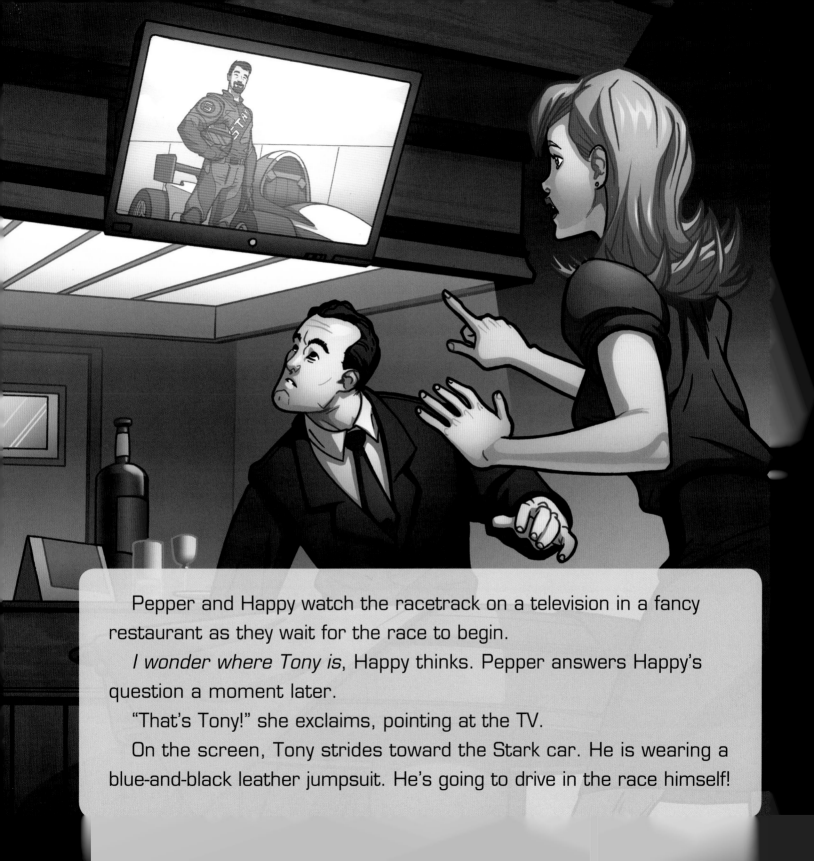

Pepper and Happy watch the racetrack on a television in a fancy restaurant as they wait for the race to begin.

I wonder where Tony is, Happy thinks. Pepper answers Happy's question a moment later.

"That's Tony!" she exclaims, pointing at the TV.

On the screen, Tony strides toward the Stark car. He is wearing a blue-and-black leather jumpsuit. He's going to drive in the race himself!

At the racetrack, the crowd in the stands goes wild, cheering and clapping. The drivers get into their cars and start their engines. They hold their steering wheels steady, waiting for the race to begin.

And they're off! *VROOM!*

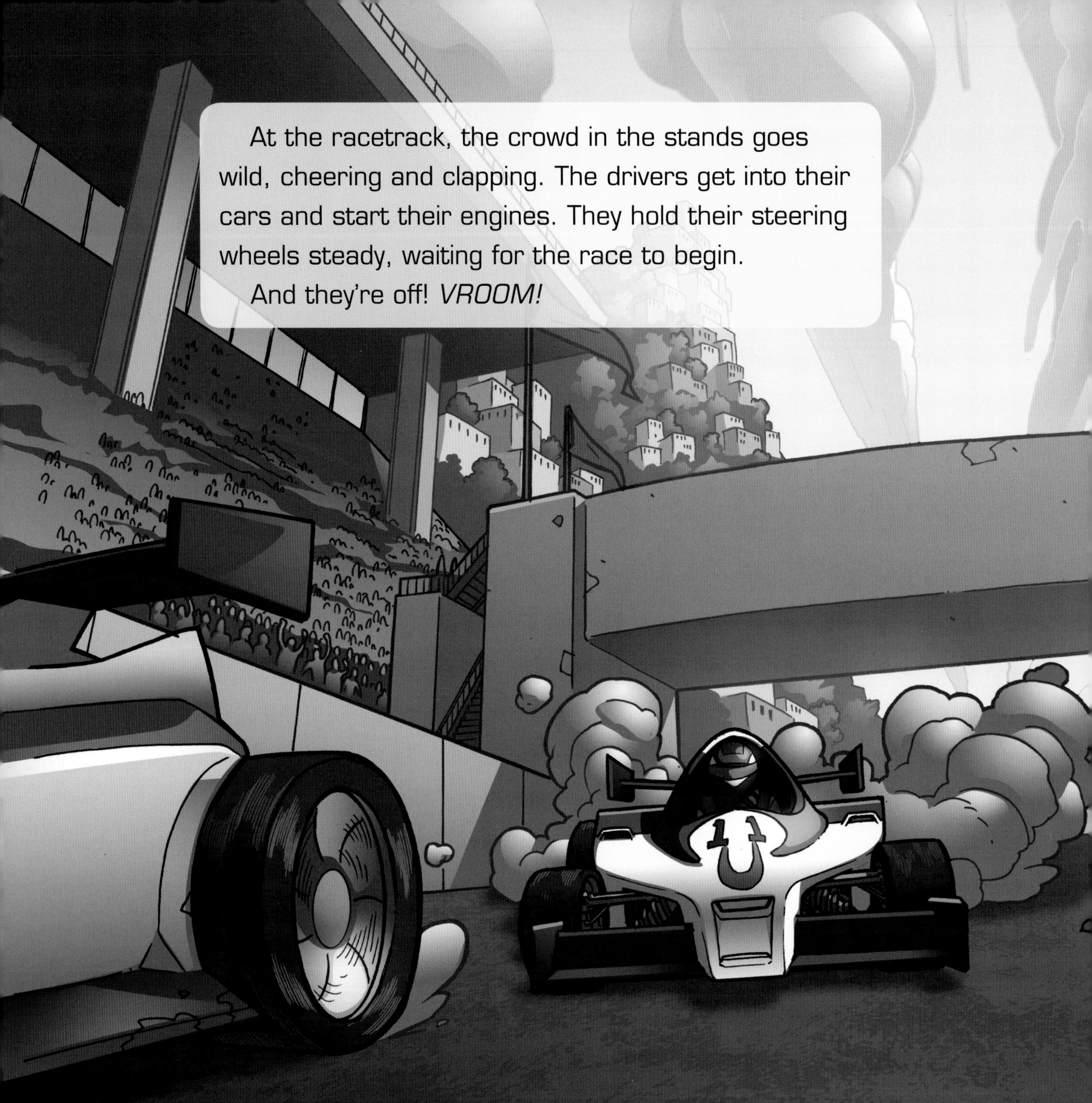

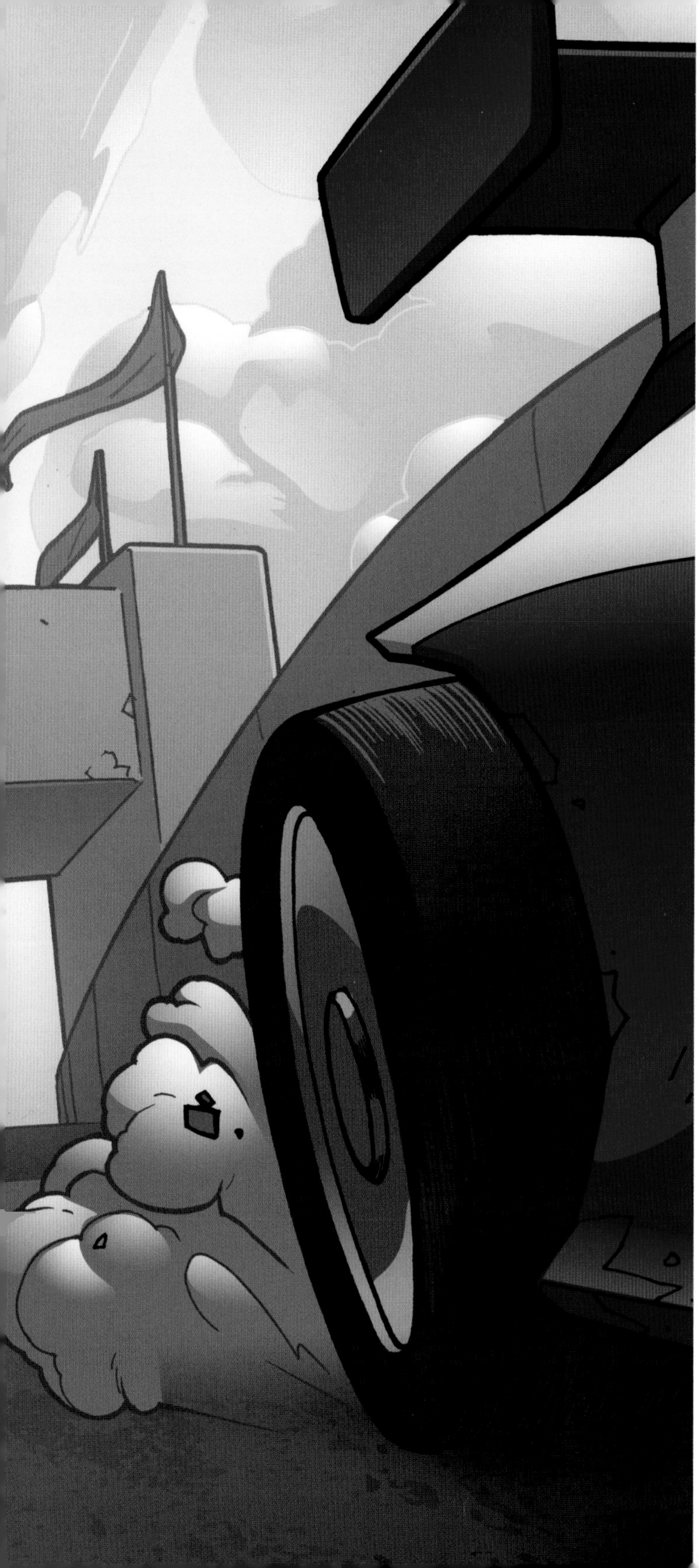

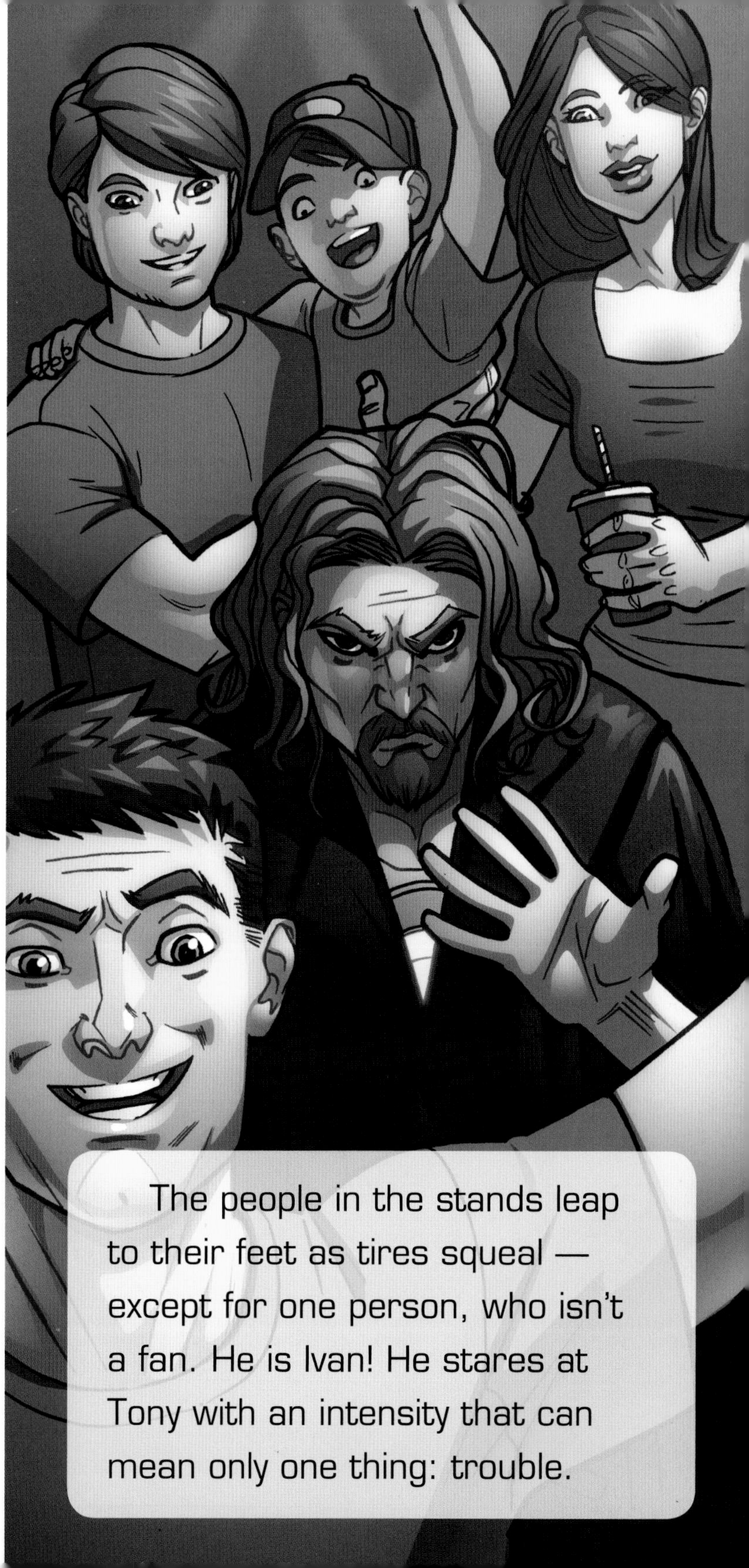

The people in the stands leap to their feet as tires squeal — except for one person, who isn't a fan. He is Ivan! He stares at Tony with an intensity that can mean only one thing: trouble.

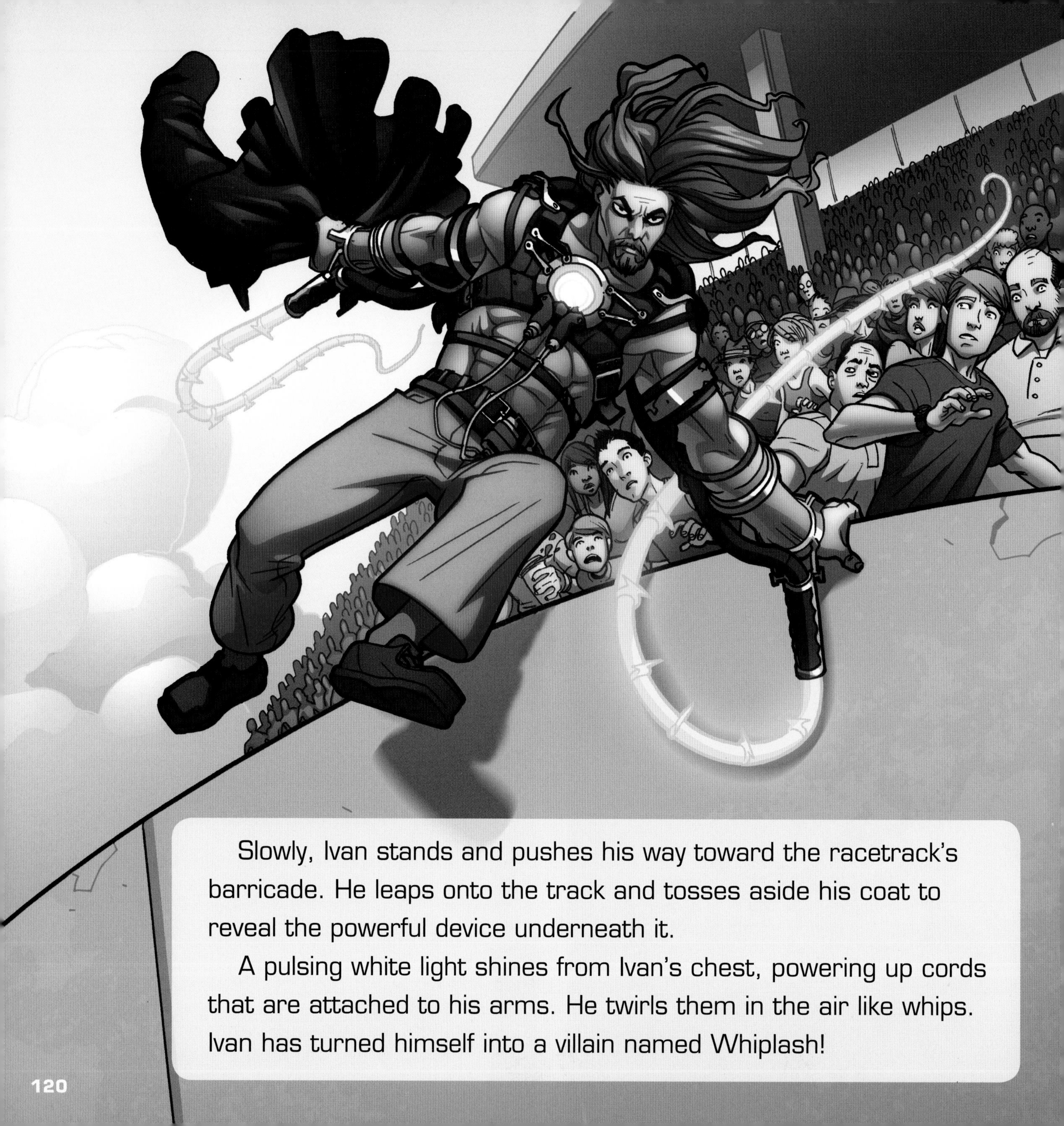

Slowly, Ivan stands and pushes his way toward the racetrack's barricade. He leaps onto the track and tosses aside his coat to reveal the powerful device underneath it.

A pulsing white light shines from Ivan's chest, powering up cords that are attached to his arms. He twirls them in the air like whips. Ivan has turned himself into a villain named Whiplash!

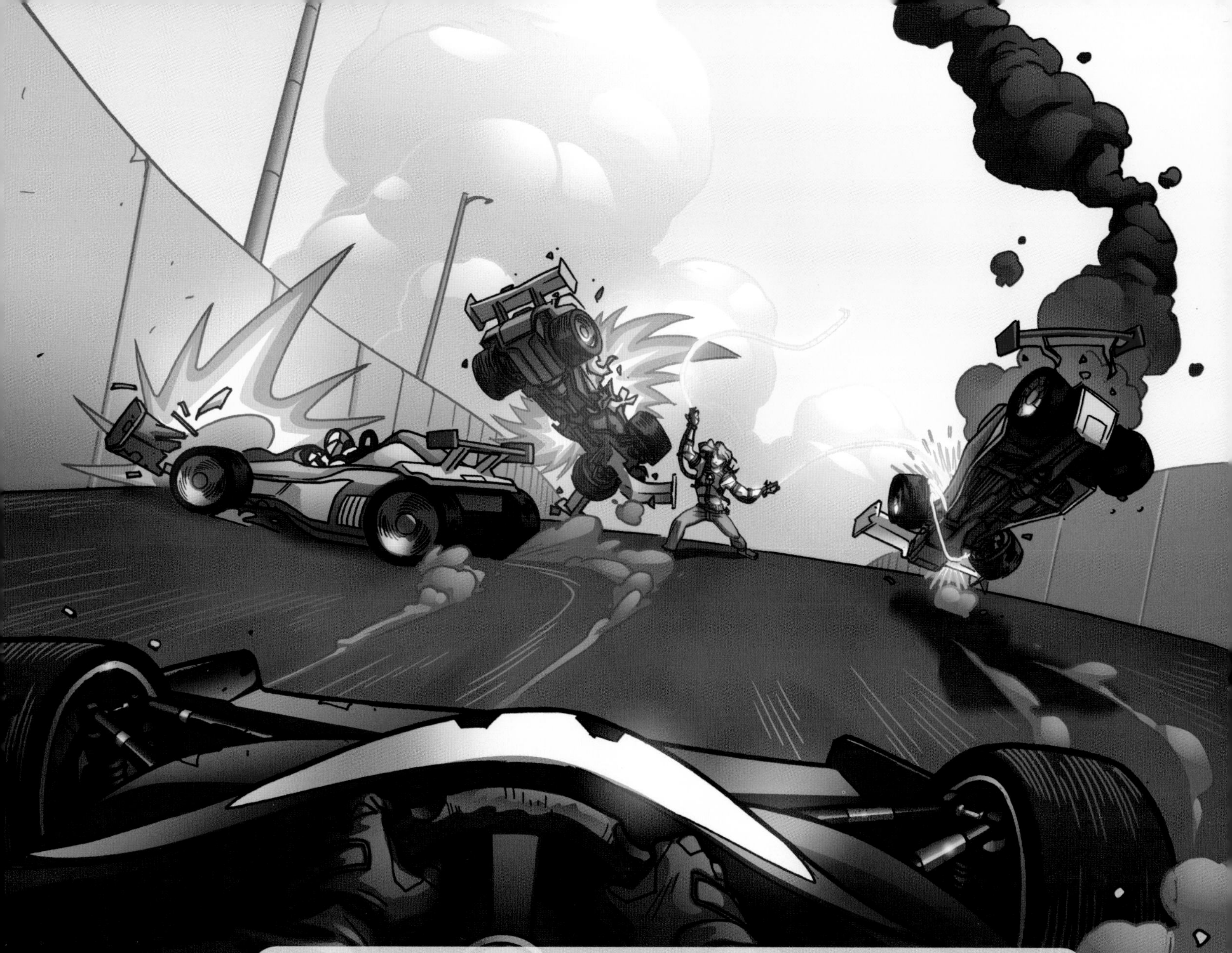

Tony zooms around the racecourse, taking curves at impossible speeds and gaining on the other drivers. He soon realizes that something is very wrong as cars ahead of him start veering around something on the track.

"What is that?" Tony says.

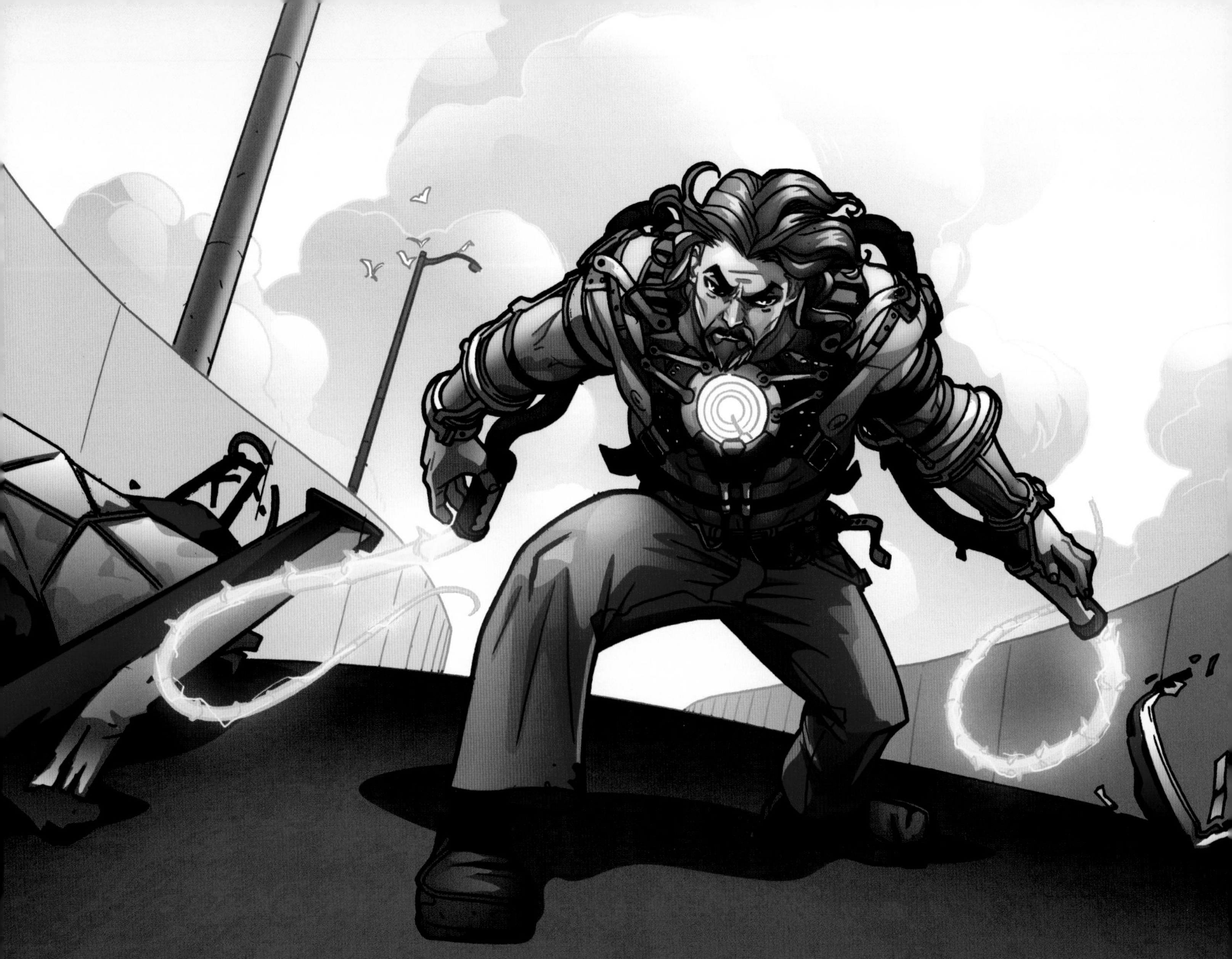

Pepper sees it, too.

"Happy, look! There's a man on the track!" she yells as she notices Ivan.

Zeroing in on Tony's car, Whiplash marches fearlessly against the flow of race traffic! Cars crash as they swerve around him.

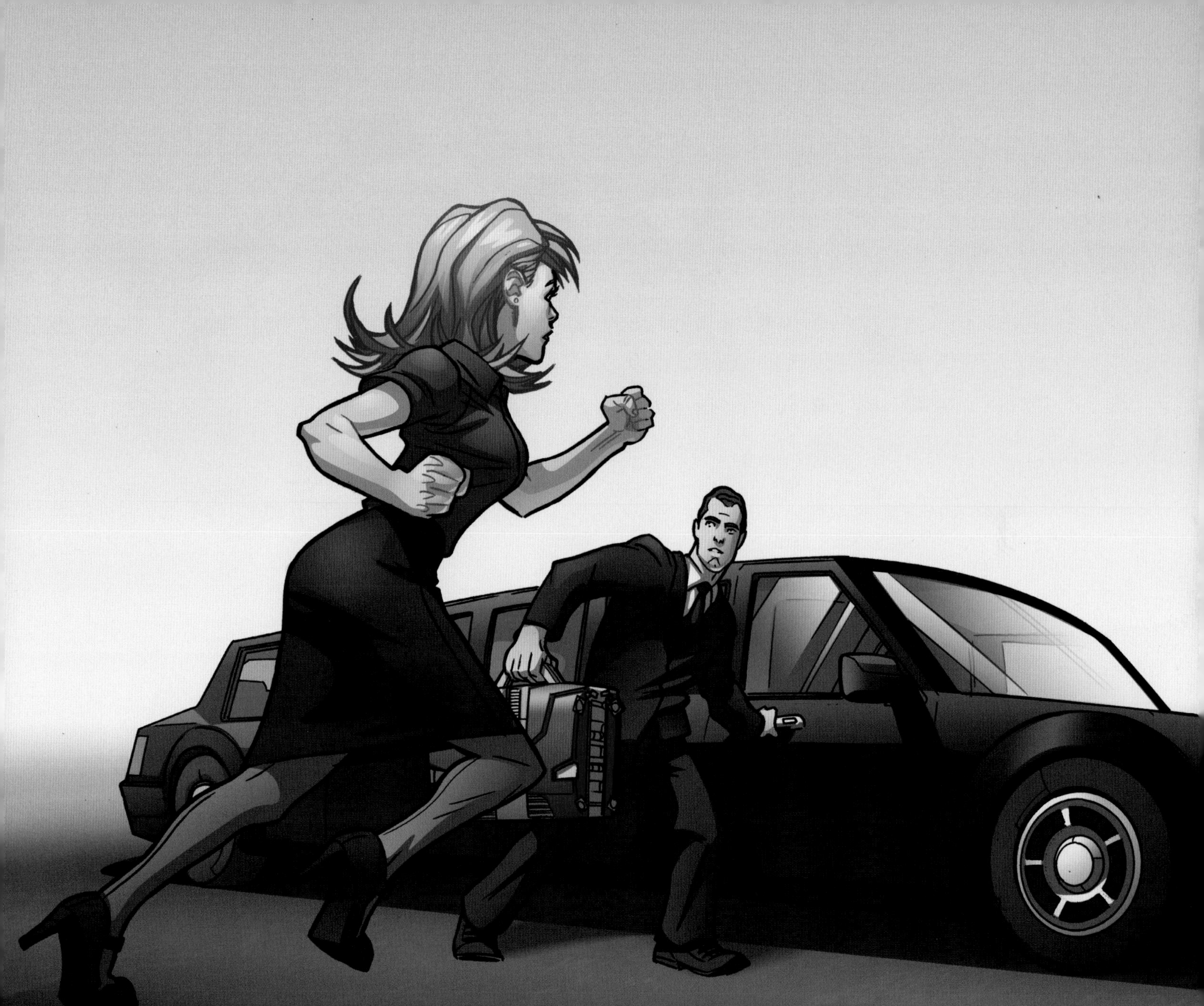

Pepper grabs Happy and makes sure he has Tony's briefcase.

Together, they flee the restaurant and jump into the Stark limo.

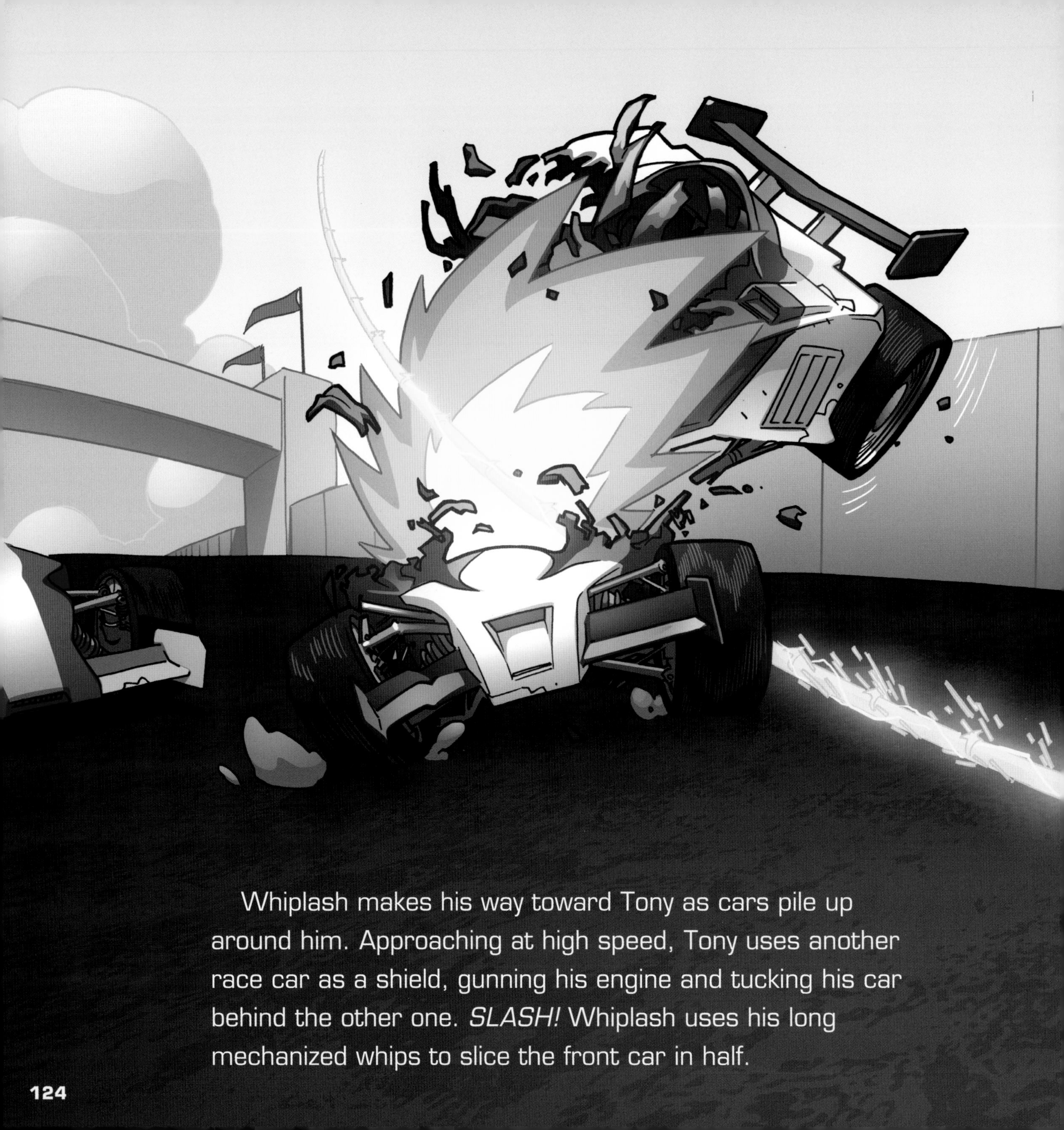

Whiplash makes his way toward Tony as cars pile up around him. Approaching at high speed, Tony uses another race car as a shield, gunning his engine and tucking his car behind the other one. *SLASH!* Whiplash uses his long mechanized whips to slice the front car in half.

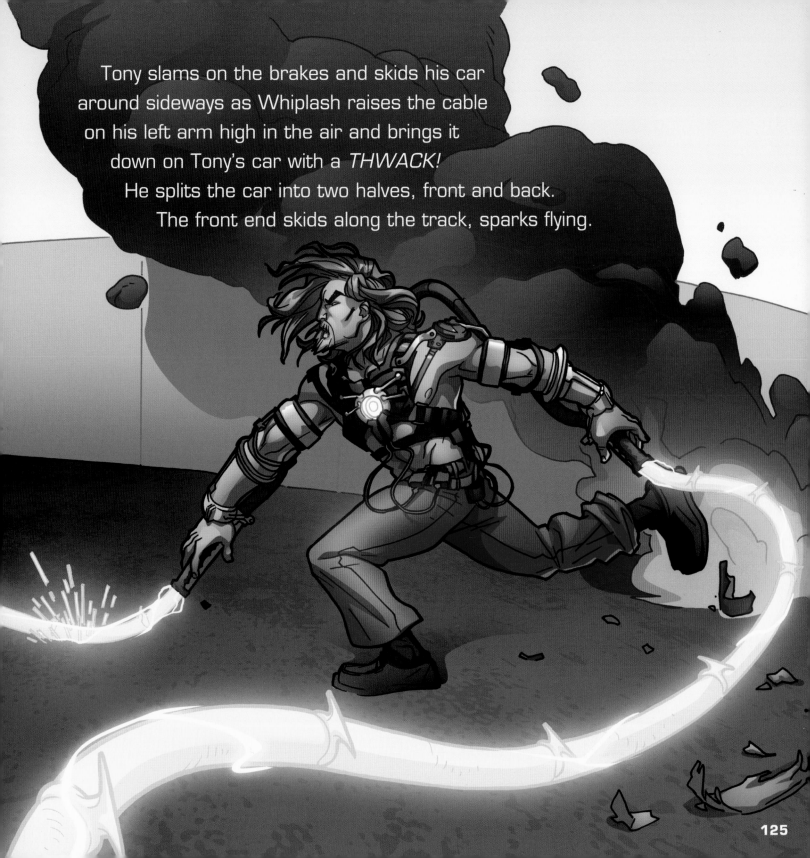

Tony slams on the brakes and skids his car around sideways as Whiplash raises the cable on his left arm high in the air and brings it down on Tony's car with a *THWACK!* He splits the car into two halves, front and back. The front end skids along the track, sparks flying.

With his prey in sight, Whiplash follows Tony, who is still in the car's front end. It tumbles and skids along the track, finally screeching to a stop upside down. Whiplash stomps toward it and grabs the steel frame with his whips. He rips it open and finds . . .

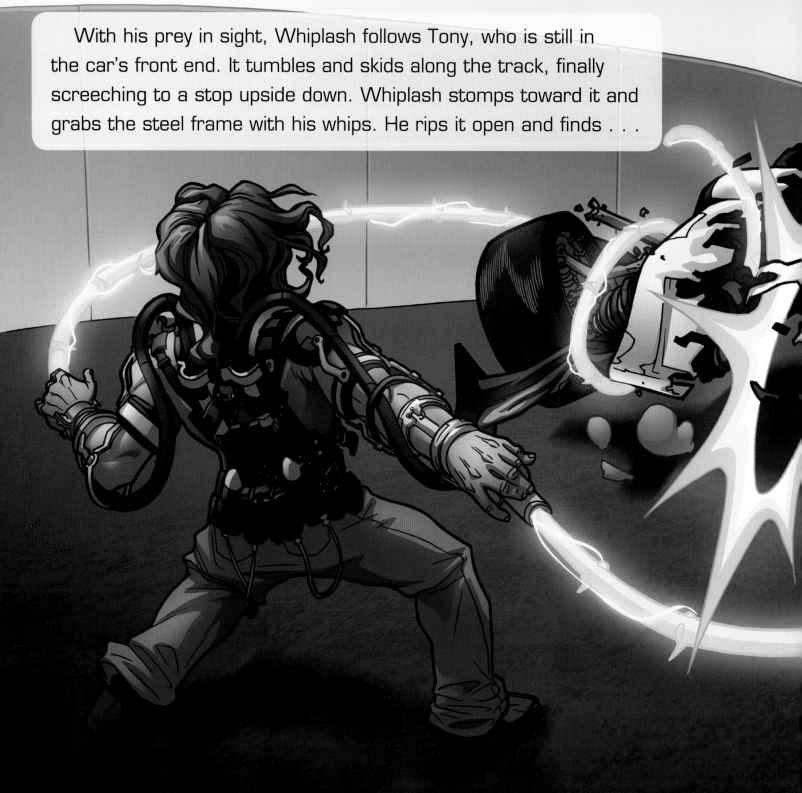

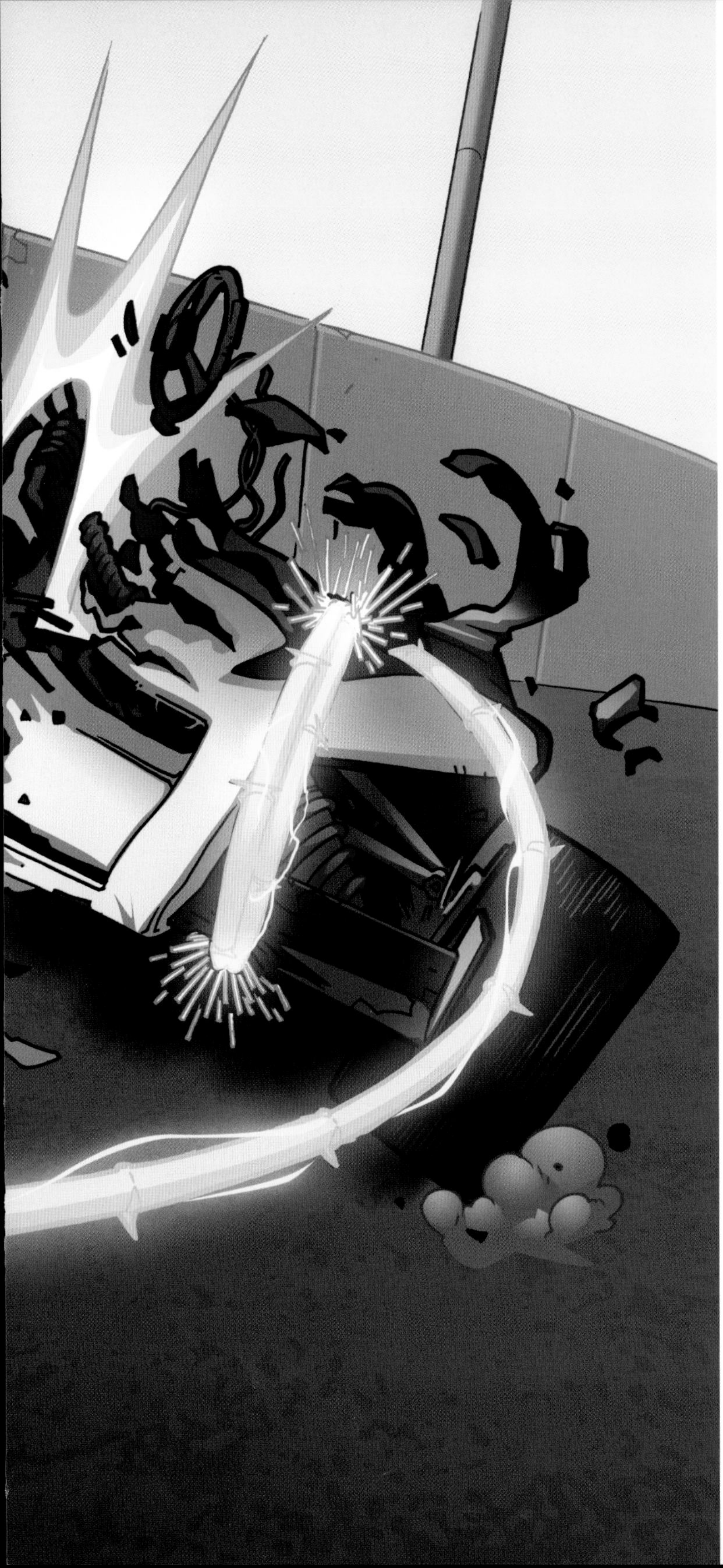

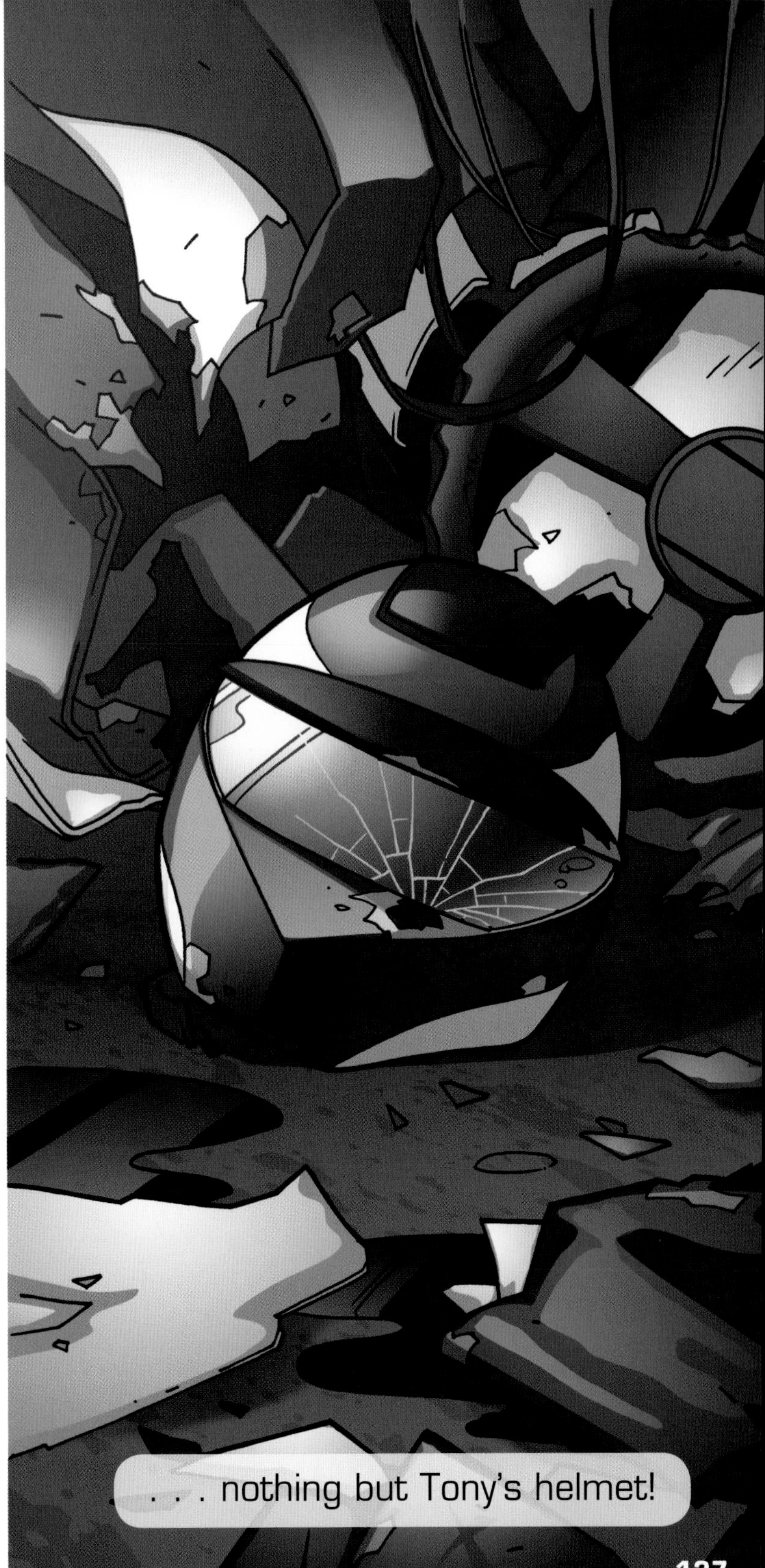
. . . nothing but Tony's helmet!

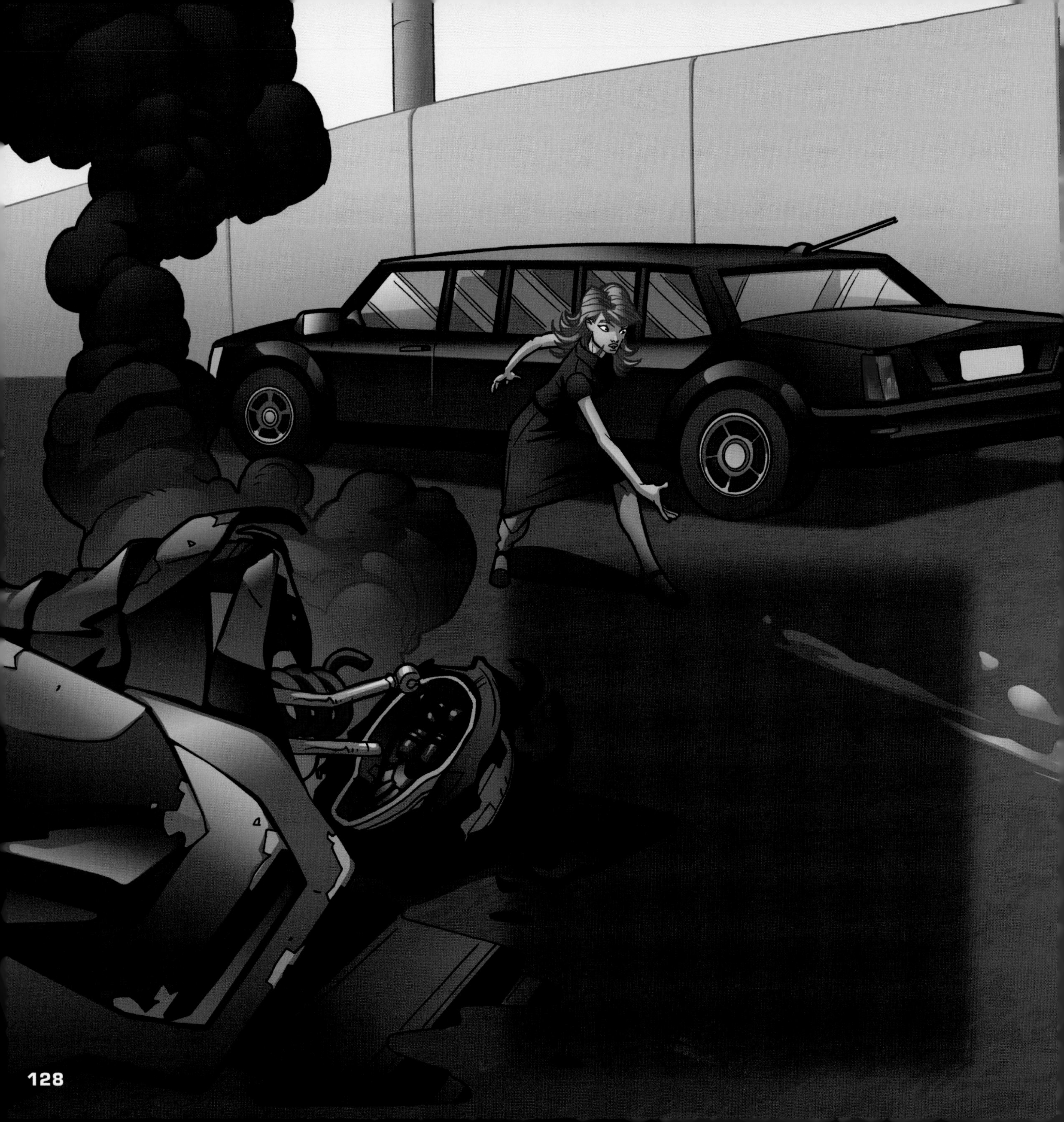

The briefcase isn't *just* a briefcase! In seconds, Tony's feet turn into boots, his legs into armor. Piece by piece, body part by body part, the case morphs into an Iron Man suit!

As the suit covers Tony's body completely, he becomes Iron Man.

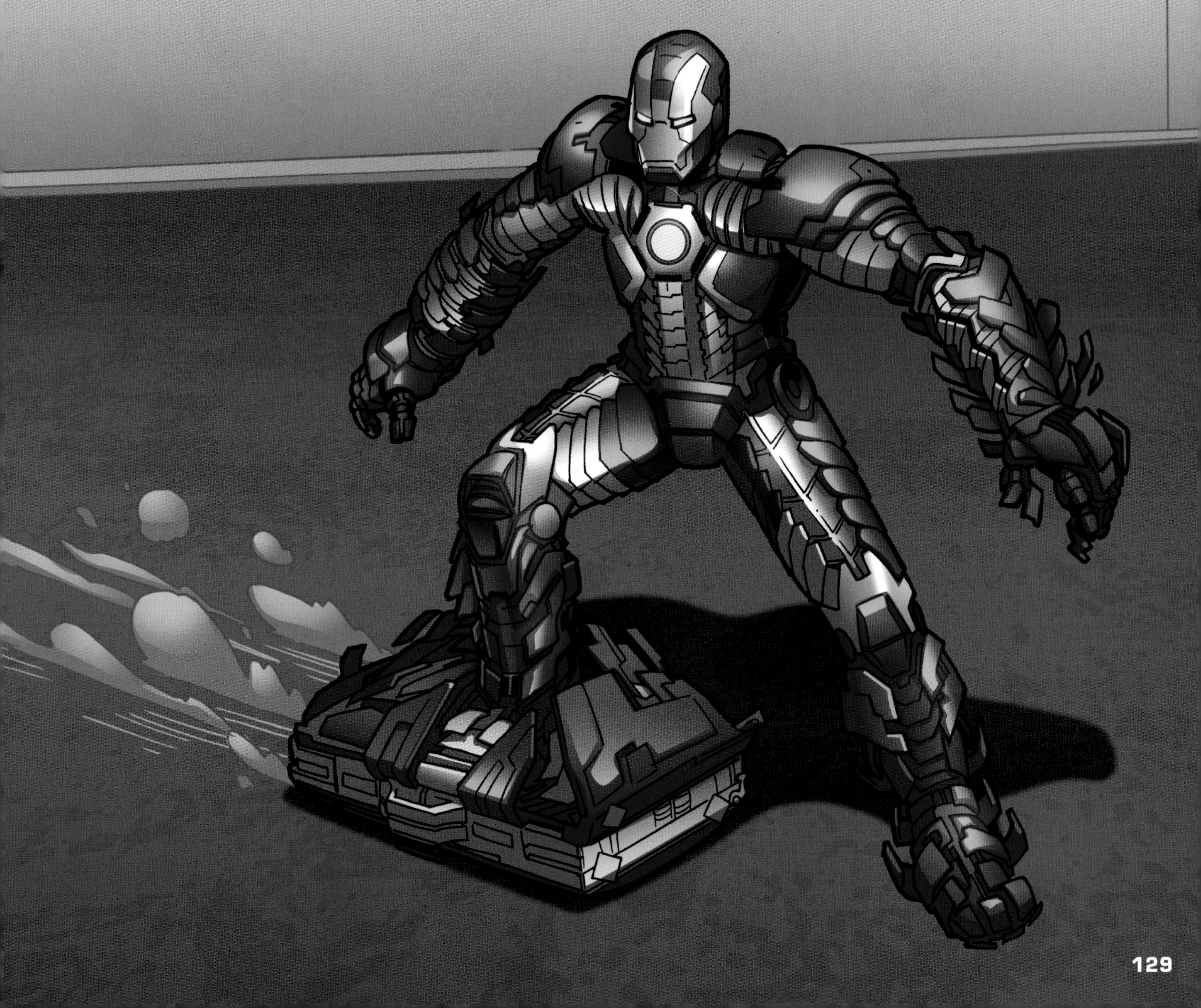

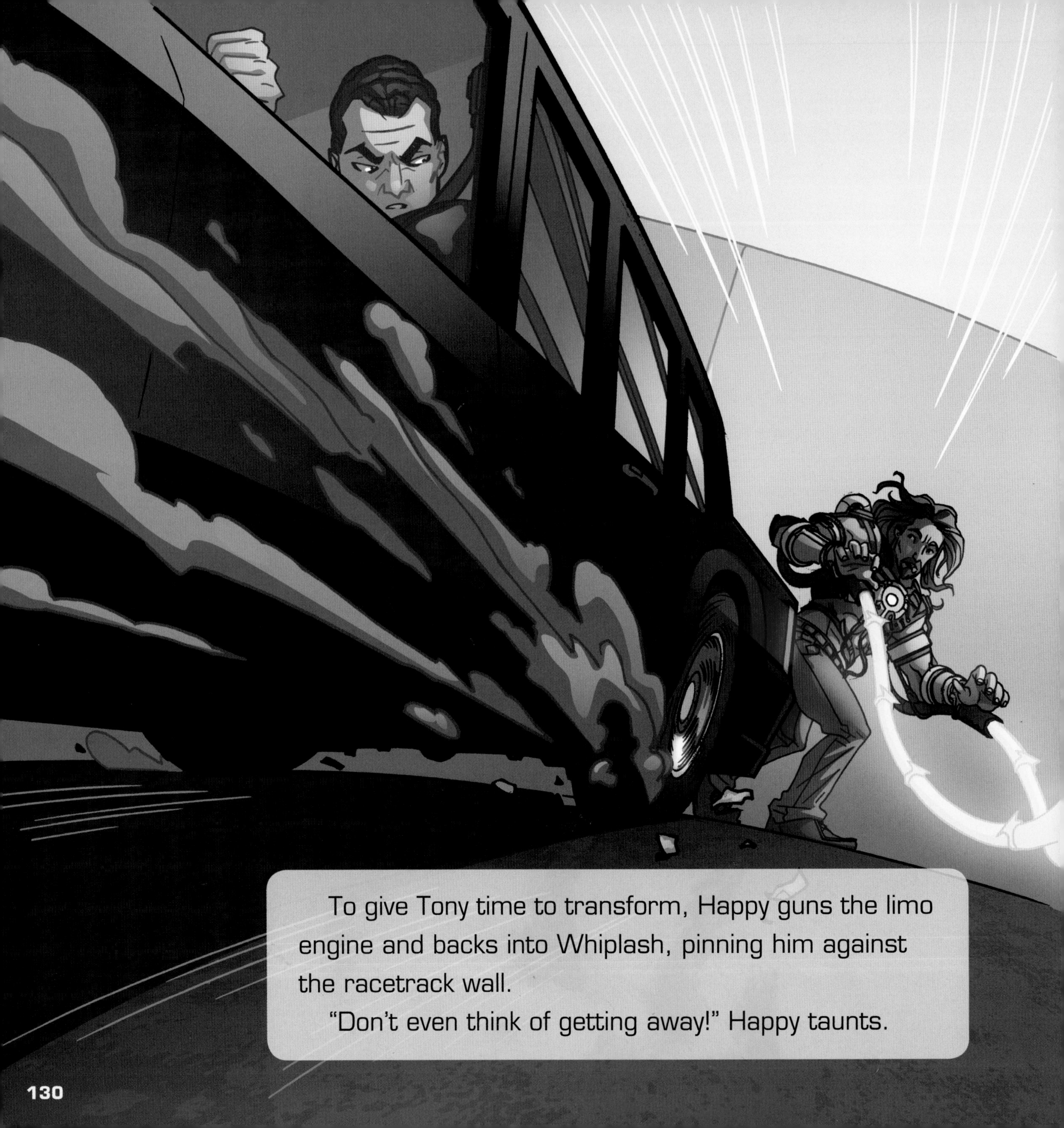

To give Tony time to transform, Happy guns the limo engine and backs into Whiplash, pinning him against the racetrack wall.

"Don't even think of getting away!" Happy taunts.

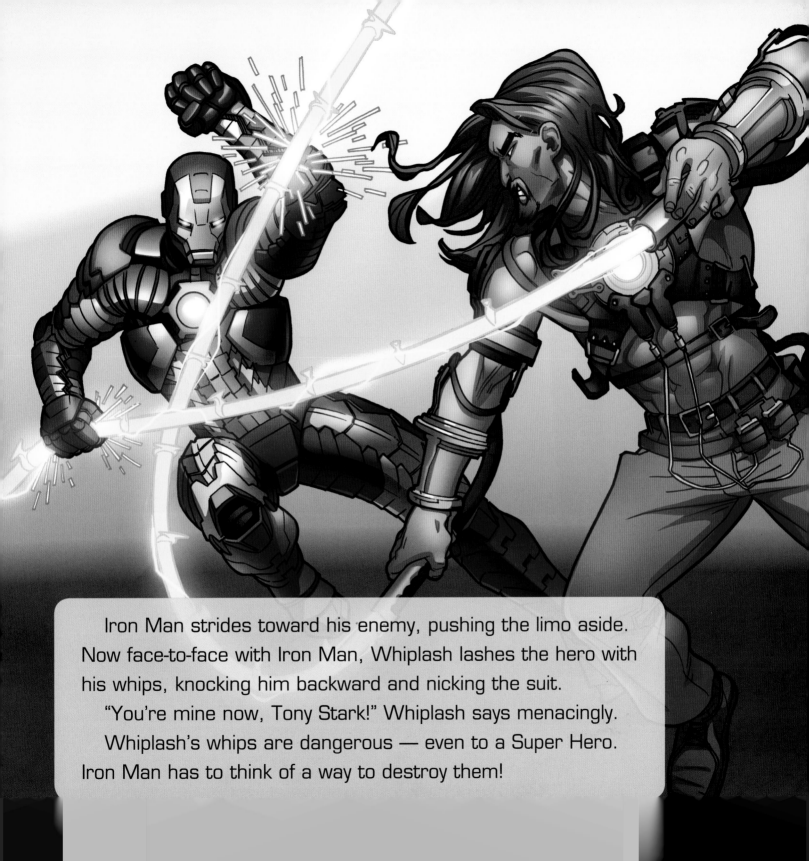

Iron Man strides toward his enemy, pushing the limo aside. Now face-to-face with Iron Man, Whiplash lashes the hero with his whips, knocking him backward and nicking the suit.

"You're mine now, Tony Stark!" Whiplash says menacingly.

Whiplash's whips are dangerous — even to a Super Hero. Iron Man has to think of a way to destroy them!

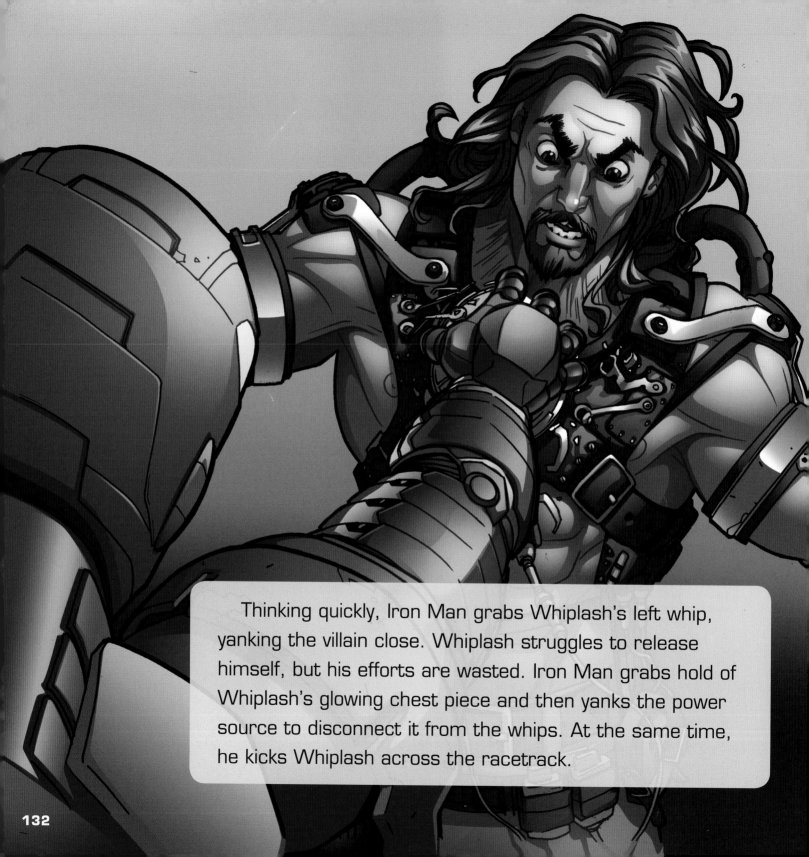

Thinking quickly, Iron Man grabs Whiplash's left whip, yanking the villain close. Whiplash struggles to release himself, but his efforts are wasted. Iron Man grabs hold of Whiplash's glowing chest piece and then yanks the power source to disconnect it from the whips. At the same time, he kicks Whiplash across the racetrack.

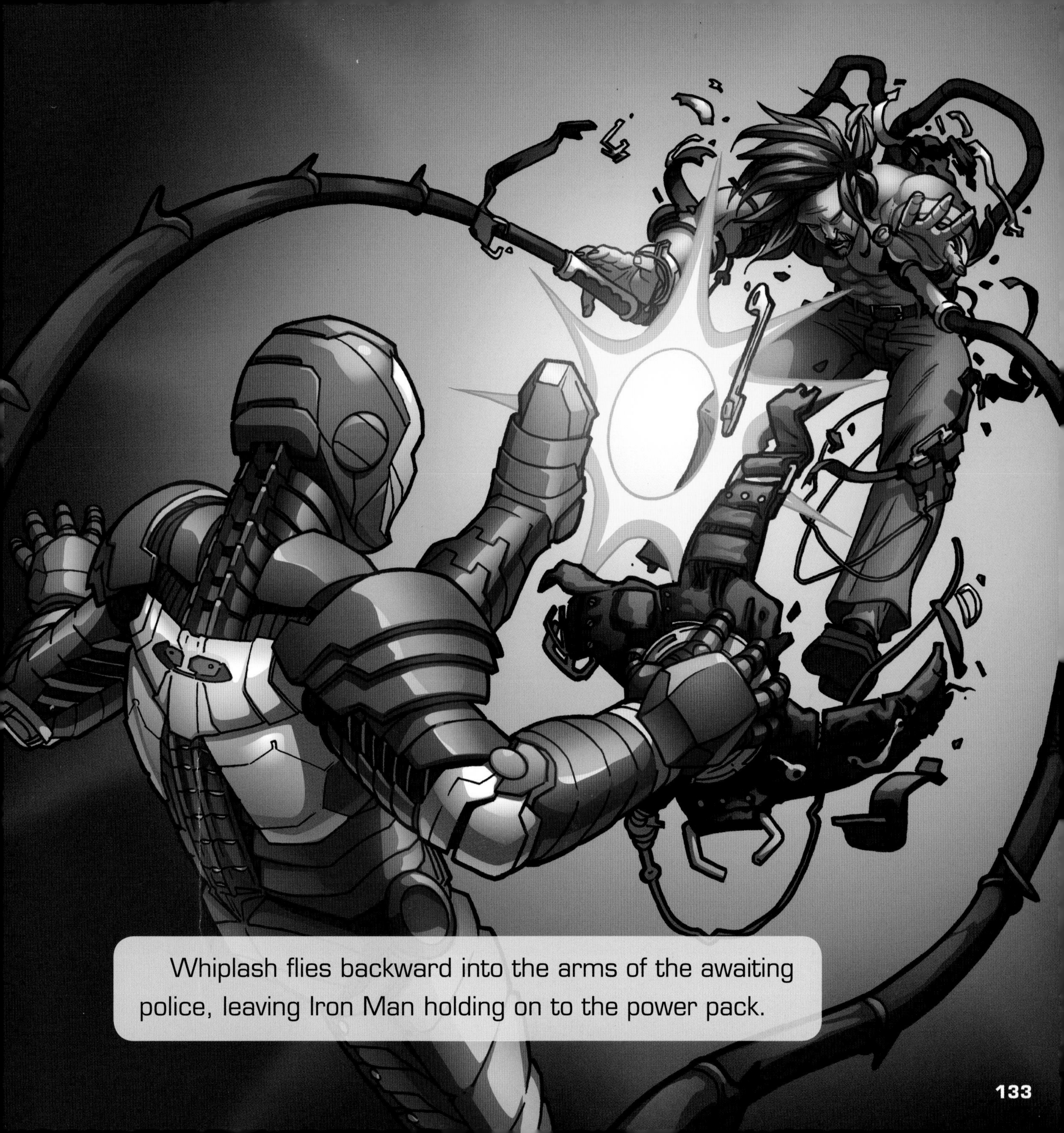

Whiplash flies backward into the arms of the awaiting police, leaving Iron Man holding on to the power pack.

The crowd cheers.

"All in a day's work," Iron Man calls out as he waves to the fans. He might not have won the race — but he won the battle!

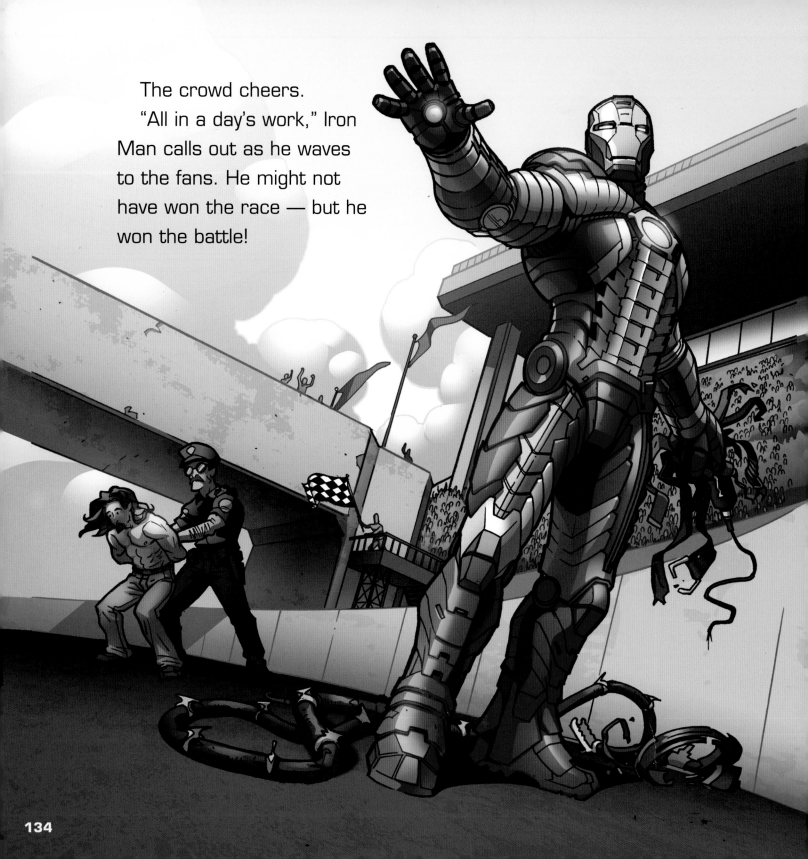

![MARVEL]

THOR™
THE DARK WORLD
WARRIORS OF THE REALMS

By **TOMAS PALACIOS** & **ADAM DAVIS**

Based on the Screenplay by **CHRISTOPHER L. YOST**

and **CHRISTOPHER MARKUS** & **STEPHEN McFEELY**

Story by **DON PAYNE** and **ROBERT RODAT**

Produced by **KEVIN FEIGE**, p.g.a.

Directed by **ALAN TAYLOR**

Illustrated by **RON LIM**, **CAM SMITH**, and **LEE DUHIG**

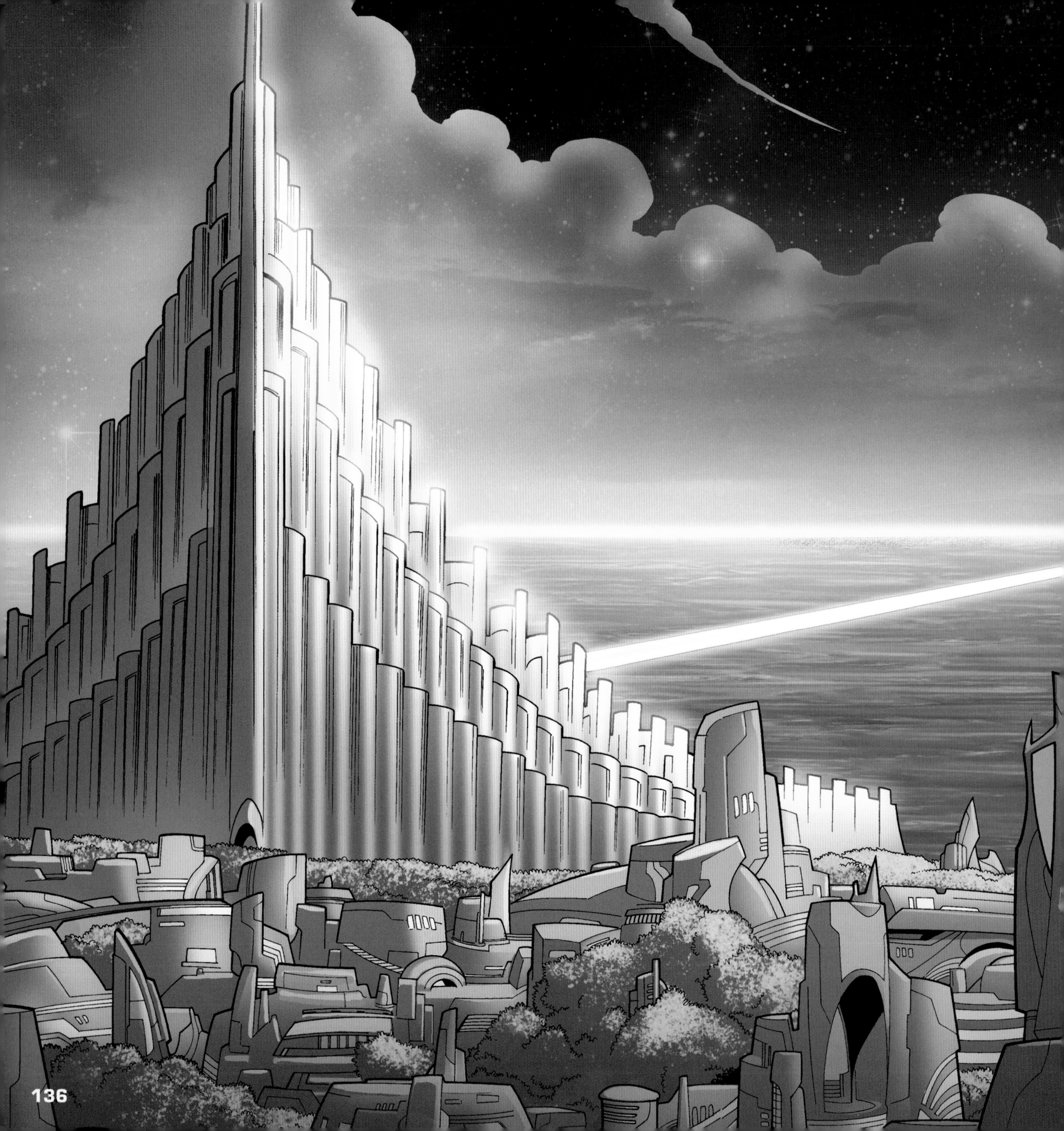

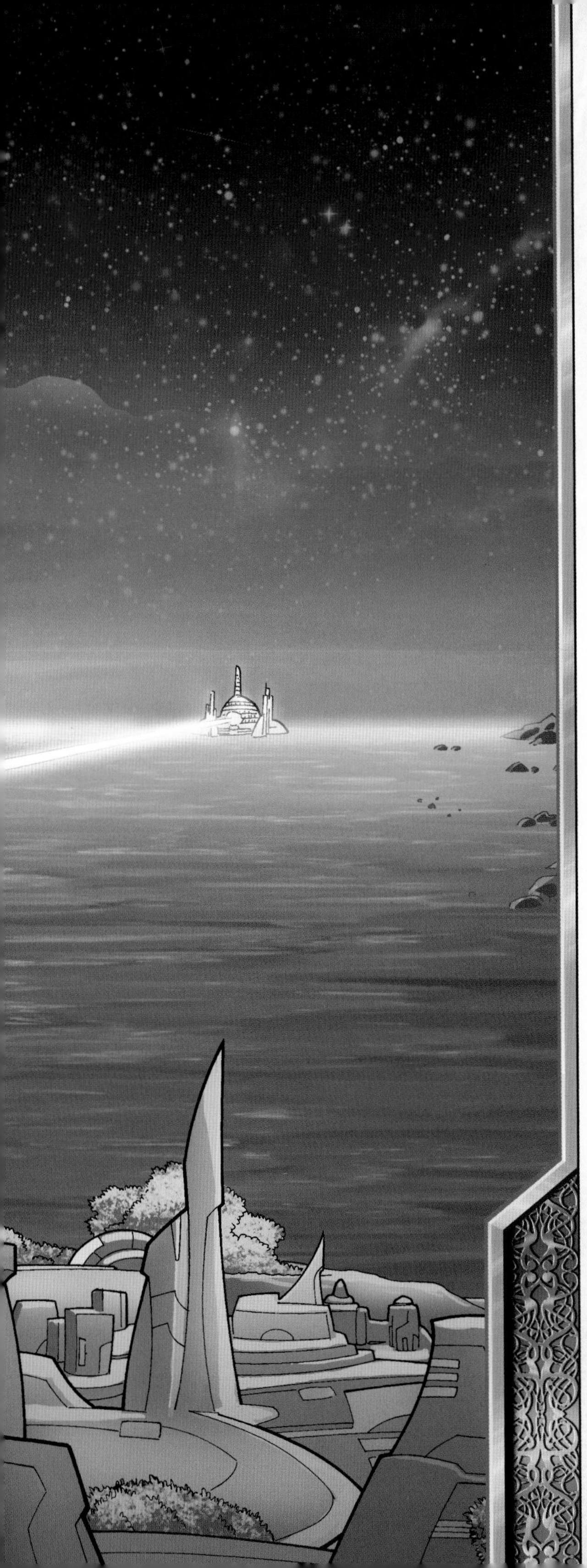

SOMEWHERE ACROSS THE UNIVERSE, there existed a realm known as Asgard. It was the land of a strong people, the Asgardians. Perched at the edge of the realm was a beautifully adorned structure, its golden dome housing the Bifrost. It was home to one of Asgard's most important and interesting individuals: the all-knowing, all-seeing Heimdall. The sentry had been here, at his post, unmoved, for quite some time. In fact, for thousands of years Heimdall had watched over his home world and guarded it from any incoming threat.

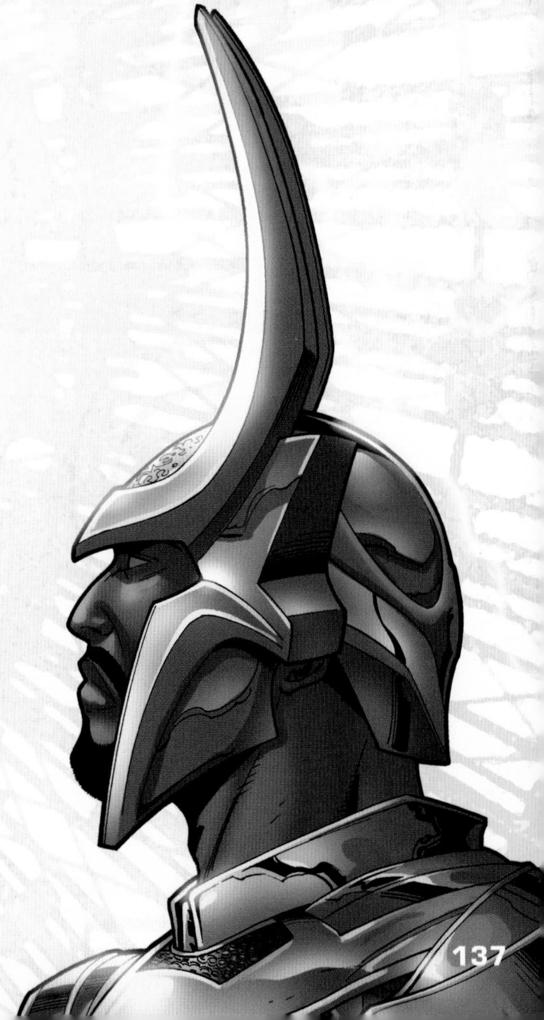

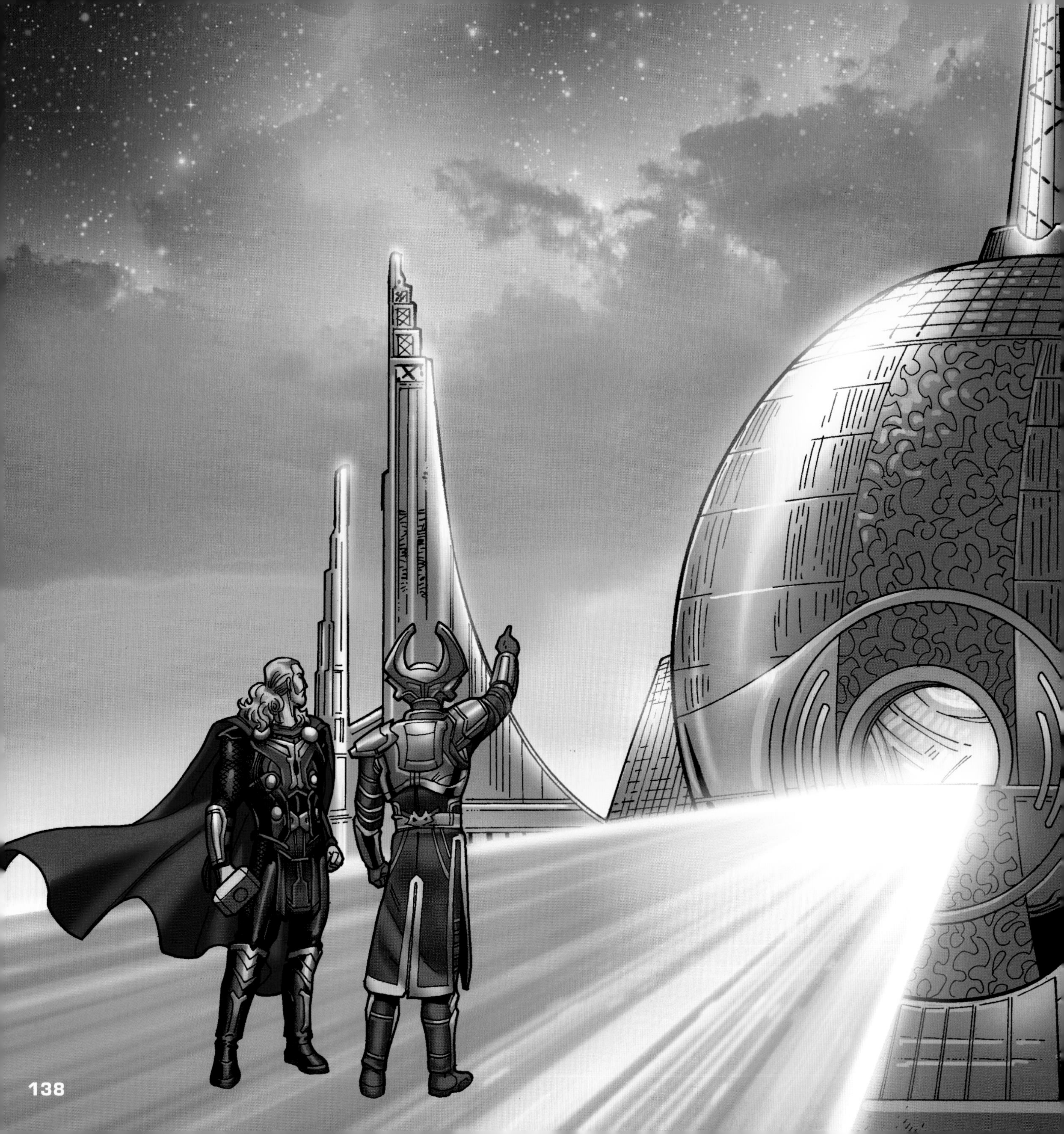

LOOKING OUT ACROSS THE UNIVERSE,

Heimdall fixed his eyes on the unending line of stars above. From here, the all-knowing sentry could see all Nine Realms and ten trillion souls—such a heavy burden for one to carry.

Heimdall thought about his last conversation with Thor, how they discussed the wonderment of the Convergence, a phenomenon that occurs once every five thousand years!

The alignment of worlds . . . it approaches, thought Heimdall.

He knew that with the Convergence approaching, Asgard and the surrounding realms would need to prepare for a great battle. For with the Convergence would come the Dark Elves, a dangerous race of creatures bent on plunging the universe into complete darkness.

LET US NOW VISIT THE HEROES AND VILLAINS OF THESE REALMS. . . .

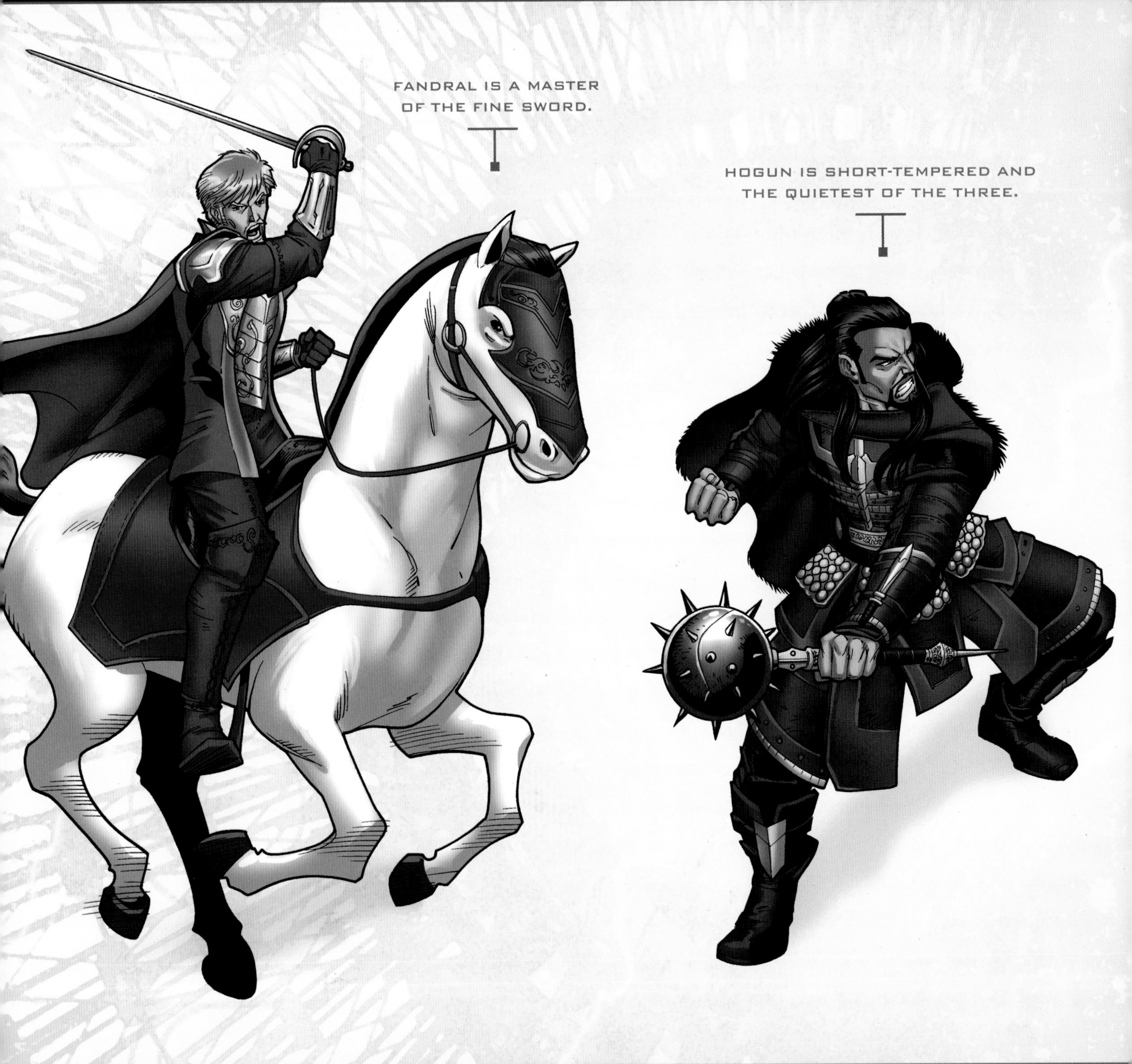
FANDRAL IS A MASTER OF THE FINE SWORD.
HOGUN IS SHORT-TEMPERED AND THE QUIETEST OF THE THREE.

WARRIORS OF THE REALMS

THE WARRIORS THREE. The name rings true. **FANDRAL** the Dashing, **HOGUN** the Grim, and **VOLSTAGG** the Voluminous form a mighty band of Asgardian warriors, each skilled in combat and with their own specific weapon. When the Nine Realms call for protection against enemies, the Warriors Three answer. Fandral, as skilled with his blade as he is with his charm, thinks very highly of himself, as do the single ladies of Asgard. Hogun, the stoic master of the mace and of throwing knives, is a quick and precise fighter who pulls no punches. And Volstagg, though equipped with the power of his mighty ax and hefty brawn, has also been known to use his massive belly as a weapon against enemies.

VOLSTAGG IS ALSO A MASTER OF THE QUARTERSTAFF, AS WELL AS A MASTER OF FOOD AND DRINK.

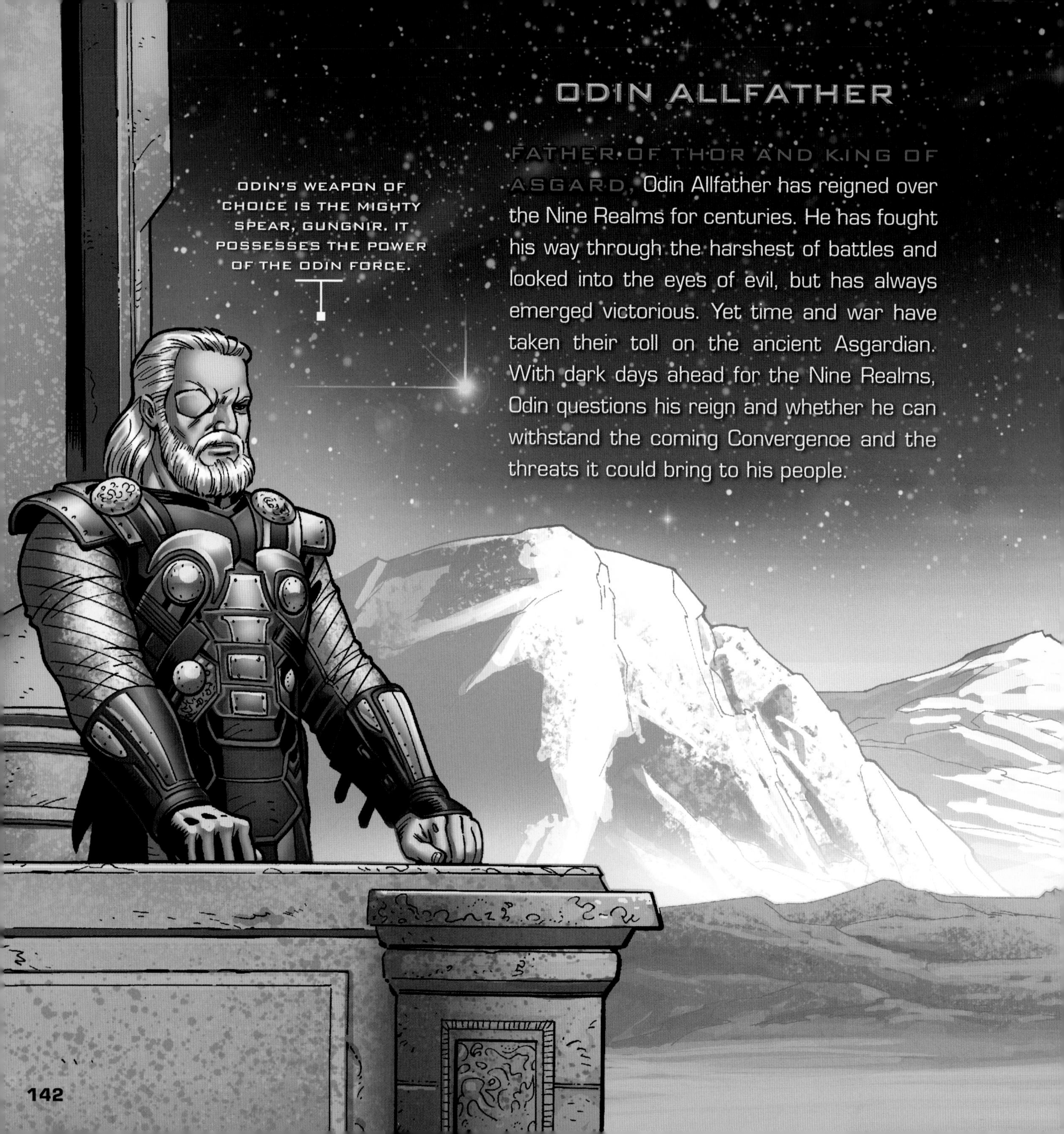

ODIN ALLFATHER

ODIN'S WEAPON OF CHOICE IS THE MIGHTY SPEAR, GUNGNIR. IT POSSESSES THE POWER OF THE ODIN FORCE.

FATHER OF THOR AND KING OF ASGARD, Odin Allfather has reigned over the Nine Realms for centuries. He has fought his way through the harshest of battles and looked into the eyes of evil, but has always emerged victorious. Yet time and war have taken their toll on the ancient Asgardian. With dark days ahead for the Nine Realms, Odin questions his reign and whether he can withstand the coming Convergence and the threats it could bring to his people.

LADY SIF

THE FIERCEST OF ASGARD'S FEMALE FIGHTERS, Lady Sif has proven herself time and time again to the Warriors Three, Thor, and the people of Asgard. With her incredible agility and her skill in the double swords, Sif is someone whom the mighty Thor is proud to fight alongside. Since Jane Foster's recent absence, Sif has tried to fill the void in Thor's heart. But Thor's heart is already taken. . . .

LADY SIF IS A MASTER SWORDSMAN. SOME SAY SHE IS THE BEST IN ALL OF ASGARD.

LOKI THE TRICKSTER

LOKI IS THOR'S BROTHER.
He hasn't been very good lately.

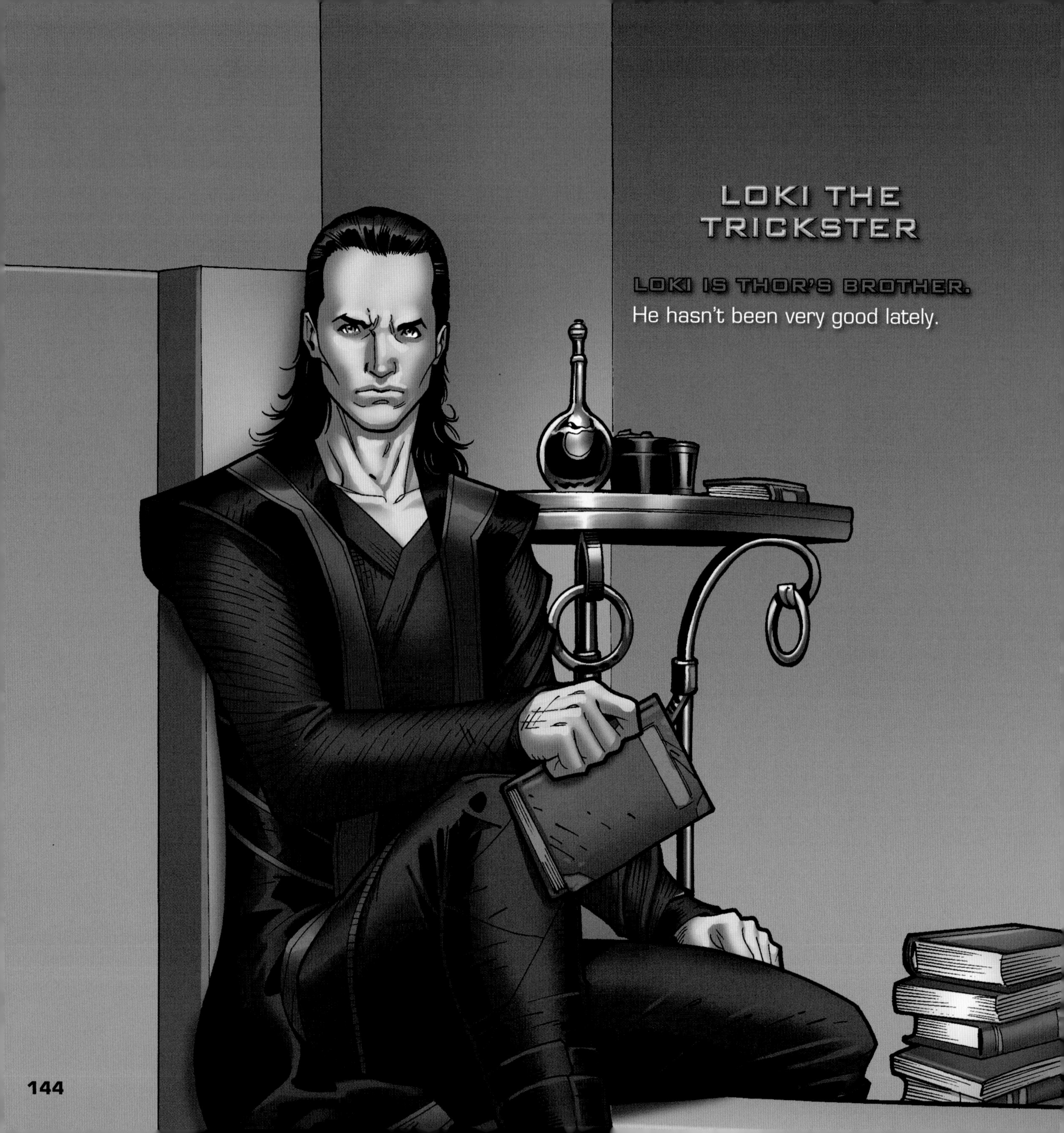

FRIGGA

FRIGGA, the mother of Thor and Loki, loves both her sons equally (even though one tried to take over Earth, and the other was banished to the same planet for starting a war with the Frost Giants). But that doesn't mean she taught them the same skills. Frigga is equally versed in the art of magic as she is with a blade. To Loki, she taught her knowledge of illusions, and to Thor, she taught how to be strong in battle, both physically and mentally. With her deep capacity to defend and love, Frigga is truly the perfect wife for Odin.

FRIGGA HAS BEEN THE WIFE OF ODIN FOR THOUSANDS OF YEARS.

HER LOOKS ARE DECEIVING. FRIGGA IS A SKILLED WARRIOR AND MASTER SWORDSMAN.

THE GOD OF THUNDER

THE MIGHTY THOR! Warrior of Asgard. Son to Odin. Friend of the Warriors Three and Lady Sif. Thor has proven to his people, and to himself, that he is ready to take on any challenge, including the throne of Asgard. After the events of New York City involving the Avengers, Thor and his band of warriors traveled the cosmos to restore order and peace. From realm to realm, Thor banished evil and reminded the universe that harmony was needed. From fighting Marauders to battling Chitauri, Thor backed down from no challenge.

THOR'S BATTLE ARMOR IS MADE FROM THE STRONGEST METAL IN THE COSMOS.

THOR CAN SPIN HIS HAMMER, MJOLNIR, AND FLY GREAT DISTANCES.

MJOLNIR

If Thor is Asgard's mightiest warrior, **MJOLNIR** is Asgard's greatest weapon. Forged in a dying star, Mjolnir is Thor's mighty hammer, made from uru metal. It lets Thor summon rain, lightning, and thunder, and when spun at a rapid rate, Mjolnir helps Thor take flight! If Thor is separated from Mjolnir, it will travel any distance, even across worlds, to return to him. Unable to be lifted by any mortal or Super Hero from any realm, Mjolnir was created for Thor, and Thor alone.

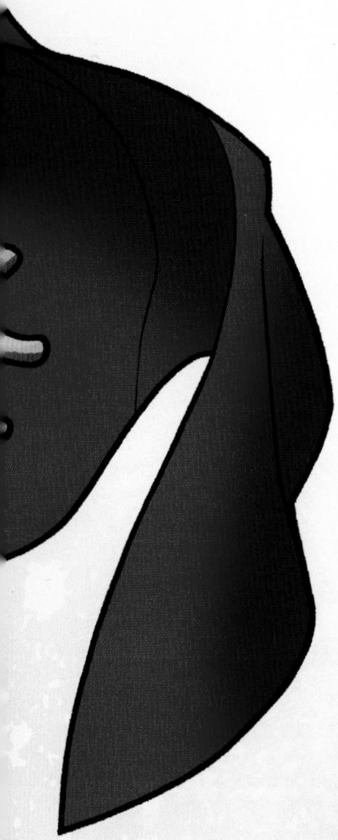

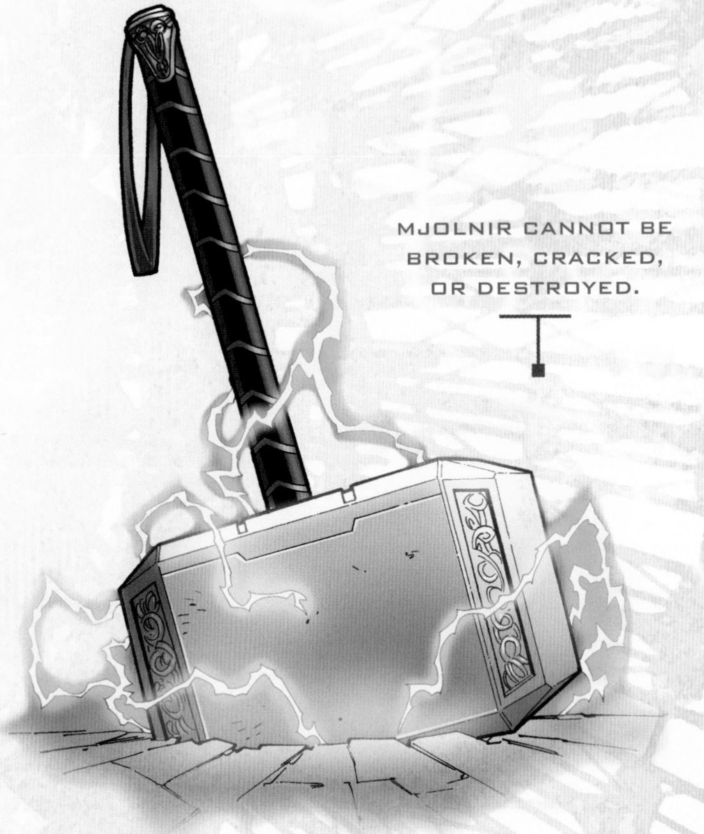
MJOLNIR CANNOT BE BROKEN, CRACKED, OR DESTROYED.

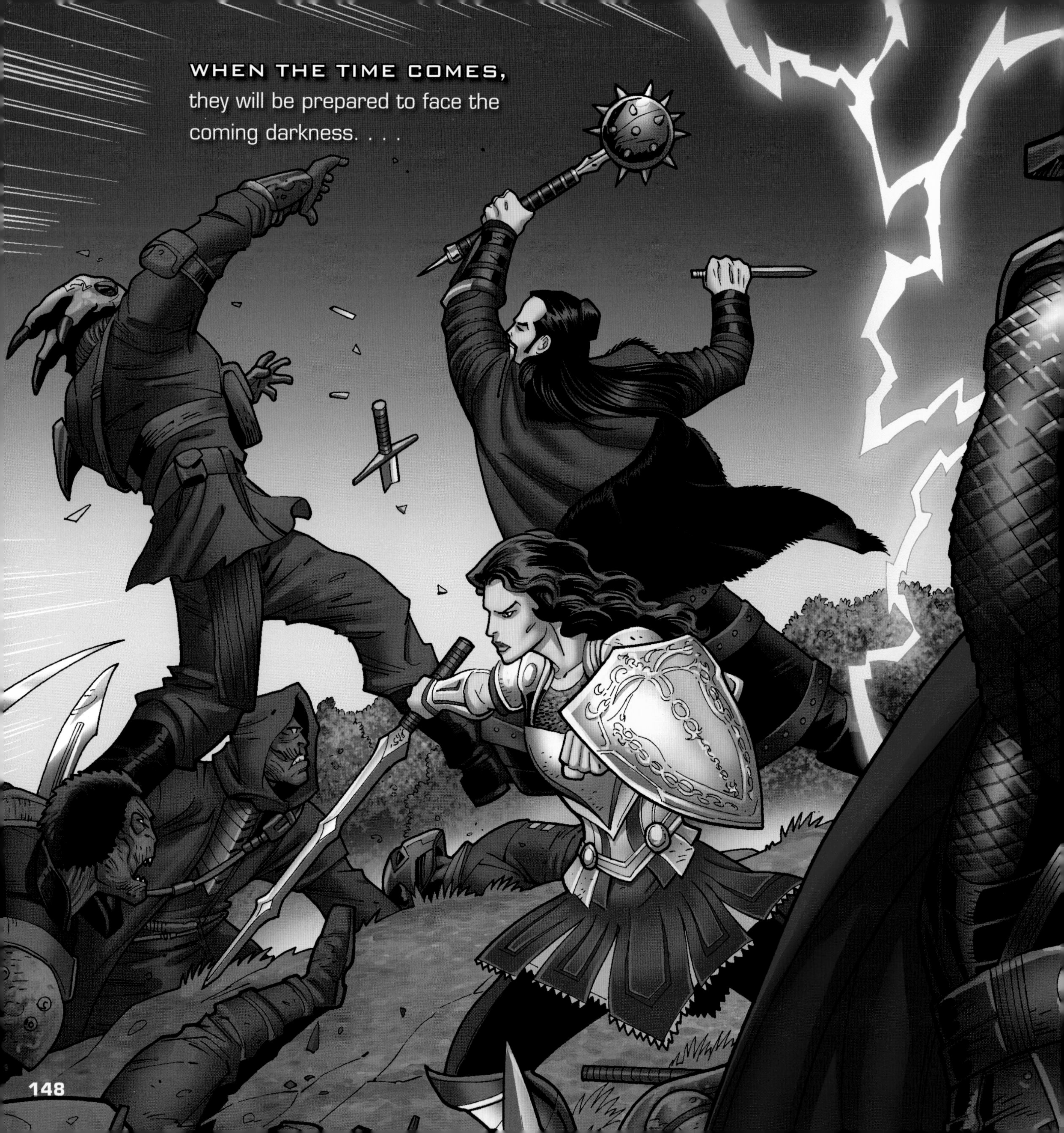
WHEN THE TIME COMES,
they will be prepared to face the coming darkness. . . .

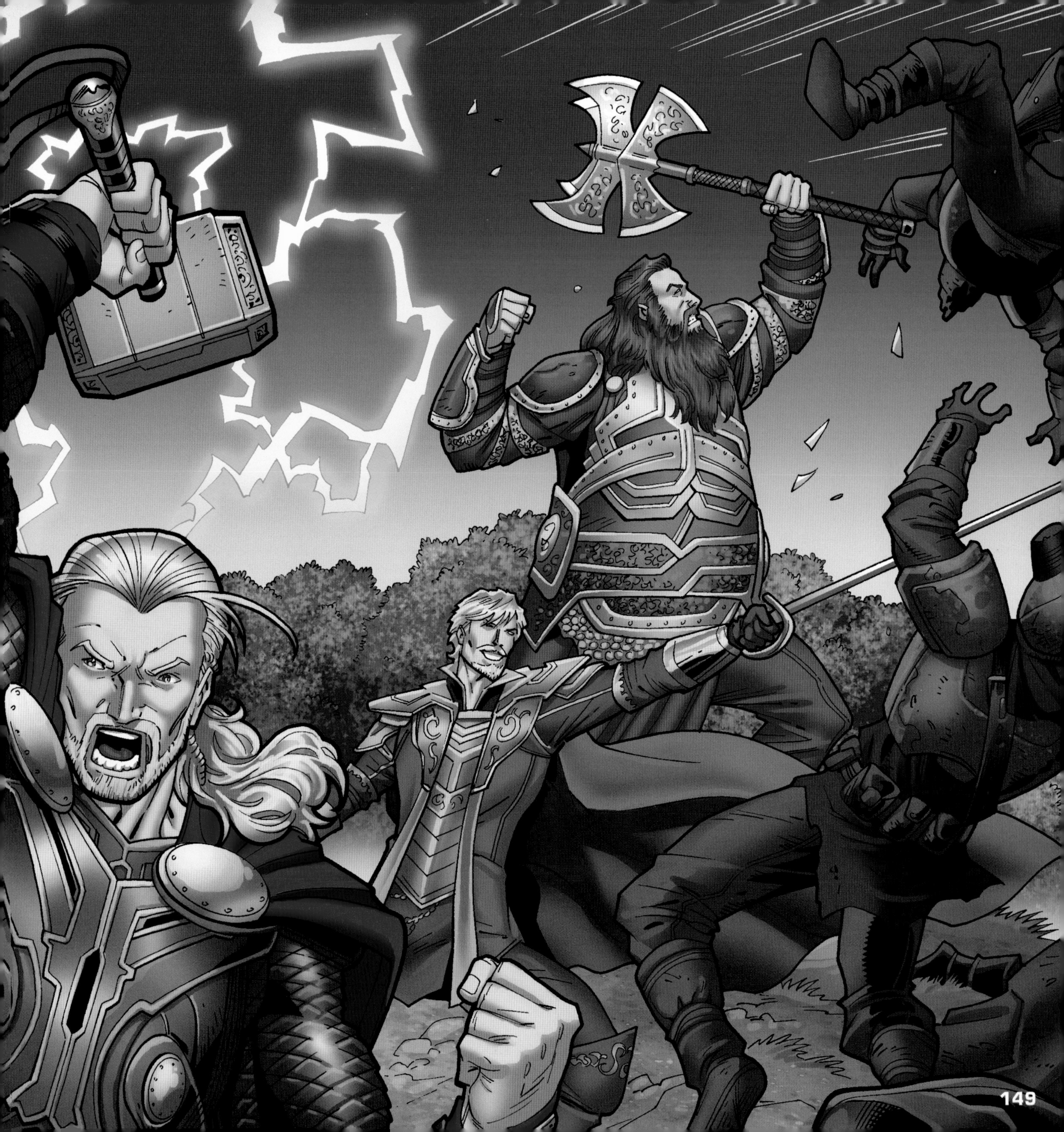

THE MARAUDERS

Vicious and armed to the teeth, the **MARAUDERS** are a band of looters that travel from world to world in search of everything and anything that planet holds dear. When word spread that the Bifrost was down, and that the Asgardians would have no way to protect the citizens of the Nine Realms, the Marauders took it upon themselves to cause chaos.

Their choice of weapons usually consists of swords and rocket launchers. A strange mix, but when you're a space pirate, you use what you can get your hands on. But the Marauders have more than a few weapons up their sleeves. . . .

MARAUDERS TRAVEL IN
GROUPS OF NO LESS THAN
A DOZEN AT A TIME.

THE DARK ELVES

THE DARK ELVES of Svartalfheim. A race long forgotten by many. But no more. Recently having been rallied by their great and powerful leader, Malekith, the Dark Elves have come together for one reason: revenge for the devastation of their home planet. Unable to breathe the air on their homeworld without their shiny, pearl-colored masks, the Dark Elves are fearless and will do anything in the name of their race and king. Armed with the mysterious dark technology, they use their ferocious guns to form black holes against their enemies, sucking them into the abyss, never to be seen again.

THE DARK ELVES SHOW NO EMOTION IN THEIR BATTLE MASKS.

MALEKITH AND ALGRIM

Before the universe, there was darkness, and in that darkness the Dark Elves thrived. The leader and king of the Dark Elves of Svartalfheim, **MALEKITH** ruled unchallenged, his dark reign touching every inch of the cosmos. But then came the birth of light and with that the end of Malekith's grip on the universe. Since then, he has been waiting . . . waiting for the right moment to come back to existence and seek revenge for his people, and his family. That moment . . . is now.

Malekith's second in command, **ALGRIM** has been in the fight since the beginning. Always willing to go above and beyond for his king, Algrim is crucial to spreading darkness back over the universe. He helps build the Dark Elf army for his king and will be at the forefront of the charge against any opponent.

ALGRIM

MALEKITH

THE ARK

A monstrous ship that once floated quietly in space has come back to life, glowing with a dark energy. This is the ARK. Malekith and his army of Dark Elves have dwelled inside the Ark for many, many years, but now that time of dwelling is over. The Ark is not only the mother ship of this dark race, but also a powerful weapon for invading planets and realms.

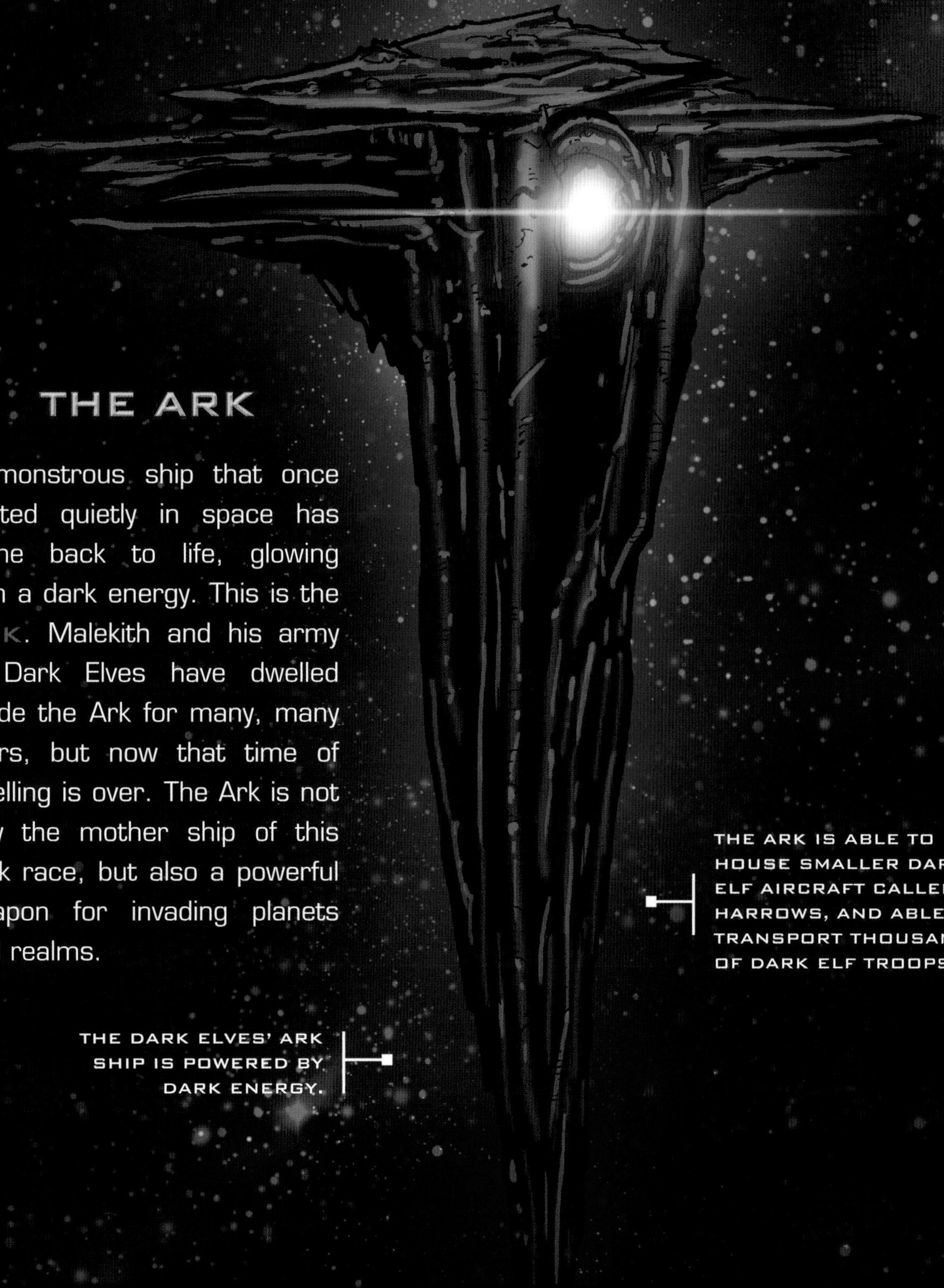

THE ARK IS ABLE TO HOUSE SMALLER DARK ELF AIRCRAFT CALLED HARROWS, AND ABLE TO TRANSPORT THOUSANDS OF DARK ELF TROOPS.

THE DARK ELVES' ARK SHIP IS POWERED BY DARK ENERGY.

KRONAN STONE MAN

When the Marauders invaded Hogun's home planet of Vanaheim, they were prepared for the weaponless Vanir people. But they were not prepared for the arrival of Thor. Nonetheless, when they needed to battle the Asgardian, they called upon their secret weapon, the **KRONAN STONE MAN**. Made entirely of rock and carrying a massive club, the Kronan beast stood toe-to-toe with Thor, ready for a battle.

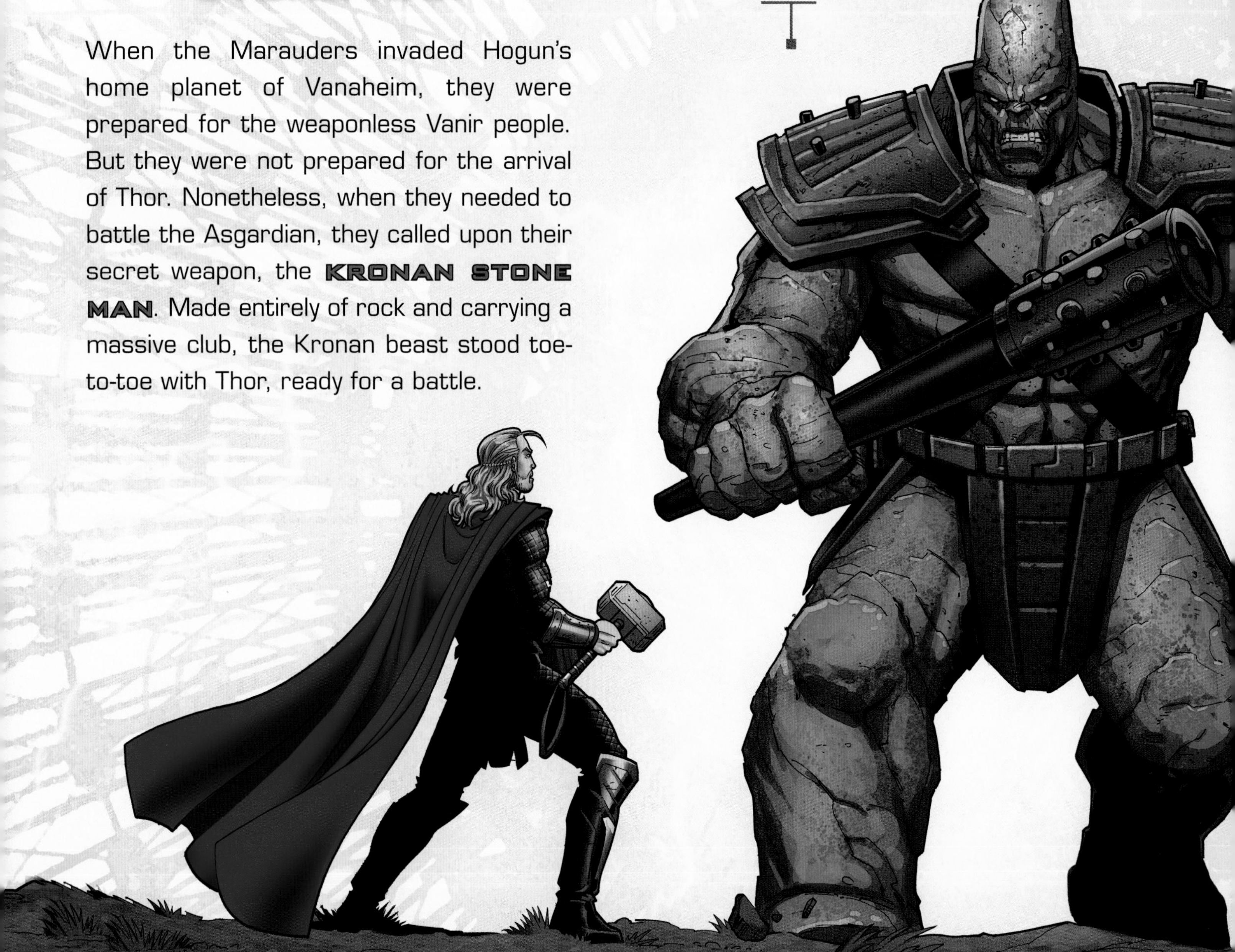

THE KRONAN MAN TOWERS OVER ALL, INCLUDING THE MIGHTY THOR.

A KURSE TO ALL OF ASGARD

KURSE is Malekith's secret weapon. Not much else is known about this brutal creature. . . .

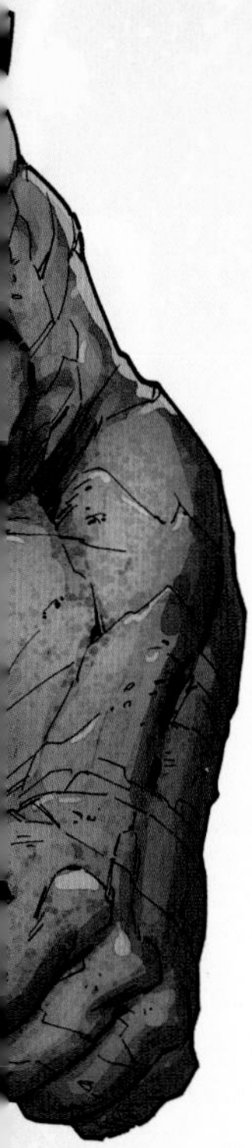

KURSE HAS THE POWER OF A HUNDRED WARRIORS.

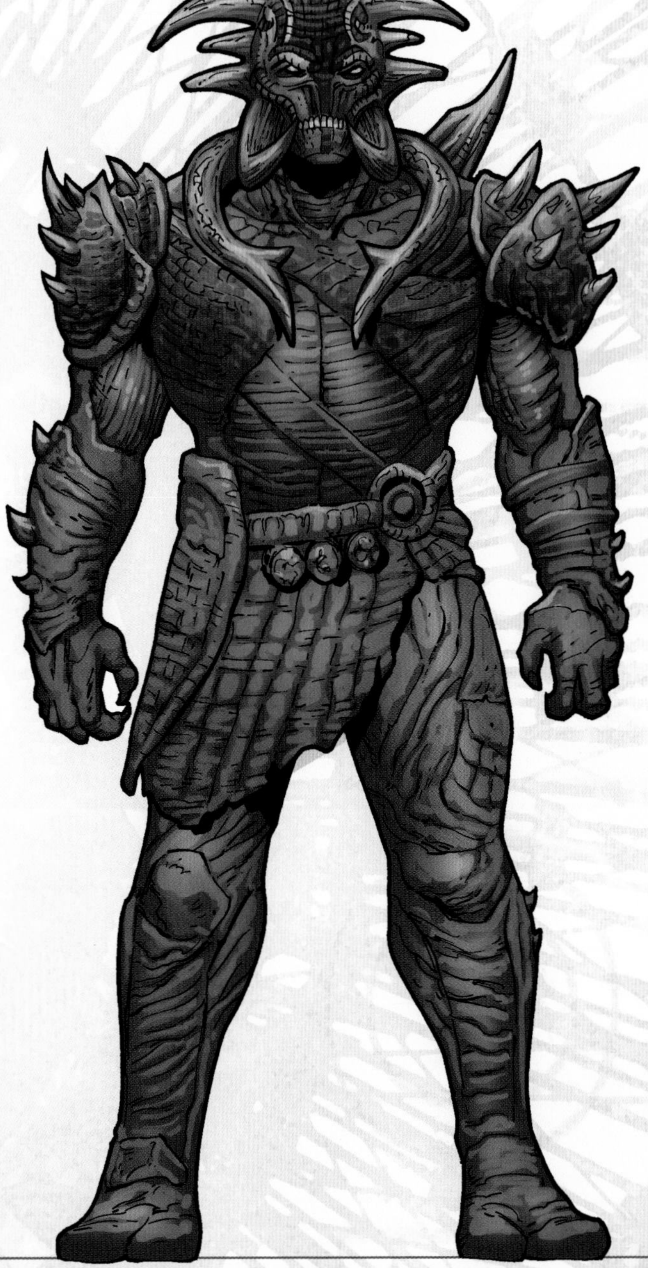

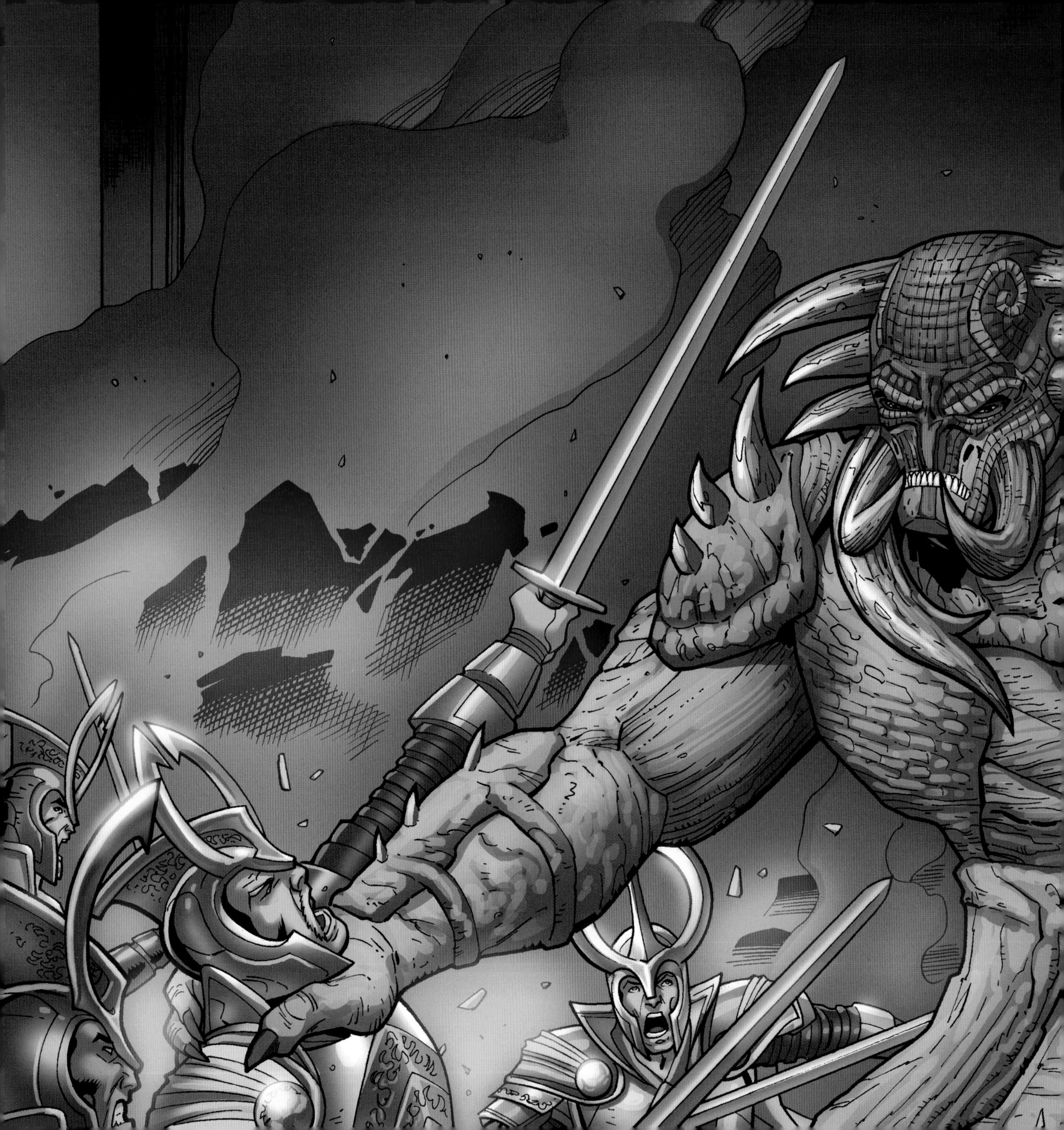

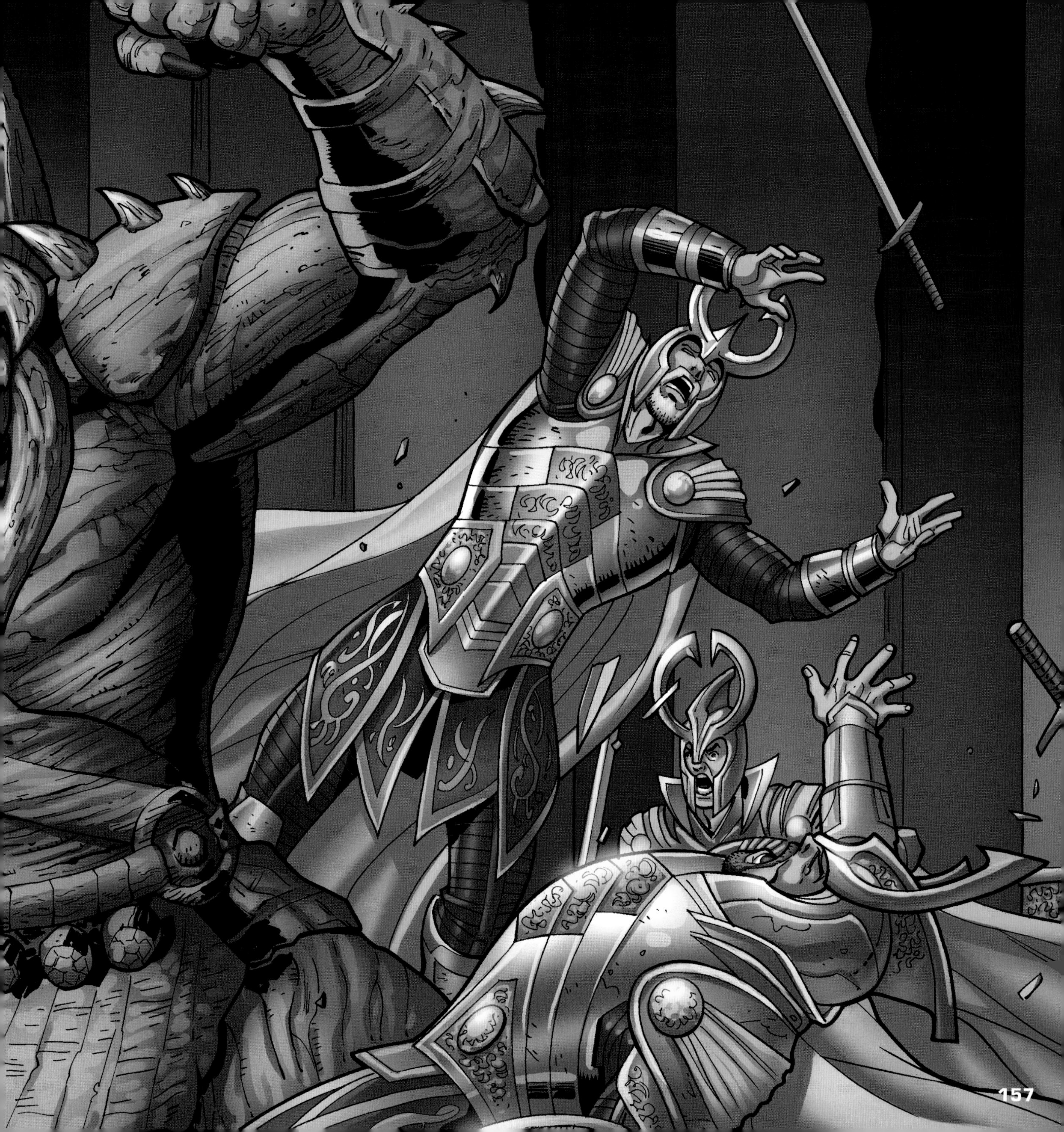

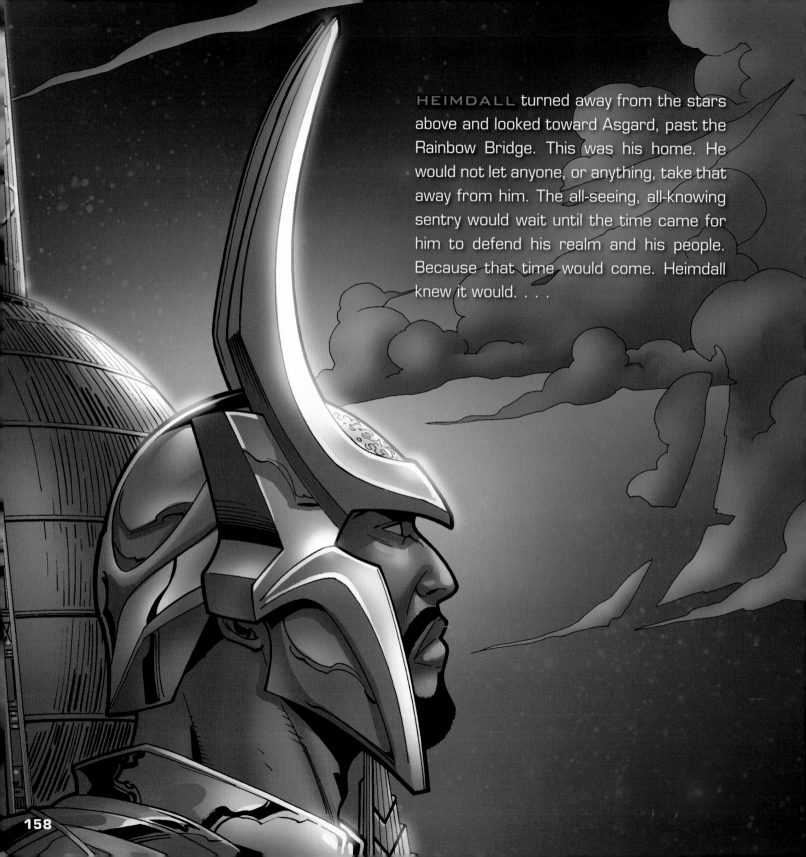

HEIMDALL turned away from the stars above and looked toward Asgard, past the Rainbow Bridge. This was his home. He would not let anyone, or anything, take that away from him. The all-seeing, all-knowing sentry would wait until the time came for him to defend his realm and his people. Because that time would come. Heimdall knew it would. . . .

MARVEL
CAPTAIN AMERICA
THE WINTER SOLDIER
RESCUE AT SEA

WRITTEN BY

Michael Siglain

BASED ON THE SCREENPLAY BY

Christopher Markus & Stephen McFeely

PRODUCED BY

Kevin Feige, p.g.a.

DIRECTED BY

Anthony and Joe Russo

ILLUSTRATED BY

Ron Lim, Cam Smith, & Lee Duhig

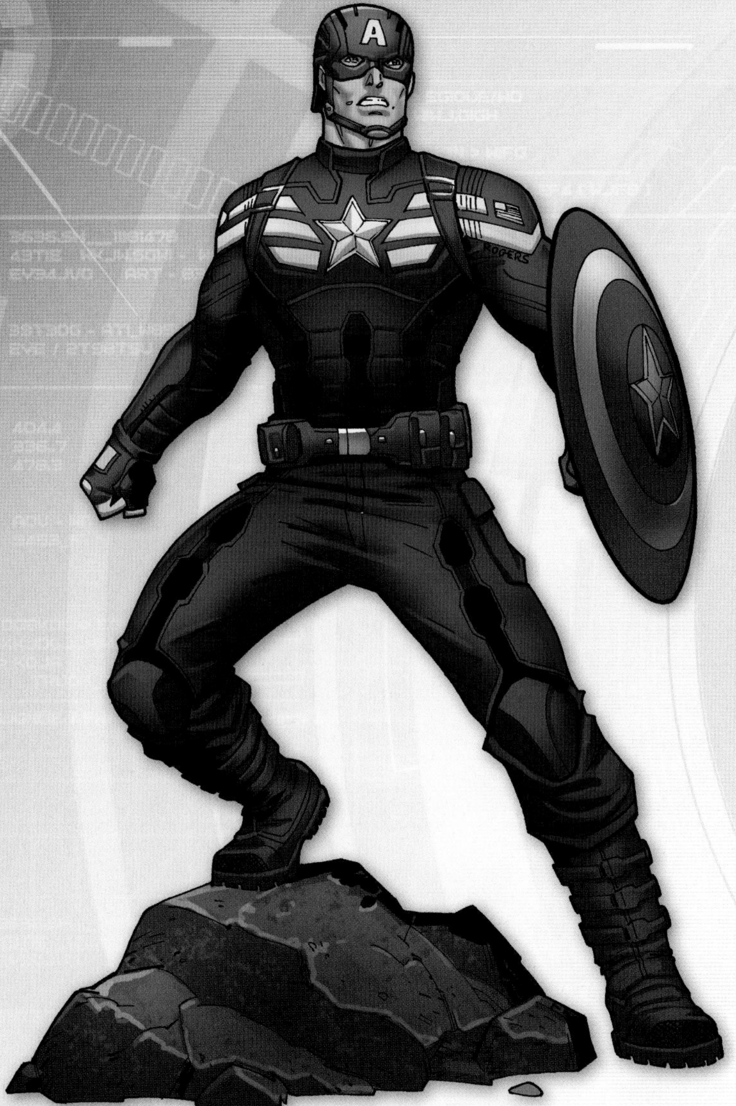
ROGERS

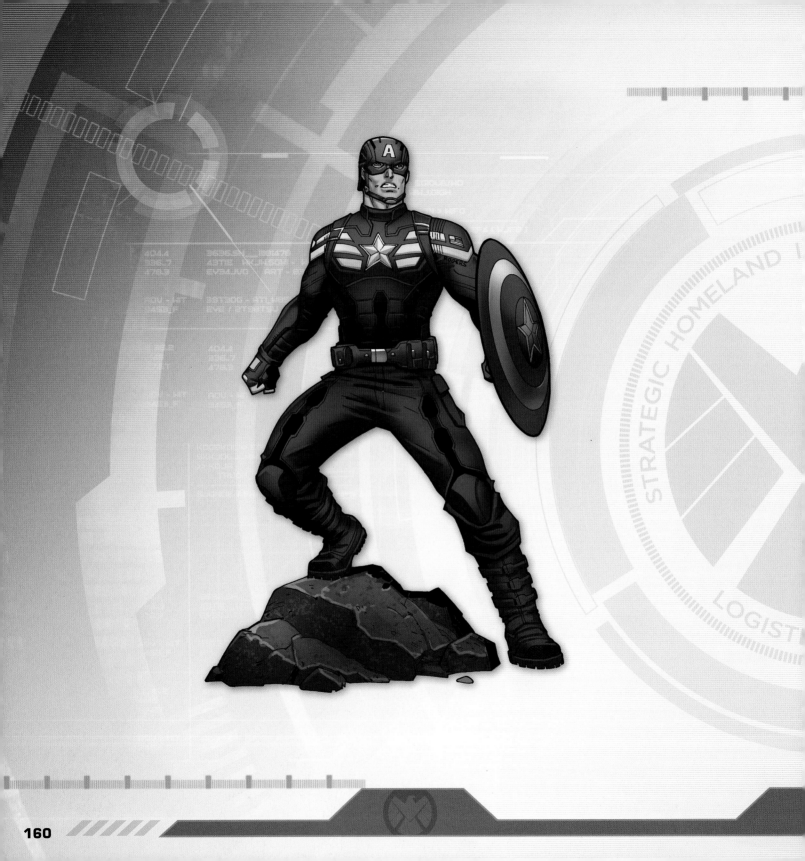

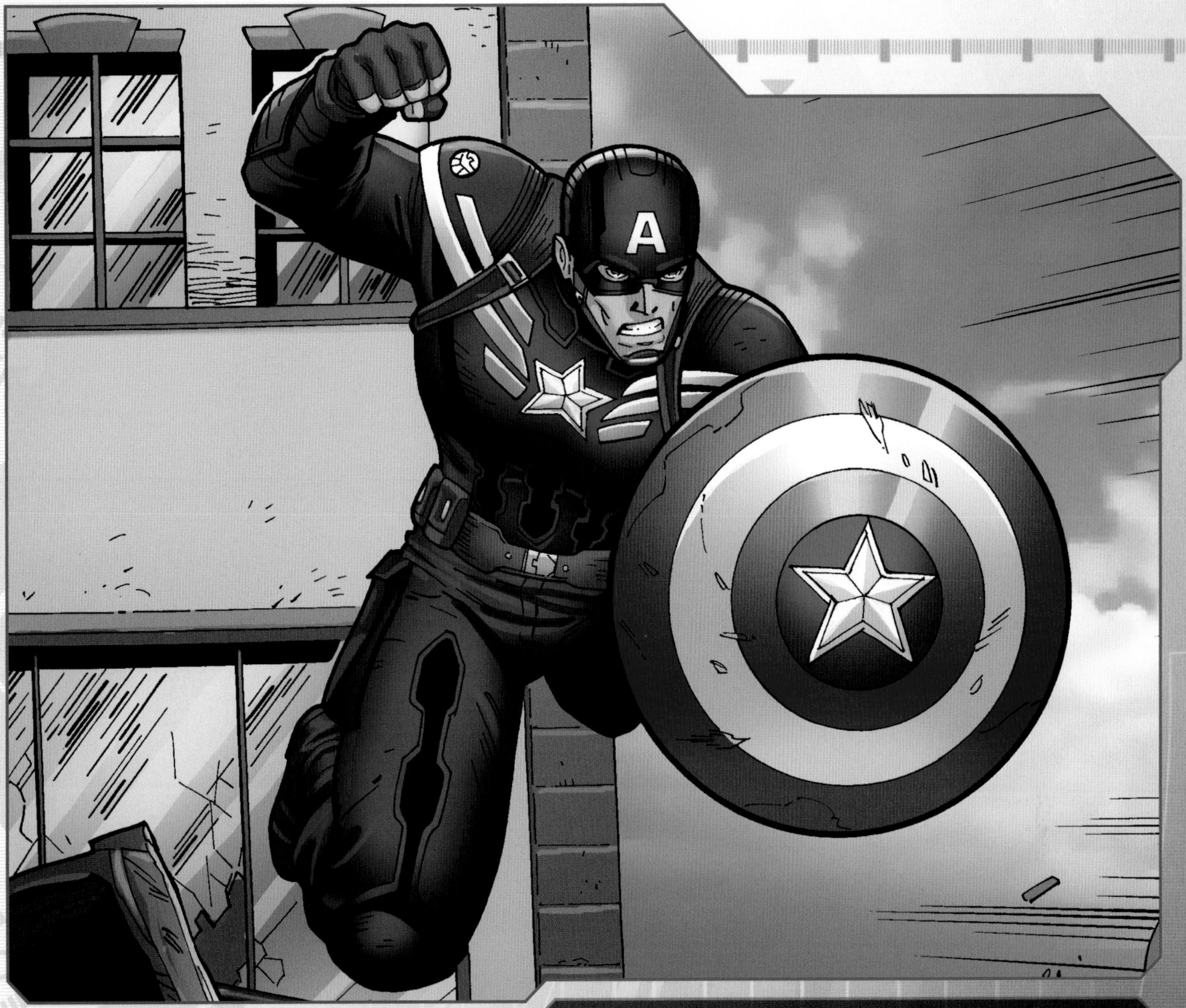

Steve Rogers was once a frail and sickly soldier, but after taking part in the top secret experiment Project: Rebirth, Steve became America's first Super-Soldier. Armed with an unbreakable shield, Steve now fights for freedom as Captain America!

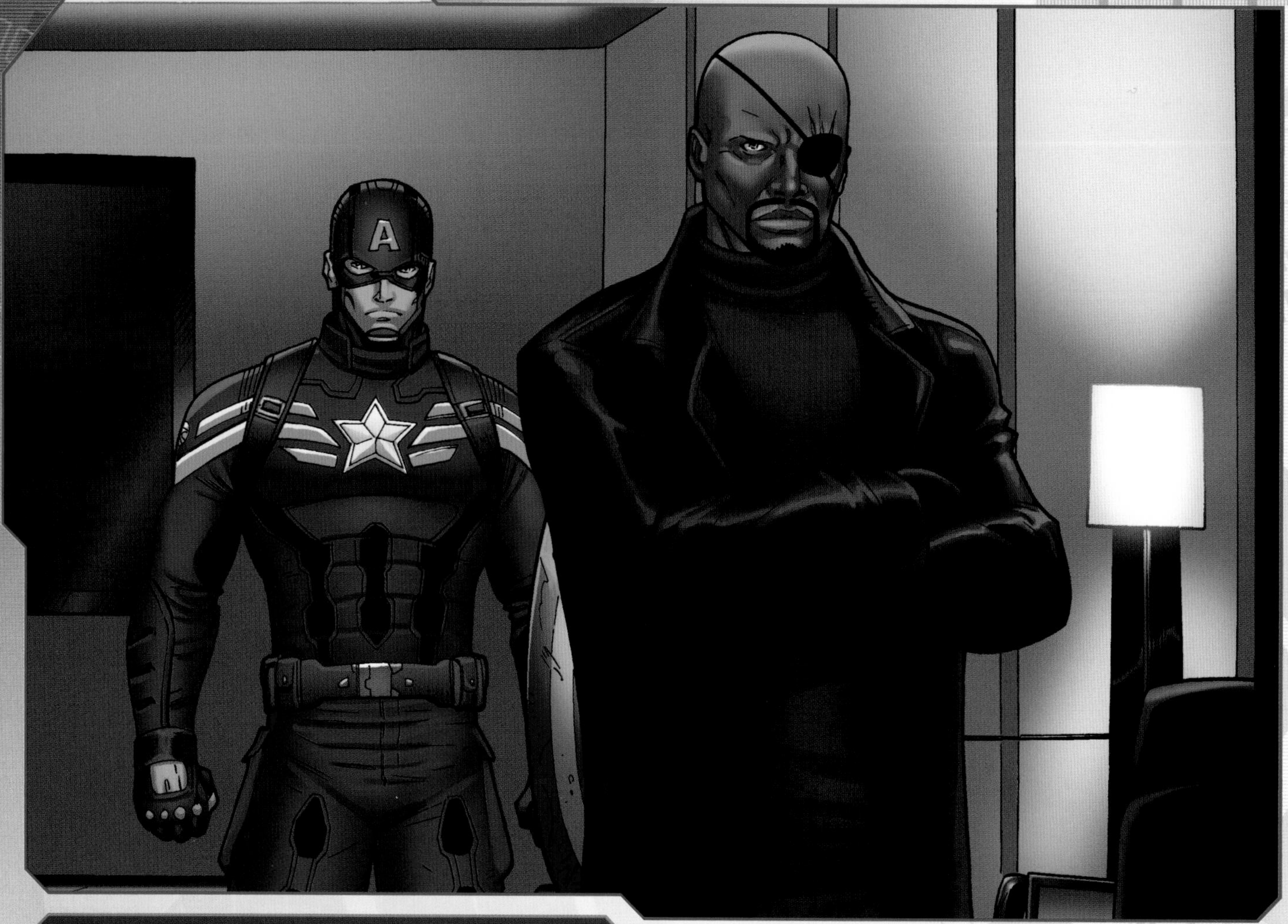

Nick Fury was worried. He was the director of S.H.I.E.L.D., and he was tasked with keeping the world safe. He had just learned that a large cargo ship called the *Lemurian Star* had been hijacked by pirates. There was only one man who could save the day: Captain America.

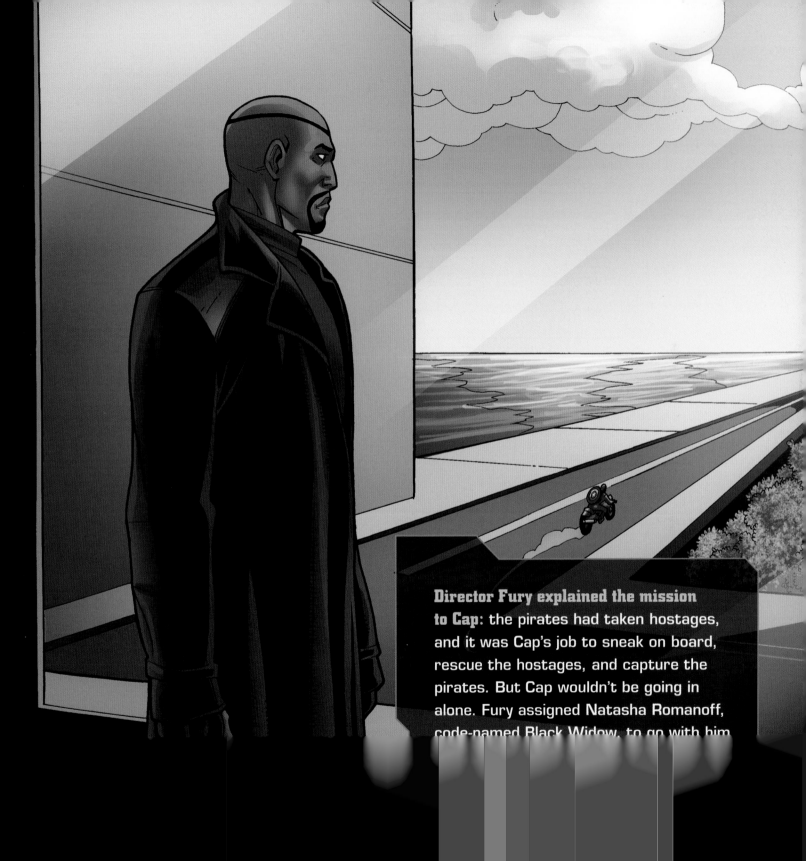

Director Fury explained the mission to Cap: the pirates had taken hostages, and it was Cap's job to sneak on board, rescue the hostages, and capture the pirates. But Cap wouldn't be going in alone. Fury assigned Natasha Romanoff, code-named Black Widow, to go with him.

Time was running out, and as Cap went to meet Black Widow, Director Fury wished them luck. They were going to need it!

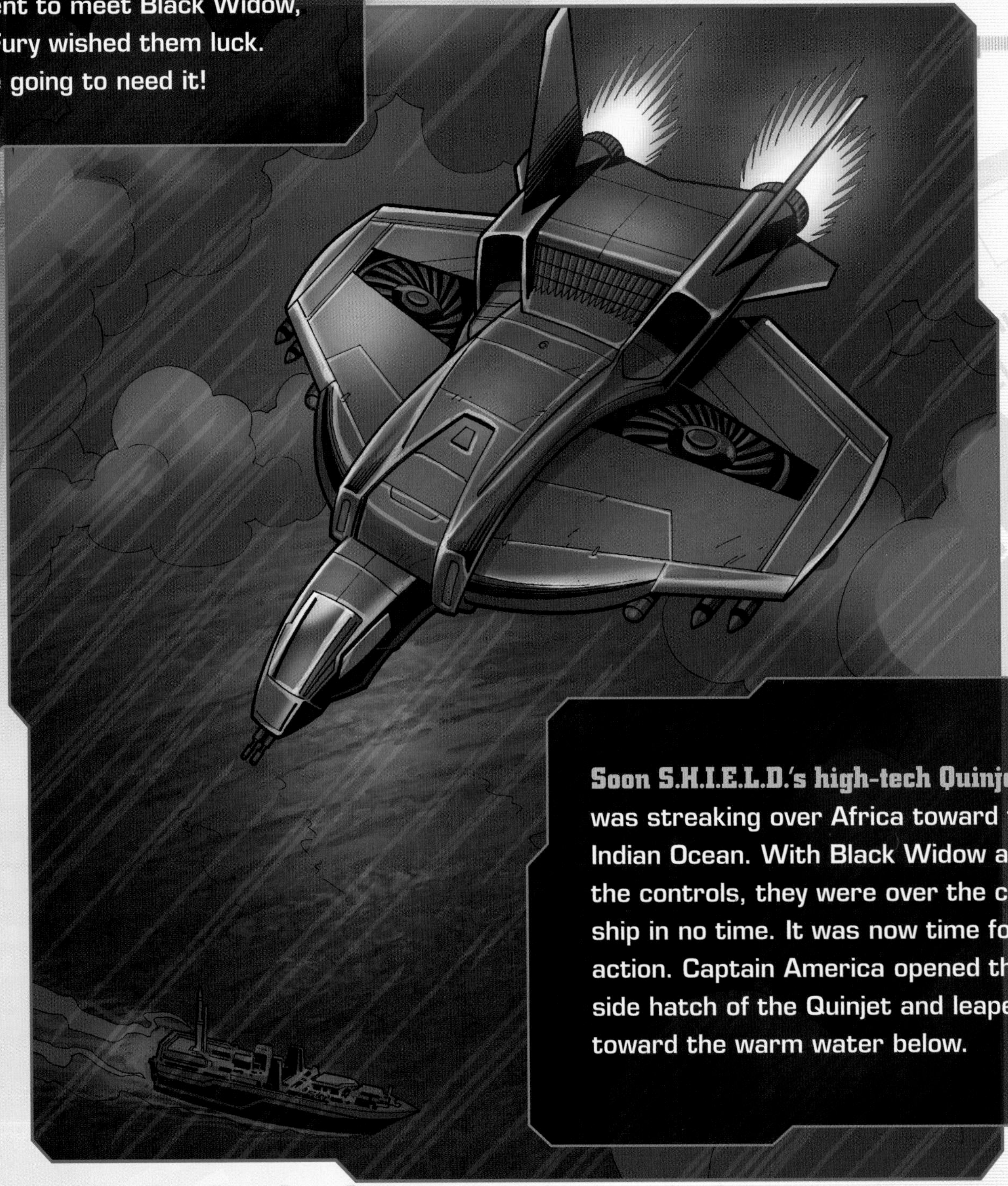

Soon S.H.I.E.L.D.'s high-tech Quinjet was streaking over Africa toward the Indian Ocean. With Black Widow at the controls, they were over the cargo ship in no time. It was now time for action. Captain America opened the side hatch of the Quinjet and leaped toward the warm water below.

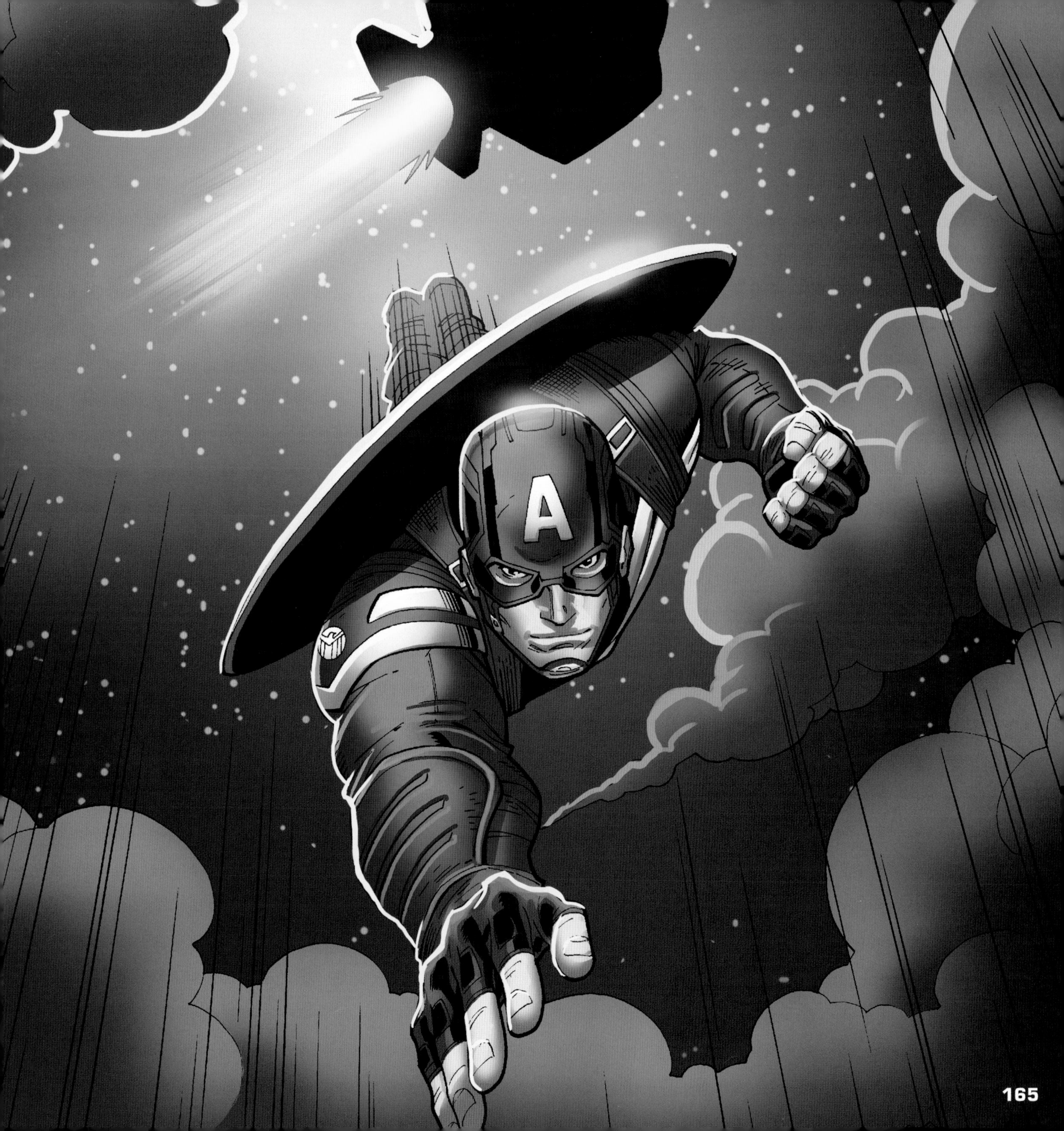

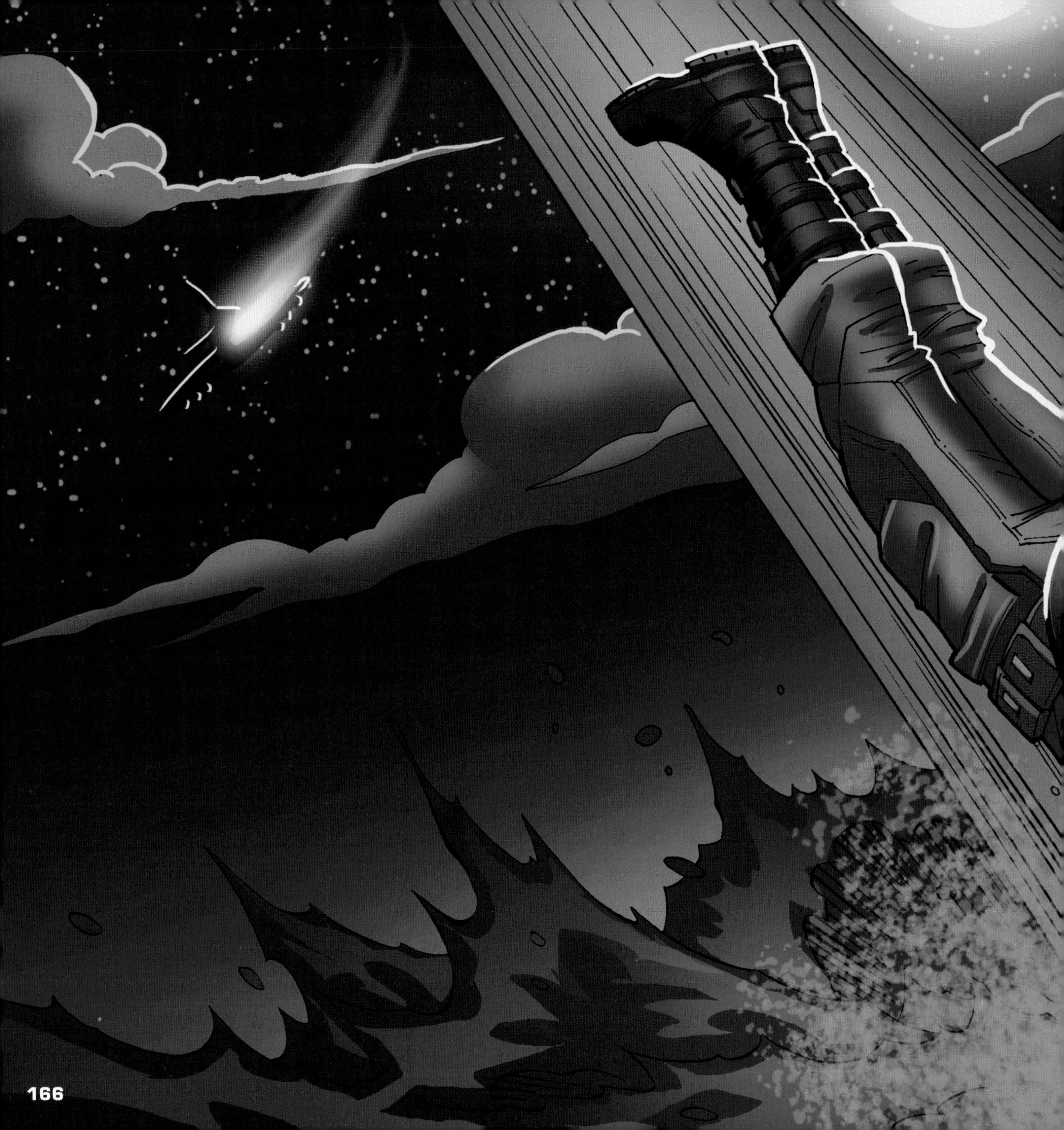

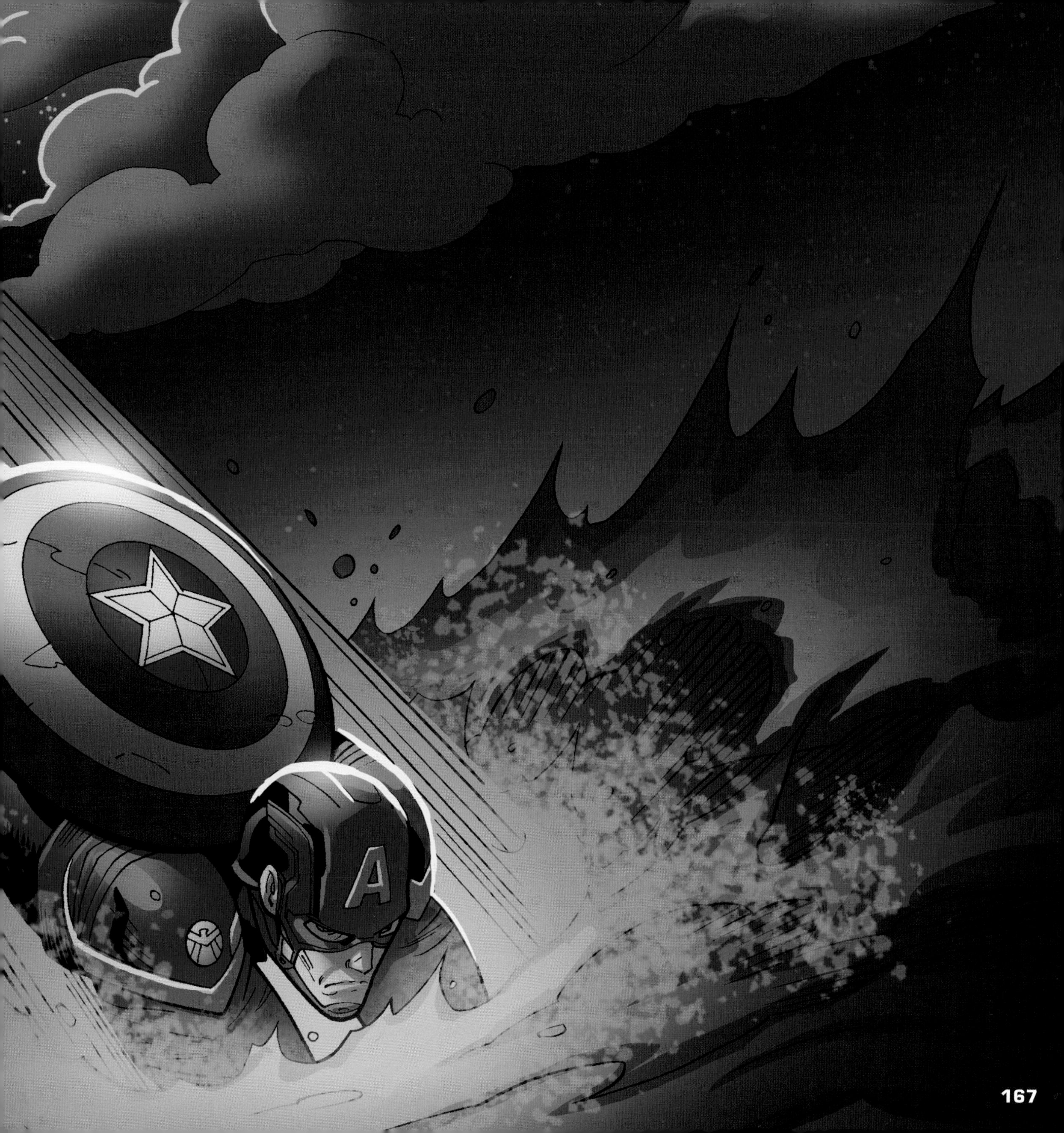

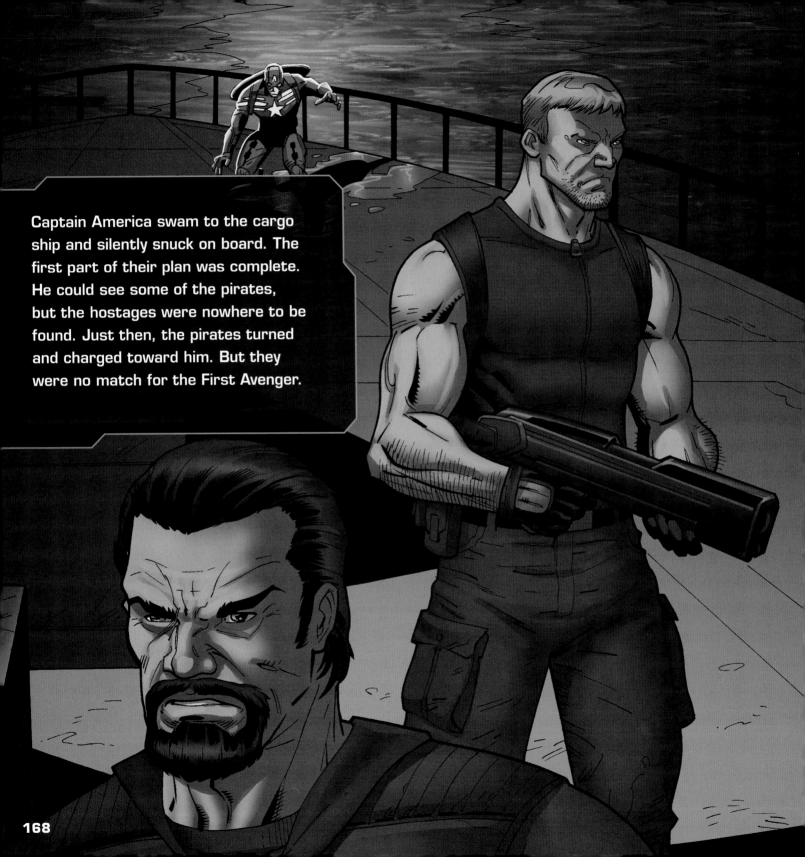

Captain America swam to the cargo ship and silently snuck on board. The first part of their plan was complete. He could see some of the pirates, but the hostages were nowhere to be found. Just then, the pirates turned and charged toward him. But they were no match for the First Avenger.

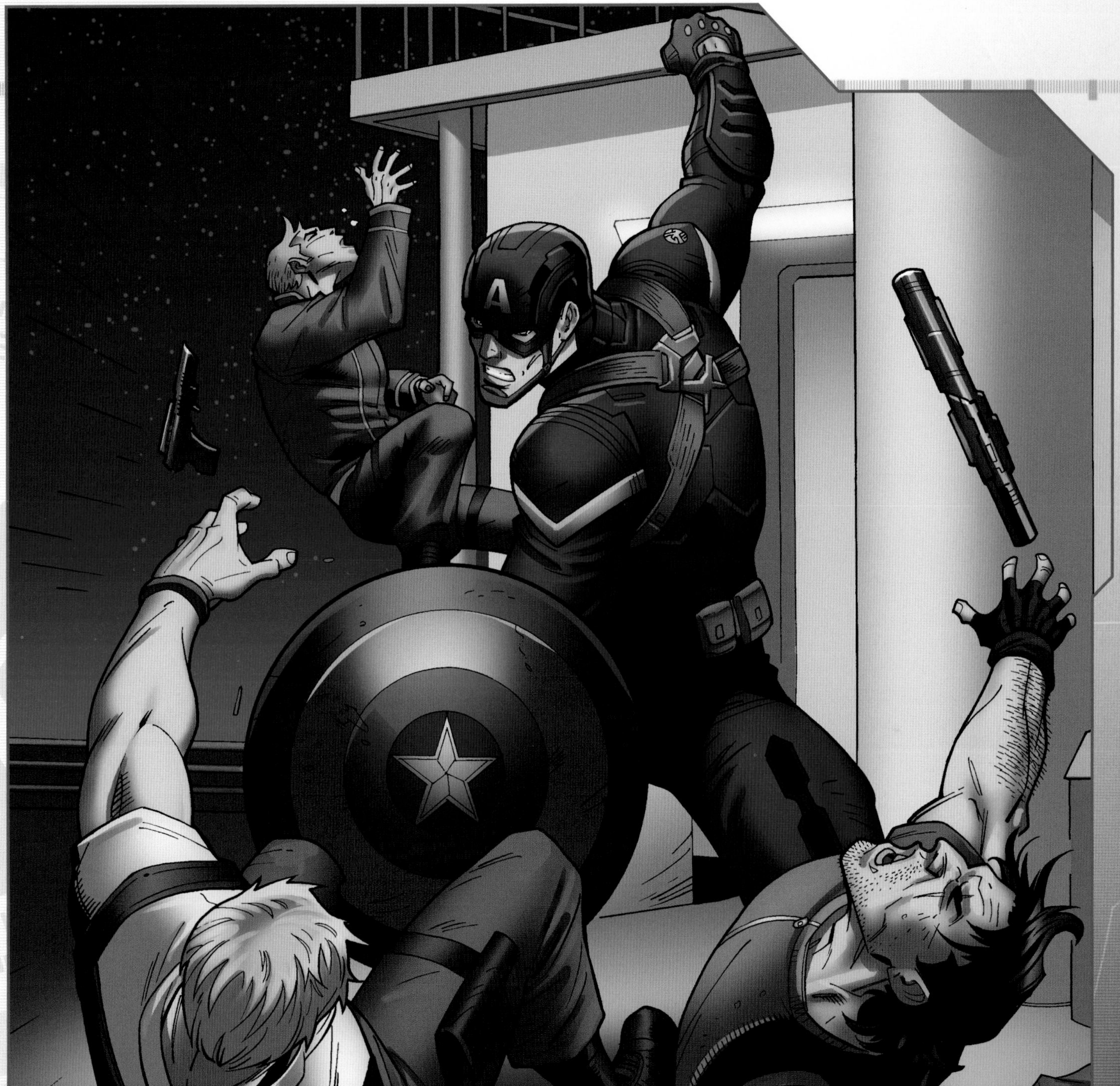

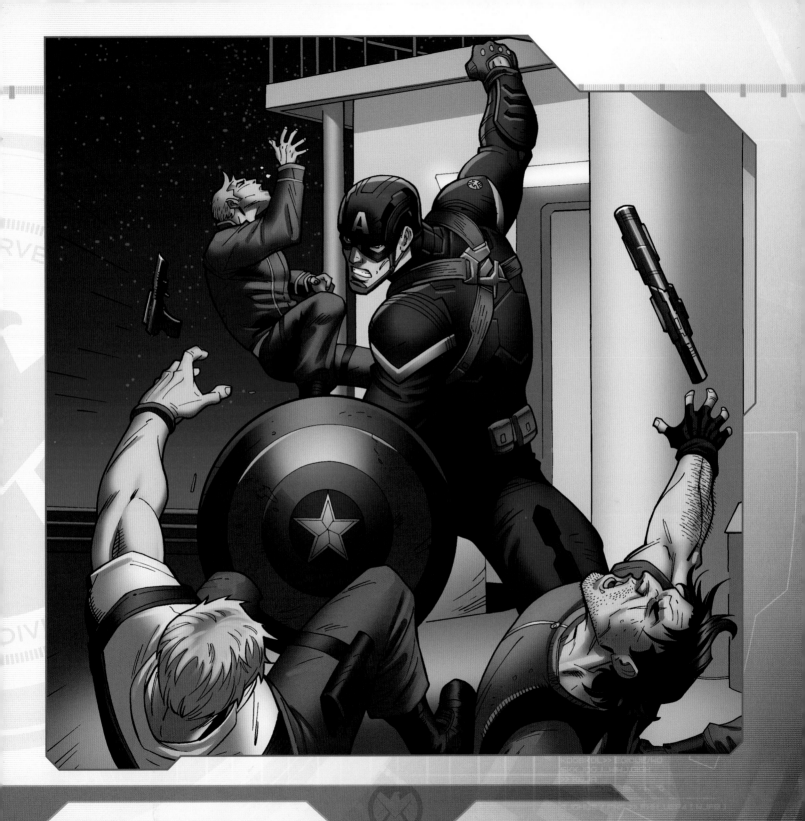

Meanwhile, Black Widow radioed Fury to report in. Fury warned her about Georges Batroc, who was the leader of the pirates. Batroc was armed and very, very dangerous.

Black Widow put the Quinjet on autopilot and radioed Cap to tell him the information about Batroc, but Cap was already on the move, searching for the hostages.

Black Widow knew she had to join her S.H.I.E.L.D. partner in case he needed help. That and he couldn't have all the fun! She put on a parachute and stepped to the back of the Quinjet. She opened the door and leaped out, falling to the ship below. Just as Black Widow was about to hit the water, she opened the parachute and quietly landed on the deck, quickly disposed of the chute, and raced off to find the pirates.

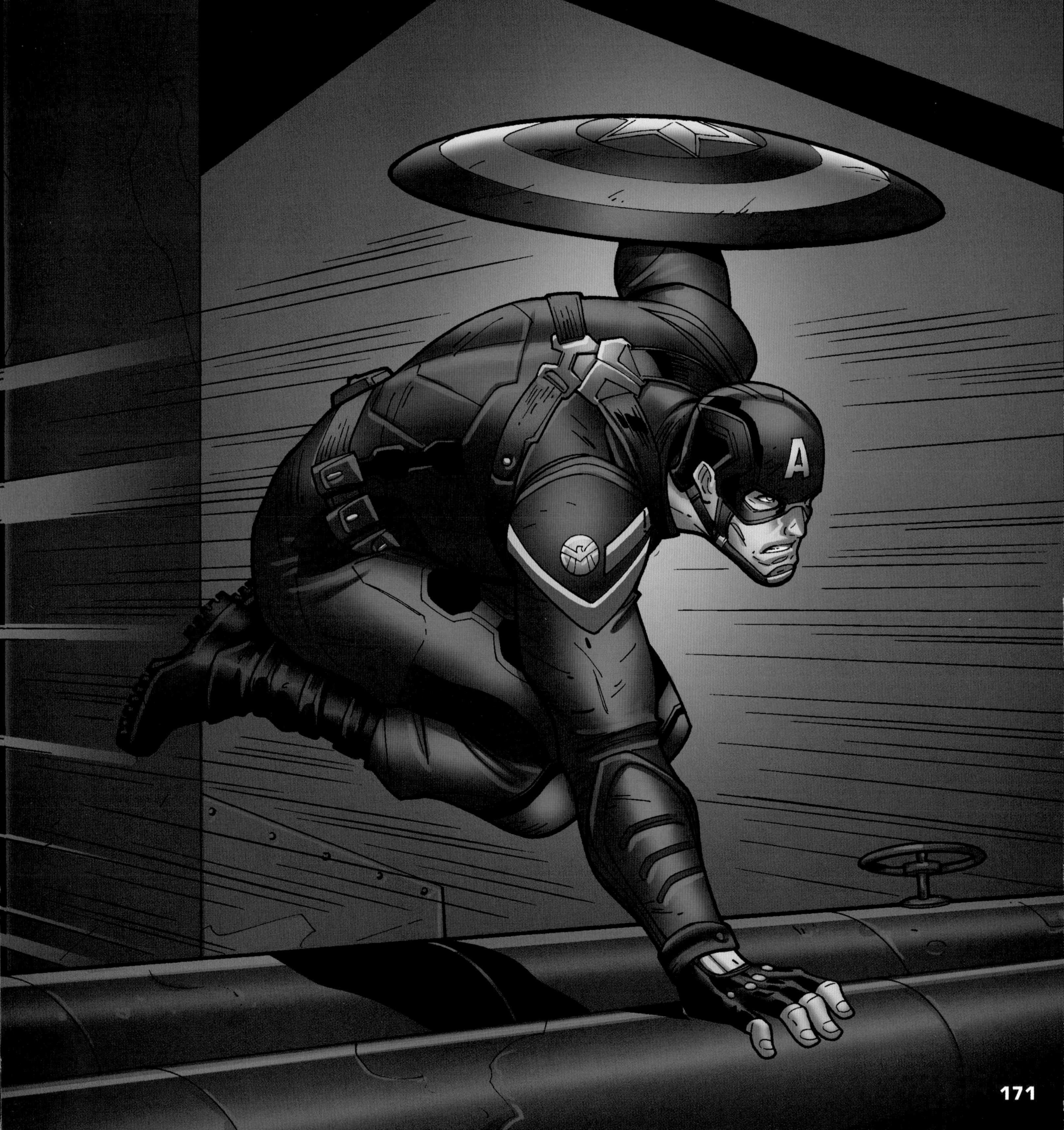

Deep within the hull of the *Lemurian Star,* inside a secret control room, Georges Batroc was making his demands. He wanted one and a half billion dollars in exchange for the hostages.

Batroc was very smart and knew that S.H.I.E.L.D. might try something, so he checked in with his men. He wanted to make sure they were all on high alert. But when the pirates in the engine room didn't answer his call, Batroc knew that something was wrong.

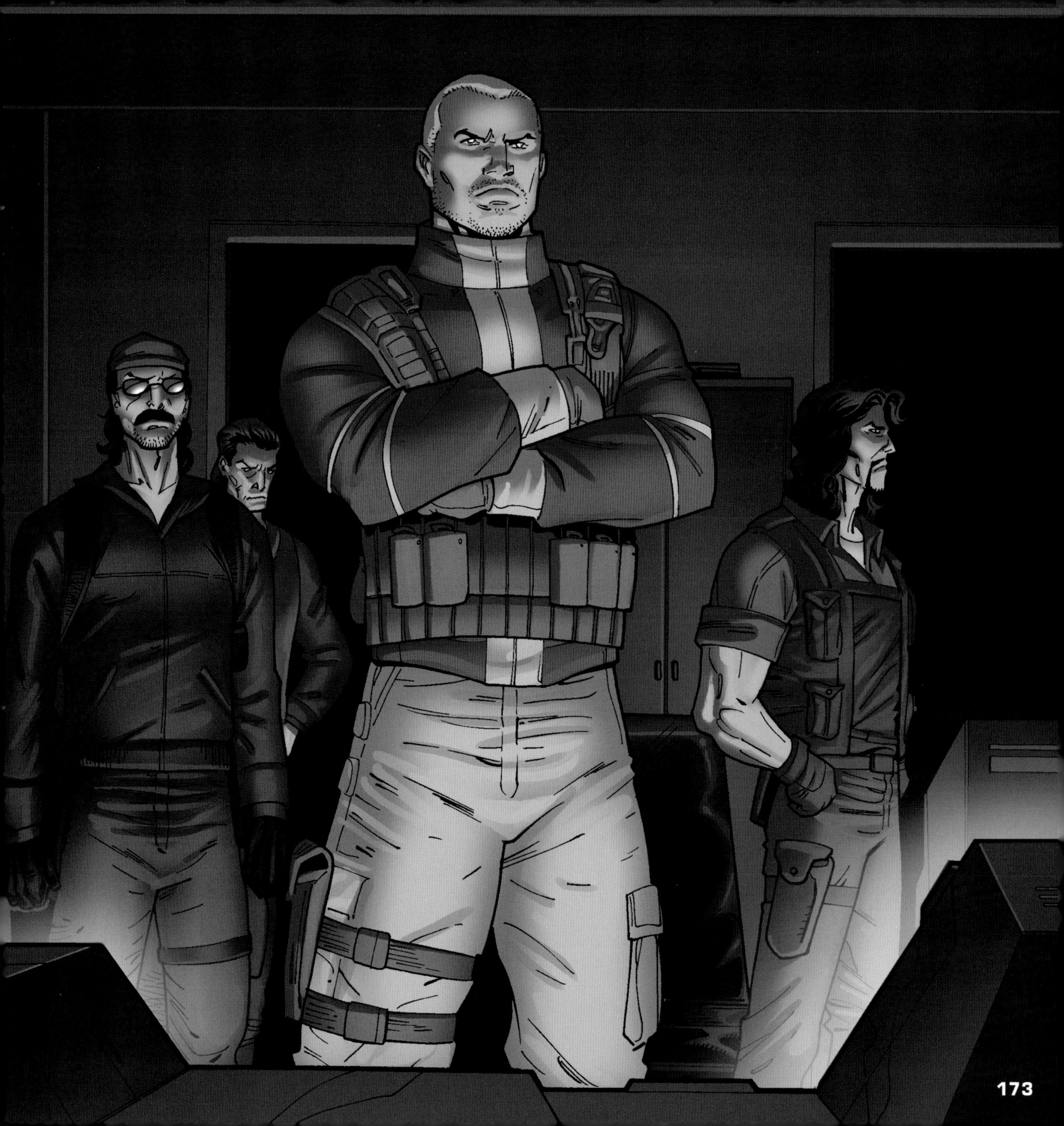

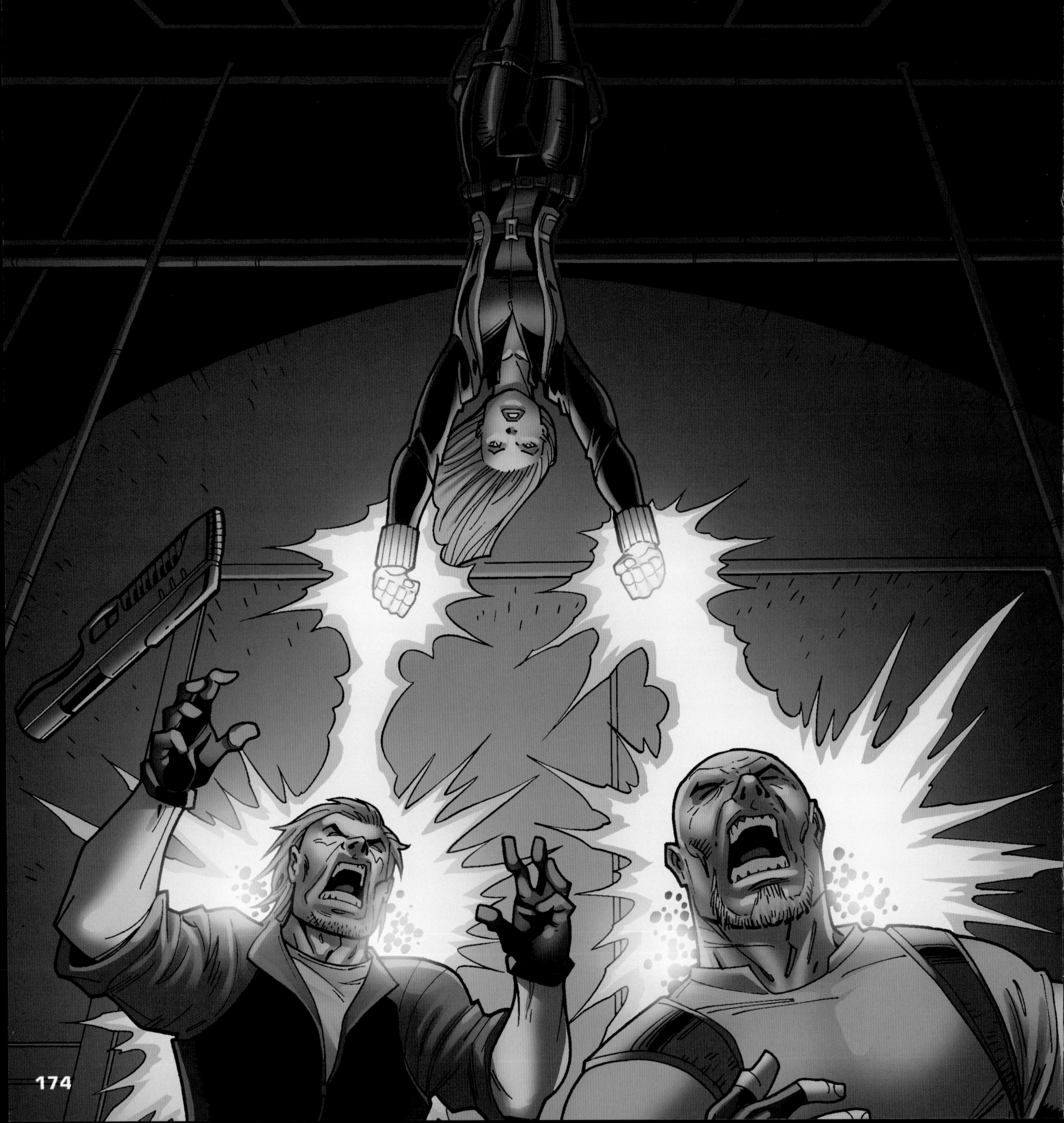

Cap had already knocked out the pirates in the engine room and learned the location of Batroc's secret control room. He contacted Black Widow to let her know what he had found out, but Natasha was one step ahead of him.

Outside the control room, Black Widow lowered herself from the ceiling and used her special bracelets to deliver small electric shocks—what she called her "Widow's Bites"—to the pirates guarding the room. Then it was Cap's turn to take out the bad guys!

Just then, Captain America's unbreakable stealth vibranium shield crashed through the control room window. It smashed into two pirates, knocking them out, then returned to Captain America.

Batroc snarled as he looked up to see Captain America standing in the doorway. He reached for his weapon, but Cap was too fast for him. The Super-Soldier jumped and delivered a mighty kick to the villain's chest, knocking him out cold.

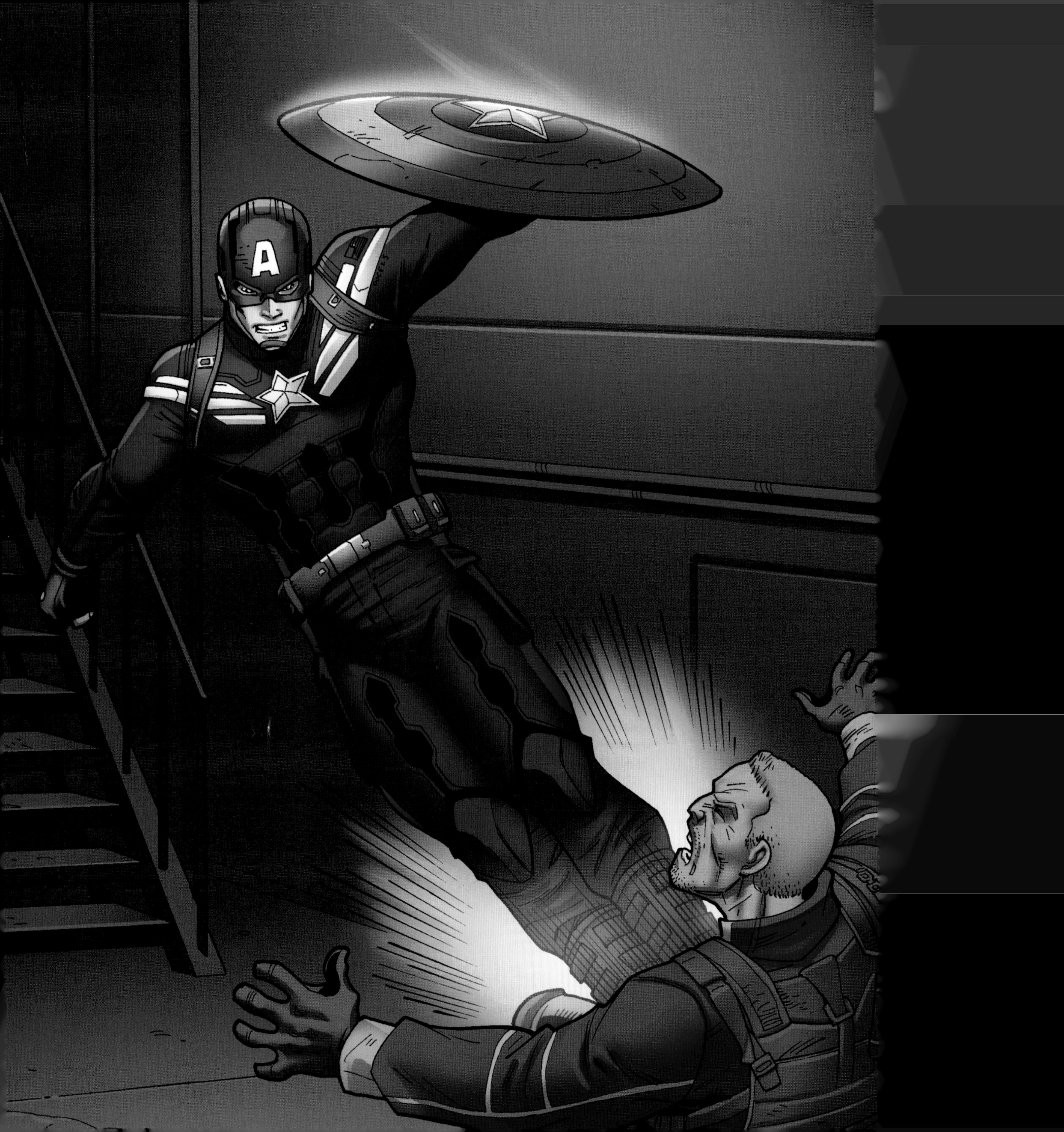

With Batroc defeated, Cap tied him up and secured him in the control room so that he couldn't escape. Then it was time to get the hostages and let them know that they were free and safe.

Black Widow joined Captain America as they made their way down to the cargo hold, where the hostages were locked up. Cap looked at Black Widow and smiled. Getting inside would be a piece of cake for these Avengers.

With a mighty crash, Captain America and Black Widow burst through a large window that led to the cargo room.

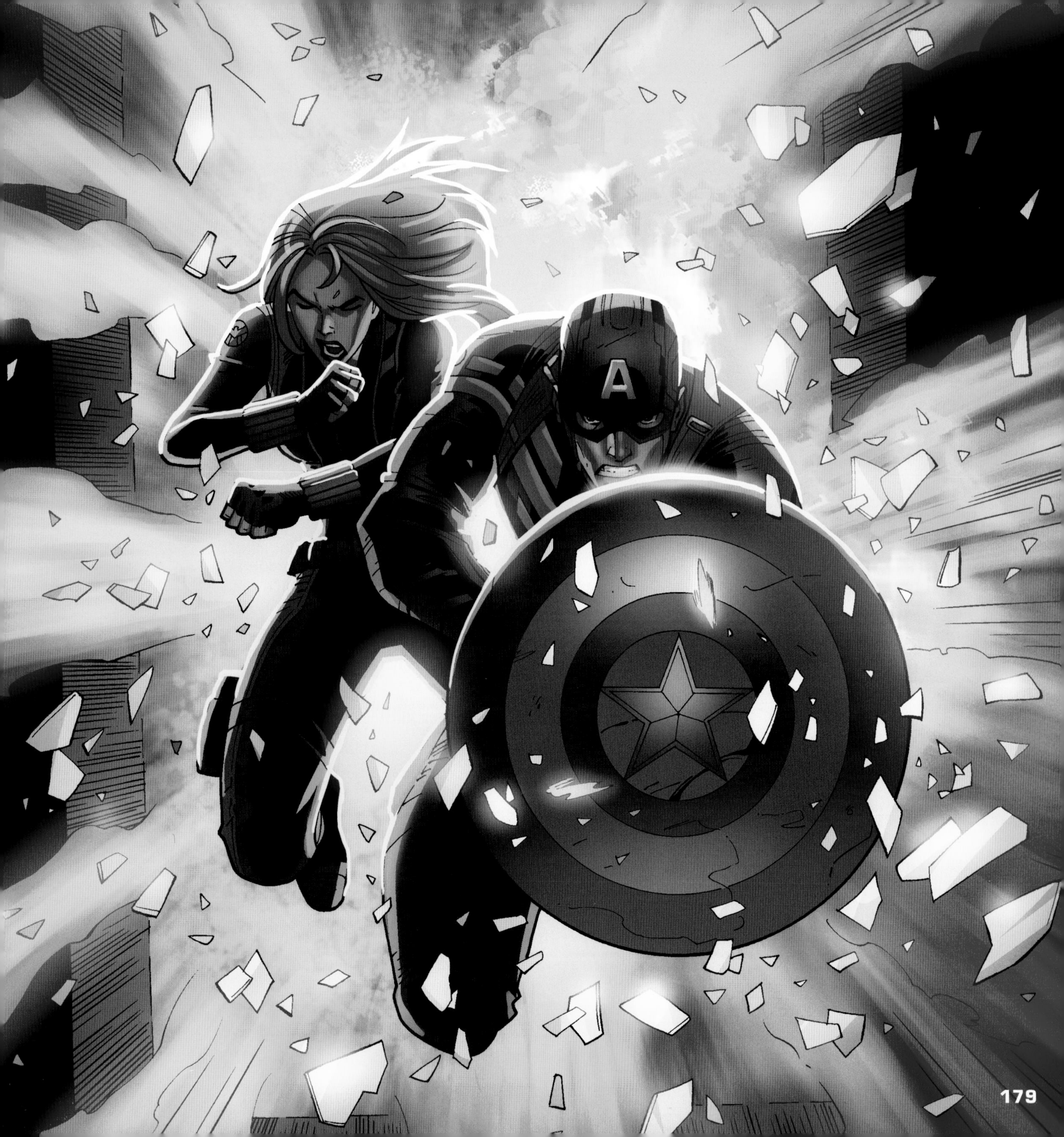

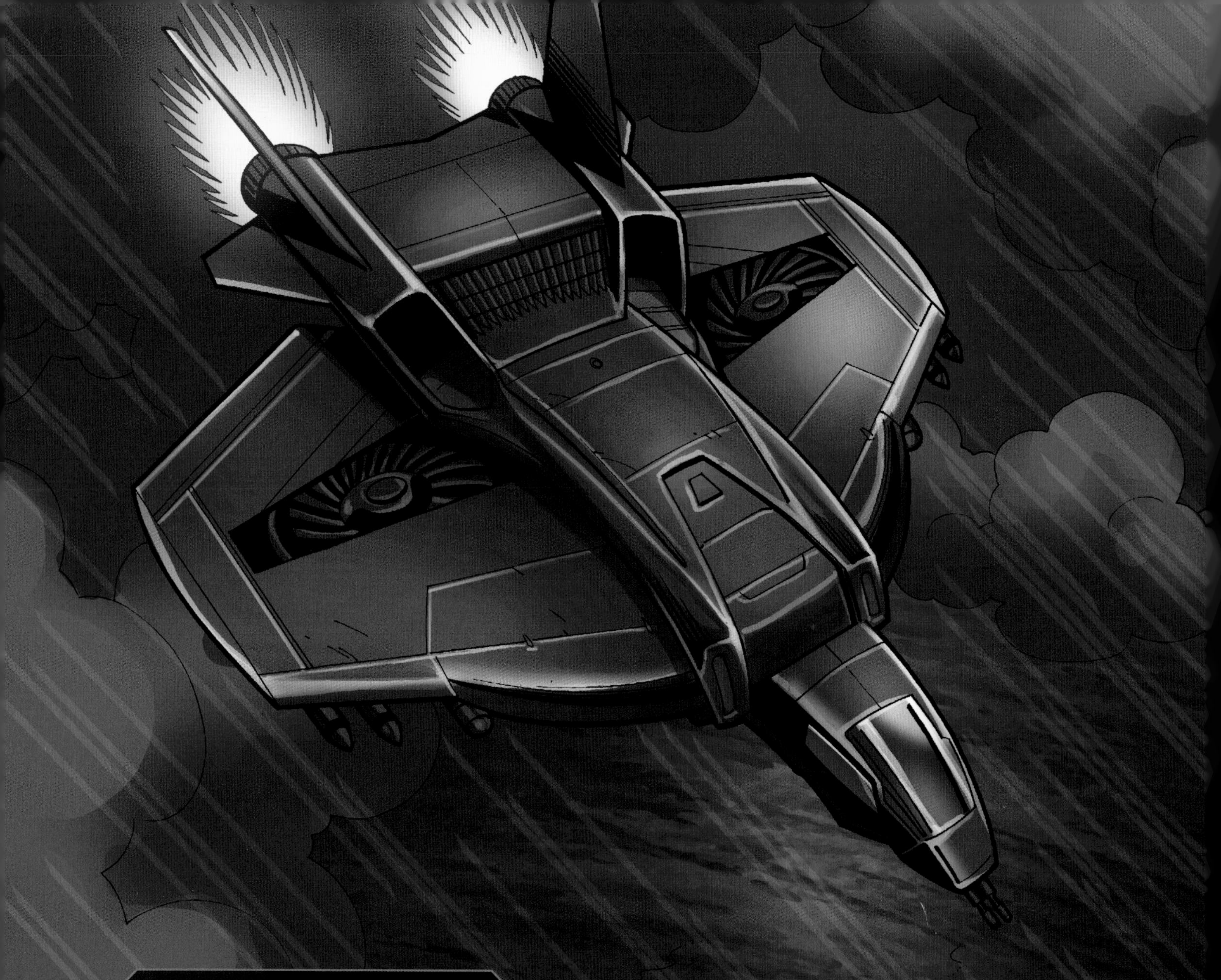

The hostages were relieved to see Captain America and Black Widow standing before them. Thanks to the two S.H.I.E.L.D. agents, the hostages knew that everything was going to be all right.

As Cap helped the men and women out of the hold, Black Widow called the Quinjet back to the *Lemurian Star*, where it safely landed on top of the ship. They would load the hostages on board and take them back to S.H.I.E.L.D. headquarters.

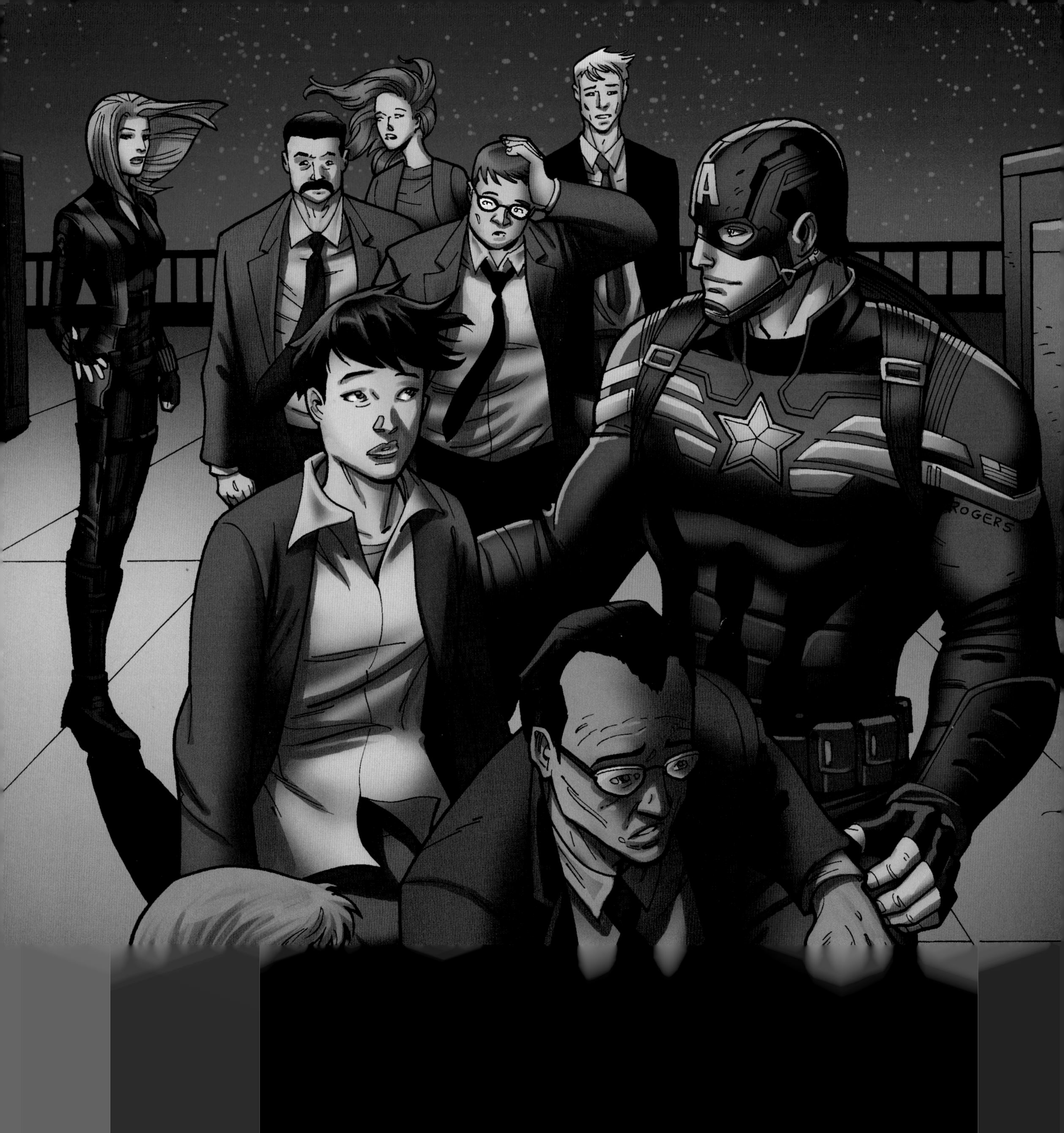
ROGERS

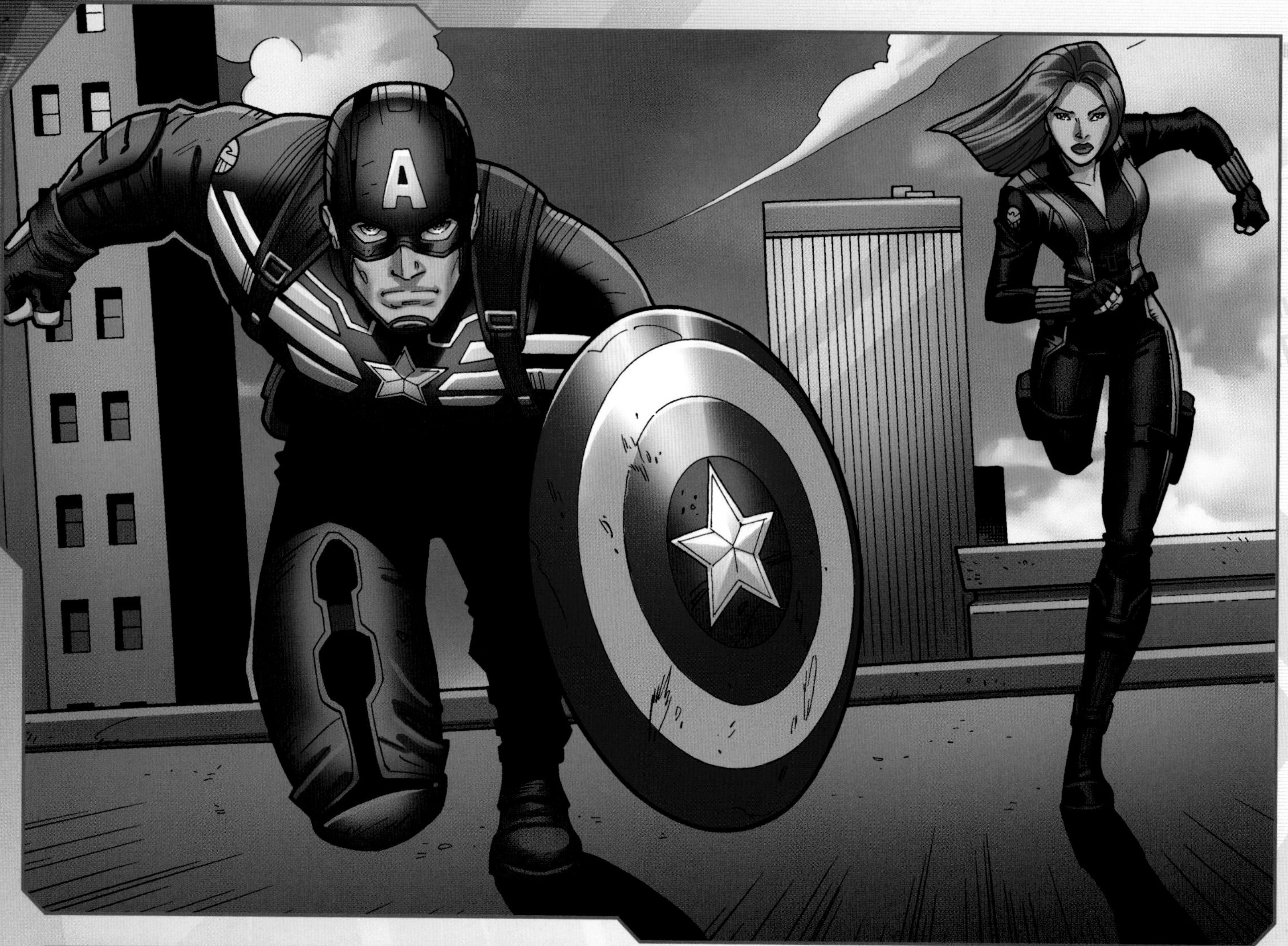

Director Fury was happy: Batroc had been captured and the hostages had been saved. The rescue at sea had been a success, thanks to the combined might of Black Widow and the courageous Captain America!

THE END

MARVEL

GUARDIANS OF THE GALAXY

MARVEL
GUARDIANS OF THE GALAXY
PASSPORT 2 TO READING
FRIENDS and FOES

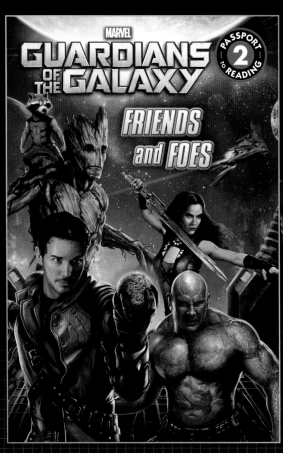

MARVEL
GUARDIANS OF THE GALAXY
BATTLE OF KNOWHERE

BASED ON THE MOVIE!

MARVEL
GUARDIANS OF THE GALAXY
ROCKET AND GROOT FIGHT BACK

Includes Rocket mask!

BASED ON THE MOVIE!

Read the books!

MARVEL
GUARDIANS OF THE GALAXY
THE REUSABLE STICKER BOOK

Based on the Movie!

INCLUDES MORE THAN 50 REUSABLE STICKERS!

MARVEL

THE AVENGERS

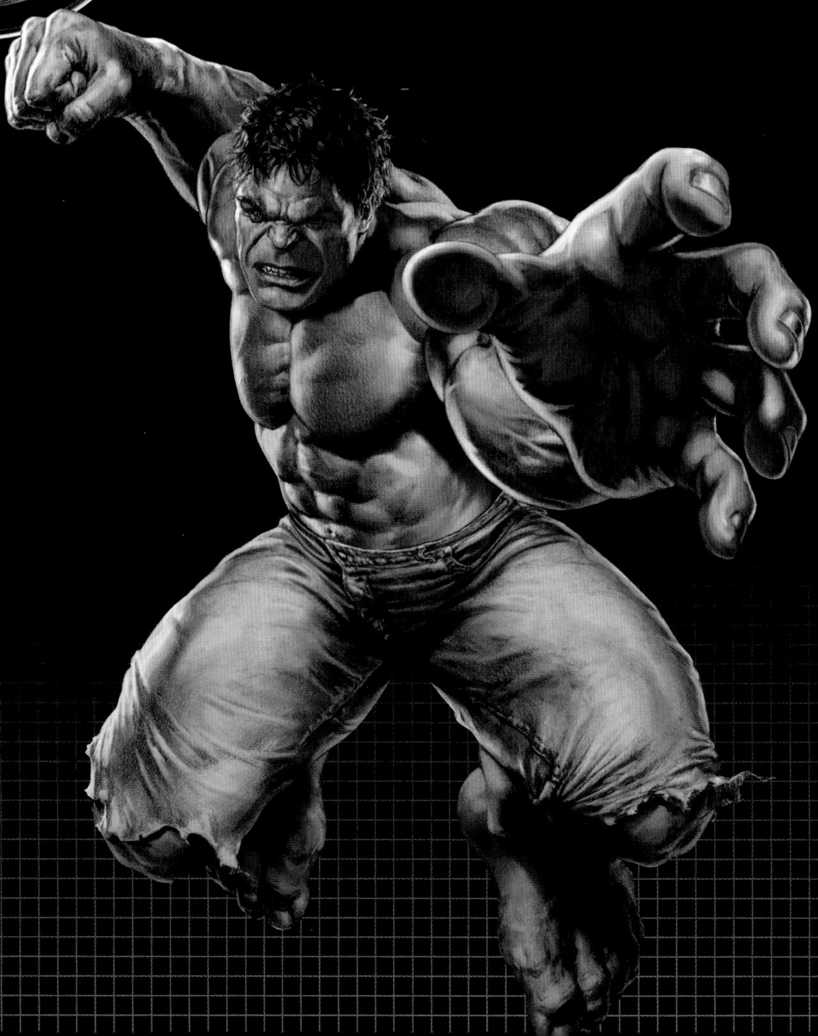

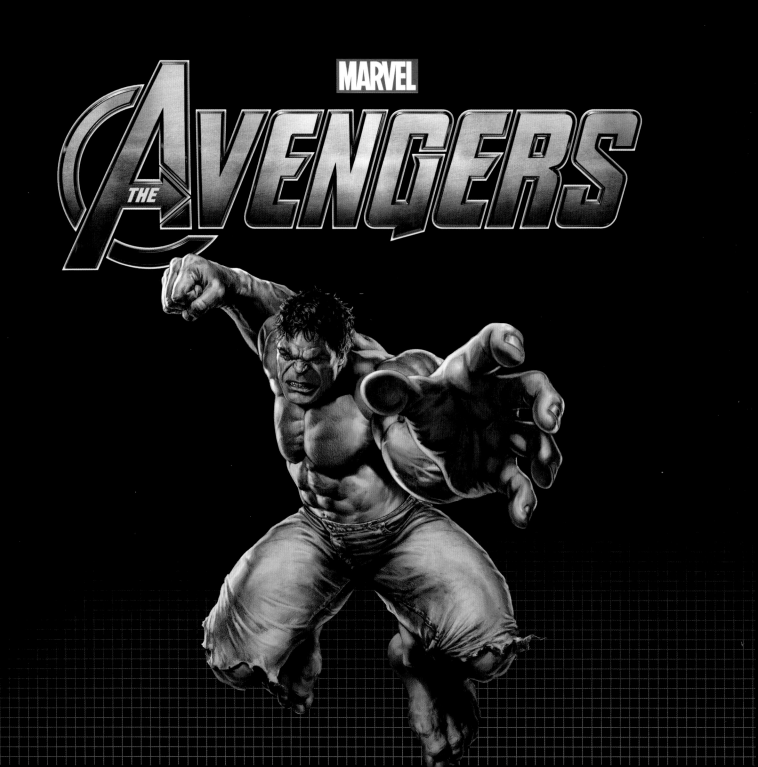

Read more Super Hero stories!

MARVEL
THE AVENGERS
PASSPORT TO READING
2
READING ADVENTURES
6 BOOKS IN 1!

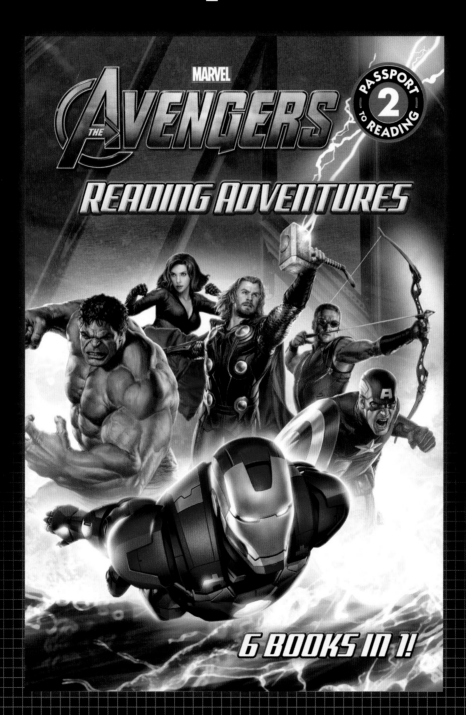

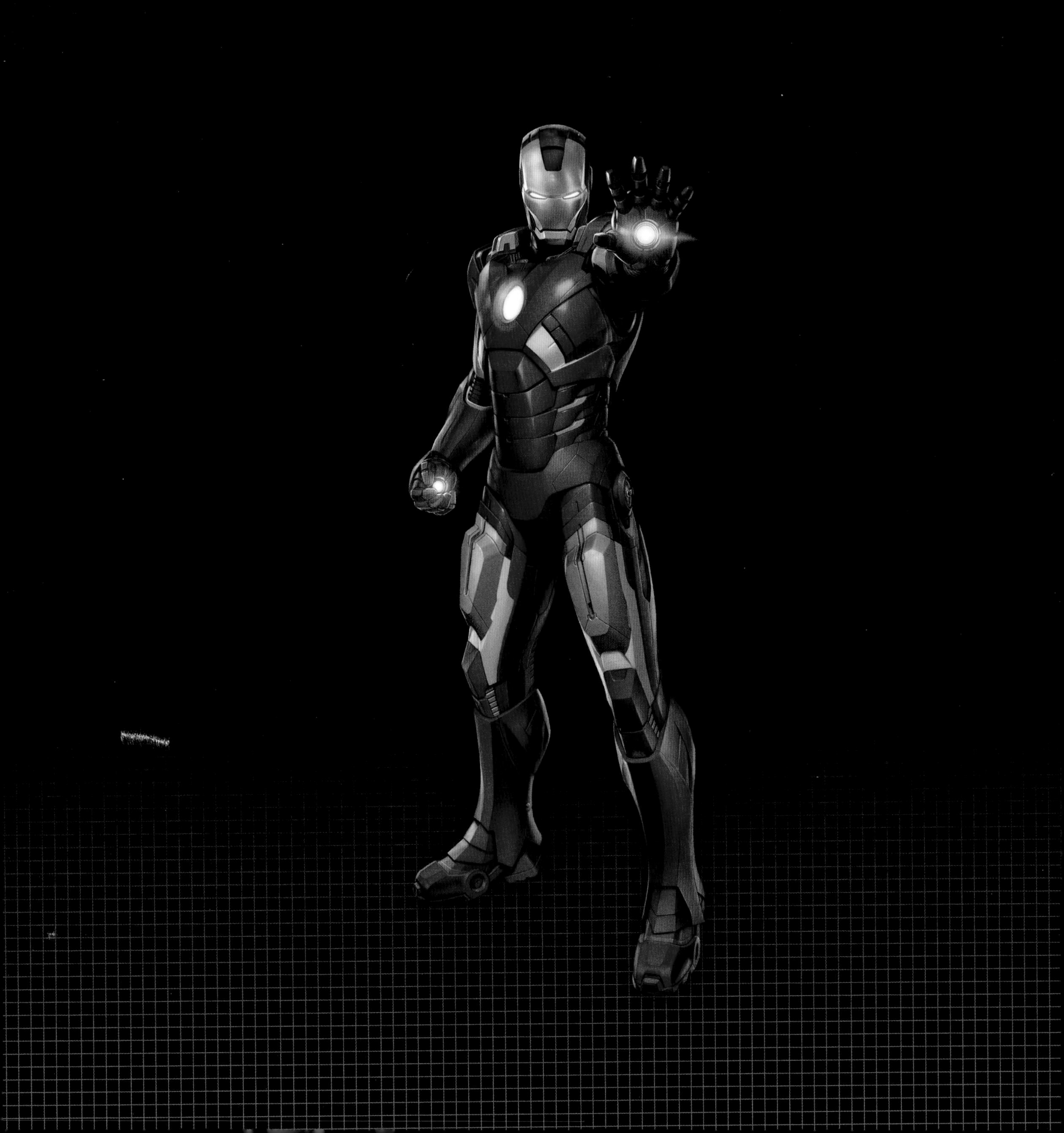

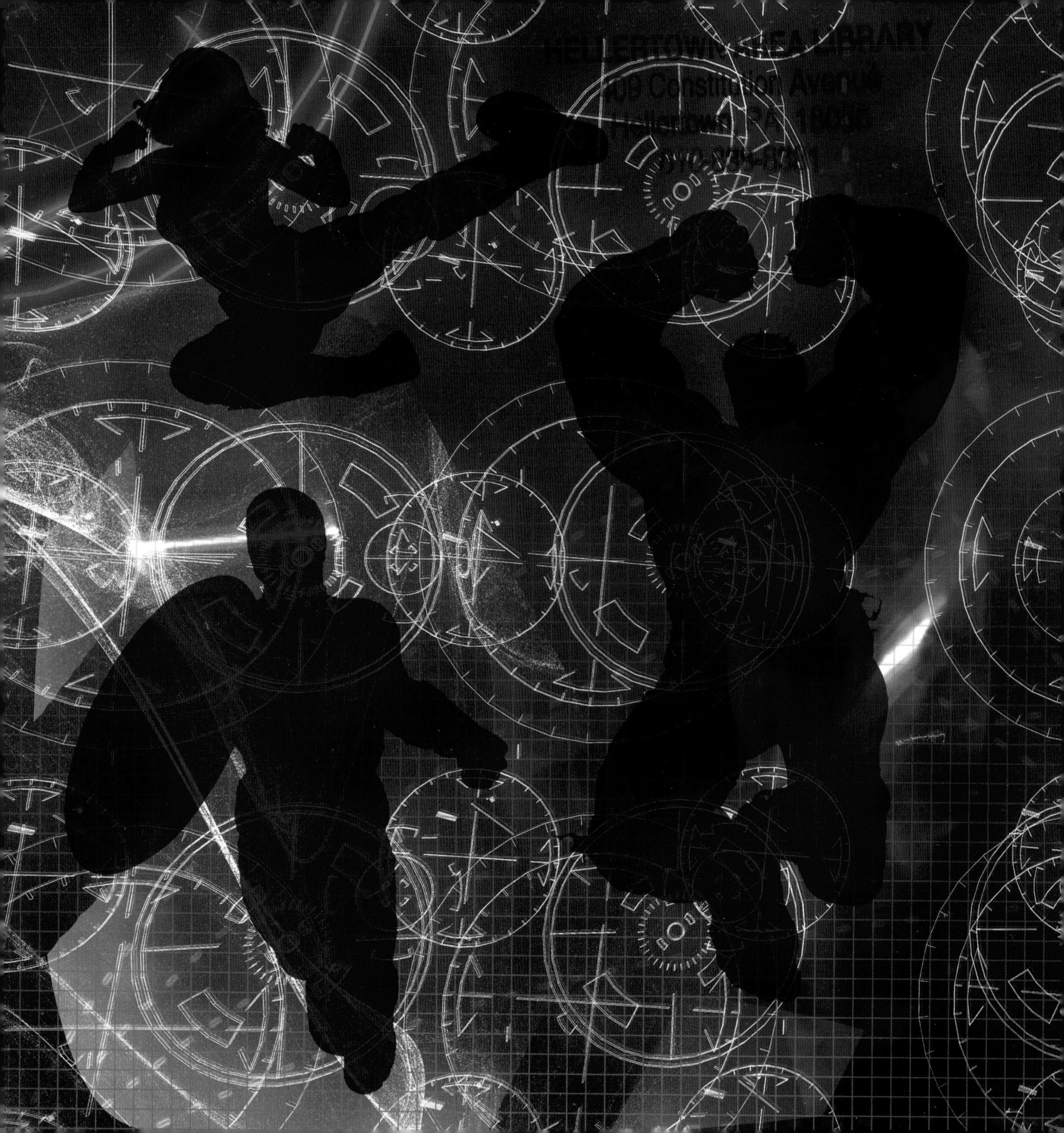